"Sensuality, passion, excitement, and drama . . . are Ms. Miller's hallmarks."
—*Romantic Times*

Two passionate lovers are ready to put their hearts on the line—if they can survive avenging murder in a blazing Arizona town. . . .

Linda Lael Miller charts suspenseful new territory in her *New York Times* bestsellers

NEVER LOOK BACK

"[An] exciting police procedural romance. . . . The return of the cast from *Don't Look Now* will excite readers. . . . [A] well-written thriller that never slows down until the final confrontation between the heroine and the killer. . . . Romantic suspense fans will look back on the two Westbrook novels as fond Miller time."
—Bestreviews.com

"Clare's wry humor gives the novel . . . zing."
—*Publishers Weekly*

DON'T LOOK NOW

"An exciting romantic suspense thriller. . . . The story line is action-packed. . . . Linda Lael Miller at her intriguing best."
—*Midwest Book Review*

THE LAST CHANCE CAFÉ

"Powerful romance flavored with deep emotional resonance."
—*Romantic Times*

"This novel is dead-on target . . . [with] suspense, down home comfort, and sizzling tension. . . . Ms. Miller has a timeless writing style, and her characters are always vivacious and appealing."
—*Heartstrings*

"An entertaining story."
—*Booklist*

"[An] enriching tale of contemporary frontiers and family fulfillment."
—*Romance BookPage*

SPRINGWATER WEDDING

"Fans will be thrilled to join the action, suspense, and romance portrayed in [Linda Lael Miller's contemporary fiction]."
—*Romantic Times*

"Pure delight from the beginning to the satisfying ending. . . . Miller is a master craftswoman at creating unusual story lines [and] charming characters."
—*Rendezvous*

"The perfect recipe for love. . . . Miller writes with a warm and loving heart."
—*BookPage*

"Miller's strength is her portrayal of the history and traditions that distinguish Springwater and its residents."
—*Publishers Weekly*

Also by Linda Lael Miller

BANNER O'BRIEN
CORBIN'S FANCY
MEMORY'S EMBRACE
MY DARLING MELISSA
ANGELFIRE
DESIRE AND DESTINY
FLETCHER'S WOMAN
LAURALEE
MOONFIRE
WANTON ANGEL
WILLOW
PRINCESS ANNIE
THE LEGACY
TAMING CHARLOTTE
YANKEE WIFE
DANIEL'S BRIDE
LILY AND THE MAJOR
EMMA AND THE OUTLAW
CAROLINE AND THE RAIDER
PIRATES
KNIGHTS
MY OUTLAW
THE VOW
TWO BROTHERS
SPRINGWATER
SPRINGWATER SERIES:
     RACHEL
     SAVANNAH
     MIRANDA
JESSICA
A SPRINGWATER CHRISTMAS
ONE WISH
THE WOMEN OF PRIMROSE CREEK SERIES:
     BRIDGET
     CHRISTY
     SKYE
     MEGAN
COURTING SUSANNAH
SPRINGWATER WEDDING
MY LADY BELOVED (WRITING AS LAEL ST. JAMES)
MY LADY WAYWARD (WRITING AS LAEL ST. JAMES)
HIGH COUNTRY BRIDE
SHOTGUN BRIDE
SECONDHAND BRIDE
THE LAST CHANCE CAFÉ
DON'T LOOK NOW
NEVER LOOK BACK

ONE
LAST
LOOK

Linda Lael Miller

POCKET BOOKS
New York   London   Toronto   Sydney

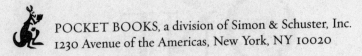

POCKET BOOKS, a division of Simon & Schuster, Inc.
1230 Avenue of the Americas, New York, NY 10020

Library of Congress Cataloging-in-Publication Data

Miller, Linda Lael.
    One last look / Linda Lael Miller—1st Pocket Books trade pbk. ed.
        p. cm.
    I. Arizona—Fiction. I. Title.

    PS3563.I413730538 2006
    813´.54—dc22   2005045935

ISBN-13: 978-0-7434-7050-6
ISBN-10:   0-7434-7050-8 (trade paper)

This Pocket Books trade paperback edition January 2006

   10   9   8   7   6   5   4   3   2   1

For information regarding special discounts for bulk purchases, please contact Simon & Schuster Special Sales at 1-800-456-6798 or business@simonandschuster.com.

For all my friends at Unity of Phoenix,
Church of my dreams.
In particular:

Julia and Kathy Kellogg
Rev. Richard Rogers and Tamis
Rev. Lei Lanni Burt and Jerry
Dorothy Moore
Jeri Royce

Thank you for your commitment to Living Love.

ONE

Pima County Forensic Science Center
Tucson, Arizona
January 7

The zipper on the body bag caught, and the technician gave it a hard, practiced yank. The stenches of death and the attendant chemicals roiled out of the cavity and, in the moment before Detective Tony Sonterra remembered my presence and eased me back with a slight motion of one elbow, the image of Jimmy's youthful, ravaged face imprinted itself, hologram style, on every cell in my brain.

Bile scalded the roof of my mouth.

My name is Clare Westbrook, and I've seen more than my share of corpses. I seemed to attract them on my own, and my association with Sonterra, who was a homicide cop at the time, merely compounded the problem.

I turned away, doing my best not to retch.

Jorge "Jimmy" Ruiz was sixteen years old. His dreams were heartbreakingly modest—he'd wanted a car, cheap housing, and a dog that would come when he called it.

Sonterra had befriended the boy eight months before, when he'd turned up in Phoenix, hungry and ingenuous, and wangled a job with Sonterra's family's landscaping business. Customs and Immigration snagged the kid a few weeks after he arrived, during a routine green-card check, and promptly sent him home to Mexico. Sonterra stayed in touch with Jimmy after that, got him a room in Nogales, on the Sonoran side, then pushed up his sleeves and waded into the red-tape matrix. Probably because of his own Hispanic heritage, he'd been determined to make a difference, if only for this one boy.

I loved that about Sonterra, the way he would lock on to an idea if he thought it was right, and never let go. Our relationship was intense, and by no means simple. I'd moved into his house, with my niece, Emma, and our two dogs, Waldo and Bernice, but I still had one foot in my old life. I'd worked hard to get through law school, schlepping drinks at a Tucson bar called Nipples, and later put in my time at Kredd and Associates, where ambulance chasing was a specialty. It had been Emma and me against the world ever since my sister Tracy's sudden disappearance, when Emma was only seven, and when it turned out that my sister had been murdered by someone close to her, my streetwise, foster-kid wariness went into overdrive.

Trusting Sonterra, trusting *anyone,* was a challenge. Hell, I wasn't even sure I could trust myself.

Now, in the stark reality of cold storage, Sonterra's voice seemed to come through a long, hollow pipe, even though we were within touching distance. "His name was Jorge Ruiz," he told the attendant grimly. "No next of kin."

The tech nodded, blandly accustomed to the unclaimed and unmourned, handed Sonterra a clipboard, watched in silence as he signed off on the attached form. Another body identified. A complex life, reduced to words and numbers. A few check marks, a couple of official signatures, and that's it. Add one more statistic to the column.

I hadn't been well acquainted with Jimmy, but I ached for him, remembering his shy smile, his ragged jeans and T-shirt, his amazing capacity for hard work. I knew he'd slept on a cot on Sonterra's dad's sunporch during his brief stay in the USA, and been pathetically grateful for a place at the kitchen table. He'd loved bologna sandwiches and lime Kool-Aid.

I swayed, gripped the edge of a nearby steel table for balance, and instantly recoiled. The slab was bare, even sterile, but I had a sudden, swift sense of all the bodies that had rested there, for a brief and grisly interval, with only a toe tag to differentiate them from the other vacant shells of humanity that had passed through that place. I'm not exactly squeamish, but I was in a morgue, and four months pregnant.

Kay Scarpetta, I'm not.

Sonterra pressed a hand to the small of my back and steered me toward the exit. Once outside in the corridor, I sank onto a bench and dropped my head between my knees.

"I asked you to wait in the car," Sonterra said with a familiar note of resignation. He waited until I straightened, then handed me a paper cup with a slosh of lukewarm water inside. None of this was new to him—he'd stood by many times, while a family member identified a victim, and even witnessed autopsies—but he was clearly shaken.

I gulped down the water, waited to see if my stomach would send it hurtling back up or simply convulse around it with a couple of good clenches. I kept down the first dose, and threw back the rest.

This would cinch it, I thought. Just the day before, Sonterra had fessed up that he'd been offered a job with a federal task force. He'd been closemouthed about the details, but I knew it had something to do with the stream of illegal immigrants flooding in from Mexico. Now, because of Jimmy, he'd accept for sure. Turn his whole life upside down, and mine with it.

"Coyotes," he said. He wasn't referring to the four-legged variety. In cop speak, coyotes are the sleazeball flesh-smugglers who run Mexican nationals across the border, into the land of milk and honey—for a price. They lock their "clients" up in the trunks of cars, in airless vans, and in "safe houses," sometimes ten to thirty to a room, with little or no food, water, or sunlight. If things go sour in transit, they often shoot them in the head and leave them in the desert for the buzzards. And that's the merciful method. The most common one is dropping them off miles from any road, without their shoes, if they had any in the first place, without water or food or any means to defend themselves. Duct tape and dehydration save on the high cost of bullets. Coyotes are in business to make money, and they do, hand over fist.

Sonterra and I left the building in silence, started across the parking lot toward his slick SUV, gleaming black in the winter sun. That's the reason we Arizonans put up with summer temperatures in the 120-degree range—for the mellow months between October and April. The door locks popped audibly when he pressed the button on his key fob.

We'd discussed the new job, of course, but it was a source of conflict. It meant leaving the Phoenix/Scottsdale area, where I had friends and a pro bono practice I loved, for a wide spot in the road well off the beaten path. I was familiar with Dry Creek, a dust bunny under the bed of life, because of its proximity with Tucson, my hometown. I'd gone there a lot, as a teenager, admittedly to party with other wild kids, and had always come away with one clear thought: *Thank God, I don't live there.*

It's ironic how fate keeps track of blithe statements like that one and uses them to slap you in the face. "Does this mean you're going to play ball with the feds and sign on as chief of police in Dry Creek?" The last chief, a man named Oz Gilbride, had disappeared into a parallel universe, a couple of months ago, under a cloud of controversy and suspicion. I remembered Oz from my misspent youth, too. He'd run a lax department, which was why kids from Tucson liked to raise hell in and around his town. Since he'd vanished, the news media had pegged Chief Gilbride as the lead dog in a very bad pack of coyotes, and maybe they were right.

Maybe they were full of bullshit, too.

I'm not a fan of talking heads, lacquered and smiling, assessing the world from behind a news desk. Most of them, in my opinion, could be a little less interested in pursuing their personal political agendas and a *lot* more interested in telling the truth. It's one thing to alert the population to corporate or government skullduggery, and quite another to back up a truck and dump a load of fear into the collective consciousness just because there's nothing else to talk about on that particular day.

The sky is falling. Film at six.

When Sonterra didn't answer my Dry Creek inquiry right away, I considered switching the subject to lunch, but it didn't seem appropriate, even if it *was* one-thirty in the afternoon, and we hadn't eaten since before we left his place in Scottsdale that morning.

Still musing, Sonterra opened the passenger door for me and waited until I was settled. His handsome features were set, his jawline hard. "Another couple of months," he reflected, "and he would have been legal. He knew all about coyotes. Why get involved with them again?"

I snapped my seat belt on. Youth is not noted for its patience, and Jimmy Ruiz had been *very* young. In Mexico, he'd worn discarded clothes and eaten other people's garbage. In the U.S., he'd tasted Big Macs and stepped, goggle-eyed, into the wonderful world of Wal-Mart.

"It's not your fault," I told Sonterra, because I knew that was what he was thinking—that if he'd done things differently, Jimmy would be alive. Given the singular dangers and depressing nature of Sonterra's work, I thought he was being a little hard on himself.

Sonterra rounded the vehicle, got behind the wheel, cranked on the ignition. Warm air blew from the dashboard, and I felt sweat drying between my breasts and shoulder blades. His right temple pulsed, and he wouldn't look at me. "*Damn* it," he rasped. "Jimmy was so bright. He could have had a good life. Contributed something."

I reached out, touched his arm. "Let it go. You can't save them all, Sonterra."

"I wasn't trying to save everybody in the world," he retorted, backing out of a parking space marked VISITORS. "I was trying to save *Jimmy*. One kid."

I withdrew my hand. I was in no position to make speeches—
I knew something about the savior complex myself. After inherit-
ing a shitload of money from the father I never knew, I'd hung out
my shingle in the worst part of Phoenix, unofficially adopted one
of my first clients, a beautiful young black woman named Shanda
Rawlings, given her a job in my storefront office, helped her beat a
bad-check rap, and bought her a secondhand car. In a few days,
she'd be entering Gateway Community College as a part-time student, financed by a combination of loans and grants. Like any
good messiah, I'd offered to pay her tuition fees and provide the
books, but she'd refused. Shanda had a lot of pride. She really
wanted to build a life for herself and her little girl, Maya, and she
had the guts and brains to make it happen.

I couldn't help imagining how I'd feel if she'd been in
Jimmy's place, and the image made me shudder.

Sonterra pulled into traffic with a slight screech of rubber.
"One kid," he repeated, as the morgue and county hospital fell
away behind us.

"I'm sorry," I said. The pit of my stomach quivered with a
combination of dread and hunger. When Jimmy was found two
days before with four other murder victims, facedown in a gulley
outside of Dry Creek, with his hands taped behind him and most
of his head blown away, the cops had checked his pockets and
found Sonterra's card. They'd called him to make an ID, which
was why we were in Tucson that burnished January afternoon. I'd
had Shanda reschedule all two of my appointments and insisted
on coming along to provide moral support.

I wasn't much help, it seemed to me.

Sonterra's cell phone chirped; he pulled it from his belt,
checked the screen, and pressed the TALK button with his thumb.
"Hi, Dad," he said, weaving through light traffic. Pause. "Yeah. It
was Jimmy, all right."

Sonterra listened soberly for a few moments, then answered,
"They'll probably donate the remains to the med school."

I cringed. True, science needs bodies. But it's a gruesome concept when the one in question belongs to someone you knew.

"I'll see what I can do," Sonterra went on, after another interval of attentive silence. "You're sure that's what you want?"

I adjusted the air-conditioning. Waited.

I hate waiting.

"All right," Sonterra said finally. "Yeah—Clare's with me. Hold on." He extended the phone, keeping his gaze on the road, and I took it.

It lifted my spirits just to hear Alex Sonterra's voice. In fact, I felt a welcome, warming rush of affection, a thawing of the marrow-freeze I'd picked up in the morgue. Like I said, I wouldn't have known my own father if I'd met him on the street, and Alex seemed a willing substitute. "Are you okay, Clare?" he asked gently.

Sentiment washed over me, and tears stung my eyes. I sucked it up, because I didn't know how to do anything else. "Yes," I replied. And it was true. I'm nothing if not resilient. Sure, I was stricken over Jimmy's death, but the nausea, a combination of morning sickness and normal revulsion, had passed, and I was thinking about food.

"You keep an eye on Tonio. Make him eat something." Alex let out a long breath. "He's taking this personally."

I nodded, even though Alex couldn't see me. "I know," I said, glancing at Sonterra. "I'll force-feed him if I have to."

Alex chuckled. "Good," he replied.

We said our fare-thee-wells and disconnected. I handed the cell back to Sonterra.

"Dad wants to bury Jimmy up in Phoenix," he said. "Catholic funeral. Family plot. The whole thing." There was a Cracker Barrel coming up on the right side of the street; he flipped on his signal and turned into the restaurant's lot—bless him. He'd gotten the food reference, then. And he'd probably heard my stomach growling.

"That'll require some paperwork," I replied. I wasn't sure, since I didn't handle immigration cases, but I figured it was safe to assume that the federal, state, and county governments would all want a bureaucratic say in the matter.

"I know a lawyer," Sonterra said, and managed a semblance of a grin. He rarely mentioned my hard-won career, at least in a positive way. He busted the perps, and as a defense attorney, I did my best to get them off. This did not make for domestic tranquillity.

We got out of the rig, and he locked it up again. Inside the restaurant, I made my way through the gift shop, heading for the restroom, while Sonterra approached the hostess for a table. He was on his cell again when I came out, and he cut the call suspiciously short.

My antennae twitched.

"Your dad again?" I asked mildly, when he didn't volunteer anything. It was that cop-lawyer, adversarial thing again. Sonterra and I could blister a mattress, but when it came to just about anything else, we were both pretty careful about showing our cards.

Before he gave up an answer, we were seated, with menus in hand.

"No," Sonterra said. Pulling teeth. That was what it was like, getting information out of him.

A waitress strolled over, ogling Sonterra the way waitresses almost always did. I ordered a BLT with extra mayo, clam chowder, and a side of sweet potatoes, and Sonterra asked for a burger and fries.

"I don't know how you can eat like that," he observed, reaching for the little peg-board game the Cracker Barrel provided to keep hungry customers occupied while the cooks worked their magic behind the scenes.

"I'm pregnant," I reminded him in a righteous and moderately affronted tone.

"Yeah," he said, with another sparing grin. "I was there when it went down." He paused, raised his eyebrows. "So to speak."

Heat flashed through my body. "You were the perpetrator."

He stabbed a green peg into a hole in the game board. "I'm taking the task-force job, Clare," he said.

My spine straightened like a dancing cobra rising out of a basket. As usual, Sonterra was piping the tune. "That means—"

"It means a leave of absence from Scottsdale PD," he interrupted, looking directly into my eyes for the first time since we'd left the morgue. "It means cleaning out a den of coyotes."

"Noble, but it won't bring Jimmy back," I insisted, thinking of my niece, Emma, my best friends, Loretta Matthews and Mrs. Kravinsky, and my practice. If Sonterra moved to Dry Creek, a polyp forty miles up the intestines of Creation, I would have to make a drastic choice. Go with him, or stay.

"No," Sonterra agreed, and waited out the food-service professional when she returned with our iced teas, lingered a little too long, and finally left. "Jimmy's gone. But I might be able to keep this from happening to somebody else."

"Get real, Sonterra," I replied, though not unkindly. I knew he was hurting, and I cared. Four months ago, he'd asked me to marry him—*before* he knew I was carrying his baby—and I'd said yes. I was wearing his late mother's diamond ring on my left hand. Damn straight I cared, even if I had been dragging my feet a little about setting an actual date to walk down the aisle. "These guys are like mushroom spores. Coyotes, I mean. Pull one up by the roots, and a hundred more spring out of the manure overnight."

Sonterra spread his hands, and his right temple pulsed. "Oh, *well* then," he said. "Let's just roll over and let them keep right on killing people!"

Two elderly couples, obviously tourists, eyed us warily from the next table. I half expected them to jump up in unison, make a dash for the old Winnebago, and lay rubber out of there.

"You've got to choose your battles," I argued, in a whisper, and slurped up some iced tea. I guess I thought that would make us seem more normal. *Oh, that's all right then,* I imagined the retirees thinking to themselves. *They're* talking *about murder, but they're drinking iced tea, so they must be all right.*

"Yeah," Sonterra agreed tersely, "and it would be nice if half of those battles weren't with you!"

I leaned in a little. "Pull in your horns, Sonterra. I'm on your side."

"Prove it," he challenged.

Out of the corner of my eye, I saw that the Winnebago crowd had lost interest in our little drama.

"Oh," I said, keeping my voice down anyway, "now we get to the old if-you-love-me-you'll-do-what-I-tell-you routine?"

Sonterra stuck another peg in the board, hard. "Call it whatever you want," he shot back. "You'll put your own spin on anything I say, anyway."

I puffed out a breath and sat back in my chair. The waitress brought our food on a tray, giving me a moderately censorious glance as she set the chowder, sweet potatoes, and BLT down in front of me. Sonterra got a sympathetic sigh along with his lunch.

Bitch, I thought, without much rancor. If I actively hated every woman who felt sorry for Sonterra because he'd hooked up with me, I'd be one big ulcer by now. Besides, I was more interested in the sweet potatoes.

"Are you coming with me or not?" Sonterra asked, in a tight voice, after munching a french fry.

I guess I could have pretended I thought he was talking about the ride back to Scottsdale, but it would have been bullshit. "What would I do in Dry Creek?"

"Relax a little, maybe. You're expecting a baby, remember?"

My temper flared. Sonterra wanted me to veg. Hang out at home, watch daytime TV. Knit booties. Sounded like a prescription for brain rot to me.

"Barefoot and pregnant," I said, aggrieved.

Sonterra swore under his breath.

I lost interest in the sweet potatoes. Then and there, I decided that, if I *did* go to Dry Creek with Sonterra, I would either start another law office or find myself a job in Tucson.

The Winnebago people pushed back their chairs and stood up to leave, chatting amiably about the next destination. Sedona or Santa Fe? Decisions, decisions.

I watched as one of the men dropped a few dollar bills in the middle of the table for a tip. His wife paused beside my chair, her eyes earnest behind her old-fashioned glasses, and for a moment, I thought she was about to ask if I'd accepted Jesus Christ as my personal savior.

She laid a hand on my shoulder. "He looks like a very nice, steady young man," she said, referring, I assumed, to Sonterra, and not Jesus. "Give him a chance."

With that, she trundled away after the other members of her group.

Sonterra chuckled. "Good advice," he said, looking bleakly smug.

"Shut up," I replied, but I couldn't help grinning.

His cell phone blipped. He sighed, checked the caller ID, and frowned. "Sonterra," he said.

I watched his face change. Dark clouds gathering over an uneasy sea.

A little trill of fear shimmied up my windpipe.

"What?" I mouthed.

Sonterra shook his head, listening intently. Finally, he said, "I'm in Tucson. I'll be there as soon as I can." Still on the phone, he signaled the waitress for the check. Clearly, lunch was over. "Tell him to hold on." He waited. "I don't *care* if he's unconscious. Tell him anyway."

TWO

Eddie Columbia, Sonterra's partner, lay still as death in his bed in the intensive care unit at Good Samaritan Hospital in Phoenix, sprouting tubes and wires like some kind of high-tech octopus. His aunt, Louise Pearson, stood next to him, smoothing back his hair.

When we entered, she looked up, tears shimmering in her eyes. "Tony," she said, on a relieved breath, and gave me a nod.

She and Sonterra hugged stiffly.

"What happened?" Sonterra asked, but it was a rhetorical question. A cop had filled him in on the details when he took the call down in Tucson—Eddie had been moonlighting as a security guard for a Phoenix nightclub, probably to meet maintenance payments to his soon-to-be ex-wife, Jenna. He'd been found behind a Dumpster that morning, beaten to the proverbial pulp.

Maybe Sonterra was hoping the story had magically changed, while we were making the two-hour drive north. Rewriting the script, so Eddie had taken a header down his apartment steps, or something innocuous like that. I couldn't blame Sonterra for wanting a different reality. This one definitely sucked.

Louise left Sonterra's question hanging. "When it rains, it pours," she said with a sniffle. "As if this wasn't enough, Eddie's divorce was final yesterday." I picked up a tissue box from the bedside table and silently held it out to her, and she gave me a faltering smile of gratitude. "Jenna got full custody of the kids, and she's marrying the boyfriend next week."

"Shit," Sonterra said. He moved to Eddie's bedside, looked down at his bruised, swollen face. Eddie was in his midthirties, like Sonterra and me, but he looked painfully young, lying there, and limp as a discarded glove. "Phoenix PD nailed the bastards, Eddie," he added, leaning in. "Somebody called in a tip, and it was righteous. Three of them, out of their heads on crank, with their brass knuckles still in their pockets."

Louise and I both winced at the reference to the brass knuckles and took another look at the mess they'd made of Eddie's face.

"Why would anybody do such a thing?" Louise asked, but she didn't sound as though she expected an answer.

In the meantime, I watched Sonterra's face, and it was as if I could see into his head. He and Eddie had been best friends since the pair of them made detective, eight or nine years back. They'd played on the same softball team, exchanged countless macabre jokes, and stood over the chalk outlines of more corpses than I cared to think about. Because of the bond between them, Sonterra was probably feeling every blow Eddie had taken.

I would have squeezed Sonterra's hand, but we were standing too far apart.

"God damn, buddy, it hurts just to look at you," Sonterra said, confirming my psychic abilities.

Louise dabbed at her eyes with a wad of tissue, still holding the box in her other hand. "I wish he'd sell shoes or something," she said. "My *neighbor's* nephew makes a six-figure income doing that, at Nordstrom. Mine's got to chase murderers during the day and get himself beat up by thugs at night!"

Sonterra didn't look up. "Once a cop, always a cop," he answered flatly. "He didn't mention taking a second job, though." A muscle twitched in his jaw. Eddie and Jenna had sold their cozy tract house in mid-November, and Eddie had moved into a studio apartment over Thanksgiving weekend. "I should have guessed why he was always watching the clock. Lent him money."

Eddie wouldn't have taken a cent from Sonterra. I knew, because I'd offered him a loan myself, after a look at his depressing apartment, furnished with lawn chairs, a rickety card table, and an air mattress. He'd bristled and told me he appreciated my concern, but I ought to mind my own business for once. Eddie and I weren't enemies, but we weren't pals, either. The "for once" still rankled a little.

Eddie's doctor stepped into the room just then. He was tall and thin, probably in his midsixties, with thinning white hair and the bluest eyes I've ever seen. He nodded to us, checked Eddie's monitors, scribbled a few notes in the chart at the foot of the bed.

I got a glimpse of his name tag. PHILLIP HAZELTON, M.D.

"There's a five-minute limit on visits in intensive care," Dr. Hazelton said, with kindly reluctance. "I'm afraid I'll have to ask all of you to leave."

I'd been easing around to Sonterra's side. I gripped his hand, squeezed.

He hesitated, then squeezed back. "Is Eddie in a coma," he asked the doctor, "or is he just sleeping?"

"There's a gray area, in between those two states," Dr. Hazelton replied. "That's where he is right now."

"You must have run a lot of tests," Sonterra pressed. He liked specific answers, and he was trained to pursue them in the same single-minded, ruthless way a wolf runs its dinner to ground. "And you must have a professional opinion. I'd like to know what that is."

Dr. Hazelton smiled sadly. "I wish I could tell you everything will be all right, Mr.—?"

"Sonterra. Eddie's a cop, as you probably know. I'm his partner."

The older man nodded. "Your friend is in critical condition, Mr. Sonterra," he said. He inclined his head toward the machines clustered around Eddie's bed. "We're picking up some brain activity, and that's a good sign. His heart rate is steady, if not particularly strong. I can't give you much of a prognosis unless and until he wakes up—"

There was an unspoken "or" dangling at the end of Dr. Hazelton's sentence.

A silence settled over all of us, heavy and electric, like the stillness before a desert storm, and so thick I could barely breathe.

Hazelton checked his watch. "Mr. Columbia needs his rest," he said. It was a diplomatic bum's rush.

Louise rose from her chair, shouldered her purse, and gave her nephew a lingering look before slipping out of the room. I let go of Sonterra's hand and followed her into the corridor.

"Are you all right?" I asked. Louise was in her midseventies, like Mrs. Kravinsky, but she looked and acted much younger. I didn't know her well; I lived in a world of acquaintances and strangers, careful not to get too close to too many people. Except for Jenna and the kids, Louise was the only family Eddie had.

She sighed. Her eyes and nostrils were red-rimmed. "Once I pull myself together, I'll be fine," she said. She started toward the elevator, distracted and still a little dazed, and I walked with her. Sonterra stayed behind in Eddie's room, with the doctor. So much for the five-minute visitor's limit. "I'm going home to change clothes and rest for a while," Louise told me, as the elevator doors opened. "Then I'll come back here and wait. Sit with him, when they'll let me."

I nodded. I was deeply worried about Eddie, like Louise and Sonterra. But I also wondered, selfishly, I know, how his partner's condition would affect Sonterra's decision to take the job in Dry Creek. I didn't want to pack up and move, but I didn't want to be separated from Sonterra, either.

Louise disappeared as the elevator doors closed, teleported to the lobby.

I stood still for a moment, recalling another hospital, when I'd stepped out of another elevator and met myself. Not a long-lost twin. Not a clone. A hallucination to be sure, but one with substance.

I shook my head, trying to throw off the memory. *Don't go there*, I thought. It was an isolated incident, the result of head trauma, and it hadn't happened again. It *wouldn't* happen again.

"Clare?"

I came out of the fog and was surprised to spot Jenna Columbia standing in the waiting room doorway, to my right. Neither Louise nor I had noticed her earlier, which only added to the surreal feeling of the whole scenario. Eddie's ex-wife looked like one of the walking dead.

I glanced toward Eddie's room, hoping Sonterra would go right on breaking the five-minute rule. Nothing good would come of it if he ran into Jenna before he had a chance to square things away in his head.

"Hello, Jenna," I said quietly.

Her face, pretty and guileless and slightly plump, crumpled. "Eddie was beaten up?"

I nodded, feeling wary. I knew Sonterra—when it came to marriage, he was a traditionalist. Because Eddie wouldn't have needed to moonlight if it hadn't been for the breakup, he was likely to blame Jenna, at least in part, for Eddie's assault behind the nightclub. Not very sensible, I know, but since when has human emotion been sensible?

As luck would have it, Sonterra stepped into the hallway at precisely that moment, and his dark gaze tracked and found Jenna like a Scud missile. His face turned to stone.

I moved slightly, hoping to head him off.

Jenna looked nervous, but she stood her ground. Thrust out her chin slightly. "I want to see Eddie," she said, for Sonterra's benefit.

"Maybe you'd like to pull a couple of plugs while you're in there," Sonterra bit out. "Finish him off, once and for all."

"Tony," I said. I linked my arm with his, and for a moment I thought he'd shake me off, but he didn't. I so rarely used his first name that it must have given him pause.

"I *care* about Eddie," Jenna said.

"Almost as much as the boyfriend," Sonterra retorted.

I gave him a jerk in the direction of the elevators.

"He's the father of my children!" Jenna called after us.

Sonterra dug in his heels. "You might have thought of that a little sooner. Like *before* you started fooling around behind Eddie's back!"

Jenna flushed.

"Let's *go,*" I urged, trying to tow Sonterra out of dangerous waters.

He raked a hand through his hair, and Jenna nearly withered under the heat of his glare, but I felt him raise anchor. "I'll be back," he warned.

The Terminator.

The ride down in the elevator was silent. Menace rolled off Sonterra in undulating waves, almost visible in that closed space. We were on the first floor and moving through the lobby before either of us spoke again.

"Jesus," Sonterra grumbled, "she's got some nerve showing up here."

I didn't answer. I did hold out my hand for the car keys, and he gave them to me. Drunks shouldn't drive. Neither should angry people.

It took a few minutes to find the SUV. When we did, Sonterra threw himself into the passenger seat, landing with an angry flop, and wrenched his seat belt into place. The metallic snap echoed like a gunshot. "I guess some women aren't cut out to be a cop's wife," he said when we were making our way toward the 101.

The remark opened a chasm between us.

I wondered if I wasn't one of those women, and I knew Sonterra was asking himself the same thing.

Half an hour later, we pulled into his attached garage. Even before the door rolled down behind us, I heard the dogs barking in the kitchen, and I felt a little better. Waldo, a one-eyed golden retriever, and Bernice, a Yorkie, could always be counted on for a welcome-home party. No matter what else was going on, or what kind of mood either of us might be in, they were glad to see us.

Sonterra slammed out of the SUV before I could shut off the engine. Simultaneously, the inside door opened, and my niece, Emma, recently turned fourteen, stood in the gap, a slender woman-child with short blond hair, fake piercings, and an attitude. Waldo and Bernice, true to form, shot past her to greet us.

I got out of the car, bent to scoop Bernice up into my arms. She wriggled and licked my cheek.

"I heard about Eddie," Emma said. "It's all over the news." She looked more like her mother every day, and I had mixed feelings about that. On the one hand, it was gratifying to know a part of Tracy lived on in Emma. On the other, the reminder was still painful. My sister had been one of the few constants in my life, and the loss of her had a way of sideswiping me when I was least prepared.

Sonterra ruffled Emma's spiky hair, something I would not have been permitted to do. "He'll be okay," he said. Emma probably wondered, as I did, whether he really believed that. He wasn't very convincing.

Emma's wide, troubled gaze shifted to me. "Loretta left a *bunch* of messages. She sounds upset."

I nodded, glumly resigned. Things are rarely so crappy that they can't get crappier. Jimmy Ruiz was dead, along with four other victims. Eddie was in intensive care. Sonterra was on the verge of a move to Dry Creek. It just figured that my best friend was in trouble, too.

I stalled. Loretta lived a charmed life. If she was in a panic, a tidal wave was probably about to submerge the Statue of Liberty. "Did you do your homework?" I asked my niece.

I was half-hoping Emma would say no, even get defiant. She liked to play the part of the rebel, but she was fiercely intelligent and enrolled in a special accelerated course at school. She'd decided to become a cop, and she was determined to double-time it through the rest of her education, before entering the police academy. While most tenth-graders were thinking about surviving adolescence, my niece was planning a career.

Emma backed up to let Sonterra and me into the house. I set Bernice on the floor, and she scampered for the patio doors, Waldo clicking after her, tags jingling on his collar.

"I couldn't concentrate on algebra," Emma said. "Not after I heard about Eddie getting pounded like that."

I nodded, reached for the telephone. My emotional reserves were running low, but Loretta was my closest friend—we went back to the Nipples days in Tucson.

I punched in the number sequence for voice mail.

Loretta's voice was oddly thick, as if she'd had too much to drink. "I need to talk to you, Clare. I tried your cell phone, but you must have it off. Why do you even *have* a goddamned cell phone if you're not going to turn it on?"

I dialed her home number. No one picked up, and the message system didn't kick in, either.

I tried her cell.

No longer in service.

My stomach began to quiver. I was trying to decide what to do next when the phone rang in my hand, nearly startling me out of my skin.

Sonterra gave me a sidelong glance and opened the fridge.

"Sonterra residence," I said, after pushing the TALK button.

"Finally," Loretta said. "Where the hell have you been?"

It didn't seem like a good time to tell her about Jimmy Ruiz, or Eddie. "I might ask you the same question," I replied moderately.

My friend gave a long sigh. "I'm at the ranch," she said. "I've left Kip."

I gripped the edge of the counter with my free hand. *"What?"* Loretta and Kip, her suave, multimillionaire husband, had one of the few good marriages I'd ever seen. Eddie and Jenna were in the swirler. Even Sonterra was divorced, though amicably, and my own romantic history, B.S.C.—before SuperCop—was lackluster to put it mildly. I hadn't realized, until that moment, when the foundations really began to shake, how much I'd depended on Loretta's example as proof that wedded bliss still existed for people who'd tied the knot after 1970.

"It's a long story." Loretta started to cry. I tried to remember the last time I'd known her to break down. We'd still been at

Nipples, serving drinks and fending off gropers—a definite challenge, since we were wearing short skirts and tight tops with bare breasts silk-screened on the front. Loretta was spunk itself, but when her cat died, she folded.

The phone was cordless, so I went to the kitchen table and eased myself into a chair. Emma and Sonterra both stared at me.

"I don't believe this," I said. "What happened?"

Loretta sniffled. "It's the old story. Kip has a girlfriend."

"No," I said.

"Yes," Loretta insisted. "Her name is Miranda Slater, may she rot in hell. She's one of Kip's vice presidents. Research and Development. She developed, and he researched."

I shook my head, still a beat or two behind. "There must be some mistake."

"No mistake," Loretta said flatly. "Clare, can you come down here? I know it's a long way from Scottsdale, but I'm all alone, and I'm bouncing off the walls."

I closed my eyes for a moment. Loretta's ranch was outside Tucson. We'd driven past her exit that day—twice. "I'll be there as soon as I can," I answered.

"Hurry," Loretta pleaded. Loretta didn't plead.

"Hold on," I said, watching Sonterra's face, and hung up.

"What?" Sonterra asked.

"Loretta's in trouble. It's a marriage thing. She wants me to come to the ranch. Tonight."

Some men would have objected, but not Sonterra. "I'll drive you there," he said.

"You've got Eddie to worry about. I'll drive myself."

"I want to go, too," Emma put in, looking anxious.

"No," I said. "You can spend the weekend with Heather or Tiffany."

Emma opened her mouth, closed it again. "That bites," she said, after a few moments of expressive deliberation.

"Right now," I answered calmly, "everything bites."

Sonterra started rustling up supper. He was a whiz with pasta.

I shook off my stupor, went upstairs, showered, and dragged a small weekender and an overnight case from the back of Sonterra's closet. Emma appeared in the bedroom doorway.

"I know I'm just a kid," she said bravely, "but Loretta is my friend, too. I need to know what's wrong." The dogs stood behind her in the hallway, like backup singers ready to do-wah.

I studied her. "You're not 'just' anything," I told her quietly. "You're one of the smartest people I know. So here's the plain truth. Loretta says Kip is having an affair. She's in a lot of pain, and she's probably mad as hell. If you're around, she might feel she has to gloss things over, put on a happy face—"

"And if you go alone," Emma finished, "she'll open up."

I nodded. Fourteen going on forty. That was my niece.

Emma's lower lip wobbled. She'd seen more than her share of trouble in her life, with her father doing periodic stretches in prison and Tracy disappearing when she was little. I'd filed a number of inquiries with the universe, but so far, no one had gotten back to me with an explanation. "First Eddie," she whispered, "and now Loretta. It seems like the whole world is falling apart."

I left my packing to hug her tightly. Security was an issue with Emma, for understandable reasons. "It's not," I said, but I wonder how good a case I made. I was pretty disillusioned myself.

She allowed herself to cling, but not for long. She took her cues from me, though the jury was still out on whether that was a good thing or a bad one. Stepping back, she dashed at her cheek with the back of her right hand. "Right," she scoffed. "People keep trying to kill you, and Tony, too." A rueful grin curved her lips. "Some childhood I'm having."

It was certainly true that I'd been a target. In fact, it was chronic with me. For Sonterra, it came with the job.

I laughed, though I was dangerously close to crying. "Make the best of it," I said. "It's all you've got."

I knew she was shifting mental gears. She was maybe a little too good at that, for a kid. "Tony says the pasta is ready," she said. "So hustle your butt."

I nodded, wishing I could think of something reassuring to say.

Emma didn't wait. She turned and headed back down the hall, toward the stairs, the dogs trotting in her wake.

I went back into the bathroom and splashed my face with cold water until my tear ducts contracted. By the time I got downstairs, I looked more together than I felt, and supper was on the table.

The pasta was delectable. So, alas, was Sonterra. I'd been looking forward to bedding down with him that night—whatever else was going on between us, the sex was better than terrific—but it wasn't to be. I resigned myself to the inevitable.

"I called Tiffany while you were in the shower," Emma informed me, slurping up a noodle. "She and her dad are picking me up at seven-thirty." She nodded toward the counter, where my cell phone was charging. "You were down to one bar," she scolded. "Be sure to plug it into the lighter in the Escalade—and take it inside with you when you get to Loretta's."

"Yes, Mother," I said, smiling a little. My heart wasn't in it, but hey, I tried.

When we were finished eating, Sonterra went upstairs for my bags, and I said good-bye to the dogs while my niece cleared the table and loaded the dishwasher. Without being asked.

The good-byes were awkward. Emma said hers quickly, then retreated to her room, taking Bernice and Waldo with her.

In the garage, Sonterra tossed my luggage into the back of the Escalade and handed me my cell phone, charger and all. "Are you going to tell me what's up?" he asked.

"Loretta says Kip's having an affair."

Sonterra opened his mouth. Closed it again. "Keep in touch," he said, with a shake of his head, kissing me through the open window on the driver's side as an afterthought.

"I was hoping for sex," I confessed.

He grinned, nibbled at my lower lip. "Slut," he said.

"You'd better believe it," I answered.

He chuckled, cupped my cheek in one hand. Brushed the pad

of his thumb lightly over my mouth. "I'll let you know if there's any change with Eddie."

I blinked back a rush of emotion. My throat felt tight, and I wanted nothing so much as to go back into the house, march up the stairs, fall into bed, and pull the covers up over my head. If Sonterra chose to join me, so much the better. "And I'll give you regular Loretta updates."

He kissed me again. "Be careful, Babe."

I nodded, pushed the visor button to raise the garage door behind me, and backed out slowly onto the darkening street.

Color me lonely.

THREE

Loretta looked terrible. Her normally perfect, salon-tinted hair stuck out in every direction. Her eyes were puffy, with great swipes of mascara underneath, and she'd swathed herself in an old flannel bathrobe that resembled an Indian blanket. Crumpled tissues bulged from one pocket, and I suspected the martini in her hand was only the latest in a series.

"It's about time you got here," she said, and belched.

I let the remark pass, setting my purse, weekender, and overnight bag down in the front entryway, taking her by the arm, and squiring her toward the kitchen. In that house, only one of half a dozen she and Kip owned, it was roughly a five-mile hike.

"You need coffee," I said.

"No, I don't," she protested. "I need Drano."

I took the martini out of her hand and kept on trekking.

She belched again, like a trucker after a six-pack of warm beer.

"Where's Kip?" I asked.

Loretta tried twice to reclaim the martini, but she was too unsteady on her feet and finally gave up. Her bare soles made a slapping sound on the expensive tiles as we crossed the living room.

"He's with *her,* of course."

"Bastard," I said, even though I liked Kip and had a hard time picturing him in the role of womanizer. If he *was* cheating on Loretta, however, then he was indeed a bastard, and worse. "How long has this been going on?"

"I found out about it last week." A tear streaked its way through Loretta's ruined makeup.

I stopped. By that time, we'd gained the dining room, which was roughly the size of a Wal-Mart superstore. My voice echoed. "*Last week?* And you were planning to tell me, *when?*"

She made another try for the martini. I held it out of reach. "I didn't want to bother you," she said. "You were busy wrapping up the Valardi case, and getting Shanda registered for college."

Shanda. Damn, I'd forgotten to call my able assistant and let her know I wouldn't be coming into the office in the morning. "You're my best friend," I reminded Loretta, a little sharply. "If Sonterra had been stepping out, you can bet I would have called you, no matter *what* you were doing."

"I was hoping it wasn't true," she admitted.

When we reached the kitchen, I poured the martini into the sink. Truth is, I could have used a stiff drink myself, but, being pregnant, I refrained. I'd never cared much about alcohol, one way or the other, but now I missed it with a sudden and poignant force that scared me a little. My mother was a drunk. I had no intention of carrying on the family tradition.

Loretta sank into one of the chairs at the long table, cupping her chin in one hand. "I was hoping it wasn't true," she repeated, looking dismal and small, like a bird just plucked from an oil slick.

The coffeemaker was complicated enough to require instrument ratings to operate, but I managed to get a pot brewing. I pulled up a chair at the table and sat down close to Loretta, taking her hand.

"Tell me what happened," I urged quietly. "Did you find them in bed together, or what?"

Loretta shook her head. "No," she said. "I called Kip's suite—he was in Aruba, 'on business.' The lovely Ms. Slater answered the phone."

Lawyer Woman leaped out of her inner phone booth, cape flying. "A suite is not the same as a room, Loretta," I reasoned. "They could have been having a meeting."

Loretta shot down my theory like a clay pigeon. "It was three o'clock in the morning there," she informed me.

"Oh," I said, deflated. "Did you ask to speak to Kip?"

"You're damn right I did," Loretta answered. "The floozy said he was in the shower, but she was sure he'd be glad to call me back."

"Did he?"

"No, the chicken-shit bastard."

"So you just took her word for it and hotfooted it down here?"

"No. I checked Kip's credit card statements. He's been shopping at Tiffany's. I didn't get any jewelry."

"Loretta, you have to *talk* to the man, if only to tell him he's a low-life, dirtbag, scum-sucking son of a bitch."

"He can talk to my lawyer." Her mascara-circled eyes widened imploringly. "You'll do it, won't you, Clare? You'll handle my divorce?"

"I'm in criminal law," I reminded her.

"Well, what he did *is* criminal. I trusted him!"

"You're getting ahead of yourself. Divorce is pretty drastic, Loretta."

"Well, *excuse* me!" Loretta erupted. "I thought you'd be on *my* side!"

"I *am* on your side."

"Then do something! File a suit. Freeze his bank accounts. Have him arrested—"

The fancy coffeemaker chortled in for a landing, and I got up to scout for cups. "Get a grip," I said. "Even if Kip did cheat—and I'm not convinced he did, since all you seem to have is Ms. Slater's questionable word and a few items charged at Tiffany's—the two of you might be able to work this out. You love each other, remember?"

"Would *you* want to 'work it out,' if Tony did this to you?"

I paused. "Maybe. After I'd done him severe and lasting bodily harm."

"You wouldn't take him back," Loretta insisted, stabbing at the tabletop with one manicured fingertip. "Don't bullshit me, Clare. I know you. And I *know* you'd go ballistic!"

I poured coffee, carried it to the table, went back for spoons, the sugar bowl, and a jug of cream from the massive refrigerator. You could hang a beef carcass inside that thing. Or an errant husband.

"You're probably right," I admitted belatedly. "But that doesn't mean it would be the best thing to do. People make mistakes. *Good* people make mistakes."

Loretta pushed away the coffee, laid her head down on her folded arms, and gave a wrenching sob.

"I see I'm not making you feel better," I said, sitting down again and laying a tentative hand on her shoulder.

Loretta wailed.

Over the din, I heard a strange noise. A flapping sound, outside and high overhead, growing louder as it got nearer. For a moment, I thought some humongous bird was homing in on the roof.

Glaring light spilled through the windows, and the flapping swelled to a roar that made the floor vibrate under our feet.

Loretta lifted her head. *"Damn* it," she said, eyes glittering. "The helicopter. He's here!"

"Who? Kip?" All right, so I wasn't quick. It had been a long day.

She jumped to her feet, swayed. "Shit, shit, shit! You've got to hide me!"

Hide her? Hell, in that place, she could have eluded him for days.

"Sit down," I yelled over the roar.

Loretta sank back into her chair.

"Did he set that thing down on the roof?" I asked.

"There's a concrete landing pad on the other side of the driveway," Loretta explained. "Look at me! I'm a mess!" She tried to bolt again, but I got her by the sleeve of her Sitting Bull bathrobe and made her sit back down.

The roar subsided to a *whup-whup-whup*.

We waited, and I, for one, was barely breathing. I wasn't used to incoming aircraft. Gunfire, maybe. But not this.

Presently, the lock on the back door jiggled.

And then Kip was there, looming in the doorway.

Loretta sent the sugar bowl wheeling toward his head. She'd been the darts champion at Nipples, and she hadn't lost her touch.

Kip ducked just in time.

I stood, planning to make a run for it.

Loretta put a hand on my shoulder and pushed me back into my chair. "Don't you dare leave!" she shouted. "I'm about to commit murder, and I want a witness!"

"Loretta," Kip said. He looked rumpled, as if he'd hung from one of the helicopter runners all the way from Aruba, or wherever he'd been in the days since the fateful phone call. Indiana Jones after a very bad week. "What in the name of God has gotten into you?"

Loretta screamed a drunken expletive, reminding me of dear old Mom, and sent the cream pitcher sailing along the same trajectory as the sugar bowl. Again, Kip was lucky. Or just quick.

"For God's sake, Loretta," Kip reasoned. "This will get us nowhere."

The fool. Didn't he know there is no getting through to an angry, inebriated woman in an ugly bathrobe?

I covered my face with one hand, but couldn't resist peering between my fingers. If the conflict escalated, I decided with an odd detachment, I would dive under the table. Kip was blocking one exit, and the others were too far away.

"Is this about Miranda?" Kip asked.

Duh, I thought.

Frenzied, Loretta looked around for more things to throw. Fortunately, the bronze quail sculpture in the middle of the table proved too heavy, though she tried to hoist it. She finally settled for the Waterford salt and pepper shakers I'd saved for weeks to buy, back in the Nipples days. Okay, I got them at an outlet, but I wasn't rich then. I hated to see my wedding present hurtling across the kitchen, shattering into expensive slivers, just short of Kip, on the tile floor.

"You're—having—an—affair!" my friend huffed.

"Loretta," Kip said, spreading his hands. "It's over. I promise it will never happen again."

A direct admission of guilt.

My mouth fell open.

Loretta froze.

Kip's beleaguered gaze slid to my face, rested there for a moment. I think it's safe to say he and I were both wishing I wasn't around. I wondered what had taken him so long to make his dramatic entrance. The ways of tycoons, I concluded in the next moment, are past understanding.

"I'll make it up to you," Kip told Loretta.

Inwardly, I rolled my eyes. There weren't enough little blue Tiffany boxes in the world to make up for *this* one.

"Get out," Loretta said. She seemed so fragile that I stopped thinking about taking cover under the table and prepared to catch her if she started to go down.

"I fired her," Kip said dismally. "Miranda is gone. For good."

Loretta flushed, then went alarmingly pale, all in the space of a few seconds. *"Get out,"* she repeated.

Kip didn't move. I almost felt sorry for him. *Almost.* But I couldn't help imagining what I would do in Loretta's position.

"I love you," he said to her, and I believed him, crazy as it sounds. Of course, Loretta didn't, and that was what counted.

Loretta gaped at him. Tears trickled down her face. Then she turned and fled the kitchen.

I rose from my chair to follow. God knew what she would do next.

"You'll stay with her?" Kip asked.

I nodded and hurried after Loretta. The roar of the departing helicopter seemed to set the walls trembling.

It took me a full twenty minutes to run my friend to ground. She was downstairs in the wine cellar, trying to pull the cork out of a vintage merlot with her teeth.

I gently removed the bottle from her grip.

"You've had too much to drink already," I said, stating the painfully obvious.

"Wrong," Loretta countered petulantly. "If that were true, I wouldn't be hurting so much."

I took her arm. "Come on," I said quietly.

Loretta's chin quivered. "I hate him," she said, and her blue eyes welled up again.

"No, you don't," I replied. "That's the problem." I set the bottle aside, thankful she'd chosen the wine cellar over the gun collection in Kip's study. "Here's the plan. You'll take a bubble bath and try to calm down a little. I'm going back to the kitchen and fix you something to eat. I'll bet you haven't had a balanced meal since you called Aruba and got Ms. Slater on the line."

"I can't eat," Loretta protested. "I intend to starve myself to death."

"No man is worth that," I said.

Loretta surprised me by giving in. "All right," she said. "I'll take a bubble bath. But I won't eat anything healthy. I want cookie dough ice cream, with whipped cream and walnuts."

"Done," I promised.

We parted ways at the top of the cellar stairs.

When Loretta came into the kitchen, half an hour later, her face was scrubbed and moisturized, and she'd exchanged the Indian blanket for a black sweat suit. Her hair was pinned up in a loose French twist. Without her makeup, she looked incredibly young. If we hadn't been in the middle of a crisis, I probably would have hated her for it.

"What am I going to do?" she asked very softly, slumping back into her chair.

"Eat ice cream until you pop," I answered. I got out two mixing bowls, retrieved the Ben & Jerry's from the freezer, and started scooping. The spray-on whipped cream and ground walnuts were at the ready, on the counter, and I'd broken into the chocolate syrup, as well, just to make the feast really evil. "It's the only sensible thing to do in a situation like this."

Loretta laughed, though it was a congested, snuffly sound. "You're bad," she said. "That's one of the reasons I like you so much."

The whipped cream made me miss Sonterra more than ever. Never mind why.

I carried my culinary creations to the table, and Loretta and I each took a spoon and dug in.

"We'll probably gain five pounds from this," she said.

"More like ten," I lamented.

She laughed again. Reached out to squeeze my hand. "Thanks, Clare. Thanks for being my friend."

"I wouldn't put on ten pounds for just anybody," I told her.

An hour later, when Loretta had gone to bed, and I was ensconced in one of the guest suites, fighting off a sugar coma, I scrabbled through my purse for my cell phone and speed-dialed Sonterra.

He answered on the second ring. "It's about time," he said. "I thought you were dead beside the road someplace. I was about to send out the State Patrol."

"I'm at Loretta's," I replied, plopping down on the edge of the bed. "The situation is critical."

"How about a rundown?"

If only he were there with me. I could have used the company, and there was still a lot of whipped cream left. "Kip's been cheating on her, all right," I said. "He actually admitted it."

"Oh, that," Sonterra replied.

I stiffened. "'Oh, *that*'? Did Emma tell you?"

Sonterra let out a sigh. "No," he said, somewhat sheepishly. "You *knew?*"

Silence.

"*Sonterra.*"

"All right. Yes. I knew."

Forget the whipped cream. I was thinking more along the

lines of blunt objects. "You knew, and you didn't bother to mention it to me?"

"I found out by accident," he said. I didn't have to see him to know he'd run a hand through his hair. He always did that when he wanted to buy time. "The commissioner belongs to Kip's country club. We had a meeting there, a few weeks ago, about this task-force thing, and I ran into Kip and the Squeeze. She was wearing a slippy red dress and he had his hand on her thigh. I jumped to the obvious conclusion."

I had to consciously relax my jaw. "Why didn't you tell me?"

Pause. One of those charged ones, the kind that crackle. "I figured you'd decide all men were scum and give back my engagement ring. I'm sorry, Clare. I should have said something."

"You're damn right you should have said something!"

"Is Loretta okay?" I could tell by his tone that he truly cared what the answer was, and I softened a little, but grudgingly.

"No," I said, the word catching in the back of my throat. "No. She's not okay."

"She will be, Clare," Sonterra promised. "Whatever happens. Loretta's tough, like you."

"Right now, I don't think she *feels* very tough. I know I don't."

"I could come down there."

I thought about Eddie, battered and broken. "No, you couldn't. Your best friend is in the hospital."

"My best friend is in Tucson," Sonterra said.

I started to cry, all of a sudden, and a few moments passed before I could say anything. "Is there any news?" I finally choked out. "About Eddie, I mean?"

"I'm at the hospital now. He's stirred a couple of times. Still unconscious, though."

"Is Jenna there? If she is, be nice to her."

"She isn't. Which is a good thing."

"This isn't her fault, Sonterra." I plucked some tissues from the box on the bedside table and wiped my face hard enough to take off a layer of skin.

Sonterra spoke moderately. "Let's save this discussion for

another time. Like tomorrow. I'm due in Dry Creek at ten o'clock, for the official swearing-in. I'd like you to be there. Bring Loretta."

I swallowed. "You're still taking the job?"

"Yes."

"What about Eddie?"

"I can't stand here and hold his hand till he wakes up, Clare. He wouldn't even want that."

I wasn't so sure, but I didn't have the will to argue. I'd had all the drama I needed for one night.

I bit my lower lip. "I'll be there," I said. "For your swearing-in, I mean."

"Good. How about the rest of my life? Will you be there for that, Counselor?"

"Depends on how long you plan to stay in Dry Creek," I answered. I was only half-kidding. The place could have been the set for one of those B-movies where everyone gets abducted by aliens. I imagined shutters creaking on rusty hinges, sagebrush blowing down the middle of the main street. Nobody at the gas station. Dust settling on the petrified pies in the diner.

"We're talking about six months, max," Sonterra said, treading carefully.

Yes. Six months—five of which I would be profoundly pregnant. I looked down at my engagement ring, turned it round and round on my finger. If I agreed to the hitch in Dry Creek, I'd not only be with Sonterra, I'd be near Loretta, too. I was almost sure she'd stay on at the ranch until she figured things out, or felt ready to face Scottsdale society, whichever came first. And the ranch was only twenty miles from Sonterra's new beat.

That left Emma, who would be only too happy to board at school and spend the weekends in Dry Creek. In the meantime, she could stay on with Tiffany and her family, if they were agreeable to the idea, of course.

"Are you still there?" Sonterra asked.

"Yes," I said.

"Look, try to get some rest, will you? And stop worrying. Everything will work out."

"I'll see you in the morning."

"I'll be the guy with the shiny badge."

I smiled, but it felt shaky on my mouth. Suddenly, I was so tired I didn't know if I had the strength to put on my pajamas or brush my teeth. Maybe I'd just stretch out on top of the bedspread and let myself sink into oblivion. "Will that be a gun in your pocket," I teased, "or will you just be happy to see me?"

He laughed. "Oh, I'll be happy to see you, all right."

We said our good-nights, and I did manage to stagger into the bathroom, shower for the second time that evening, and dress for bed. I even remembered to plug my cell into the charger.

The moment I crawled under the covers, I was out.

I dreamed Loretta and I were wandering in the desert, with our feet bare and our hands duct-taped behind our backs.

Suddenly, a loud, high wind came up.

We heard the familiar *whup-whup-whup* of helicopter blades.

Kip! We were about to be rescued. Overjoyed, weeping with relief, we jumped up and down, the dream Loretta and me, trying to shout through the thick tape covering our mouths.

But then the helicopter tipped ominously in our direction, and the blades came at us like a giant buzz saw. We stumbled, tried to run, but it was too late.

I woke with a start and a cry that hurt my throat.

Wasn't it me who said it?

Things are never so crappy that they can't get crappier.

I was awake, but the nightmare lingered. My heart stumbled and slammed to a stop, and my eyeballs dried as I tried to make sense of what I was seeing.

Myself, standing at the foot of the bed.

I clenched my fists, just to make sure they were still attached to my arms.

I blinked, but the vision didn't go away. The other Clare wore jeans and a gray sweatshirt, and she was bleeding from a nasty gash in her head.

She didn't speak.

She didn't move.

She just stood there, bleeding.

My heart started up again, pounding so hard I thought it would rupture. My breath was too quick and too shallow. I knew I was hyperventilating, but I couldn't get control.

I hugged myself, too stricken to scream, and squeezed my eyes shut. This time, it worked. When I looked again, she was gone.

I waited for my knees to solidify, then stumbled into the bathroom and hurled up the ice cream.

FOUR

I didn't sleep the rest of the night, and when Loretta wandered into the kitchen at six-thirty in the morning, I was pouring cold water into the well on the coffeemaker. I'd already swept up the broken crockery from last night's Kip bombardment.

"You don't look so good," she said. Loretta and I rarely minced words. "Are you feeling all right?"

"Morning sickness," I answered. It was only a partial lie. I was hungover from the ice-cream binge; then there was the helicopter dream. Semibullshit reasons. The main one was the hallucination. She'd been so real, the other Clare. Not shimmering and see-through, like your average apparition.

I should have told Loretta what happened, right then, but she had problems enough without having to worry that I was losing my sanity.

And I should have told Sonterra—but he, too, had a lot on his mind, because of Jimmy Ruiz and Eddie and because it was the first day of his new job. Besides, he hadn't told me about seeing Kip with Miranda Slater at the country club. If he wanted to play keep-a-secret, he'd find himself seriously outmatched.

I decided to wait for a decent hour and put in a surreptitious call to Mrs. Kravinsky on my cell phone. My good friend and former neighbor was psychic, among other things. She would know what to do.

I bit my lower lip, fumbled for coffee mugs.

Loretta took a loaf of bread from the freezer and set her course for the toaster. "Have you spoken to Tony?"

I couldn't meet her eyes. Sonterra had known about Kip's affair. Granted, he hadn't told me, but I still felt guilty, as though I'd been the one to withhold information. "Yes," I said. "He's being sworn in as chief of police today, over in Dry Creek. Ten o'clock. Care to come along and help celebrate?"

Loretta was clearly taken aback, but she recovered quickly. She didn't look half as bad as I felt. In fact, she didn't look bad at all. Bitch.

"Chief of police—Dry Creek—Clare, what the heck are you talking about?" She took the coffee carafe out of my hand and poured a mugful for each of us.

I explained about Sonterra's career change, leaving out the task-force part. Since the feds had arranged the gig, I wasn't sure if it was supposed to be top secret or not.

Hope sparked in Loretta's eyes. I wondered what cost-the-earth cream she'd used to prevent puffiness. I was a Maybelline girl myself. "You'll be just down the road from here," she said. "You *are* planning to live with Tony in Dry Creek, right?"

"Right," I said with a sigh.

"Show a little enthusiasm. The man is seriously attractive."

I smiled, took a sip of hot, fresh coffee, and felt a little better, that quickly. As a detective, Sonterra worked in plain clothes. Now he'd probably wear a standard cop suit. "I do have a thing about uniforms," I said.

Loretta giggled. It was a thick sound, painful to hear. "Sit down and drink your coffee," she said. "You still seem a little peaky. I'll make breakfast."

Loretta didn't usually cook. In Scottsdale, she had Rosa to keep house and make the meals. It finally occurred to me that I hadn't seen any sign of the middle-aged couple who managed the ranch.

I asked about them.

The toast popped up, and Loretta buttered it before answering. "They're spending a month in Seattle," she said without looking at me. "Their daughter had a baby last week." Her voice caught on the word "baby." She put the toast on a plate and brought it to me. "Eat this."

"What about Dry Creek? Are you coming with me?"

Loretta shook her head. "I think I'll stay here. Maybe have one of the cowboys saddle Cherokee. Take a ride."

"Loretta, you're talking like a telegram."

She cracked six eggs into a skillet, and, munching toast, I watched with interest as she picked out little pieces of shell with her nail. We took a cooking class together once. We were the first people ever physically expelled from the Williams-Sonoma at Fashion Square Mall.

"I'm not up to celebrating anything today, Clare," she said.

That was the end of the subject.

After breakfast, Loretta donned jeans, boots, and a chambray shirt and retreated to the stables.

Though it was still early in the day, I snagged my cell and put that call through to Mrs. K just the same. I first met her when I started my indentured servitude with Harvey Kredd—Harvey had picked up the tab for my three years of law school, with the proviso that I'd work *five* years for him, at an abysmally low salary, with all the worst cases funneled straight to my desk—and I knew by long experience that she'd be up and around.

"Clare," she chimed, another devotee of caller ID, assuming that she'd even bothered with such mundane technology. Mrs. K might not have been Irish, but she definitely had the Sight. I'm the skeptic's skeptic, but I've seen her in action too many times to discount her unique talents. "I was just thinking about you."

"Good things, I hope," I said, putting on my makeup while we talked. I didn't wear much, but meeting yourself can definitely take the color out of your cheeks.

"Well, I did have a rather disturbing dream," she said carefully. She didn't like to scare the uninitiated, or even the *partially* initiated, like me. "Your head was bleeding."

A chill did a Cirque du Soleil number down my spine, and

for a second I was afraid to turn around, afraid my spare self would be standing there, eyes pleading, hair soaked crimson.

"Funny you should mention that," I said, once I caught my breath. "I saw myself again last night, Mrs. K."

She gasped, which did nothing to make me feel better. This was the third hallucination. I'd confided in Mrs. K after the first two episodes, several months before, and, unlike most people, who would have recommended immediate medical attention, she believed the phenomenon had a deeper meaning. I'm not given to flights of fancy, strange or otherwise, and sometimes my elderly friend seemed to be the only person in the world who never forgot that. She'd told me gravely to let her know right away if it ever happened again.

"Tell me exactly what you saw," she said crisply.

I recounted the details. The clothes, the blood, the imploring eyes.

"This is not good, Clare," she concluded.

I felt a touch of impatience, despite the aforementioned high regard for Mrs. K's unusual abilities. I'd figured that much out for myself. Perhaps I'd even hoped she'd ascribe it all to hormones, strain, and my imagination. "It's probably just stress. There's a lot going on in my life right now." I told her briefly about Sonterra's new job and the move it would require, and hinted that Loretta was having problems, without betraying her confidence.

"There is *always* a lot going on in your life," Mrs. K retorted flatly. "Things will turn out fine for Loretta. The new job is just what Tony needs right now—what you both need, actually. But we're talking about you, specifically. The first thing I want you to do is call your obstetrician. The second is, tell Tony, if you haven't already."

I was taking my prenatal vitamins, even though they made me gag. I avoided alcohol, consumed less than half my usual quota of caffeine, and never took over-the-counter medications. I wasn't going to tell my doctor that I was seeing things. She'd either lock me up in a rubber room or slap me in the hospital for a bunch of tests—or both—and I wasn't about to let myself in for that.

"Okay," I said, drawing the word out to twice its normal length. I figured it wasn't exactly a lie, since I hadn't said "yes" to cluing in either Sonterra or my doctor.

"In the meantime, I'll look into the matter." When Mrs. K "looked into the matter," she lit candles, burned herbs, and talked to spirits. It sounds crazy, I know, but she got answers. "How can I get in touch with you, Clare?"

"Call my cell," I said, as I swabbed on some mascara, taking care not to put out an eye, and forced a cheerful note into my voice. I'm not naturally perky. "How's the secret-shopping biz these days?"

Recently, Mrs. K had taken a part-time job as a mystery shopper. It was one of those serendipity things. She'd found her niche in the career world and promptly started her own company. She ran the operation from her kitchen table, and within weeks, she'd taken on three employees.

"Booming," she said proudly.

"That's good."

"I couldn't have done it without your loan, Clare. I should be able to start paying you back by next month."

I didn't care if she never paid me back—the few thousand dollars I'd given her hadn't made a dent in the interest on my inheritance, let alone the principal. Still, like Shanda, she had her pride. I understood pride, having so much of it myself, and stepped lightly whenever I encountered it in others. "That'll be great," I said.

"Be careful," she replied seriously.

"I promise I will," I said in all good conscience.

How was I to know somebody would try to kill me before the day was over?

FIVE

The population of Dry Creek had not, as it turned out, been sucked up into a flying saucer since my last visit, as a problem teenager. From the looks of some of the people on the streets, though, there might have been a few instances of intergalactic crossbreeding.

The Escalade drew curious glances as I cruised down Main Street, careful to stay within the speed limit. Not that I would have minded seeing Sonterra, even if he was writing me a ticket. It was 9:47 by the clock on my dashboard—I'd killed a little time shopping for maternity clothes in Tucson after leaving Loretta's. The swearing-in was scheduled for ten sharp.

I was right on time.

I eyed the Bijou, the town one-plex—I think it closed about the time Disney released *Old Yeller*—then came two combination gas station–convenience stores, the Doozy Diner, three taverns with redneck names, a hair salon, an insurance agency, and a seedy-looking supermarket with discarded flyers and crippled shopping carts littering the nearly empty parking lot. Most people probably went to Tucson for everything but bread and milk, and those could be purchased at the gas-and-go's. The American Legion occupied the same squat log building it always had, bravely advancing the cause of blackout bingo on a reader board out front. There were several more recent additions to the landscape, but one stood out—an antique store called Danielle's Attic. The building was new and expensive, with a faintly startled look to it, as though it had gone to sleep in Scottsdale's oh-so-upscale gallery district and awakened to find itself in Dry Creek.

The place was doing a brisk business. I counted six RVs out front, all with out-of-state plates, as I passed, headed for the police station, which was at the far end of Main Street, unless they'd moved it, across from Dry Creek High School. The barbershop had closed, though the red-and-white-striped pole was still clinging to the wall like a sailor on a sinking ship. There was a FOR RENT sign in the smudged window, and my spirits lifted a notch. Good place for a law office.

A couple of squad cars waited in the gravel lot outside the cop shop, and quite a crowd had gathered for the swearing-in. Sonterra's arrival was big news, and everybody in town probably wanted a good look at Oz Gilbride's successor.

Anthony Sonterra, chief of police. I had to admit it had a certain ring. And hadn't Mrs. K as much as said the job was part of his destiny, as well as mine?

Two old ladies squinted at my vanity plate as I headed for a space between a rusted-out truck and a minivan. Since they didn't seem to be in any immediate danger of figuring it out, I didn't worry.

A deputy with a round face and a serious belly spotted me as I approached the entrance to the station, and tugged politely at the brim of his Smokey hat. He had a pair of sunglasses hooked in his shirt pocket, and the skin around his eyes sagged, as if he'd seen too much in his time, and his flesh couldn't support the weight of it anymore.

I smiled warmly. If Sonterra and I were going to live in this town for six months—and at some point I had resigned myself to the fact that we were—it was important to get off on a friendly foot.

"I'm Clare Westbrook," I said, putting out my hand.

"Dave Rathburn," the deputy replied. His grip was crushing, but, through long practice, I didn't wince. "Chief Sonterra asked me to be on the lookout for you. He's inside, doing an interview with some woman from the *Arizona Republic*." He resettled his hat. "They didn't bother with us much when Oz disappeared."

I offered no comment on that. I had seen file footage of Oz Gilbride on a few newscasts, after he took an alleged powder, but Rathburn was essentially right. There hadn't been any big splash.

After engaging in a sigh, Deputy Rathburn took a loose grip on my elbow and squired me inside the police station. It was small, with old-fashioned wooden railings separating it into sections, three visible cells, and an honest-to-God potbellied stove. I almost expected Andy Griffith to appear, whistling, with Don Knotts ambling along at his heels.

Sonterra was indeed wearing a uniform, and he was every bit as hot as I'd anticipated. The reporter from the *Republic,* a pretty little thing who looked about seventeen, gazed up at him in wondrous appreciation of every golden word that fell from that sensual Latin/Irish mouth of his. She and I had butted heads recently, when I'd won an acquittal for David Valardi, a client accused of writing a computer virus and sending it out to gobble up hard drives.

Eat your heart out, kid, I thought benignly, admiring Sonterra. *He's mine.*

He turned, spotted me, favored me with one of his lethal grins. There was a promise in that grin.

Maybe I should have picked up a can of whipped cream along with the maternity tops and expandable pants.

Sonterra cut the interview short and made his way toward me.

"How's Loretta?" he asked, at the same time I blurted, "How's Eddie?"

"Eddie's awake," he said with relief. "He's going to be okay." Sonterra's eyes were warm, watchful. I felt like a rat for not telling him I was having hallucinations. Then I remembered he hadn't told me about seeing Kip and the girlfriend at the commissioner's country club. In my opinion, we were even-steven.

"What about Loretta?" he asked.

"Very depressed. I invited her to come along, but she didn't feel like leaving the ranch. She was saddling up for a horseback ride when I left."

Sonterra took my upper arms in his hands. "Thanks for coming, Clare," he said quietly. "It means a lot to me."

I wanted to rise on my toes and kiss him, but there were too many people around. "Where, exactly, are we going to live?" I asked sweetly. "Not the Hidy Tidy Trailer Park, I hope." I'd seen a sign for the Hidy Tidy on my way into town and been surprised to know it was still in business. Even way back when, it was tacky to the max.

The grin flashed again, wicked and warm. "Didn't I tell you? The town council ponied up for a house. It has a screened-in sunporch and a big yard with lots of grass. The dogs love it." He leaned in close, and his warm breath brushed my ear, sending a sweet shiver through me. "There's no furniture yet, of course. Just a blowup mattress in the middle of the living room floor. Don't think for a minute you're going back to Loretta's before we break it in."

I blushed. I do not blush.

"I told her not to expect me before midnight," I whispered back.

He made a low, growling sound, audible only to me. I noted, out of the corner of my eye, that Kelly Staben, Ace Reporter, was watching closely, though. The old acid-wash glare.

I've had that from the best, practicing law. She was hardly intimidating. I waggled my fingers at her.

She scowled back.

A pudgy bald man, who could only have been the mayor, cleared his throat loudly, preparing to orate.

"Ladies and gentlemen," he boomed, as the crowd settled into an interested murmur. "As you know, the fine community of Dry Creek has been subjected to scandal and unfair speculation in recent months, but this is a new and better day . . ."

I glanced over and saw Deputy Rathburn's jowls quiver, and

a faint pink flush rose in his thick neck. The two old biddies from the parking lot were nearby, too, watching me narrowly.

Guess they figured out my license plate.

MJRBCH.

Major Bitch.

I smiled engagingly.

SIX

After the swearing-in, there was a community picnic at the park, down by the dry creekbed from which the town had taken its name. Sonterra had to hobnob and press the flesh, and eat a lot of fried chicken, so everyone would know the new chief of police was approachable, a regular guy. I wondered if the mayor or Deputy Rathburn knew that Sonterra was drawing a second paycheck from the feds, and made a mental note to ask him for the lowdown later on.

Not that I had a hope in hell he'd tell me anything sensitive.

I was tucking into a second helping of potato salad at one of the picnic tables when a tall, skeletal woman with a sleek cap of black hair materialized out of the milling citizenry and put out a bejeweled hand in greeting. Even though dusk was gathering, she wore sunglasses, so I couldn't see her eyes. By my best guess, she was in her midthirties.

"Danielle Bickerhelm," she said, by way of introduction.

I felt a jiggle of familiarity in the pit of my stomach, but I couldn't remember meeting her before.

"Clare Westbrook," I replied, intrigued.

Her lips formed a twitchy smile. "Not 'Clare Sonterra'? Are you one of those modern women who don't take their husband's name?"

It was a reasonable question, I suppose, but it definitely rubbed me the wrong way. And I was only half in the conversation, since I was still trying to figure out how I knew her. "Not Sonterra," I confirmed, putting down my paper plate.

"Well," she said. "That's interesting."

I figured it was Sonterra she found interesting, but being the soul of polite decorum, I didn't comment. Instead, I made a deductive leap. "You own Danielle's Attic," I said, recalling the swanky antique store on Main Street.

"Yes," she answered. I wished she'd take off those damn glasses, so I could get a read on her. Maybe, if I saw her whole face, I'd recognize her. "You must stop in sometime. I've got some furniture that would look lovely in the chief's house."

The chief's house. As though I didn't fit into the equation.

"Have we met before?" I asked.

"No," she answered, without hesitation.

"I'd swear—"

"I tried to buy that place," Danielle broke in, and her voice seemed to tighten a little, as though some little demon was twisting a screw, deep down in her psyche. Meanwhile, my legal brain flipped through the files—law school, college, even high school. Nothing, but still the déjà vu persisted. "The city council refused to sell," Danielle complained. "It's the only house in town with trees in the yard."

Life is hard and then you die, I thought uncharitably. Then, *Rein it in, Clare. You're being hormonal.* "I like trees," I said, because I was still snagged on placing her.

"Cottonwoods," Danielle said dreamily. "Lovely and green."

I began to feel restless. I looked around for Sonterra, spotted him playing horseshoes with half a dozen old boys in billed caps. Our gazes connected, and I sent a silent message. *Damsel in distress.*

Fortunately, he picked up on it, excused himself, and headed in my direction. Danielle lingered. Maybe I couldn't see her eyes, but I could tell by the angle of her head that she was watching Sonterra's approach.

"Hello, Chief," Danielle said sweetly. "I was just telling—"
She paused, as though she'd forgotten my name, and maybe she
had. Plainly, I was not the focus of her attention. "—*Clare* that I
put in a very generous offer on the house you'll be living in. It was
turned down flat."

Sonterra's grin was affable, but his eyes were on the alert.
"That's too bad," he said lightly, and took my hand. "We'd better
go and check on the dogs," he told me. "They've been alone since
this morning. God knows what they're up to by now."

There were other people to meet before we could make a clean
getaway, of course. Leaving Danielle behind, we made the acquaintance of Father Morales, who officiated at St. Swithin's Catholic
Church and was surrounded by an adoring retinue of small, eager
children, mostly Latino. Madge Rathburn, the deputy's wife. Various
business owners and community leaders.

When we could make a graceful departure, Sonterra and I
hiked for the parking lot, and I still couldn't get Danielle out of
my mind, even knowing any pertinent data would surface eventually if I left it alone.

"I've met that woman somewhere before," I mused aloud.

"What woman?"

"Danielle Bickerhelm. The one in the sunglasses. Do you
know her?"

Sonterra pondered a moment, looking somber, then shook
his head. "Nope."

Big Chief had driven his SUV to the celebration, and I'd
brought the Escalade, so we wouldn't have to go back to the cop
shop to pick up one vehicle or the other.

"I don't like her," I said, as he opened my driver's door for me.

Sonterra didn't answer. I could tell he was thinking about
other things. Like Oz Gilbride's disappearance and the five bodies found in the desert outside Dry Creek, one of them Jimmy
Ruiz's.

Suddenly, he grinned gloriously. The sun had come out from
behind the clouds. "Follow me, Counselor. I've got an air mattress
I want to show you."

I felt infinitely better and immediately forgot Danielle. "Lead the way," I said.

He left me to get behind the wheel of his SUV, and we caravanned it out of the parking lot, down Main Street, and onto a side road marked Cemetery Lane. It gave me a little chill, seeing that street sign. I put it down to tension, pregnancy, and too much potato salad.

Though it was still midafternoon, the house was all lit up, inside and out. It was a sizable white Victorian with gabled windows and a wraparound porch, flanked by the lush cottonwoods Danielle had mentioned. There was a picket fence, and the mailbox beside the front gate was one of those elegant iron mail-order jobs, a large, ornamental box with curlicues and a door with a brass handle.

I was charmed already, and I hadn't even been inside.

As a kid, living in shabby, backstreet rentals with my mother, then a series of foster homes and, finally, blessedly, in my grandmother's double-wide mobile, I'd dreamed of houses exactly like this one. Once, I'd even carried around a picture ripped from an outdated magazine in my caseworker's office, like the kid in *Miracle on 34th Street,* hoping Santa Claus would hook me up with just such a place, complete with a pair of sober parents.

Not that I ever believed in Santa Claus—or sober parents.

"Cemetery Lane?" I asked Sonterra, because, for some inexplicable reason, I couldn't comment on the house. I felt a rare, raw yearning, just looking at it, and any but the most ordinary words would have stuck in my throat.

Sonterra grinned, pocketing his keys. "Didn't I mention that there's a graveyard on the other side of the back fence?" he asked.

I shook my head, let him take my hand. "There are a lot of things you didn't mention," I said. I could hear Bernice and Waldo barking happily inside the fantasy house, and my heart did a funny little flip behind my breastbone.

Sonterra opened the gate, and we started up the walk.

"You should stay the night," he said, as we mounted the front steps.

"I didn't bring pajamas," I replied. An inane excuse, I know, but it was all I could come up with.

Sonterra wriggled his eyebrows. "You won't need pajamas, Counselor," he said. He opened the front door, which had a stained-glass oval in the middle, without using a key. Bernice and Waldo sprang out at us in furry, ecstatic welcome.

Hell, I thought tremulously. *All we need is an old lady holding a Thanksgiving turkey on a platter and we've got a Norman Rockwell painting.*

Sonterra lifted me into his arms with an exaggerated grunt of effort and carried me over the threshold.

Careful, warned my inner foster kid, *don't get too happy. Let the universe guess that you want something, and it's as good as gone.*

Sonterra didn't put me down again until we'd toured the whole first floor, with its spacious kitchen, formal parlor, cozy living room, and a small den, where his computer and mine were already set up, along with a fax machine.

Pinch me. The floors were all hardwood, tongue and groove, and the windows were leaded.

I was in love, and I kind of liked Sonterra, too.

At the foot of the front stairway, he set me back on my feet. I recalled the ice-cream binge at Loretta's the night before and wondered, albeit belatedly, if I really *had* gained ten pounds.

The upstairs, like the first floor, was straight out of that old magazine picture. A big front bedroom ran the length of the house, and it had window seats, for God's sake. There was only one bathroom, which would be a major problem when Emma was around, but the claw-foot tub was the size of a horse trough, and the pedestal sink and chain-pull toilet finished off the nostalgic scene. Lastly, there were two other bedrooms, both considerably smaller than the master but screaming with character.

"What do you think?" Sonterra asked very quietly, as we

stood in the upstairs hall. "There's a basement, too, but it's pretty gloomy."

"I think," I said carefully, because my emotions were still too close to the surface, "that I know why Danielle Bickerhelm wanted to buy this place."

"We've got first option," Sonterra said, turning me to face him, catching my chin in his hand so I couldn't look away. "One of the perks of being the new police chief." He squinted, and I knew he'd catch any nuance of emotion that showed in my face. "What's going on in there, Clare? You've been on the verge of tears ever since you got out of your car."

"I'm just tired," I hedged. "Tired and pregnant."

"Bull," he said gently. "It's something to do with the house."

I bit my lower lip and wished Sonterra would let me go. At the same time, I was glad he didn't. "It's just—well—it's not what I expected."

A grin quirked one corner of his mouth. "We could always move into the Hidy Tidy Trailer Park instead," he said.

"I think I'd feel more at home there," I admitted. I was serious, that's the pitiful thing.

He hooked a hand in the waistband of my jeans, right over the button and zipper, and pulled me against him. The contact promised a hot time on the old air mattress tonight. "Time you got over that," he drawled. I'd told him about my childhood, of course, and I knew he saw past the grown-up lawyer I'd become to the scared, difficult ward of the state I'd once been. "You're a big girl now, Clare. No need to play by the old rules."

The button on my jeans gave way, then the zipper. I groaned. I was all grown-up, all right, and perfectly willing to be distracted from the sentimental emotions the house had aroused in me.

"I want a bath first," I said.

Sonterra slid his hand inside my panties and played with me until my breath caught. "Are you sure about that?" he teased.

"Oh, God," I whimpered. Just then, I, the queen of certainty, wasn't sure of anything.

His finger made a slow, wet circle. I smoldered in a delicious misery of need. Then the flames erupted, and I was at flash point in no time.

"Really, really sure?" he asked. He backed me up against the wall, really working me now.

I didn't—couldn't—answer.

Sonterra buried his face in my neck, nuzzling, then started nibbling at my earlobe.

My hips began to grind, seeking his hand.

"I've been thinking about this all day," Sonterra told me, pulling up my cotton blouse, not even bothering with the buttons. The front catch on my bra popped open. "Give it up, Clare. Let it happen."

Heat suffused me, spreading from the apex of my thighs to race along my nerve endings and pulse in the marrow of my bones. I felt a couple of Sonterra's fingers slide up inside me, while his thumb continued the slow, sweet revolutions around my clitoris. I swear I would have slid down the wall, like so much warm wax, if he hadn't been holding me up.

He bent his head, took one of my nipples into his mouth, and sucked.

That was it.

I went over the edge, consumed, clinging to him with both hands, bucking against his hand, sobbing with the ferocious release of tension.

When it was over, I could barely stand.

Sonterra looped an arm around my waist and took me into the bathroom, setting me carefully on the toilet seat. While I sat there, my insides still reverberating with the force of that multi-level orgasm, he put the plug in the tub and started the water running.

I was to have my bath after all.

I figured I was in real danger of disintegrating and spiraling down the drain.

"No candles?" I joked lamely. "No foaming bubbles?"

He looked back at me, over one shoulder, and grinned. "I

could make a run to the supermarket for bubble bath and a candle or two," he said, "or I could just lay you out on that air mattress downstairs and go down on you until you lose your mind. Take your choice."

I'm nobody's fool.

I took door number two.

It was hard to leave Sonterra, hard to get up off that blow-up bed and pull my clothes back on, but I did it. Somehow, legs quivering, I did it.

"Stay with me tonight," Sonterra said.

"I can't," I answered miserably, digging my cell phone out of my purse and checking it. I'd thought I'd heard a muffled tune while Sonterra and I were making love. Sure enough, the message light was blinking.

Sonterra sighed, reached for his wrinkled uniform pants, and made himself decent. "There's probably a law on the books," he said, standing up to zip and button. "Driving under the influence of an orgasm. I counted seven."

I swayed, willing my knees to come back online with my central nervous system and hold me upright. "Six," I corrected. My personal tally was nine, but he didn't need to know that. "Cocky bastard."

He laughed, but he didn't sound all that amused.

I put the cell phone to my ear after pushing the appropriate buttons. My fingers were awkward, and I had to start over twice.

Message one: Loretta. "Clare? You should have been back by now. I'm getting worried."

Message two: Loretta. "Turn on your damn phone, will you? I'm in crisis, here."

Message three: Guess who. "Okay, I'm just going to eat all this freaking pizza by myself!"

I sighed. "Damn it," I said, "I think she's been into the martinis again."

"How long do you think she'll keep this up?" Sonterra

asked. I gave him points for leaving it at that. Some men would have complained that they should have come first, but Sonterra understood the bonds of friendship.

I shook my head. "I don't know. Until she gets it out of her system, I guess." How long would it take for her to get *Kip* out of her system? She really loved him, and like any red-blooded woman, she enjoyed his money, especially since she'd never had much of her own, but I knew Loretta. She'd have married Kip Matthews if he'd been selling Slurpies at 7-Eleven.

I found my car keys, started reluctantly for the door. The dogs meandered in from the kitchen, where they'd curled up on a hooked rug to wait out the sex marathon, and I bent to ruffle their ears in farewell. I'd call Loretta from the Escalade, I decided, let her know I was on the way. Tell her to lay off the booze.

"Maybe I should drive you to the ranch," Sonterra fretted.

"I'll be fine," I answered. He had to work in the morning, even though it was Sunday. "Anyway, it's only fifteen minutes from here." I stood on tiptoe to kiss him. "I'll call to say good night."

He walked me outside to the Escalade. There weren't any near neighbors, which was probably good. It wouldn't do for the populace to see their new police chief in crumpled uniform pants and nothing else, fresh from a lengthy session of mattress mambo.

"I hate this, Clare," he said, as I hoisted myself into the driver's seat and turned the key in the ignition.

"Me, too."

He leaned in, kissed me, closed the door with a slight bang. "Call."

"I will," I promised.

I didn't look in the rearview mirror as I pulled away.

I'd left Dry Creek behind when I remembered my cell phone, got it out of my purse, and called Loretta.

She didn't answer.

I tried again.

Same result.

I felt a twinge of fear, as well as irritation, hung up, and hit REDIAL once more.

In the next instant, headlights suddenly burst on behind me, flooding the interior of the Escalade with a harsh, invasive glare. I barely had time to drop the phone and grip the wheel with both hands before the driver of the other car rammed me hard enough to rattle my teeth.

My car swerved with a screech of tires, headed for the ditch.

I fought to keep it on the road, succeeded, for what that was worth, and the other vehicle struck again, harder this time. The Escalade spun a figure eight in the middle of the highway, and the engine died.

Sonterra, I thought desperately, wishing I'd held on to the cell phone. It was on the floor somewhere, immersed in shadow and out of reach.

I peered through the driver's-side window, one hand resting on my abdomen in an instinctive attempt to protect my baby. It was dark, and I couldn't see much of anything but the vague outline of what was probably a truck, and those headlights, flaring in the gloom like the devil's eyeballs. I watched, stunned into temporary immobility, as the lights receded. There was more squealing of tires, then my attacker gunned the engine, and I realized, in horror, that they were coming at me again. I was a sitting duck, broadside on that lonely road.

In the split second before the crash, I must have unhooked my seat belt and dived to the other side of the car.

That was where I woke up, crouched on the floor in a fetal position, blood dripping into my eyes, my arms wrapped around my knees.

SEVEN

The beam of a flashlight swept the inside of the Escalade, glittering across a snowfall of broken glass.

"Holy Christ, Lanna!" a voice shouted, youthful and male. "There's blood everywhere!"

I hugged myself, trembling with cold. Other than that, I was numb.

My baby, I thought, dazed.

The car shook violently.

I couldn't move. I looked up, saw a face peering at me through a fist-sized hole in the windshield.

"Lady!" the face yelled. "Unlock the door! The gas tank is leaking!"

When I didn't move, a hand reached down through the hole, groping for the release button on the armrest.

Another face appeared, that of a young girl, with long, dark hair. For a moment, I thought I was having another weird experience, seeing myself again, this time as a teenager. But no—the boy had called her "Lanna."

Then I smelled the gas.

The premonition of an explosion rocked my bewildered mind, so vivid that I thought the Escalade had already disintegrated, taking me and the baby with it. I must have clicked the lock, because the next thing I knew, I was tumbling out the door.

Strong hands caught me before I could strike the pavement, dragged me roughly over the asphalt and into a ditch.

I was befuddled with shock and confusion. They'd saved us, the baby and me.

Or had they? Maybe they'd been the ones to ram me from behind. Maybe this was a kidnapping, not a rescue.

I struggled wildly, trying to scream, but all that came out was a primitive, senseless sound.

Then there was a whoosh, followed by a horrendous roar, and heat blistered my back, singed my hair. Chunks of burning metal showered down around me, like a firestorm in hell.

My vision zoomed in to a pinpoint, then nothing.

"Clare?"

The voice was familiar. Verbal sanctuary. I struggled upward, toward it, through the black void that had swallowed me whole.

Sweeping lights, blue, then red, rushed across my eyelids.

The voice again, more urgent this time. "Clare!"

The effort to open my eyes was monumental, but I did it.

Sonterra was leaning over me, rimmed in the flashing lights.

"The baby?" I whispered.

"I don't know," he answered gravely.

I realized I was on a gurney, and it was moving.

Sonterra kept up.

Invisible hands loaded the stretcher into an ambulance, and Sonterra scrambled in beside me, along with a paramedic, who kept calling out numbers to somebody up front. I heard the siren shriek, and we shot forward at warp speed.

"Can you tell me what happened?" Sonterra asked, when I'd had a few minutes to connect with current reality.

I struggled to remember the details of the incident. It was as if my memory had been tucked away on some internal shelf, just out of reach.

I felt his fingers entwined with mine. Good. I still had at least one hand. My head began to ache savagely, reaching a new crescendo with every hard beat of my heart.

It came back, a piece at a time.

The headlights.

The first crash into my rear bumper.

Spinning out.

The lights, the engine of the other car roaring like a dragon as it surged toward me a second time, then a third.

The kids, pulling me to the roadside.

Oblivion.

"Somebody came up behind me," I said carefully, feeling my way from one word to the next. *Please, God, let the baby be all right.* "Flashed their lights. Then—then they hit me." I paused. My lips were so dry they hurt, but nobody offered me water. Maybe they thought I'd spring a leak. "Kids. There were two teenagers—"

Sonterra stroked my cheek. His eyes glistened. "Michael Brown and Lanna Peterson. They saved your life. Came around the corner and saw the Escalade in the middle of the road." He sighed. "Whoever slammed into you took off before they could get a plate number or a model. They said it was an old truck, and they didn't see who was inside. They were busy getting you out of the wreck."

I drifted.

The paramedic called out more numbers.

"What about the baby?"

Sonterra didn't answer, so I turned to the paramedic.

"What about the baby?" I repeated.

The man's glasses glinted strangely in the light. I couldn't see his eyes. I thought, oddly, of Danielle Bickerhelm.

"Try to relax, Ms. Westbrook," the paramedic counseled. "We won't know much until we get you to the hospital, where you can be examined."

A sob rose up in my throat, spiky, like a giant burr.

Then, perhaps mercifully, I lost consciousness.

Awareness came and went, after that. It was as if I were on some crazy carnival ride, now in shadow, now in light.

I felt myself being jostled.

There was a blinding dazzle, and I screamed—or, at least, I meant to scream—sure that I was back in the Escalade, with that other car speeding toward me. Needles pricked my arms. Sonterra's face loomed and receded, loomed and receded.

The effect was dizzying. I seemed to have no equilibrium.

It was the pain that finally woke me up for real.

I felt as though I'd been tossed into a low-speed cement mixer.

My eyes flew open, my hands went to my abdomen.

Every bone and muscle in my body throbbed.

"Clare."

I focused. I was in a hospital bed, and Sonterra was there, pale and gaunt, with a shadow of beard darkening the lower half of his face.

"Clare," he repeated. "It's all right."

"Did I lose the baby?"

He shook his head. Smiled wearily. "No," he said. "The kid is tough, just like his mama."

I let the tears go then, the tears I'd somehow been holding inside, awake and asleep, ever since the horror began. Sonterra held me while I sobbed.

A nurse came in, gave me a shot.

The sobs subsided to hiccoughs.

There was so much I needed to know. "How long—when—?"

Sonterra stroked my hair. I felt fine grit rolling over my scalp, and realized it was probably broken glass. "It happened last night," he told me gently.

"I was so scared." I groped for him again; he held me close.

"It's okay, Babe." When I stopped trembling, he settled me gently back onto the pillows. The shot was taking hold; I was getting groggy.

I hadn't lost the baby.

My mind slipped backwards, toward the waiting darkness. I fought to stay awake, and lost the battle, but even as I sank, I knew I'd won the most important one.

I was still carrying my child. My child, and Sonterra's.

EIGHT

"It's a miracle you didn't break any bones or rupture something," Mrs. Kravinsky fretted, as I dressed to leave the hospital. Sonterra was working, so I'd had to bum a ride with friends.

"Freakin' A," Shanda added, gathering the bouquets of flowers that had been arriving steadily since last Sunday morning. I'd spent most of my childhood and all of my life pissing people off. Who'd have thought I had so many friends?

Mrs. K, resplendent in one of her caftans, with her dyed hair sprayed into submission, had dropped her latest secret-shopper gig to be there, picking Shanda up at her apartment as she zoomed south through Phoenix.

Shanda looked striking in blue jeans, a red silk blouse, and high-heeled boots. She'd had her long hair braided since I'd seen her last, and she was, as Emma would say, "stylin'." Every line of her seemed to say, "black is beautiful," and no one with eyes in their heads would have disagreed.

Despite her own problems, Loretta had come through in the clinch, too, driving up to Scottsdale to fetch a terrified Emma, now fussing at the foot of my bed, and bringing her back to Tucson, so they could both hover and stare at me whenever Sonterra wasn't around. He didn't say much about it, but I knew he was personally inspecting every dented pickup in Pima County, looking for the one that had smashed into me.

I also knew he hadn't had any luck.

I'd tried to distract him with questions about the coyote investigation, but he wasn't easily distracted.

I signed the release papers, and a male nurse wheeled me out of the hospital in a chair. Loretta went to get her Lexus from the parking lot, and Shanda was right behind her, with Mrs. K and Emma and most of the flowers—I'd left behind what we couldn't carry, for the other patients on my floor.

We had our own little parade going, all the way back to Dry Creek.

I knew the movers had arrived during my confinement, and all the rooms in the tree-shaded Victorian were furnished with pieces from Sonterra's place up in Scottsdale. Most of my own stuff was still in storage, and I felt a twinge of guilt. I was still on the emotional fence, one foot in the old life, one in the new.

What the hell was I so afraid of?

Bernice and Waldo rushed down the stairs, yelping with joy, while we were still in the entryway.

I laughed and crouched to ruffle their ears and let them lick my face.

"This is some house," Shanda remarked, crossing the threshold with a vase of flowers in either arm. Mrs. K was behind her, carrying more.

"Sit down, Clare," Mrs. K insisted, relieving herself of a couple of bouquets to take charge. "Emma, please help Shanda bring in the rest of those flowers. Loretta, make tea."

Nobody gave her any guff. Maybe it was that helmet hair of hers. You could have hung a bucket on the side curl.

Mrs. K pressed me into a chair in the living room. Sonterra's big-screen TV took up one whole wall, almost dwarfing the fireplace.

We were going to have to talk about that TV.

My friend the psychic secret-shopping magnate plopped down on the hassock in front of me and took both my hands in hers.

"I have good news and bad news," she said, gazing thoughtfully at the tiny row of stitches visible through my bangs. With a chill, I remembered the apparition I'd seen at the foot of my bed in Loretta's guest room. She'd been bleeding from the head. I was sure Mrs. K had made the connection, too, but mercifully, she didn't mention it.

Recovering from the insight, I let out my breath. "Let's start with the good news." I could hear Loretta in the kitchen, clattering around, trying to make tea.

Mrs. K smiled. "Your pregnancy will continue."

"Okay," I said, much comforted, "what's the bad news?"

The smile faded. Mrs. K leaned closer and lowered her voice. "When you saw yourself at Loretta's, it was a warning," she said. "And this isn't over."

I didn't want to believe that, for understandable reasons, so I went straight into denial. "It was probably road rage. The guy was drunk, or high on something. My bad luck to be there when his switch tripped."

"Nonsense," Mrs. K said firmly, squeezing my hands for emphasis. "It was a deliberate attack, and you know it." She drew a deep breath, exhaled slowly. "Loretta has a house in Sun Valley, doesn't she? Get her to take you there. You and Emma. You can come back to Dry Creek when the danger is past."

Emma and Shanda ambled in, carrying two bouquets each. Both young women were all eyes and ears, and I knew they'd been listening from the doorway. I hoped they hadn't caught the whispered parts.

"I'm staying right here," I said. If there was one thing this incident had taught me, it was that I wanted—okay, *needed*—to be near Sonterra. And it had taught me something else, too.

There were no safe places.

NINE

"I'm coming here to live," Emma announced that night in the brightly lit kitchen of Sonterra's Dry Creek digs. He was still working, so it was a hen gathering—Loretta, Mrs. K, Shanda, and me. And, of course, my very adamant niece.

"I think I'll check in at the bed-and-breakfast," Loretta said. "I want to keep an eye on you, and the ranch depresses me anyway."

I was a little choked up by all this devotion. I didn't have much trouble giving, but receiving was more of a challenge. I felt strong when I was taking care of other people and weak when the tables were turned.

I do not like feeling weak.

"What bed-and-breakfast?" I asked, leaving Emma's statement about moving in strictly alone while I collected my thoughts. She'd been staying with her friend's family up in Scottsdale, but she was scheduled to move into the dorm in a few days.

"It's three blocks over, on the other side of Main Street," Loretta answered, reaching for her glass of iced tea. "It's a great place. There's a lodge, but the rooms are cabins, with little patios and kitchenettes."

Shanda looked at her watch. "I'd better call Mama. See how Maya is doing." Her little girl was nearly three years old now, and every bit as smart and good-looking as her feisty mother.

I nodded, and Shanda excused herself from the table, taking her cell phone from its holster on the side of her purse as she went out the back door.

"That girl has come a long way since she walked into your office with a bad-check charge hanging over her head," Mrs. K observed. My eldest friend had been a little subdued, ever since I'd refused to hightail it to Loretta's ski chalet and hide from the bogeyman.

I smiled, proud of Shanda. She had indeed come a long way, and mostly under her own steam, too, though she'd had some help from me and from Father Mike, her favorite priest and mine. We'd discussed my plan to telecommute, for the duration of my stay in Dry Creek, and she was enthusiastic. I meant to head up to Phoenix on Friday to help her close my storefront office and set up a new command station in the apartment she shared with her mother and Maya. My caseload was minimal at the moment, and I could handle most of it via telephone, e-mail, and fax. When I needed to make a court appearance or interview a client in person, I could make the drive.

And I still intended either to find a job or set up some kind of temporary practice.

I thought of my totaled Escalade and felt a pang. "Major Bitch" bites the dust. I hoped it wasn't some kind of cosmic metaphor.

"You don't have to do this," I told my niece lightly. "Move to Dry Creek, I mean." Part of me wanted her to stay in Scottsdale. Another part yearned to have her close by, within the range of my eyes and ears, not just my heart. I'd missed her, and I knew Sonterra had, too. And then there were the dogs—to them, Emma was a goddess. They'd been following her around since her arrival, sniffing at her shoes. The canine version of holy writ.

"I'm moving here," my niece reiterated, more forcefully than before. I saw Tracy in her again. And I saw my own stubborn self. "You need me, Clare. Besides, every time I let you out of my sight, you get into trouble."

I laughed. "What about your accelerated study program?"

Emma's slender shoulders rose and fell in a graceful, womanly shrug. Dear God, they grow up so fast. One minute, they're seven, asking when Mommy will be back, and the next, they're looking after you. "It'll keep," she said, in a that's-that tone of voice. "I'll go to Scottsdale with Shanda and Mrs. K tonight. Stay on with Tiffany and her folks until you come up this weekend to close the office. But when you head back here on Sunday, I'm coming with you."

"Sounds like a plan," I said, but I was nervous. After all, somebody in or near Dry Creek wanted to kill me, and they'd damn near succeeded. What if Emma got caught in the cross fire?

There are no safe places, I reminded myself. *Not for you, not for Emma. Not for anybody.*

Shanda came in through the back door, smiling and putting away her cell phone. "You ready to hit the road, Mrs. K?" she asked. "I'm missing my baby girl something fierce."

Mrs. Kravinsky's gaze slid to my face, thoughtful and worried. "Yes," she said with a sigh. "I've got a big project on for tomorrow. I need my rest."

"Doesn't anybody want cheesecake?" Loretta inquired mildly.

"Well, now," Shanda said, sitting down again. "Cheesecake. That puts a whole new slant on things."

"Not to mention a whole new layer of cellulite," I replied.

"I'll take the dogs outside for a run," Emma said. I thought it was ironic that she was the one member of the group who could have eaten that whole cake without putting on an ounce, and she wasn't interested.

God, I dreaded saying good-bye to her, even for a few days, and I knew Waldo and Bernice would mope after she was gone.

The crowd was down to Loretta and me by the time Sonterra turned up, tired from a hard day's work. He hung up his service belt, revolver and all, and looked askance at the leftovers from the deli. "Who's been cooking?" he joked, bending to kiss me on the cheek and touching Loretta lightly on the shoulder. When nobody confessed, he built himself a grilled cheese sandwich.

Loretta looked from me to him and back again, and sadness flickered in her eyes. "I'd better go," she said. She smiled at me. "I'll be at the Wagon Wheel B&B if anybody tries to kill you."

I squeezed her hand. "I'll be sure and let you know," I said. "If anybody tries to kill me, that is."

She kissed me on top of the head, found her purse, and left.

"Emma's coming to live with us," I told Sonterra, when we were alone. By that time, his sandwich was ready, and he was pouring a glass of milk to wash it down with. "She insists."

Sonterra gave me a wry look. "Gee. No more monkey sex in the upstairs hallway."

My throat got tight. To Sonterra, Emma and I were a package deal, and his easy acceptance of her moved me deeply. I waited a few moments before I spoke again. "So, how was your day?"

"Long," Sonterra said.

"Any leads on the coyotes?"

"No," he admitted with a sigh. "I've been concentrating on pickup trucks. Checking paint chips and databases, and all that. Interestingly enough, there have been a couple of similar incidents in the last few months."

"Better let it go for now, Sonterra. The feds want coyotes. They'll be on your back if you don't produce."

"Screw the feds," he replied, chewing.

"Great attitude."

He looked me over, his eyes warm and weary. "How are you, Babe?"

I had to swallow again. "I'm okay. Honest."

Sonterra looked doubtful. "What's with Loretta checking into the Wagon Wheel?"

"She wants to babysit me." I paused, smiled sweetly. "Have I mentioned, in the course of our relationship, that if you ever cheat on me, I'll shoot off your kneecaps?"

He chuckled. "Numerous times. I'm clear on that."

I frowned, thinking of Loretta moving into a cabin over at the B&B. It was as if she no longer had a home, and that gave me a bereft feeling. Was there nothing permanent in life? Nothing a person could count on to stay the same? My pragmatic side said "no" to both questions, but my emotions had trouble making the leap.

"What do you suppose got into Kip—fooling around like that? I thought he loved Loretta."

"He does," Sonterra said, finishing off his sandwich.

"Pardon me?"

"Don't get me wrong, Counselor. I'm not saying what Matthews did was all right. That boys-will-be-boys bullshit is just that—bullshit. But there could be a lot of factors operating here—anything from problems with the IRS to not getting it up to finding a bald spot one morning when he was combing his hair. The bimbo catches him in a weak moment, far from home, and bingo. He's over the fence and lost in the woods."

I narrowed my eyes. "If you're ever away from home, having a 'weak moment,' suffering from erectile dysfunction, and you happen to find some of your hair missing, just remember that life is *very* difficult without kneecaps."

He picked up his plate, carried it to the sink, rinsed it, and set it in the drainboard. For about the millionth time, I silently blessed his late mother for training him so well. Sonterra never left his clothes on the floor, belched on purpose, or forgot to put the toilet seat down.

"Let's get married," he said bluntly.

I bit my lower lip.

"You chicken?" he asked. He spoke lightly, but I knew he wasn't kidding.

I looked away, looked back. Blushed. "No, I'm *not chicken,*" I lied.

"Okay, then. Let's do it."

"I'm all for doing it. It's *getting married* that worries me."

It was a joke, but Sonterra didn't seem amused. He ran a hand through his hair, and he looked even wearier than before. "Why?" he asked. It wasn't the first time he'd put that question to me in this context and many others, but there was something new in the way he said it.

"You're busy with a new job. There's Eddie, and Jimmy's funeral—"

"None of which have anything to do with our tying the knot."

I took a deep breath. Let it go. "Okay," I said, and I don't know who was more surprised—Sonterra or me.

He crossed the kitchen, pulled me gently to my feet, held me. Kissed the tender spot on my forehead. "You mean it?"

I nodded against his shoulder.

Sonterra lifted my chin, looked into my eyes. I blinked back tears. He frowned inquiringly.

"Hormones," I explained.

He chuckled. "Why can't you just admit you're scared?"

"All right. I admit it. I'm scared."

He kissed me. My body, in a state of suspended animation since the assault, came alive. "Don't be. You up for a little slow, easy sex, Counselor?"

"I can tell that you are," I said, feeling the evidence against my belly.

His eyes danced. "Very astute observation."

"Slow and easy, huh?" I caressed him.

"You just got out of the hospital. You're bruised and scraped. If it weren't for that, I'd probably bend you over the table and slam into you like a battering ram."

I went right on handling him. I loved the low groan he gave, loved the way his eyes smoldered with lust. "I might not be as delicate as you think," I teased.

"Don't tempt me, Clare."

I nibbled at his lower lip, unfastened his belt. "Let's go upstairs," I crooned. "Right now."

He took my hand, tugged me toward the back stairway, switching off the kitchen lights as we passed. The dogs curled up on the hooked rug, in front of the stove, resigned to human mating rituals.

The master bedroom was all set up, the bed made, the covers turned back. Talk about service—those must have been some movers.

Sonterra undressed me tenderly, peeling away my clothes garment by garment, pausing to admire and caress me every time he uncovered another part of my body. I shivered with anticipation. I had been so close to death. This was life, and I was drawn to it like a poor wayfarer to a fire on a cold winter's night.

He laid me down on the bed, ran a hand over me, pausing to rest his palm against my abdomen. I reached for him, wanting to tear off his uniform, but he caught hold of my wrists, pressed them gently back to my sides. I watched, already quivering inside, as he stripped. The sight of his erection made my hips rise a little way off the mattress, as though magnetized to the corresponding part of his anatomy.

He turned off the bedside lamp, stretched out beside me. Fondled my breasts while he kissed me senseless.

"I'm not particularly delicate," I told him, when I could breathe again.

He grinned. Tongued my nipples in slow, torturous turns, until I whimpered.

He stopped tonguing and sucked, taking his time.

"I really, really need an orgasm," I gasped. The battering-ram idea was sounding better and better.

"I aim to please," he murmured, and started kissing his way down my belly.

I knew where he was going, and the mere prospect of the pleasure to come rolled along the length of my body like a huge, invisible fireball. I tried to turn over onto my knees, so I could grip the headboard and take him inside me from behind in one hard thrust, but he wouldn't let me.

He parted my legs, made me dance on the tip of his tongue. I begged. I moaned. I cursed.

I wanted him bad, and he was making me wait.

"Ummmm," he rumbled, and sucked.

Zero to sixty in ten seconds flat. Wheels throwing sparks, I crashed through the guardrail and tumbled over the cliff in a blaze of glory.

Hot damn, it was good to be home.

• • •

The phone woke us up around midnight, jangling on the bedside table. Sonterra and I unwrapped ourselves from each other, sorting out whose arms and legs were whose, and he sat up, swearing under his breath.

"Sonterra," he barked, into the receiver.

I waited.

"Shit," he said, groping for his uniform shirt, which was in a heap on the floor, and pulling a pad and ballpoint pen from the pocket. "Where? Yeah. Yeah, I'll be right there. Try to keep everybody calm. Is there an ambulance on the way?"

The pit of my stomach opened like a trapdoor, and the rest of my vital organs fell through.

Sonterra slammed down the phone and crossed the room to yank open a dresser drawer and pull out jeans and a sweatshirt.

"What happened?" I ventured to inquire.

"Nothing you need to worry about," Sonterra said, fastening his jeans and tugging the sweatshirt on over his head. "There was a free-for-all at one of the bars on Main Street, and it went from fists to pool cues."

I winced, imagining the damage. No sense trying to go back to sleep. I'd only lie there, staring at the ceiling.

Sonterra planted a kiss on my mouth, grabbed his badge, and boogied.

"Dead-bolt the door when I'm gone!" he yelled from the kitchen.

I waited until I heard his SUV screech out of the driveway, then helped myself to a pair of his boxers and a T-shirt. Downstairs, I followed orders and secured the heavy-duty lock on the back door.

"This situation calls for cheesecake," I told the dogs.

They seemed to agree, so we shared the leftovers.

When the phone rang again at six-thirty the next morning, I was still in the kitchen with the countertop TV blaring. There was nothing about the bar brawl on the Tucson news, so I'd spent the last thirty minutes staring at the Food Channel and wondering why on earth anyone would want to make their own pretzels when they could be bought at any mall.

I lunged for the receiver, expecting an update from Sonterra. This was ridiculous. I needed to get a life.

"Did you hear?" Loretta asked.

"Hear what?" I asked, peevish in my disappointment.

"Kip's been arrested."

I couldn't have been more surprised if she'd said he'd grown an extra ear. But, then, his infidelity had taken me completely off guard. Life was full of surprises—and lately, most of them had been nasty ones.

"What?" I asked stupidly, certain that I must have heard wrong.

She started to cry. "It was on CNN a few minutes ago. He's been charged with insider trading and stock manipulation."

"Oh, my God," I whispered. "Are you still at the B&B? I'll be right over!"

"You don't have a car."

"Loretta, the place is four blocks away. Hold on—I'm on my way."

"I'll get dressed and wait for you out front," Loretta said despondently.

I dressed hastily in a sweat suit and sneakers, splashed my face with cool water, brushed my hair—very carefully, because of the stitches—fed and watered the dogs, and set out. I felt a little light-headed, and stopped once to grip somebody's front gate with one hand, steadying myself.

Danielle Bickerhelm appeared on the porch of the house next door, wearing sleek white silk pants, a silvery tunic, and designer sunglasses. I felt that worrisome sense of familiarity again, and wondered whimsically if anyone had ever seen her eyes. Maybe she was born wearing shades.

"Are you all right, Clare?" she called, and picked her way down the steps of her small stone cottage. English roses bloomed tenaciously on either side of the walk, and the grass in the yard was overgrown, sprouting dandelion ghosts on tall, spindly stalks. "I heard about your accident. I'm so sorry you were injured."

My hand convulsed on the gate. "It wasn't an accident," I heard myself say, though I had not intended to bare my soul. Nor did I feel inclined toward idle chitchat. Loretta had just had another shock, and she was expecting me. "I was attacked," I clarified.

Danielle tripped lightly toward me, her mouth pulled into a little O of surprise. It seemed odd that she wouldn't have heard the details, Dry Creek being so small; but I was focused on getting to my friend, doing whatever I could to help, so I didn't dwell on that one wispy thought. "How terrible!"

"Yes," I agreed, with a slight shudder as the memories assailed me, weakening me further. "It *was* terrible. I'm looking for the Wagon Wheel B&B—can you tell me where it is?"

"I'll drive you there," Danielle said, jangling her keys. Presumably one of them would start the BMW parked at the curb. "Forgive me, but you don't look as though you're in any condition to be walking around."

Relief rushed through me. I hadn't exactly taken to Danielle, but riding certainly seemed preferable to crawling the rest of the way to the B&B, and besides, a little time in her company might stir my memory.

"Thanks," I said, and got into the car.

Danielle took the wheel. "I suppose you've heard about the mess at Bubba's Place last night," she said cheerfully, as we zoomed away. "Even the women got involved. Lots of hair-pulling." She paused. "They say women are meaner in a fight than men."

"Sounds as if you were there," I commented.

Danielle shook her head. "Police scanner," she tossed off, as we whipped up in front of a large, rustic lodge. "Here's the Wagon Wheel," she said. "Have a good day, Clare. And do take better care of yourself. Children are a precious gift, you know."

Children?

Was my pregnancy common knowledge? I hadn't mentioned it to anyone in Dry Creek, but maybe Sonterra had.

"How did—?"

She looked at her watch. Lady President, with diamonds. Expensive car, pricey jewelry. The antique business must be thriving. "Sorry I can't chat," she said, briskly perky. "I need to make some calls before I open the store. I do have a wonderful cradle you might want to look at. Early Victorian. A museum piece, actually. *Ciao* for now!"

I got out of the car, still feeling a little wobbly. I *would* visit her shop as soon as I could, I decided. I wasn't much interested in the cradle, however old it was, but I did want to know more about her. It bothered me, knowing I'd met her before and wondering where and under what circumstances. And I still wanted to know how she'd learned I was pregnant.

"Thanks for the ride," I said, closing the car door.

I had barely stepped back before she raced off, leaving me in a cloud of road dust.

As promised, Loretta was waiting on the lodge steps when I turned around. She looked remarkably composed, for someone who had just learned that her estranged husband might be headed for a federal hoosegow.

"Who was that?" she asked, frowning after the BMW. Loretta wore a Chanel suit and matching Manolos, and her makeup, either smudged or nonexistent in recent days, was perfect. The effect was rather like that of Ms. Bickerhelm's sunglasses—I felt distanced. Shut out.

I put it down to hormone fluctuation.

"Danielle Bickerhelm," I replied, taking in the lodge as I started up the walk. It was a solid structure, more like a transplant from some evergreen environment than anything endemic to the desert. Like the antique store on Main Street, it seemed amazed to find itself in unfamiliar surroundings.

I shifted my focus back to Loretta, taking in the outfit again. "When you said you were going to get dressed, you weren't kidding. What's with the corporate getup?"

"I'm going to New York to see Kip. That's where he's being held."

Inwardly, I sighed. *Who are you?* I demanded silently. *And what have you done with Loretta?* On the outside, I smiled. "He must be out on bail by now," I said.

"You look terrible," Loretta said, ignoring my remark and rushing forward to take my arm, as though she thought I might collapse right there in front of the B&B.

"Thanks a whole heap," I said.

"I'm dropping you off at home. You should be in bed, Clare. I don't know what I was thinking, letting you come over here—"

"If you want to drop me somewhere," I said, "make it the cop shop."

Loretta pondered that. "All right," she agreed reluctantly, squiring me up the steps and setting me in the nearest porch swing. The view from there was truly uninspiring—a derelict gas station stood across the unpaved street, plastered with rusting metal signs that would have sold for a small fortune on eBay. The grass was even more out of control than Danielle's yard, and scattered with broken bottles, old tires, and other debris.

Loretta took hold of the latch on the screen door leading into the lobby of the Wagon Wheel. She paused, flushed. "I wish you could go with me. I know it's a lot to ask, but—"

"It's a good idea," I said.

Loretta shook her head. "No, it isn't," she said with a sigh. "You just got out of the hospital. And this isn't your problem, it's mine."

"You're my best friend, Loretta. Your problems are my problems."

She smiled wanly, but shook her head again. "No," she said decisively. "Sit tight. I'll have my car brought around. They're already loading my bags."

I didn't argue. I really didn't feel up to tackling the Big Apple, but I would have done it, at a word from Loretta.

I chose my words carefully. "Do you think this is wise? Rushing off to New York, I mean? Did Kip actually ask you to come?"

She pretended not to hear, which was answer enough.

Fifteen minutes later, we pulled up in front of the police

station in her Lexus. Sonterra's SUV was parked beside the entrance, coated with dust. Equally scruffy squad cars, the usual Crown Vics, were nosed in on either side, at odd angles, as though they'd been shot helter-skelter from some huge longbow.

I turned to Loretta. "Stay in touch," I said. I knew it was useless to point out that she might be rushing into something better left alone. In her place, I probably would have done the same thing.

She reached over, squeezed my forearm. "You'll be all right, won't you? If I didn't think Tony would look after you—"

"I'll be fine, Loretta. Go." I opened the door, got out. My legs felt stronger now. It took a lot to keep me down—which only encouraged my enemies to try harder.

I watched, waving once, as she drove away.

"You must be here for the bad coffee, Counselor."

I turned to see Sonterra standing in the doorway of the station, grinning wanly. I nodded. Started in his direction.

"Where's Loretta off to in such a hurry?" he asked, as the Lexus vanished from view.

"Kip's been arrested in New York," I answered, "and if you say you already knew, I'll kill you. Insider trading and stock manipulation."

Sonterra whistled and came to take my arm. He led me solicitously into the front office, and I took a chair. He perched on the edge of his desk, with a creak of his service belt, arms folded. "Okay, besides the bad coffee, you wanted—?"

"Information," I said. "I don't like being out of the loop."

Sonterra's jaw tightened. "It was your average bar brawl. Extensive damage to people and fixtures."

"Danielle knows I'm pregnant." I threw that out casually. Waited for a bite.

"Danielle?" Sonterra looked honestly puzzled. I could see that he was riffling through some mental index and coming up dry, and that pleased me more than it should have.

"Bickerhelm. Tall, bony. Owns the antique store."

"Oh," Sonterra said, grimly enlightened. "Her."

"I was wondering how. How she found out about the baby, I mean."

He went to fetch the coffee, didn't answer until I'd taken a couple of nerve-jangling sips. The stuff certainly lived up to its reputation—it could have qualified as toxic waste.

"I might have mentioned it to Dave and Jesse," he admitted quietly, referring to his deputies. "It's the kind of thing a guy tends to be proud of."

"Maybe one of them passed the word," I said, looking around. The place was empty, except for Rathburn, who was at his desk, on the phone, and Jesse, the younger of the two, dressed up in a spiffy new uniform and operating the fax machine.

Sonterra studied me. "You're going crazy, aren't you?"

"You've got that right," I admitted. "I need a job."

"How about a hobby?"

I gave him a look. "Like what? Crocheting?"

He grinned. "My aunts make lace doilies. Looks pretty challenging to me."

I rolled my eyes.

Dave hung up the phone and hoisted his bulk out of his desk chair. "I'd like to run by the house and look in on Madge, if it's all right with you, Chief," he said. "She wasn't feeling too well when I left for work this morning."

Sonterra nodded, and Rathburn took his leave.

Jesse hummed a country-western song as he fed more documents into the fax machine. He was out of earshot, so I figured it was safe to prod Sonterra a little about the federal task force.

"Any leads on Oz Gilbride and the coyote situation?" I asked.

"Nice try," he said.

"I think I have a right to know what my future husband does for a living."

"He's a cop."

I persisted, of course. "Damn it, what do the feds want you to *do,* exactly? And why did they have to pick on you in the first place?"

Sonterra sighed, glanced in Jesse's direction. His back was to us, and he was still humming. "I was accepted at Quantico, remember?" Sonterra said. Thanks to an on-the-job injury that nearly cost him his life, he'd had to drop his plans to join the FBI. "I guess they liked my application, and it might have something to do with my being part Latino. This place is a corridor for coyotes, and the illegals are more likely to trust me than a gringo, even if I *am* wearing a badge."

For Sonterra, this was a virtual soul-baring. I needed a few moments to take it in.

I think he liked it when I was speechless. He grinned.

I scanned the cells, all empty. I'm rarely stumped for words, and when I am, I recover quickly. "Didn't you arrest anybody? After the fight at the tavern, I mean?"

"Yeah," he said. "They all made bail."

I leaned in a little. "Do you think Oz Gilbride was really involved with the coyote ring?"

Sonterra narrowed his eyes. "Are you writing a book or something?"

I grinned. "Maybe. The love scenes would certainly be hot."

He looked cocky. "Damn straight," he said.

I figured I wasn't going to get any more details out of him, not for the time being, anyway. So I changed the subject. "I need a car."

He ran his eyes over me. "Not today, you don't."

Just then, there was a flurry at the door, and a woman stumbled into the station. I sat up straight at the sight of her, and Sonterra cursed under his breath.

Her face looked like fresh-ground hamburger, and the front of her blouse was stained with blood.

"I want to press charges against Bobby Ray Lombard," she said.

Both Sonterra and Deputy Jesse rushed toward her, caught her by either arm just as her knees gave way.

"Geeze, Micki," Jesse blurted, as he escorted her to a chair. "Did Bobby Ray whup you again? I told you last time this happened you ought to show him the road."

I took a professional, as well as personal, interest. Got up, went into the restroom, wet a wad of clean paper towels at the sink.

Micki looked up at me with shame and gratitude as I elbowed my way between Sonterra and Jesse and started cleaning her up as gently as I could.

"My name is Clare Westbrook," I told her, "and I'm an attorney."

"Micki Post," she replied numbly. Her eyes were rapidly swelling closed, but I saw a plea in them as she studied me. "People always think it's so easy to get rid of a guy like Bobby Ray," she told me miserably. "They don't know what he's like."

"You heard the woman, Officers," I said, dabbing away with the paper towel. "Ms. Post wants to press charges."

"Pick him up," Sonterra told Jesse.

Jesse was ready to roll, flushed with conviction. "Last time we brought Bobby Ray in, he was high on something, and Dave and I had to mace him just to get him in the car."

"You want me to go along?" Sonterra asked.

Jesse's flush deepened. He shook his head. "I'll call Dave on my cell phone or raise him on the radio. Have him meet me."

"Is there a doctor in this town?" I asked Sonterra, as Micki took the wad of paper towels, wiped her mouth with it, and checked to see if she'd spit out one of her teeth. "If so, get him over here. Now."

"Doc Holliday's number is in the Rolodex," Jesse called in parting, as he dashed for the door. "She's been visiting her folks in Iowa, but she ought to be back by now."

Doc Holliday, I thought. *Now, that's colorful.*

Doc Holliday, as it turned out, was not a consumptive gunfighter holding a dead man's poker hand, but a woman, a diminutive pixie-type sporting jeans, a blue cotton work shirt, a buzz cut, and a chip on her shoulder. When she caught sight of Micki, her eyes shot fire. She slammed her bag down on the nearest surface, opened it with one deft hand, and pulled out a stethoscope without looking.

"If you don't press charges this time, Micki," she warned, checking the patient's heartbeat, "I swear I'll have to take matters into my own hands."

A tear trickled through the blood streaking Micki's poor, swollen face. "I will," she said. "But his sister will just bail him out, like she did last time, and the time before that."

Last time, and the time before that.

"This isn't going to be like last time," Sonterra vowed, drawing closer.

Doc Holliday took him in. "Isn't it?" she asked icily. Then she turned to me, clearly sizing me up. "Who are you?"

"Micki's attorney," I said, and gave her my name.

"I don't have money for no lawyer," Micki put in.

"You don't need money for this lawyer," I answered.

"Here we go," Sonterra said with a sigh. Maybe he'd hoped my initial offer to represent Micki was an idle one, that I'd go straight home and start crocheting doilies.

He should have known better.

"I think I like you, Clare Westbrook," the doctor told me, before shifting her attention back to Micki. "You need stitches, and that means a trip to my office. Can you stand on your own, or should the chief here carry you to my car?"

"I can get myself to the car," Micki said, looking askance at Sonterra. She clearly didn't want to be manhandled, and after what she'd been through, I could empathize.

"Maybe your lawyer ought to come along," Holliday said.

I nodded. Together, she and I hoisted Micki out of the chair and headed for the exit. Sonterra followed with the doctor's medical bag. I knew he wanted me either to go home or stay where he could keep an eye on me. He'd already figured out that he wasn't going to get his way, though. I could tell that by the grim set of his jaw.

Outside, Doc Holliday helped Micki into a red Volvo, and I climbed into the backseat, waving to Sonterra as we sped out of the parking lot.

The doctor practiced out of an old house on a side street

called Cottonwood Drive. There wasn't a cottonwood in sight, of course, since they were all in Sonterra's yard.

"Do you live here?" I asked when we went inside. The living room had been converted to a waiting area, with the requisite uncomfortable chairs and outdated magazines, but there was no receptionist to make appointments and file insurance claims. I didn't even see a telephone.

Holliday led the way into an adjoining examining room. "No," she said, and left it at that. She didn't seem unfriendly, just focused on the task at hand, which was attending to her patient.

Micki climbed resolutely onto the table. Her body language seemed to offer an apology for taking up space. "You missed a bunch of patch-up work last night," she told the doctor gamely. "There was one hell of a fight at Bubba's Place."

Holliday rummaged for disinfectant, gauze, and other tools of her trade. "Thank God for small favors," she replied. Then, apparently for my benefit, she added, "I just got in from Iowa this morning. My sister got married."

"Bet you wish you were *still* in Iowa," Micki said. She sounded ashamed, and that saddened me. Bobby Ray Lombard was the one who should have been ashamed, not her.

"Wish in one hand," Judy said, and left it at that.

She was ready with a hypodermic when Micki's shock gave way to pain, and made short, efficient work of cleaning her up and stitching the gashes on her lower lip and along the top of her forehead.

I watched in silence, trying not to wince.

Presently, Doc started the conversation rolling again, though tentatively. "There are good shelters in Tucson—" she began.

Micki interrupted with a quick shake of her head and said, "I'm not leaving my trailer. It's all we've got, Suzie and me. I make the payments—*me,* not Bobby Ray, that no-good son of a bitch—from my tips at the Doozy Diner." She gave me another sheepish look. "Suzie's my little girl."

Dr. Holliday sighed. She and I both knew Micki had been all too right, back at the station, when she said Bobby Ray would be out of jail right away. We'd be lucky if his fingerprints dried on the booking forms before he was free again; guys like him always had a sister, or a buddy, or some other well-meaning idiot, to post bond. "Then at least get a restraining order."

Micki looked fearful. "How much does that cost?"

How well I understood her position—I'd been a waitress once myself, after all. I'd fought like a scalded cat to keep the lights on, gas in my old beater of a car, and the rent paid. "For you, nothing," I said. I would cover the filing fee myself, and do the small amount of work pro bono.

"In the meantime," Doc Holliday said, "let's see if there's any other damage."

I borrowed a pen and a piece of paper and took down the pertinent information. When I got home, I would call the appropriate judge and get the legal ball rolling. Maybe I was running on adrenaline, but by then I felt strong enough to take on Bobby Ray Lombard and all his inbred cousins.

I wrote out my name and cell number on another sheet of paper, handed it to Micki. "If you have a problem with Bobby Ray, call the police first and me second."

Micki stared at the paper. "And I'm not going to get a bill for this?" she asked carefully.

I laid a hand lightly on her shoulder. "I used to work at a place called Nipples, in Tucson, serving drinks. A real dive. Every month, when the first rolled around, I prayed I'd be able to keep a roof over my niece's head and my own. I'm on the level, Micki. I said this would be free, and I meant it."

"Thanks," she whispered.

I moved closer, so I could look straight into her bruised, fist-ravaged face. "Bobby Ray's likely to have a whole slew of sob stories ready, once his sister springs him. All about how he didn't mean to hurt you, but you just pissed him off *so bad,* he couldn't help himself, and he'll never, ever do it again. He'll try to make it your fault. Don't you believe it, Micki. You let that snake back into your life, and one of these days, he'll kill you. So if you won't keep him out for yourself, do it for Suzie. Worst case, he'll hurt her, just the way he hurt you. Best case, she'll grow up believing it's okay to live with a man who hits her."

Micki blinked. "I don't want her thinking that."

"Of course you don't," I said, and over her head, Doc Holliday and I exchanged glances. I figured the doctor was probably thinking the same thing I was—that Micki had taken Bobby Ray back before, and there was a good chance she'd do it again.

It was time I went home. "Nice meeting you," I said to Judy Holliday, putting out my hand.

We shook. "Same here. Don't be a stranger."

I walked the six blocks back to Cemetery Lane, and when I got there, Sonterra's SUV was parked in the driveway, and there were two identical vehicles at the curb—plain black sedans with government plates. The federal version of subtlety.

I went around the side of the house and entered by the back door, not wanting to interrupt anything top secret.

Not much, anyway.

Waldo and Bernice greeted me in a frenzy of noisy joy.

I petted them, let them out into the yard to do all the things dogs do in backyards. I grabbed my Day-Timer off the kitchen counter, dug my cell phone out of my purse, and went to gaze over the fence at the cemetery while Waldo and Bernice took care of business.

I called a judge I knew in Tucson. While I was in my last year of law school at the University of Arizona, before Fred Tucker's appointment to the bench, I'd clerked in his Tucson office for six months. We'd never been buddies, but we got along well enough. Not something I can say about everybody I've ever worked with.

I told Judge Tucker about Micki's case.

"You have a fax machine handy?" he asked.

I gave him the number of Sonterra's fax, in the den. I'd get the documents signed and file them in the morning.

"What are you doing in Dry Creek, anyway?" Tucker wanted to know.

I explained briefly, leaving out a few details, like my pregnancy and the attack that had put me in the hospital.

"So you're on hiatus from your practice up in Phoenix?"

"I'm telecommuting." No point in mentioning that it was pretty much a one-way deal. Hell of a thing when you can't even *give* legal advice away.

"Pima County could use somebody like you, Clare," Tucker said smoothly. "Why don't you talk to the prosecutor about a job? I could put in a good word."

I considered Bobby Ray, and all the scum like him, and I was tempted. Oh, indeed, I was tempted. Once, I'd delighted in the argument that the accused deserves a good defense, but lately, that was changing. If I'd been called upon to represent the men who'd beat Eddie senseless, for example, I couldn't have done it. Ditto for the fiends who'd shot Jimmy Ruiz and his companions down like so many rabid dogs.

Sonterra's nail-the-bastards attitude was rubbing off on me.

"I'll think it over," I said.

We chatted for a few minutes after that, then I went inside and started building a sandwich. Between Loretta's departure for New York and the episode with Micki, I'd forgotten all about lunch.

Sonterra popped his head through the inside doorway just as I was about to take the first bite.

"Lombard's booked and behind bars," he said. "Guess who his sister is?"

I took a wild stab. "Danielle Bickerhelm," I threw out, talking with my mouth full.

"Damn," Sonterra retorted, "you're a regular Mrs. Kravinsky. Next, you'll be out there secret shopping."

I laughed, and almost choked on a mouthful of white bread, mayo, and bologna. "Process of elimination, Sonterra. I don't know any other woman in town by name, except for Madge Rathburn, so it had to be her."

A Tommy Lee Jones type appeared behind him. The kind of guy you want on a plane with you if somebody suddenly jumps up and starts brandishing a box cutter.

"Any more of those sandwiches?" the newcomer asked.

Sonterra stepped aside to let him into the kitchen. "Special Agent Timmons, my fiancée, Clare Westbrook. Help yourself to whatever you find in the refrigerator."

"Thanks," Tommy Lee said, after nodding to me.

Four more agents trailed in, looking hungry, and Sonterra issued the same invitation. Pretty soon, there was a bologna sandwich assembly line going on at the long counter next to the fridge.

Everybody sat down except Sonterra, who brewed a pot of coffee, then put some kibbles out for the dogs.

"So," I said brightly, "what do you think happened to Oz Gilbride? Is he in a shallow grave, or whooping it up someplace in South America on the coyote profits?"

A silence fell.

Special Agent Timmons, whose real name, alas, was George, not Tommy Lee, sat across from me, munching away. His gaze slid to Sonterra, then back to my face. "I trust Chief Sonterra has explained that this situation is—well—delicate?"

"I guessed that much on my own," I said. "I can't help wondering, though, why you'd park two government vehicles in front of Sonterra's house, in the broad light of day, and think for one moment that the whole town didn't know about it."

George smiled. "I am well acquainted with the nature of small towns, Ms. Westbrook. I grew up in Northport, Washington. You can spit from one end of the place to the other." He paused. "Sometimes it's a good thing to stir up a little gossip in a place like this. Let folks speculate a bit. Usually loosens their tongues."

"Got it," I said. "Anybody want more bologna?"

Everybody did. I made the second round of sandwiches and poured the coffee. When everybody left but Sonterra, after about forty-five minutes of food and small talk, I spoke first.

"Give it to me straight, Sonterra. You know I can keep a secret."

I watched while Sonterra struggled visibly with his better judgment. And I knew what he'd decided before he answered. "I gave you the high points at the station."

"But it's more than that."

"It's a lot more, Clare, and right now, that's all I can tell you." He approached, kissed the crown of my head. "I've got to get back to the office. I'll grab a hamburger for supper."

"Translation," I said glumly, "don't wait up."

Sonterra thrust out a heavy sigh. "Yeah."

He left, and I sat there thinking about women who weren't cut out to be married to lawmen.

TEN

I was making my breakfast—tuna salad and chocolate ice cream—when my cell phone played a chorus of "Folsom Prison Blues." I squinted at the caller ID panel. "Hello, Loretta."

"Hello, yourself," my friend answered. I couldn't get much from her tone, but at least she didn't sound tear-clogged, or drunk. "I'm an idiot."

I was ready to say I wouldn't go *that* far, since she wasn't the first wife to dash off to rescue a louse of a husband from the consequences of his own actions, but before I could get started, Loretta went on, sounding more dispirited with every word.

"I should have taken a shuttle to the airport and left the Lexus for you. A couple of the guys from the ranch will pick it up in the long-term lot and bring it to Dry Creek."

I felt a rush of gratitude. With all her troubles, Loretta was thinking of me. "Thanks," I said. Our neck of the woods wasn't exactly packed with car dealerships, and I didn't know when I'd get around to choosing and buying a new ride. I had Micki's restraining order to file, and Sonterra and I were scheduled to leave that evening for Scottsdale. We planned to attend Jimmy's funeral the next afternoon, and afterward I would devote the rest of the weekend to getting my Phoenix office packed up. Sometime on Sunday, Sonterra, Emma, and I would motor back down to Pima County and dig in for whatever came next.

"I saw Kip last night," Loretta announced. She must have dropped her bags at the hotel and boogied straight to the courthouse.

"How was it?"

She sighed. "Dismal. I ran into Miranda Slater as I was leaving the federal building. We almost had a scratching match, right there on the hallowed steps of justice."

I closed my eyes. Behind my lids, I saw Loretta opening a can of whup-ass on Little Miss Homewrecker, and I had to smile, albeit sadly. I hated that my friend had to go through all this in the first place; she flat-out didn't deserve it. "What was *she* doing there? I thought Kip fired her, sent her away."

"He did," Loretta said. "But she's a persistent type."

"You should have punched her lights out."

"And end up in the cell next to Kip's? I like the Plaza a lot better."

"I hope you're in a suite, and charging it to him."

"I am," Loretta replied, "but there's a possibility my credit cards will be cut off if the government freezes his bank accounts."

There are times when being a multimillionaire comes in handy. Silently, I blessed my late and virtually unknown father.

"I'll take care of the hotel bill, Loretta. That'll give you one less thing to worry about, and we can always settle up later."

Loretta paused, and even though there was no sound, I could tell that she'd choked up. "Thanks," she managed, after a few moments.

"So what else is going on? What does Kip have to say for himself?"

"That he's sorry. He asked for your e-mail address, Clare. I hope it was okay that I gave it to him."

"Why would he want to send me an e-mail?"

"You're my best friend. He'll probably ask you to look out for me."

"Goes without saying," I replied. If Kip was really concerned about Loretta's well-being, he and I could deal. If, on the other hand, he planned to make lame excuses and try to win my sympathy and support, I'd be ready for him. "What about the lawyers? Did you talk to them?"

"Briefly. Kip's basically screwed, financially, at least. By association, so am I. I'll tell you more about it when I get back to Arizona."

I felt sick. Loretta had been a cocktail waitress at Nipples when she met Kip. She was smart as hell, but she had no recent work experience and no education beyond a few halfhearted semesters at a junior college. How was she going to earn a living?

I rallied. "When will that be?"

"Soon," she said.

I'd been scanning Headline News, keeping up with Kip's spectacular fall from glory out of loyalty to Loretta, but there hadn't been much. Just a lot of fifteen-second video clips, showing Kip entering the federal building in Manhattan, surrounded by lawyers, and a voice-over promising to outline the calamity in depth when more facts were in. So much for hard news.

"This whole situation seriously sucks," I said. "I'm so sorry, Loretta."

"High five, girlfriend," Loretta answered glumly, but with a touching effort to raise the cheer level. "What's going on in Dry Creek?"

"I just signed up a new client. Her boyfriend knocked her around."

"I'm sorry I asked," Loretta said.

"Sonterra and I are heading for Scottsdale in a few hours. Worst possible time for him to leave town, but Jimmy's funeral is tomorrow. I'm going to close my office while I'm there and make sure Shanda has everything she needs to run things from her apartment. Oh, and since Emma has decided to move to Dry Creek for the duration, we'll be picking up her stuff, too. It's at my old place."

"Where are you staying? While you're in Scottsdale, I mean? Tony's house is stripped to the walls, isn't it?"

"My house," I said, and felt a pang of sadness. I'd left the modest abode, with Emma and the dogs, soon after my neighbor,

Waldo's original owner, was murdered. Moved in with Sonterra. Except for a few hasty forays to fetch files, cosmetics, and clothes, I hadn't been back. Definite case of avoidance, but now some decisions had to be made. Like, keep my house, or let go and put it on the market.

I'd said I'd marry Sonterra—soon—and even though we hadn't talked about it again since, I knew there was a wedding on his agenda. If I didn't show up at the church on time, he'd probably start without me.

"You could always go to our—Kip's house. Rosa's there. Do you want me to call and tell her you're coming?" That was Loretta. Always ready to help, even when her own life was falling apart.

I hesitated. "No," I said simply. "But thanks."

Loretta didn't push it, and I was grateful. Just the same, it was decision time in Clareworld. "By the way, I spoke with Rosa last night," Loretta went on. "It turns out that she has a cousin in Dry Creek—her name is Esperanza Lopez, and she's looking for a housekeeping job. You in the market?"

I considered. "Can she cook?" Rosa made a mean enchilada. Maybe it ran in the family.

"Probably," Loretta said.

I wondered what the townspeople would say if the chief of police and his woman hired themselves a housekeeper. It might be construed as big-city stuff, highfalutin and all that. To hell with them, I decided. I was cooking-challenged, and I didn't do windows, toilets, or floors. "Give me her number. Esperanza's, I mean."

"She doesn't have a number," Loretta replied. "All I know is she lives at the Hidy Tidy Trailer Park, in a rental, with twelve or fourteen of her closest friends and relations. She'll get in touch with you."

I frowned. "Is she legal?"

"Maybe, and maybe not," Loretta said. "You know how these things work."

"Loretta, I'm a member of the bar association and therefore

an officer of the court," I countered, "and Sonterra is the chief of police. We have to operate within the law."

"Whatever," Loretta responded, sounding distracted. "The other phone line is lighting up, and it might be Kip's lawyer. I'd better go."

"Take care. Keep me posted. And thanks for the loan of the Lexus."

As soon as that call ended, I put one through to the Plaza and gave them my credit card information. They promised to put all Loretta's charges on my Visa, and I rang off.

By ten-thirty, Micki's restraining order was in place, and I was out of reasons to stay home.

I decided to take a walk and check out the old barbershop on Main Street, see if it would work as an office. I leashed up the dogs and took them with me, praying we wouldn't meet somebody's roving Rottweiler along the way.

The route took us past Danielle's Attic, and the famous Victorian cradle was prominently displayed in the window. There were plenty of tourists inside, their cars lining both sides of the street. I tried to slip past but, since fate is perverse, Ms. Bickerhelm spotted us and came out, sans sunglasses, leaving her customers to their own devices. She looked at Bernice and Waldo with obvious distaste.

Waldo lifted his leg against the lamppost in front of her shop.

"Come in and see the cradle," she said, recovering quickly.

I wasn't going to get out of this one gracefully, so I wrapped Waldo's leash loosely around the post he'd just christened and scooped Bernice up in one arm. No way I was leaving my Yorkie on the street. Hazard of owning a little dog; big dogs sometimes eat them.

Danielle started to protest Bernice's entry, then stopped herself visibly.

Waldo, who was a lover-not-a-fighter and therefore could not be relied upon to protect an eight-pound sidekick, settled onto the sidewalk with a philosophical sigh, and Bernice and I ventured boldly over Danielle's threshold.

The interior was dimly lit and jammed with pricey stuff, all of it polished to a buy-me shine. Between the merchandise and the eager buyers, there wasn't a spare inch of floor space, and yet the shop didn't seem either cluttered or crowded.

My attention was immediately drawn, not to the cradle, but to a very old painting on the wall behind the counter. It was big, maybe forty-eight inches square, and showed a young matron surrounded by four golden children. These kids had known they were loved, even adored. I could almost see them breathing, and something in the woman's eyes filled me with a deep, spooky sorrow that curled acridly around my heart, like smoke.

Suddenly, it was as if Danielle and I were alone in the place. The tourists seemed to fade like so much smoke, though I was vaguely aware of a younger woman ringing up sales at a second register, in the back.

"That's not for sale," Danielle said quickly, as though she expected me to hoist the portrait down off the hook, lug it right out of the shop, and toss it into the back of a U-Haul.

I refrained from mentioning that I had no intention of buying the thing—just looking at it made me want to cry—but I stepped closer, just the same. "Is this someone famous?" I asked, referring to the stunning, dew-fresh mother.

Danielle was back in chatty-proprietor mode, nodding pleasantly to two older ladies as they departed with their purchases in brown paper bundles. "No," she said. "But she's beautiful, isn't she?" She sounded as though she and the haunting Renaissance woman were well acquainted, maybe lunching together once a week, lending each other shoes and handbags, and sharing soul secrets.

I ignored a niggling shiver. I wanted to touch the images even more than before, but I refrained—I had an armload of dog, and, besides, I sensed that Danielle would fling herself bodily between me and the painted family if I so much as lifted a finger in their direction.

"Yes," I said softly. "The children—"

"You'd never think, to look at them," she responded, lowering her voice to impart a confidence, "that the poor things would be murdered before the paint cured, would you?"

These little ones had been dead for centuries, but I felt the shock of their slaughter as a blow to the solar plexus. I might have known them myself, and read about them in that morning's newspaper, so immediate was the effect.

"*Murdered?*" I looked into their trusting eyes, noted again their plump little cheeks, their shimmering, flaxen hair. It was as if real blood flowed beneath those flawless complexions, through countless tiny arteries and veins as supple as my own.

"I know a little of the history," Danielle said, with a sort of weighted lightness, gazing at the painting while I turned my full and stricken attention on her. "Or, at least, I'm familiar with the legend. She was a contessa, from one of the wealthiest and most influential families in Venice. Her husband had been trifling with the children's governess, and one night, after he'd spurned her, the odious creature pitched all four of those babies into a canal. Three of them drowned, and one was rescued by a servant, only to contract some sort of virulent fever and die a few weeks later. The governess was sentenced to burn at the stake for the crime—but someone helped her escape."

I shuddered, barely registering the word "escape." My mind was full of horrific images. "Awful," I said. "What happened to the children, I mean. And the idea of burning someone at the stake—"

I was too choked up to go on.

Danielle turned and looked into my face, and I noticed that her eyes were gray and oddly opaque. She might as well have been wearing the signature sunglasses. "She deserved to die a horrible death, wouldn't you say?"

Naturally, I didn't condone what the governess had done, but I was, after all, a defense attorney. The woman must have been demented to murder those kids, but did *anyone* "deserve" such a hideous, agonizing death? "No," I said hesitantly. And then again, more strongly, "No."

"Four innocent children died," Danielle said evenly.

I shook my head. "There is such a thing as mercy," I reasoned.

"Did she show *them* mercy? They must have been terrified. Imagine being betrayed by someone you trusted—water slowly filling your lungs—the darkness closing around you as the weight of your clothes pulls you under—"

It was almost as though Danielle were weaving a spell. For a moment, I felt as though *I* had been cast into a canal, in the depths of some starless night. I fought my way to the surface, back to a bright winter morning in southern Arizona, where the sun was shining and the air was fresh and there were flowers nodding in people's yards.

"She must have been insane," I said firmly, and I wondered why Danielle would want to have the painting around at all, when it clearly reminded her of something so tragic, and that was when I picked up on a fact that had been jumping down in the back of my head, trying to get my conscious attention. "You're Bobby Ray Lombard's sister," I recalled aloud.

She blinked. "*Step*sister," she clarified, and had the decency to blush.

"Have you bailed him out yet?"

Danielle bristled, though her lips curved into a strange little smile. "Not yet," she said. "I was going to, but Tony persuaded me to wait."

"Tony?" I asked blankly. "Oh, you mean Sonterra."

She tilted her head to one side, examined me with a feline air. Cat, sizing up mouse. "Why do you call him by his last name?"

According to my therapist, it was because I wanted to keep Sonterra at a certain distance, physical intimacy notwithstanding, but my neuroses were none of Ms. Bickerhelm's damn business. My evil twin came out. "It's a sexual thing," I said in a confidential whisper.

Danielle pulled back, mentally if not physically. "Oh," she said.

I looked at my watch. "Gotta go."

"What about the cradle?"

I glanced at the window display and shook my head. "Bad vibes," I said, and I wasn't being flippant. The thing gave me the creeps. Generations of babies had rested in that cradle, and not a few of them must have died there, the infant mortality rate being what it was in those times. No way *my* child was going to be immersed in that kind of energy.

Sonterra was right. I was getting to be another Mrs. Kravinsky.

"But there are *years* of history in that cradle," Danielle protested.

"That's the problem," I answered on my way out. Waldo rose off the sidewalk, relieved to see Bernice and me pop back into his dimension. I put Bernice down and untied Waldo, taking a couple of moments to pet him. "Thanks for telling me about the painting," I told Danielle, in parting.

Yeah, I thought. *Thanks* a lot.

"The Dry Creek Literary Club meets at my house on Tuesday night," she called after me, as though we hadn't just been talking about drowned babies, fevers, and a governess who'd barely escaped being spit-roasted in a Venetian piazza. "We'd love it if you could join us. We're reading a new book—Oprah's latest pick."

I wondered if it came with a razor blade. Oprah seemed so well adjusted on TV, but she must have had a dark side. My first instinct, obviously, was to refuse Danielle's invitation, but I had Sonterra's position in the community to consider. It was important for the police chief's soon-to-be-wife to fit in well with the locals, and fair or unfair, whether I liked it or not, everything I did reflected on him. "I'll let you know," I answered, as cheerfully as I could, and hastened away.

In front of the barbershop, I memorized the phone number of a real estate company in Tucson, planning to call for rental information when I got back to the house.

Sonterra's SUV wasn't in the parking lot when the dogs and I reached the cop shop, so we made a U-turn and started for home. When we reached the house on Cemetery Lane, Loretta's Lexus gleamed in the driveway and a small Mexican woman sat quietly on the top step of the front porch, arms wrapped around her knees.

She was a study in patience. A thrift-shop madonna, *sans* infant.

"You must be Esperanza," I said, opening the gate and letting the dogs off their leashes. They ran to the visitor, sniffed her cheap but dazzlingly white sneakers, and dashed off to chase each other through the fragrant grass.

Without giving an immediate answer, she stood, smoothing the skirt of her simple cotton dress, oft-washed, neatly ironed, and probably homemade, her glossy black hair tamed into a thick braid resting over her left shoulder and reaching past her waist. Presently, she smiled and gave a shy nod of acknowledgment and greeting, but said nothing.

While I marveled at the speed of Loretta's personal network, another part of my brain took Esperanza's measure. Hardly bigger than a child, she could have been any age between twenty-five and seventy. While her manner was diffident, I sensed a vast, almost elemental dignity behind it, and that made me like her instantly.

"I'm Clare Westbrook," I said, approaching and putting out my hand.

She shook it readily, her grip firm. I was a head taller, and still street-kid strong, despite years of relatively easy living—if you don't count the numerous attempts on my life—but I figured she could have forced me to my knees if she wanted. "Esperanza Lopez," she replied. "My cousin Rosa sent word that you wish for a housekeeper. I can clean and cook." She'd left her white vinyl purse on the step. It was tiny, the kind of beruffled, fussy thing little girls carry at Easter, and Esperanza was probably not its original owner. "I have green card," she added hurriedly, and opened the purse. She brought out a rosary, a pack of Juicy Fruit, and a pristine pair of gloves, before she produced the documentation.

I examined the card—which, for the record, isn't actually

green—but that was a formality. I liked Esperanza Lopez, and the instant she'd said she was legal, I'd decided to hire her.

I smiled as I handed back the card. "When can you start?"

Esperanza beamed with delighted relief, her hands trembling as she hastily returned her belongings to the purse. "Anytime," she said.

"Great. Come inside, and I'll show you around."

I noticed that Esperanza crossed herself as she stepped over the threshold ahead of me, but I didn't really register the gesture. I bent to retrieve the keys to Loretta's car, which had been pushed through the mail slot in the door, and Waldo and Bernice ducked in after us.

I gave Esperanza the tour, and we finished in the kitchen, where I put on a fresh pot of coffee. We came to terms quickly; she would live out, and start on Monday morning, at nine o'clock. It was only after she'd gone that it occurred to me to wonder how Sonterra would react to the news that we now had a housekeeper.

Since he wouldn't be paying Esperanza's wages, I didn't worry about it.

I was making a fried peanut butter and banana sandwich for lunch when the landline jangled. I didn't check the caller ID; Sonterra was due to check in, and I assumed it was him.

"No way I'm buying that cradle," I said, instead of "hello." "And Loretta loaned me her Lexus, so I have wheels."

A short silence reverberated on the other end of the line.

Oops, I thought. *Not Sonterra after all.*

"Ms. Westbrook?" The caller was male, and probably middle-aged, judging by the seasoned timbre of his voice. If a redwood could talk, it would sound like that.

I propped the receiver between my shoulder and my ear and flipped the sandwich in the skillet. It smelled like heaven, and my stomach rumbled. "Yes. Who is this?"

"My name is Eli Robeson, and I'm—"

Everything inside me leaped to attention. "The Pima County prosecutor," I finished for him.

He chuckled warmly. "I'm flattered," he said.

I lifted the edge of the sandwich with a spatula and peered at the underside to see if it was brown and crisp, the way I liked it. "Your reputation precedes you," I told him. I must have seemed a lot cooler than I felt. This guy was legendary, a courtoom barracuda. Sensible crooks took one look at him, bent over, and kissed their sorry butts good-bye.

Robeson laughed again, à la James Earl Jones. I'd never met the man in person, but of course, with his trial record, he was a regular in the media, so his image took shape in my mind right away. "I could say the same thing to you," he said. "Masterful work, getting the charges dropped against David Valardi in that computer-virus case. You never would have gotten away with it if I'd been across the aisle."

I smiled and plopped the sandwich onto a plate. "Fortunately," I said, still quivering inside, "you weren't."

He chuckled warmly. "Obviously, I've been following your exploits, Ms. Westbrook, on television, in the newspapers, and via the grapevine, and when Judge Tucker told me you were in the vicinity, I decided to take a chance. I've got a rather novel proposition for you."

My heartbeat quickened and I swear my ears twitched. "I'm listening."

"I've got all the lawyers I can use," he went on, "and I don't need any more, but I *could* do with another investigator. And based on your track record, you're the ideal choice."

I caught my breath. For a moment, I even forgot about the sandwich, dripping with melted peanut butter and steaming with the aroma of sweet ambrosia.

An investigator?

Great God Almighty, it was a license to snoop.

"Tell me more," I said.

The dogs drew near, looking wistfully at my lunch. Fat chance.

I shook my head sternly, and they slunk off to their big pillow-bed in the corner.

"We get a number of cases in and around Dry Creek,"

Robeson said, without missing a beat. "I've got the files on three or four good old boys, and a couple of good old *girls,* right here on my desk. It seems there was a brouhaha the other night at a place called Bubba's?"

"Yes."

"And then there's a fish I've been trying to hook for several years now. Bobby Ray Lombard. He's got a record back in Oklahoma, and he's been up on assault charges several times since he decided to honor Pima County with his presence. Somehow, he always manages to slip through the net. I'd like you to get the goods on him, Clare. He needs putting away."

Of course. Judge Tucker had told him about the restraining order I'd filed on Micki Post's behalf.

"I agree," I said, trying to contain my excitement. "But I'm used to working for myself. I thought I could get back into office-mode, but now, frankly, I have some doubts. I can do the occasional staff meeting, and I'm up for consultations and reports with individual prosecutors, but if this is a nine-to-five kind of thing—"

"Strictly case by case," Robeson broke in.

Bringing down Bobby Ray Lombard was certainly an attractive prospect; I'd need to get a current mug shot of Lombard, fix his image in my mind. With the authority of Pima County behind me, virtually nothing would be off-limits.

Oh, man, Sonterra was going to hate this. I broke off a chunk of the sandwich and chewed quietly on that as well as Robeson's offer. "I'm pregnant," I said, and braced myself for the whole sweet dream to go right down the tube. Women have made a lot of strides in the workplace, and everybody tries to be politically correct, but the old-boy network is hardwired into the system. Pregnant women are still considered an employment risk, and anybody who thinks otherwise is up for next year's Pollyanna Award.

I figured Loretta was a shoo-in for *this* year.

"Congratulations," Robeson replied. "But I still want to hire you."

I wanted to accept then and there, which was a sure sign that

I needed time to think. I've made plenty of impetuous decisions in my life, and not many of them panned out. "Can I give you an answer next week?"

Robeson had already won, and he knew it. He exuded self-assurance; it came snaking right through the phone lines into my ear. "Shall we say Tuesday?" he asked smoothly. "I'll tell my secretary to expect you at ten o'clock."

I pretended to check my Day-Timer. Tuesday was a blank, except for Danielle's book club meeting, which I would probably attend because one, I was still curious about her, and two, I am a glutton for punishment. "I think I can make it," I said moderately.

To Robeson's credit, he didn't laugh again. "Good." He gave me the address—as if I didn't know it already—and we rang off.

I finished my sandwich in a daze.

Five minutes later, Sonterra called. I put him on speaker.

"He's out," he said.

I was setting my plate in the sink, and it almost slipped out of my hands. "Lombard?" I asked, though I already knew the answer.

Sonterra's voice sounded heavy. "A judge set bail, and Big Sister wrote a check. As of now, Bobby Ray is a free man."

I closed my eyes for a moment, absorbing reality. I shouldn't have been surprised, but I was. "Shit," I said, thinking of Micki and her daughter. Restraining order or none, they were very much at risk. I wondered if Robeson had already known Bobby Ray had made bail when he called to offer me a place on his staff.

"I've warned your client," Sonterra went on, "but we don't have the manpower to protect her, and she knows it."

"This sucks," I said. I wanted to smash the plate against the nearest wall, but it would scare the dogs and, besides, it was part of a luncheon set that once belonged to Sonterra's mother.

"Yes," Sonterra agreed with a sigh. "It does. I called Dr. Holliday. Micki and the little girl are going to stay with her for the next few days. You know something, Counselor? Sometimes I really hate being a cop."

It was all I could do not to call Robeson back and sign on as an investigator then and there.

"Any breaks in the coyote case?" I asked, though I knew by Sonterra's mood that there hadn't been.

"Zip," he said. "Nothing on the pickup that bashed into you, either. If I look at one more paint-chip comparison, my eyes are going to cross. Are you packed for the trip up to Scottsdale?"

I wasn't. "Yes," I answered. Jeans, a couple of T-shirts, underwear, and a nightgown. And, of course, a black suit for the funeral. Not a big deal.

"Okay," Sonterra said. "We might as well leave early, then."

"Right," I said.

We ended the call, and I sprinted up the back stairs to throw my stuff into a suitcase. When Sonterra pulled in, five minutes after hanging up, I was just snapping the catches on my week-ender.

I heard the back door open and some clumping of feet, then he was standing in the bedroom doorway. I blushed guiltily, still standing over the suitcase. He grinned.

He took the bag, without a word, collected his own hard-sider, already packed, from the floor of the closet, and headed out again.

I followed him down the steps. "Two things happened today," I said hastily, anxious to prove myself a truth-teller. "I hired a housekeeper—her name is Esperanza Lopez, and she's starting on Monday—and Eli Robeson offered me a job. Kind of a freelance gig."

Sonterra paused in the middle of the stairway, looked back at me, over one shoulder. "I'd say there were three things," he said. "Is that Loretta's car blocking the driveway?"

I nodded. "She's lending it to me until she gets back from New York."

"Great," Sonterra said, and descended into the kitchen. The dogs were waiting at the back door, ready to travel.

"What do you think?" I prompted.

"About what?" Sonterra countered. "The housekeeper, the job, or Loretta's car?"

"The housekeeper and Loretta's car are done deals," I said.

"If I accept the job with Robeson, I get to work out of Dry Creek, except for the odd staff meeting at his office in Tucson, and Bobby Ray Lombard's bad ass is mine on a platter."

Sonterra made it as far as the middle of the kitchen floor before he set down the suitcases. "Suppose I said I'd rather you didn't mess with Lombard?" he asked too quietly.

"I'd say your opinion matters to me," I hedged. "I understand that he's dangerous, Sonterra. I got a good look at his handiwork when Micki came in to file charges against him."

"*Do* you understand? You have a proven history of getting in over your head. Should I start listing examples?"

"No, but I still need to *do* something. The next thing you know, I'll be watching daytime television."

Sonterra didn't speak. He just stood there, looking ominous.

"I promise I'll be careful. Double-dog, hope-to-spit, *swear.*"

"What exactly would you be doing?"

"Robeson wants an investigator."

"Shit," Sonterra said. He shoved a hand through his hair, then huffed out a sigh, probably of resignation. "Take the dogs and get in the car," he said, picking up the suitcases again. "I'll lock up, then load these in back."

We were going to let the whole investigator subject ride, then. Probably a good idea. Give us both a chance to get some perspective.

Sonterra might even get me to change my mind before my meeting with Robeson on Tuesday.

And Elvis might be deep-frying Twinkies in some Southern diner, at that very moment.

"I'd like to talk to Micki before we leave town," I said, when Sonterra joined Bernice, Waldo, and me in the SUV. "Make sure she's okay."

Judy Holliday's house, like her office on the other side of town, was modest: a little cement-block affair with a rock yard and an ancient, half-decayed cactus out front. A child—Suzie Post, I presumed—watched us pull up, curious but not afraid. Probably six or seven years old, she wheeled her pink bicycle off the walk and waited. She was delicate as a rose petal, with Micki's brown hair, and when Sonterra got out of the SUV, she smiled, not at him, I suspected, but at Waldo and Bernice, who were on their hind legs at the back window, longing to make her acquaintance.

"Hey," Sonterra said easily, stopping at the gate, respecting what she'd no doubt been taught—beware of strangers.

"Are you Suzie?" I asked, stepping up beside him.

She nodded. "Who are you?"

Just then, the front door of the stucco house opened, and Micki stood on the threshold. "Clare," she said, and broke into a smile. For Sonterra, she spared a brief nod. "It's okay, Suzie. I told you about Miss Westbrook. She's my lawyer. And that's Mr. Sonterra, the chief of police."

Suzie looked us both over. "Can I pet the dogs?" she asked.

"Sure," Sonterra said. He glanced up at Micki's face, which was healing, but still swollen and bruised. "If it's all right with your mom."

Suzie checked with Micki and, at her mother's nod, sprang forward to open the gate. Sonterra let Waldo and Bernice out of the car, and the little girl crouched, laughing as they licked her face.

At Micki's beckoning gesture, I moved toward the house.

"Come in," she said. "Doc's in the kitchen."

I followed her into a small entryway, looked up at the huge, wrought-iron chandelier overhead. It was incongruous in that tiny, austere cubicle of a house.

Micki chuckled, following my gaze upward, to the light fixture. "One of the Mexicans gave it to her," she said, in a confidential whisper. "For setting his son's broken arm."

I nodded, just as Judy Holliday stepped into view from what must have been the kitchen. She looked pleased, and a little relieved, to see me. Her trim, wiry body fairly vibrated with controlled tension. Had she been expecting Bobby Ray?

"Clare," she said. "It's good to see you. Come in and have some coffee."

"I can't stay long," I replied. "Sonterra's outside, with the dogs. I wanted to let you know that we'll be out of town for the weekend. Make sure everything was all right."

Judy's smile slipped a little. Her shirtsleeves were rolled up, and there was a dish towel tied around her waist for an apron. "I guess we'll just have to depend on the deputies," she said.

Micki lowered her head. "I ought to take Suzie to her dad, over in Bisbee," she said. "I would, if I wasn't afraid Dan wouldn't give her back."

I put an arm around Micki's shoulder, felt her shrink away slightly, trembling. Given her life experience, it was no surprise that she wasn't the touchy-feely type. Neither was I, except when it came to Sonterra.

"If you want to, you can ride up to Phoenix with us," I told her gently. "You and Suzie both. You might feel safer there. We'll find you a place to stay."

Judy gave her a hopeful look. "That's not a bad idea, Micki," she said. "Bobby Ray wouldn't know where to look for you."

"Bobby Ray *always* knows where to look for me," Micki whispered miserably, ducking her head again as if to escape some unseen fist.

We passed through a minute dining area, decorated with diplomas and family photos, into a little kitchen.

"You have my cell number," I reminded them both, when a silence fell.

Judy took a mug from a rack on the wall and held it up.

I shook my head. "No time," I reminded her.

She nodded, and her shoulders stooped for a moment.

"We'll be back Sunday night," I said.

Nobody seemed reassured.

Stay, urged a voice in my mind.

I didn't. It's not the things we do that we regret, according to popular wisdom. It's the things we *don't* do.

This was certainly a case in point.

Within ten minutes or so, Sonterra and I were on the road, barreling north. I couldn't get Micki and Suzie and the doc out of my mind.

"I think Robeson's going to swear me in and give me a badge," I commented.

Sonterra's fingers tightened on the steering wheel, and his jaw looked hard, but he didn't glance my way, and he didn't speak.

"Say something," I said.

"What good would it do?" he snapped back.

I slumped back in the seat and drifted off.

We were just outside of Phoenix when my cell phone played the familiar riff.

"He called!" Micki gasped. "Bobby Ray, I mean."

I glanced at Sonterra, but he hadn't mellowed in the time I'd been napping. He was still ignoring me.

"Did he threaten you?"

That drew a quick glance from Sonterra.

"Not in so many words," Micki answered. "I think he just wanted me to know *he* knows where we are."

"Are you and Suzie still at Dr. Holliday's place?" I asked.

Micki gave a bitter, high-pitched laugh. "Yes." She was nearly hysterical, and the fear spilled out of her in a dark litany. "First thing Bobby Ray's going to do is trash my trailer, so I won't have any place to go. We can't stay with Doc forever and, besides, Bobby Ray thinks she's a lesbian. He might hurt her, just for that." She paused, and when she spoke again, her voice was small, barely more than a whisper. "Sometimes I wish he'd just kill me and get it over with."

"Whoa," I said, sitting up straight again. "Don't talk like that, Micki. What would happen to Suzie if you weren't around?"

Sonterra darted another look in my direction, his eyebrows raised.

"Maybe she'd be better off."

"Micki!"

"Well, her daddy's remarried. He's got a nice house and a good job. Maybe I'll call him. Have him come pick Suzie up."

My heart fell apart in two bleeding chunks. This was what it was like to be Micki, and a few million other women just like her.

I wanted to find Bobby Ray Lombard, rip his gizzard out, and dip it in battery acid.

"It might be a good idea to send Suzie to stay with her father," I said carefully. "And you need to get out of Dry Creek, too. At least until Lombard is behind bars for good."

Micki started to cry. It was a bleak, thick sound, a hopeless snuffling. I could picture her bruised and stitched face all too easily. "I'll be dead before that happens," she said. "When Bobby Ray finally goes down, it'll be on a murder charge, and I'll be the one he killed."

"Promise me you'll get out of Dry Creek, Micki. Tonight."

She sniffed. "It won't do any good."

"Listen to me," I said firmly, struggling to keep my cool. "This is no time to feel sorry for yourself. You've got to pull yourself together."

She hung up on me.

Sonterra pulled into a convenience-store parking lot, and I filled him in on Micki's part of the conversation. He listened, got out his cell phone, and called Deputy Rathburn. Gave the order for round-the-clock surveillance on Micki, Suzie, and Dr. Holliday. Rathburn was to call in the State Police if he needed backup.

"Feel better?" Sonterra asked when the call ended.

"No," I said.

I'm a smart woman.

I ought to listen to myself more often.

ELEVEN

The back of the SUV was crammed with stuff from my office, our suitcases, and half of Emma's earthly belongings. She sat quietly in the backseat, with the dogs, Sunday-night tired, jamming to the hip-hop flowing into her ears through a pair of headphones.

It had been a long, hectic weekend, and Sonterra and I hadn't had much time to talk, between Jimmy's funeral and the packing. While I worked at the office, with Shanda's help, he'd spent time with Eddie Columbia, who would be getting out of the hospital in a few days. Eddie's ex-wife, Jenna, had eloped with the boyfriend, and they were honeymooning in San Miguel de Allende.

When it rains, it shits.

I'd called Judy Holliday's house several times, and been reassured by either her or Micki, but I was still uneasy.

We'd managed to make a few concrete decisions in Scottsdale, at least. Sonterra and I would be married in Dry Creek, as soon as Loretta got back from New York, with his whole family in attendance. I would forget about leasing the barbershop and starting a new practice, and accept Robeson's offer, on a trial basis.

Sonterra and I had discussed the wedding, and said as little as possible about the new job with the prosecutor's office. If I'd had to guess, I'd have said he was thinking about Jimmy Ruiz, the coyotes, and/or whoever it was who totaled my Escalade on that lonely country road and almost snuffed me in the process. I remember clearly that I was wondering if Micki and Suzie were still all right, and whether or not I should ask Sonterra to stop at the supermarket so we could lay in some groceries, or wait and send Esperanza for provisions in the morning.

Sonterra's cell phone bleeped, and he answered curtly.

"Christ," he said, after listening for a few moments.

I turned to him, waiting to be filled in. Every small hair on my body stood upright, like wire, all systems screaming, *Trouble*.

"Handle it," he went on, ignoring me. "I've got my family with me, but I'll get there as soon as I can." Another grim pause. "Just secure the scene. If the press shows up, keep them out."

He paused, listened. His jaw was hard. "Where the hell were *you* when this went down?"

My stomach did a free fall.

Sonterra hung up with a curse and a jab of his thumb, and shoved the phone into a nook on the dashboard.

"Talk to me, Sonterra," I said, as we rolled into Dry Creek.

He glanced back at Emma, and so did I. She was still blissed out on her music.

"Judy Holliday is dead," he ground out. "Micki and the little girl are gone."

I put a hand to my mouth. Holliday's house was only a few blocks off the main drag, and I saw the flashing lights of the squad cars as we started past the turn onto her street.

"Stop!" I yelled, flinging off the seat belt and shoving open my door, just in case Sonterra thought I wasn't serious.

I knew he'd planned on taking Emma and me home before heading to the crime scene, but it was plainly a lost cause. "All right," he said. "Shut the door before you fall out."

I did what he asked and he made the turn, pulling in behind the squad cars. He swore as I jumped out of the SUV and ran toward the house, and I heard him order Emma to wait in the car.

Deputy Jesse was hurling up his socks in the yard.

I was through the front gate and onto the porch before Sonterra caught up with me. My face was wet with tears.

Sonterra grabbed me by the upper arms and turned me around. "Stay here," he said.

I nodded.

Sonterra's face was terrible, in the bug-spangled porch light. "Think about the baby," he said calmly. "Think about Emma."

My knees wobbled.

He let go of my shoulders and went inside.

I followed on his heels.

Judy Holliday's dead body dangled from the wrought-iron chandelier, spinning slowly to the left, then to the right, with an eerie creak of the yellow plastic rope digging deep into her neck. Her hands were duct-taped behind her, her face was purple, and her tongue protruded from one side of her mouth.

Dave Rathburn stood gazing up at her. When he looked at Sonterra, I saw a veil go down behind his eyes, and a flush rose under his jowls.

"Did you call the ME?" Sonterra demanded. He was pale.

Rathburn nodded. "Yes, sir," he said, putting a slight and surly emphasis on the "sir."

Sonterra's words were swift and clearly differentiated, like bullets. "Who found the body, and when?"

Rathburn's flush deepened, but his eyes were cold. "I did. Jesse and I were changing shifts. I figured it would be okay if we stopped by the diner for a decent meal. That was at about five o'clock. When I got back, just after six, the front door was open. I came inside to check things out, and here she was. I called Jesse right away, but he hasn't been much help. One look at this, and he started gagging. I sent him outside, so he wouldn't puke all over the crime scene."

Sonterra went still. "I told you I wanted somebody keeping an eye on this place at all times," he said carefully. "Even if that meant calling in the State Police."

"We were only gone for an hour," Dave said.

Sonterra looked up at Judy Holliday's body. A muscle bunched in his cheek. "I guess that was long enough," he replied.

He took me by the arm, about to hustle me outside. I heard sirens, and figured reinforcements had arrived.

"What about Suzie and Micki?" I asked, digging in my heels.

"No sign of 'em," Rathburn said, giving me the once-over. He obviously didn't approve of my presence, and I didn't give a damn what he thought.

I glanced desperately at Sonterra.

"I'm taking you home," he said, and pulled me out onto the porch.

I lifted my chin, squared my shoulders. "You've got work to do," I answered, sounding a lot calmer than I felt. "Are the keys still in the SUV?"

Sonterra nodded grimly, and his eyes were slightly narrowed, as though he suspected a trick. The truth was, I'd seen more than enough, and I knew I'd only get in the way if I stayed.

"We'll be at the house," I told him, and headed for the car.

The coroner's van was just pulling up at the curb, along with two state patrol cars, as I climbed behind the wheel.

"What's going on?" Emma asked from the backseat.

No point in hedging; she'd find out soon enough. "There's been a murder," I said as we passed Deputy Jesse, just finishing up his vomit fest.

When we got home, I had one of my own.

Esperanza paused beside my chair at the kitchen table the next morning, to touch the back of one hand to my forehead. Sonterra had been gone all night, busy at the crime scene, and there had been no reports. Emma was upstairs in her new bedroom, sound asleep. Later in the day, I planned to drive her to Dry Creek High School in the borrowed Lexus and make sure she was properly registered and situated.

"You not feel good, Mrs. Clare?" Esperanza asked with concern. The "Mrs." came out sounding like "Meesus," and I didn't bother to correct her with an explanation of my status as a live-in girlfriend, not a wife.

She'd arrived at eight-forty-five, crossing herself at the threshold and entering the house with an air of determined bravery. Already wearing an apron, she'd immediately switched the countertop TV from CNN to a Spanish soap opera, and from my viewpoint, one made about as much sense as the other.

"I'm fine," I lied, in belated answer to Esperanza's inquiry. Actually, I felt as though someone had scraped my insides out with a scythe. Judy Holliday's body hung in my mind. She couldn't have been dead long when I saw her, but she'd already been bloated.

"Was terrible thing, that doctor was murdered," Esperanza said, and crossed herself again, murmuring a rapid and unintelligible prayer. "She was kind to us. Take care of Maria, when she have fever." Her eyes were haunted, but then, suddenly, she brightened. "I make you green tea. Is good for all troubles."

I figured I was safe nodding, because I knew there wasn't any green tea in the house. I hate that stuff, but I enjoyed being fussed over just a little. "Thank you."

Esperanza opened the first cupboard, beginning the futile search, just as Emma came down the back stairs, still in her pajamas, and trailed by both dogs.

I introduced her to Esperanza, and Emma joined in the cupboard opening.

"Isn't there anything to eat in this place?" my niece fussed. "God, it's Scottsdale all over again!"

I smiled, albeit wanly. "Esperanza will go to the grocery store later," I said. I would have liked to hibernate, but I had to get my niece into school and put away some of the stuff in the back of Sonterra's car. Life goes on. Ready or not, here it comes. "In the meantime, stop carrying on like Old Mother Hubbard and make do."

Emma sighed expansively and got out the peanut butter. The jar was as hollow as my insides; I'd been hitting the banana sandwiches pretty hard ever since I got home from the hospital. Building up my strength.

"Maybe I could qualify for the breakfast program at school," Emma said. "On the basis of, my aunt never buys food."

"Poor child," I lamented. "I think the trust fund might get in your way."

Emma rolled her eyes, found a butter knife, and finished off the dregs of the peanut butter. "Maybe you could home-school me," she said very casually.

"Maybe pigs really do fly," I countered.

Esperanza came across the last of the plain tea and settled for that.

Emma tossed the denuded peanut butter jar into the trash and went on scrounging. Starvation averted: saved by breakfast bars.

"Has Tony been home?" she asked, plunking two of them into the toaster oven and breaking off pieces of a third for the dogs. They'd already had kibbles, but they were doing a good job of looking pathetic.

"No," I answered, and even though I knew, intellectually at least, that Sonterra was under no obligation to keep me updated, I still felt a twinge of annoyance. Judy Holliday was dead. Micki and Suzie were missing. If Lombard *had* killed Holliday, and he was the most likely suspect, they must have seen the murder. He'd surely abducted Micki and her little girl, maybe even murdered them, too.

The teapot shrilled, startling me out of my black musings.

The only number I had for Micki was the one at her trailer. I'd called several times, last night and this morning, and gotten no answer. Esperanza set a cup of tea down at my elbow as I reached for the phone and tried again, getting the same dismal results.

It was only as I disconnected that my tired, distracted brain kicked in. Loretta had told me that Esperanza lived at the Hidy Tidy Trailer Park. So did Micki—and so had Bobby Ray Lombard.

Rocket science.

Lombard was the prime suspect. Esperanza might be willing to talk to me, fill in some pertinent details.

"Esperanza," I said, leaning to push back the chair beside mine, "sit down."

She looked alarmed. Glanced nervously at the TV, where two lovers embraced, gazing deeply into each other's eyes and murmuring *en Español.*

"No problemo," I said to reassure her.

She smiled weakly and sat. Her fingers made rosary motions, even though they were empty, and her gaze strayed to the basement door and bounced off instantly.

I laid my hand on hers. "This isn't about your work," I said, as Emma meandered back upstairs with her breakfast bars, presumably to dress for school. Because of last night's traumatic events, I'd given her permission to go in late. "Were the police at your trailer park last night or this morning? Did they talk to you?"

Esperanza swallowed, nodded. *"Sí,"* she said. Tears brimmed in her eyes. "Last night, they come. They look for Micki and the *niña.* They ask, do I see them? I tell them no. Today there is yellow tape around their trailer." The housekeeper paused and covered her face with both hands for a moment. Her thin shoulders trembled as she met my gaze again. "The *niña,* Suzie, she play with my Maria. I stop at church today, before I come here. I speak to Father Morales. I pray and light a candle."

I squeezed her hands. "You didn't see Micki or Suzie at all?"

Esperanza sniffled. "I see them Saturday morning. The doctor, she bring them in her car. They go inside, and come out with suitcase and two garbage bags. Micki wave to me, then they get in car and drive away." She paused and did the crossing routine again, glancing toward the stairs and dropping her voice to a whisper. "I not tell police this. Maria, she see Suzie. In the night, standing beside her bed. Suzie say Maria, she can have Suzie's bike."

My logical brain immediately categorized this as a child's nightmare, and the subconscious desire for a bicycle, nothing more. The chill trickling down my spine must have come from some other part of my psyche—most likely the sector that had seen the other Clare in Loretta's guest suite at the ranch.

With a shiver, I reached for my tea and took a careful sip.

"Maria must have been dreaming," I said. But I was remembering another occasion, a year before, when I'd glimpsed my late sister, Tracy, in the same guest room at the Matthews ranch. Whether I'd seen her ghost, or simply projected the image, I didn't know, but it wasn't the sort of experience one takes lightly.

I watched the inner debate play out in Esperanza's dark eyes. Agree-and-leave-it-alone versus tell-the-truth. I knew by the pallor washing out her face that she'd chosen the latter, and at considerable cost. Esperanza probably needed her job desperately, and she had no way of knowing whether or not I would fire her if she said something too weird.

"Was not dream. Maria, she see grandmother last spring, in same way. Grandmother say good-bye and kiss her forehead. Two week later, we get letter from Juarez. Grandmother die, same night Maria see her."

I didn't know what to say to that. Usually, I have an answer for everything.

Esperanza stood up. Smoothed her apron. "I do beds now."

I nodded woodenly.

Half an hour later, decently dressed and with my mind tracking marginally better than before, I dropped Esperanza off in front of the supermarket. She didn't have a car, and I knew she'd walked to work. I gave her cash and a long list, and took Emma to Dry Creek High School. After making the necessary arrangements, I told my niece to have a good day and backtracked to pick up the maid.

Esperanza was seated stoically on a bench in front of the store, surrounded by bulging grocery bags. I was impressed that she'd completed the task so quickly; she'd confessed, shyly, that reading English was a challenge for her.

I pulled up nearby and together we loaded everything into the trunk of the Lexus. Then Esperanza hurried back inside to reclaim the ice cream and other frozen items the manager had stashed in one of the freezers, at her request.

When we got back to Cemetery Lane, Sonterra was prowling around the kitchen, opening and closing cupboard doors. His hair was wet from a recent shower, and he was barefoot, with only a pair of time-softened sweatpants to keep him decent. The strain of a long night's work showed in his face.

He looked startled when he spotted Esperanza coming in behind me, but he recovered quickly. Recognition flickered in his eyes before he shifted his attention to me.

"There's nothing to eat," he said. Complain, complain, complain. From the way he and Emma acted, anybody would have thought I was solely responsible for keeping the refrigerator stocked. My question was, if they expected that, why were they always so wary of anything I cooked?

Esperanza and I set our bulging grocery bags on the counter and went back for more. Sonterra came out to help.

"I make eggs," Esperanza volunteered, when all the loot was inside. It seemed to me that ever since Sonterra appeared, she'd been trying to make herself smaller. That she might have disappeared entirely if it had been possible.

I wondered why, but only in passing. No doubt Esperanza, like many immigrants, legal or otherwise, was wary of anyone with a badge.

Meanwhile, Sonterra stood around looking glum. He was definitely half-a-sandwich low.

I touched his bare shoulder. "Bad night?" It was rhetorical, of course, something to kick-start the conversation. Finding a dead body hanging from a chandelier meets anybody's criterion for a substandard universal performance.

"The worst," he said, watching thoughtfully as Esperanza set milk and eggs on the counter, along with mushrooms, onions, and cheese, then put the ice cream into the freezer.

"I take it you didn't find Lombard," I pressed, but I stepped lightly.

Esperanza pretended not to listen, now busily peeling and chopping onions. She already had a skillet warming on the stove, and it smelled cozily of melting butter.

"He might as well have slipped into an alternate reality," Sonterra replied. He looked up at me. "No sign of Micki and her little girl, either. Her ex-husband's all over this. He came as soon as he heard, got in the way a lot, and refused to leave, so Dave let him spend the night in one of the cells. He said he wanted to be there if we got a call about Suzie."

I felt a stab of sympathy for Dan Post. He must have been frantic. "Esperanza said they left the trailer park Saturday morning with a suitcase and a couple of garbage bags. You didn't find any of their stuff at Dr. Holliday's?"

Sonterra shook his head, still pensive, still watching Esperanza as she worked.

"Of course you talked to Danielle Bickerhelm," I said.

Sonterra gave me a look. "Gosh, no," he answered, with an edge to his tone. "She's Lombard's stepsister and has a history of posting bail every time he gets in trouble with the law. Why didn't *I* think of that?"

I went to the cupboard, got out a mug, and poured him some lukewarm coffee. Some people drink warm milk when they need to chill out. Sonterra responded the same way to strong doses of caffeine, probably because he'd been a cop for so long. "No point in getting sarcastic," I said mildly.

"Then why is it always *your* first line of defense?" Sonterra retorted.

If he hadn't been under extreme stress, I might have poured the coffee over his head. "I'm only trying to cover the bases."

He made an almost inaudible snorting sound as he accepted the coffee. He thanked me, though grudgingly, and took a sip.

Meanwhile, my mind was clipping away on its own little hamster wheel. Sonterra hadn't slept the night before, which meant he'd probably crash for a couple of hours. I could slip away while he snoozed, mosey on over to the Hidy Tidy, and take a look around Micki's trailer. See if I could find something he and the deputies had missed.

Okay, so I wasn't *officially* an investigator for the prosecutor's office. Call me an eager beaver. I was too worried about Micki and Suzie to wait until I had county credentials—Sonterra had checked the place out, but, being a man, he might have missed something a woman would catch.

In Scottsdale, there might have been uniforms watching the place twenty-four/seven, but this was Dry Creek, and Sonterra had only two deputies, neither of whom were any great shakes at surveillance. One of them would be off duty, and the other, most likely, manning the station.

I would just duck under the crime-scene tape Esperanza had mentioned, satisfy my professional curiosity, and be gone again before anybody noticed.

Except, maybe, the other Hidy Tidy inmates.

I suddenly realized that Sonterra was watching me suspiciously. "What are you up to?" he demanded.

"Nothing," I said.

"That'll be the day," he shot back.

"I was merely thinking that you look like you might fall over at any moment. You need a nap, Chief." Not the whole truth, but part of it. Sometimes, that has to do.

He sighed and thrust a hand through his shower-damp hair. Looked away, then back. "While you do what?"

I managed a shrug. "Plan my interview with Eli Robeson?"

I didn't expect him to bite, but he did. He must have been more tired than I thought. "Okay," he said.

Esperanza dished up the omelet and set it in front of him, along with a knife, fork, and cloth napkin. Since I usually went with paper towels, he probably thought she was putting on the Ritz.

I had been hovering like a hummingbird. Now, for the sake of keeping Sonterra lulled into a false state of masculine complacency, I sat down next to him and watched fondly as he ate.

He put down his fork and stared at me as if to say, *What?*

I reminded myself that it never paid to underestimate Sonterra's powers of perception. They were well honed, since he'd spent his adult life dealing with every possible variety of sleazeball. I drummed up an innocent expression, stopping just short of batting my eyelashes. "Don't be cranky," I said.

He glanced at Esperanza, who was running water at the sink, and lowered his voice to a breathy growl. "Why do I get the idea you're plotting something, Counselor?"

I tried to look stunned, even affronted, but with subtlety. Back at Nipples, I played some poker, and I learned to bluff. "Like what?"

He waggled his fork at me. "Like messing around with my case," he said.

Esperanza shut off the water, put the skillet in to soak, and zipped across the kitchen toward the back stairs. "I get back to work," she blurted, and vanished.

"What's she doing here?" Sonterra asked, as soon as she was out of earshot.

I blessed Esperanza, in absentia, for creating just the diversion I needed. "I told you I hired a housekeeper."

Sonterra glowered. "And it's a coincidence that she lives directly across the street from Micki's trailer?"

That I could say, unequivocally. It *was* a coincidence, because I'd met and hired Esperanza on Friday afternoon, well before Doc Holliday was strung up. I said as much.

Not surprisingly, this did nothing to improve Sonterra's pissy mood.

"I don't like it," he said.

"Right now," I answered sweetly, "you wouldn't like anything."

An evil grin crooked one corner of his mouth. "Not so, Counselor," he said. "There's one thing I would like a lot. How does a nap sound?"

I blushed. "We're not alone," I reminded him.

"We'll be quiet," he whispered back.

"Maybe you will," I argued, "but I have a history of making noise." Now that Emma was back from Scottsdale for the duration, I'd have to curtail the climactic verbiage, but it didn't serve my purpose to clarify the matter at that point.

He sighed. He was going to let me have this round. I resisted a motherly urge to test his forehead for fever.

TWELVE

Imagine my surprise when I finally located the Hidy Tidy Trailer Park—after driving fruitlessly around town in Loretta's car for half an hour—running almost exactly parallel to Sonterra's place, on the other side of the cemetery. I'd have sworn they'd moved it since my last teenage foray to Dry Creek.

Micki's single-wide was easy to spot. It was the one with yellow plastic tape strung around it, from bush to wall to teetering rural mailbox. As far as I knew, no crime had been committed there, but the place was clearly off-limits to civilians. There were no uniforms on duty, I'd been right about that, though the locals were out in force, walking dogs, puttering in yards, watching with squinty eyes as the Lexus cruised by.

I'm bold, but I'm not stupid. I figured if I parked and crossed the tape line in broad daylight, somebody would be on the horn to the station house quicker than I could say "mobile home." Being top cop, Sonterra would be among the first to get the word, and I would be in a world of hurt. I decided to bide my time.

I made a stop at the town library, which was about the size of Loretta's favorite purse, applied for a card, and checked out the most current volume on child care. Dr. Spock, circa 1962. Guess they didn't get government funding.

By the time I got home, Emma was back from school, looking sullen, and Esperanza had clocked out for the day.

Emma had breaking news. "You're going to get a call from
the principal," she announced, leaning against the kitchen sink
and swilling chocolate milk.

I laid Dr. Spock on the table and looked her in the eye. "Great,
Emma," I said. "You're there one day, and already you're in trouble."

"She started it," my niece said.

"Who, pray tell, is 'she,' and what, precisely, did she 'start'?"

"Her name is Kathy Wilson, she's a junior, and she said you
were shacking up with the chief of police."

I felt a peculiar jiggle in the pit of my stomach, reminiscent
of the bad old days in Tucson, when kids used to make remarks
about my mother on the playground. It shouldn't have mattered,
that feeling, but it did. "And you responded by—?"

"Shoving her into her locker."

I hung my purse over the back of a chair and sat down with
a plop. "You know better," I said.

Color climbed Emma's elegant neck and swelled in her
cheeks. She spread her hands, soliloquy style, and I thought, *Here
it comes. The bullshit. The tap dance.*

She learned it from me.

"Of course she was *right*. You *are* shacking up with the chief
of police." Her gaze fell, heated, on Dr. Spock. She had eyes like
a hawk, and I knew she'd taken in the title, even from that distance. "Did you check that out at the *public library?*"

I bristled. "As opposed to the private one, reserved for my
personal use? Yes, Emma, I did. What of it?"

"Well, if everybody in town didn't already know you're pregnant, they will now!"

Before I could come up with an answering shot, Sonterra was
on the scene, looking spiffy in a fresh uniform. He whistled through
his teeth. "Time-out," he said. "Back to your corners."

I bit my lower lip, fighting tears.

"What's going on?" Sonterra asked, looking from me to
Emma and back again.

"Emma's just discovered one of the many wonders of small towns," I said evenly. My temper was cooling, but I still felt as though I'd been crammed into a cage and poked with a stick.

Emma folded her arms. Her face was rock-hard, and I knew she wasn't going to give an inch. "I've got detention all week," she told Sonterra, "because you *guys* aren't married!"

"You've got detention all week," I pointed out icily, "because you pushed Kathy Wilson into her locker!"

Sonterra whistled again, put up a hand to both of us. "Clare and I are getting married Saturday," he said.

Sure, we'd made a plan. But we didn't even have a license, or a church lined up, and Loretta was still away, so I hadn't thought about it much. I dropped into a chair.

His gaze pinned me there. "Aren't we?"

"Whose side are you on?" I snapped.

"Did we or did we not agree to get married?"

"Yes," I admitted, after unlocking my jaw.

"Well, then, I don't see a problem," Sonterra said reasonably.

I gave Emma a scathing glance, and she flung it right back.

"I want Loretta to be here," I said. "Furthermore, I don't like the idea of being steamrolled!"

Emma threw up her hands and stomped past Sonterra, headed for the stairs. The dogs followed, uncertain but loyal.

"That certainly went well," Sonterra said.

I hadn't intended to cry, but my face was already wet. "Damn it, Sonterra, this is my *wedding* we're talking about. Emma might as well be forcing me down the aisle with a shotgun!"

Sonterra approached me cautiously. All those weekend seminars with the bomb squad were finally paying off. "Easy," he said, and pulled me close. He smelled deliciously of aftershave, deodorant soap, and the starch in his uniform shirt. "Take it easy, Babe. Nobody is going to strong-arm you into anything."

I looked up at him, searching his face. "It wouldn't be right without Loretta," I said. I wasn't stalling then. I meant it.

He dried my tears with the heel of one palm. He spoke gently, but his words went through me like a spear. "And if Loretta shows up, you'll think of another excuse."

"*No,*" I protested, sniffling. I wanted to bury my face in his shoulder and bawl at full throttle, but there was his clean shirt to consider, and the snot factor. "I love you, Sonterra. I *want* to get married. I do."

"Okay. We'll get a special license tomorrow, and you can call Loretta in New York."

I'd forgotten my appointment with Eli Robeson at 10:00 the next morning. I wondered if Sonterra had, too. Not likely, I decided. He was probably hoping the whole job subject would blow over if he just didn't bring it up.

"What about the church?" I fretted. "What about the dress?"

Sonterra kissed the tip of my nose. "We can be married by a justice of the peace," he said. "And I don't care if you wear a feed sack."

"You've got murders to solve. Coyotes to catch. Call me crazy, but I was sort of hoping for a honeymoon."

"Excuses," Sonterra insisted quietly. "The average wedding is over in twenty minutes, and once I wrap things up here, we can go anywhere you want. Paris. Honolulu. Timbuktu. You name it, Counselor, and I'll buy the tickets."

I gnawed at my lower lip. "Do you solemnly swear that you won't turn out to be a rotten husband, like Kip Matthews and about a hundred other men I could name?"

Sonterra chuckled, and his eyes shone. "I do," he said.

For all my misgivings, I sort of liked the sound of that.

It was easy enough to sneak out after supper. Sonterra had gone back to the cop shop and Emma, still not speaking to me, had locked herself in her room for the evening, after nuking a frozen dinner.

Even the dogs had defected, throwing in their lot with my niece.

I was persona non grata.

I waited for dark, snagged a flashlight and a pair of disposable gloves from under the sink, and let myself out, locking the back door behind me and crossing the yard like a stealthy shadow. After taking a careful look around, to make sure Emma wasn't watching from her bedroom window—in her present mood, she'd tattle to Sonterra in a heartbeat—I went over the fence.

Since a flashlight in a cemetery might attract unwanted attention, I made my way around the headstones and markers as best I could, given that there was only a sliver of moon. I dodged sprinklers and silently chided myself for acting like the heroine of a bad Gothic novel—all I needed was a snow-white nightgown, an ax murderer, and a candle.

What did I expect to find in Micki's trailer, anyway?

Damned if I could say. All I knew was, I felt compelled to go there, pick the lock, and toss some drawers. It wasn't just curiosity, either. It seemed urgent.

A few dogs barked halfheartedly as I made my way along the cemetery fence, on the other side, and finally came to a gate. The hinges creaked, of course, and I gritted my teeth, waiting for somebody to jump out of the shrubbery and demand to know what I was doing, prowling around the neighborhood.

I would have been stuck for an answer, a rare thing for me.

For once, luck was on my side. Most of the trailers were dark—maybe it was bingo night at the American Legion—and the curtains were drawn on the few lighted ones.

I stayed close to the fence until I spotted the telltale crime-scene tape. Unless there had been yet another murder, I was in Micki's backyard.

I almost fell over Suzie's bike, lying on its side in the tall grass. The last time I'd seen it had been at Judy Holliday's, before the murder. How had it gotten here?

I stood still, drying my damp palms on the legs of my jeans, sucking in deep breaths, and remembering Esperanza's account of her daughter's nightmare.

If it was a nightmare.

A man's voice called out, in cheerful, heavily accented English, and every muscle in my body seized with tension. Sweat broke out on my upper lip, and between my breasts and shoulder blades.

Another man answered.

My brain kicked in, made sense of the exchange.

First man: *Going to the poker game?*

Second man: *No. Lost too much last week.*

I let out my breath, and the release left me limp as the proverbial rag doll.

Maybe I was losing my edge.

"Bullshit," I whispered, and put on the disposable gloves Esperanza had bought that morning at the supermarket.

Somebody ought to do something about locks. They're entirely too easy to manage, especially on trailers.

I was inside in less than thirty seconds.

The place smelled of rancid cooking oil, stale cigarette smoke, and despair.

I waited for my eyes to adjust to the darkness and my nerves to stop bouncing off the underside of my skin. The curtains were drawn, so I crouched a little and switched on the flashlight, praying the few neighbors at home were too preoccupied to notice.

For one instant, I was back in Gram's double-wide in Tucson, a mouthy little kid, hurting big-time, with two scraped knees and a screw-you attitude. The sensation passed with the next heartbeat, but I would have given my law degree to hear my grandmother's voice. *Wash your hands and face, Clare. It's time for supper.*

"Focus," I told myself.

I went through the junk drawer in the kitchen first. It's funny how they're all in pretty much the same place, in every kind of house, a grubby little universe of diverse information—matchbooks from restaurants and bars, loose batteries, usually double-A, bills and receipts, subscription cards from magazines, outdated raffle tickets, Suzie's most recent report card.

Three A's and two B's.

That made my breath catch. The kid had a good future—if she had a future at all. *Don't be dead,* I pleaded silently, remembering her delight in meeting Waldo and Bernice. *Please, don't be dead.*

I moved on to the first bedroom, a tiny cubicle smelling faintly of urine. The flashlight played over the bed under the high, narrow window, with its familiar little plastic crank. Pink-and-white-checked comforter, tossed back, and a telltale stain on the sheet. Suzie was a bed wetter.

Odd that Micki had left without changing the sheets. I barely knew her, but she certainly hadn't struck me as a neglectful mother.

The closet and built-in dresser drawers were empty.

I went on, checked out the bathroom—cosmetics scattered on the counter, ring in the bathtub. Micki wasn't a housekeeper. So maybe the wet sheets hadn't been a big concern.

Most likely, she'd left the makeup behind on purpose, when Judy Holliday picked her and Suzie up on Saturday morning. Given the state of her face, after Bobby Ray got through with her, that wasn't surprising. I checked the medicine cabinet.

Birth control pills. Half a bottle of aspirin. No toothbrushes, no paste.

Very odd that she hadn't taken the pills, even if she didn't plan to have sex anytime soon. Maybe Judy had promised her samples.

The only remaining room was Micki's, and it shot down the bad-housekeeper theory. It was as neat as Suzie's was messy. Nothing in the closets or drawers. I couldn't be sure, of course, that she'd taken all her belongings with her when she left. The police could have bagged and tagged any remaining items as part of their investigation.

I was chewing on that thought when I heard a car door slam in front of the trailer. A couple of moments later, somebody was walking across the porch.

Damn, I thought, thumbing off the flashlight and scrambling under the bed. It was a tight fit, and there were dirty socks and dust bunnies to keep me company.

Even you can't be this unlucky, I told myself. I had visions of Doc Holliday's killer showing up, pissed off at my interference, followed by thoughts of Sonterra or one of his deputies catching me in the no-no zone. One scenario was only slightly more attractive than the other.

My heart thundered in my ears as I waited, every cell in my body suddenly freeze-dried. Dust tickled my sinuses, and I closed my eyes for a moment, fighting a visceral urge to sneeze.

The front door opened and closed. More time passed.

Finally, footsteps sounded in the short, narrow hallway. I caught a whiff of familiar perfume and peeked under the bedskirt to see a pair of high-heeled shoes and, in a stray glimmer of moonlight, a gold ankle bracelet with a dainty "D" suspended provocatively from the chain.

Danielle Bickerhelm? If the visitor *was* Danielle, she wasn't being particularly subtle. She hadn't turned on the lights, but I'd distinctly heard her car door click shut, which meant she was parked in the street and, like me, she'd ducked under the tape barrier.

She sat down on the edge of the bed with a sigh, and the mattress springs dug into my back. I swallowed a grunt, along with more dust, and fought the sneeze battle all over again.

She sighed once more.

I waited.

She got off the bed, and I heard her opening the dresser and closet. The fact that she hadn't done that first thing was a clue that her visit wasn't primarily investigation-oriented.

I peered from beneath the dust ruffle. It was Danielle, all right.

I felt a surge of irate energy. I wanted to confront her, demand to know what she was looking for, but I was hardly in a position to do that. My own presence would be tough to explain.

I did some more waiting, and my nervous bladder began to fill.

Danielle came back to the bed, but this time she kicked off her shoes first and stretched out full length on the mattress. In the midst of all that motion, I heard the front door open again, and more footsteps. Danielle laughed, a low, throaty sound.

"Don't be shy," she said.

It was no great leap to work out that the newcomer was a man. He said nothing, but I felt the floor sag with his weight and smelled his aftershave. The cheap stuff, from the drugstore.

The mattress wriggled, and I figured Danielle was hiking up her skirt.

I lodged a silent protest with the heavens. *Not that. Please. Not that!*

"I'm a very bad girl," Danielle crooned.

No answer, but I heard a zipper give way, then the mattress springs came down on me again, hard, forcing all the air from my lungs in an audible rush.

I tried the universe again. Instant redial. *Get me out of here.*

Zip from the celestial realm. Guess it was busy spinning off new planets and blowing up stars. Or maybe it was a cosmic comment on my tendency to get myself into situations like that one.

I became conscious of my cell phone, which I'd tucked into the front pocket of my jeans just before I left the house, and tried to remember if I'd switched it off. Hell of a note if I got a pathos call from Loretta, or an olive-branch ringy-dingy from my niece.

Pretty likely on the first.

Fat chance on the second.

Meanwhile, Danielle and Mr. Strong and Silent went at it. Fortunately for me, Mr. S & S was no Sonterra. The whole thing was over in about a minute and a half. Slam-bam, but evidently, no "thank you, ma'am" was forthcoming.

I decided to deal with the emotional trauma of the experience later and lifted the bed ruffle again when I felt him rise off the bed. I wanted a look at Danielle's boyfriend.

It was dark, but I could make out a pair of scuffed running shoes and the cuffs of his jeans.

Say something, I urged Lover Boy silently, hoping I'd recognize his voice. I didn't dare stick my head out from under the bed, but the temptation was overwhelming.

"See you around," Danielle said, when the debacle was over.

Damn the luck, he didn't say a word. I heard him walk back down the hallway and leave the trailer. Cross the porch. No car door, so he must have come on foot.

Danielle began to cry.

I wasn't sympathetic. My bladder was screaming for relief, and images of what had just gone on directly over my head seeped into my brain. Nausea kicked in, overdue.

What the hell would prompt a woman to choose somebody else's bed for a tryst, especially when that someone else might well be the victim of a brutal crime? It was flat-out weird.

It was probably only a couple of minutes before Danielle arose, put her shoes back on, and left, but it seemed like an elephant's gestation period. I was vaguely surprised that my stomach hadn't grown.

As soon as I heard her car start, I was out from under the bed. I made a pit stop in the bathroom, took a chance on flushing, and crouched back to the front door. Then my cell phone rang.

I answered, simply to silence the thing. I guess I was too flustered to simply turn it off.

"Where are you?" Sonterra demanded. He rarely bothered with formalities like "hello."

"Just out," I answered.

"Emma said she saw you climb over the back fence, into the cemetery."

My jaw clenched. "Stool pigeon," I muttered.

"Funny thing," Sonterra went on, "but I'm sitting right in the middle of Peaceful Meadows. No sign of you."

"It's dark," I offered. My palms were sweating inside the plastic gloves. I wanted to work the latch on the trailer door, let myself out, and boogie, but I was afraid Sonterra would catch the sound and somehow figure out where I was.

"Front and center, Counselor. Come out, come out, wherever you are."

"Give me five minutes," I bargained.

"I don't have much choice, do I?" Sonterra countered.

"Just go home. I'll meet you there."

"Like I'd fall for that one."

I disconnected.

I put away the cell phone, grateful for small favors. I was in hot water, but at least Sonterra hadn't called while Danielle was still in the trailer, thus alerting her and Mr. Romance to my presence.

The immediate problem was to get out of the trailer park without being seen by any of the neighbors. If they'd heard Danielle's car, or caught a glimpse of her arrival and/or departure, they might be watching for further developments.

The secondary challenge would be to explain my sudden penchant for nighttime cemetery visits to Sonterra. That would be tougher.

Uselessly, I wiped my plastic-shrouded palms on the thighs of my jeans.

I don't think I took a full breath between opening the door of the trailer, bolting around the side, and tumbling gracelessly over the fence. Squinting through the brush, I saw the headlights of Sonterra's SUV gleaming in the middle of the cemetery.

I took the long way around and came out of the bushes on the other side. There, I turned on the flashlight and made my way between the headstones, thinking on my feet.

Sonterra finally spotted me when I was about a hundred yards out and opened his door. Stood in the glow of his interior lights. I didn't need to see his face to read his mood; even his shadow bristled.

"Start talking," he ordered, when I approached, silently whistling a happy tune.

My palms felt wet again, and I realized I hadn't taken off the gloves. Drat. Another tactical error. His gaze went right to my hands, of course. I felt his eyes ricochet to my face, and flushed in the darkness.

"Don't tell me," he said.

"Okay," I answered.

"You went to Micki's trailer." There were times when I regretted Sonterra's keen instincts, and that was one of them. In fact, except in bed, they were pretty much a pain in the ass.

I let out my breath. "Yeah," I admitted. "And I had company."

That distracted him, but only for a few moments. "Who?"

"Danielle Bickerhelm and some guy. I was under the bed."

Sonterra's grin flashed white in the gloom. It was a temporary phenomenon, and so was his good humor. "Serves you right," he said.

"They boinked," I told him.

He laughed.

"It's not funny."

"The hell it isn't," Sonterra retorted, taking me by the elbow and steering me around to the passenger side. I snapped off the gloves as I went and jammed them into my hip pocket. Out of sight, out of mind.

l hoped.

"Who was the boyfriend?" Sonterra asked, once I was buckled in and he was behind the wheel again.

I sighed. "No idea," I said forlornly. "He didn't say anything, and I couldn't get a good look at him, under the circumstances."

"He didn't say *anything?*"

"*Nada,*" I answered.

Sonterra put the SUV in gear with a sharp motion of one arm. "What were you doing there in the first place?"

So much for the respite. "I was hoping to find something you missed," I said.

"Gee, thanks," he said.

"It's been known to happen."

"Do you realize that I could arrest you for trespassing and a whole shitload of other things?"

"Yes," I answered. "I'm a lawyer, remember? But you won't, because then everybody in town would know, and that would be bad for public relations."

"I'm not worried about PR right now, Clare. And I have enough to do without keeping track of you."

I ran a hand through my hair. God, I wanted a shower, and not because of the dust under Micki's bed. "Then stop trying," I said.

"In your dreams."

We drove out of the cemetery, and Sonterra left the car to close the gate behind us. I used that time to consider my options but, once again, I came up dry.

"I think we should just forget this," I ventured when he returned.

"I imagine you do," he replied. No discerning if he'd mellowed, but I was guessing not, from his tone.

"I could use an Oreo Blizzard," I said.

"You really freaked Emma out," Sonterra said. Since he didn't turn the SUV in the direction of town, I deduced that my craving was not to be indulged.

"Emma," I countered, feeling testy again, "is a tattletale."

"She's adjusting to a new town and a new school. She loves you, and she's afraid you'll get yourself killed. How about cutting her a break?"

"When is somebody going to cut *me* a break?" I shot back, but I did feel a little guilty. Emma was my niece, and I loved her like my own child. I hated being on the outs with her.

"Not anytime soon," Sonterra said. The SUV bumped into the driveway, came to a stop behind Loretta's Lexus. "If you interfere in this investigation again, Clare, I *will* bust you for it, on general principles, and damn the fallout. Do I make myself clear?"

No point in reminding him that after tomorrow, I'd be able to investigate just about anything I damn well pleased. I unfastened my seat belt and opened the car door. Every light in the house was on, and I could hear the dogs yapping in the entryway. "Abundantly," I said. "And it wouldn't have killed you to buy me a Blizzard."

Sonterra didn't respond to that. He left the SUV running, opened the gate, and squired me up the walk to the porch. For all my planning, I hadn't brought a house key, but it didn't matter, because the door flew open, and there was Emma standing on the threshold, arms folded, flanked by the dogs.

"Rat," I said.

"Great start," Sonterra remarked. Then, to Emma, "Give me a call if she makes a break for it."

Emma nodded.

"Don't kill each other," Sonterra said. Then he turned and strode back down the walk to the gate, still ajar, got into his rig, and drove away.

Emma and I just stood there for a few moments, staring at each other in the eerie yellow glow of the porch light.

Atypically, Emma was the first to give ground. She stepped back, so I could come into the house.

"Are you mad at me?" she asked. Her tone didn't match the question or her body language, which put me in mind of the world wrestling championship.

"No," I said, realizing that I wasn't. "Do we have any Oreos?"

THIRTEEN

I wasn't exactly at my best when I arrived at Eli Robeson's Tucson office the next morning at ten o'clock, straight up; Emma and I had OD'd on our improvised version of cookie milk shakes the night before, so I was hungover from the influx of sugar, and Sonterra's poor attitude lingered right through breakfast. He left without saying good-bye.

At least I was on good terms with Esperanza and the dogs, I reflected, checking out the prosecutor's waiting room.

Robeson came out to greet me personally. He was even more impressive in the flesh than on television, well dressed, polished, and roughly the size of an upright freezer. He put out a meaty hand, and boomed, "It's good to see you, Clare." If we hadn't had an appointment, I would have thought he was startled to find me there.

We retired to the inner sanctum. Like most government offices, Robeson's was short on decoration and long on paperwork. It was a tidy sort of chaos, with files stacked on every surface, the computer screen flashing, and every line on the telephone lit up.

"Sit down," Robeson said cordially, moving four thick folders out of the chair facing his neatly cluttered desk.

I sat. Since the visit was his idea, I didn't say anything, just waited until he was seated, hands folded, smile bright as headlights on high beam.

"I need bright, motivated people like you on my team, Clare," he said.

I shifted in the chair. Smiled back.

Robeson cleared his throat and dimmed a little. "Nasty business, that doctor being murdered," he lamented. "She was a credit to the community, looking after the migrant population *gratis* the way she did."

The image of Doc Holliday hanging from the chandelier sprang into my mind. I headed off a shudder midway up my spine. "Yes," I agreed. Talk about understatements. "The suspect hasn't been apprehended yet."

Robeson nodded solemnly. "Judging by his history with the judicial system, I'd say Bobby Ray Lombard isn't sufficiently bright to avoid capture for long."

"His sister bailed him out repeatedly," I answered. Sonterra had warned me off the case, but as a member of the prosecutor's investigative team, I could dig to my heart's content. I planned to start by attending Danielle's reading group that evening. It was a safe bet that Sonterra had already questioned her about Lombard's probable whereabouts, but he wasn't inclined to share information at the best of times, and he was still smoldering over my visit to Micki's trailer.

No problem. I had a little pop quiz of my own planned for the adventurous Ms. Bickerhelm.

"What's your take on the situation?" Robeson asked, leaning back in his chair. He was a bulky man, but he moved with a certain graceful elegance. "Is Lombard our man?"

"I'd bet on it," I said. "Right now, though, I'm a lot more concerned about Micki Post and her daughter, Suzie. They disappeared from Dr. Holliday's house around the time of the killing, and as far as I know, there haven't been any leads." If there were, Sonterra was keeping mum.

Robeson tented his fingers under his several chins. "They may have been witnesses to the murder."

"I'm afraid so," I agreed. My heart clenched just to think of a little girl seeing such a thing. Bad enough for an adult.

The prosecutor pondered my response gravely, drumming his fingertips on the desktop. Then, in an instant, the political smile was back, so dazzling I nearly had to shade my eyes. "You'll be paid a modest consultation fee," he said. "Case by case, as we agreed on the telephone last week."

I had my issues, but money wasn't one of them. I probably would have paid *him* to let me have this job. "I understand," I said.

After that, we went over a few other terms, and I signed the customary forms. As soon as I left Robeson's office and hit the street, I called Sonterra.

He didn't even say hello. "Tell me you're in Tucson," he said.

"Okay," I replied, heading for the Lexus. "I'm in Tucson. I just left Eli Robeson."

I could almost hear Sonterra's jaw tightening. "Right," he said. "Did you take the job?"

"Of course I took the job." I pushed the button on the key fob, and the locks popped inside Loretta's car.

Silence from Sonterra's end. I guess his dreams of me settling happily into the *hausfrau* role and learning to crochet doilies died hard.

I got behind the wheel, relocked the doors, and started the engine, all without a word from SuperCop. "Speak, Sonterra," I prompted. "We're burning satellite minutes."

"You called me, remember?"

"So I did." I checked the side mirrors and rearview and popped the car into reverse. "Any leads on Micki and Suzie?"

"No, not that it's any of your business."

"I'm with the prosecutor's office now, Sonterra. It definitely *is* my business."

"Whoopee."

I let the sarcasm pass. "How about the coyotes? Have you and the feds gotten anywhere with that?" I looked both ways and pulled out into light midmorning traffic. It was a beautiful, crisp day. *Blue skies, smilin' at me.*

"Also not your business."

"Wrong again. You bust them, and I'll nail their balls to the floor."

"It's federal," Sonterra reminded me. "Out of your jurisdiction."

"Go figure," I countered, shaking my head. I so seldom had a professional advantage over Sonterra that I wanted to relish the experience. God knew when, or if, it would happen again. "Robeson seems to think otherwise. You are aware, I presume, that I can investigate with impunity, now that I work for Pima County?"

"I'm aware," Sonterra bit out. "But I don't have to like it."

"And you don't have to cooperate, either, but I think you will, because you want to see Lombard, not to mention Jimmy Ruiz's killers, in leg irons as much as I do."

"You've got me there." I thought I heard a note of goodwill in his voice, but I wasn't sure, and I wasn't jumping to conclusions. "We've got a meeting with Father Morales at two o'clock," he went on. "The license is already in the works. All you have to do is sign on the dotted line."

"You still want to marry me?" I asked lightly, glancing into the mirrors again before switching lanes. One thing about playing "it" in a deadly game of bumper cars on a dark country road—it makes a person alert to other drivers.

"Amazing as it sounds, yes," Sonterra allowed.

A sedan whipped in behind me, following too close. Tinted windows, no plate in front. In Arizona, they're required only in back.

I tapped the brakes. I hate tailgaters.

The sedan backed off, but not far. I heard the engine rap out. Was that yahoo about to take a run at me?

"Clare?" Sonterra sounded too calm. Maybe he sensed danger too, even from that distance.

I glanced in the rearview. The sedan revved again, and the headlights flashed, bringing back some very unhappy memories. My spinal fluid chilled by a couple of degrees. "I'm here," I said.

"What's wrong?"

"Somebody's riding my rear bumper."

"Description," Sonterra said. Cop forever, alpha and omega, amen.

"Blue sedan," I answered. "Toyota, I think. Late-model, but the hood is rusted out. Crumpled, like it's been in an accident." The car surged forward again, with another, even more aggressive roar of the engine.

"Plates?" Sonterra asked.

"Can't see them."

The sedan tapped the Lexus, almost playfully, like a boa constrictor nuzzling the mouse it intends to swallow.

Fear gave way to irritation. I swore.

"*Clare,*" Sonterra said.

"He just hit me. Broad daylight, in the middle of downtown. What the hell?"

Sonterra was all business. "Location," he said.

I gave him the cross streets. The sedan whacked me again, this time harder.

"I'll get you a black-and-white," Sonterra told me. "Whatever you do, don't stop. This is a classic car-jacking technique."

"Thanks for the crime-stoppers bulletin," I replied.

"I'll be back on the line in a second," Sonterra promised.

"Check," I said, put the phone on speaker, and tossed it onto the passenger seat. The sedan was backing off for another run at my bumper, and I needed both hands on the wheel.

Other drivers stared and honked furiously as I swerved, tires screeching. Then the other car swung into the left-hand lane, whizzed up beside me. I ducked instinctively, prepared for a bullet, thinking frantically of my baby. I could hear Sonterra shouting my name from the cell phone, then the faint, welcome bleat of an approaching siren.

I peered over the dashboard just in time to see a red light coming up. Automatically jammed on the brakes and fishtailed into the intersection. I squeezed my eyes shut, expecting either to be shot at through the windshield or crunched between oncoming cars.

"Clare!" Sonterra yelled.

Shaking, I fumbled for the phone. "I'm all right," I gasped, hoping the conclusion wasn't premature. I thought the sedan was gone, but I had no way of knowing for sure, so I ducked again, just in case there was a bullet in my future.

Somebody pounded at the driver's-side window, and I looked up, half-expecting to see a gun barrel pointed at my head. Instead, it was a cop, peering through the glass.

"It's okay," I told Sonterra. "The police are here."

Sonterra heaved a sigh. "Good."

The uniform, a tall young man, nodded for me to push the lock button. I did, and he pulled open the door. "You all right, ma'am?" he asked.

I nodded, but when I recovered the cell phone, thumbed the speaker button, and stepped out of the Lexus, my knees buckled. The officer passed me off to his partner, got into Loretta's car, and drove it out of the middle of the intersection, so traffic could flow again. When the other cop and I reached the curb, I sat down, heedless of my panty hose and straight skirt, and concentrated on not passing out.

The cell phone was glued to my ear.

"Put somebody on who can talk," Sonterra counseled.

Wordlessly, I handed the cell to my escort. There was no sign of the Toyota. I would have put my head between my knees if I could have gotten them apart. Impossible in that skirt.

I heard the officer talking to Sonterra, but I couldn't make out the words. It sounded like an alien radio transmission, with lots of static.

"We're taking you to the station," the other cop informed me, after he'd parked the Lexus in the lot of a corner convenience store.

I blinked. "Am I under arrest?"

The officer smiled benevolently, reached down to help me to my feet. "No, ma'am. Mr. Sonterra asked us to keep you in protective custody until he can pick you up. In the meantime, though, we've got a few questions for you."

• • •

A few questions.

Two *long* hours later, I was in the SUV with Sonterra, headed for Dry Creek. He must have been worried about me, because he stopped for an Oreo Blizzard without even being asked.

"What happened?" he asked, once I'd been primed with ice cream and crumbled cookies.

"We've been over it a hundred times, Sonterra," I said wearily. Automotive harassment makes me testy. "I told you, I told the whole damn Tucson PD. A blue sedan pulled in behind me, rammed me a couple of times. I didn't see the driver or the license plate. What else is there to say?"

"*Somebody* must have seen *something*," Sonterra insisted. I knew he was wondering, as I was, if the two attacks were connected.

A couple of drivers had watched the whole incident, and so had a clerk in the convenience store, along with a guy filling his gas tank at a rival company on the other side of the intersection. As far as I knew, none of them had been able to add anything useful.

"There wasn't a scratch on that car when Loretta loaned it to me," I lamented. "Do you think it will be safe in that neighborhood? Until a towing company can pick it up and get it to a shop, I mean?"

"I don't give a damn about the freaking Lexus," Sonterra said. "You could have been killed!"

"Well, I wasn't," I said reasonably.

Sonterra swore.

"I'm hungry," I announced.

"You just had a Blizzard," Sonterra pointed out.

"Melted," I told him.

We stopped at a chain restaurant for fish tacos and pancakes with extra syrup, both of which were mine. Sonterra didn't have an appetite, and he kept glowering at my food and shaking his head.

"I think I have morning sickness," he said, as we left.

"It's afternoon," I reminded him.

He checked his watch. "Holy crap," he muttered. "We're supposed to be in Father Morales's rectory in twenty-five minutes."

"We could reschedule," I suggested lightly.

Sonterra gave me a scorching glance. "As if," he said.

We pulled up in front of St. Swithin's Catholic Church half an hour later.

By that time, the Blizzard, fish tacos, and pancakes were at war in my stomach. My knees were still wobbly, I had a headache, and I kept reliving the moment when the Lexus came to a shuddering stop in the middle of a busy intersection. All in all, I did not feel much bridal anticipation.

"I'm going to puke," I told Sonterra.

"Go ahead," he said. "There's the gutter."

What a romantic.

A tiny priest came out of St. Swithin's, smiling. I recognized him as Father Morales and guessed we'd been absolved of the sin of unpunctuality.

Sonterra helped me out of the car and hustled me across the church's rock lawn. A few sprouts of dog-christened grass poked up here and there, bravely trying to look green.

"My fiancée," Sonterra explained, virtually holding me upright, "has had a hard morning."

Father Morales looked sympathetic. About time somebody was. "Come inside," he said, in a thick Spanish accent. "Sit down."

I made it as far as the back pew.

The priest studied me, then glanced questioningly at Sonterra. "Perhaps we should do this another time?"

Sonterra hipped me aside and sat down. Put a proprietary arm around my shoulders and squeezed. "Tell the man we want to get married, Clare," he said.

"We want to get married," I parroted.

Father Morales frowned. "Usually there is more—enthusiasm?"

I smiled blandly. If Sonterra wanted Stepford, he'd get Stepford. "We want to get married," I repeated.

Sonterra elbowed me. "Cut it out," he said.

"I'm under stress," I whispered back.

"Did you say you are under duress?" Father Morales asked.

I had to go home with Sonterra, so I decided enough was enough. "No," I said. "I'm here of my own free will." A bit of a stretch, but it was time to throw SuperCop a bone.

"You have a marriage license?" the priest inquired.

Sonterra whipped out a copy. Sure enough, he'd done all the legwork. Nothing lacking but my signature.

"I usually like to do premarital counseling," Father Morales imparted, after scanning the paperwork. He cleared his throat diplomatically. "But since Chief Sonterra says you are in a delicate condition—"

This time, I was the one doing the elbowing. I gave Sonterra a good jab. "Yes," I said. "I'm—pregnant." I'd wanted to say knocked up, bun-in-the-oven, or something even cruder, just to spite Sonterra, but, like I said, I had to go home with the man.

"You are Catholic?" Father Morales wanted to know. Seemed like a reasonable question to me.

"Yes," Sonterra said.

"No," I replied.

Father Morales crossed himself.

Sonterra tossed a statement into the ensuing silence. "Your secretary said the church is free Saturday afternoon."

"Yes," Father Morales said. "There will be guests, flowers, decorations?"

"Yes," Sonterra said.

"No," I answered.

Father Morales crossed himself again. Sighed. "Very well," he said. "Two o'clock, Saturday afternoon."

"What if Loretta can't get here by then?" I demanded of Sonterra, a few minutes later, as we left the church.

"She'll get here," Sonterra said, opening the SUV door and practically shoving me inside.

"What makes you so sure?" I asked suspiciously, when he got in and turned the key.

"I called her. She's flying in as soon as she can get away."

"I don't even have a dress."

"Good thing," Sonterra said. "The way you're eating, you wouldn't fit into anything bought more than a week ago."

"That was uncalled for."

Sonterra didn't answer. The back tires grabbed a little as we lurched away from the curb.

Maybe it was the pressure. Maybe it was feeling as though I was being railroaded into getting married. "Are you saying I'm fat?"

He muttered something in Spanish. English was not Sonterra's second language.

"I didn't catch that," I pressed.

"Do me a favor," he said. He didn't say what, but I could guess.

"You think I'm fat," I accused, folding my arms.

"Holy Mary, Mother of God," Sonterra prayed. At least, it had *better* have been a prayer.

Not another word passed between us until we got home. He left me in Esperanza's flustered, fluttery care and went back to work. I hated that he got to be the one to make a grand exit. *I* was the woman. I was the one who had survived an attack on my life, and I was the one quivering with prenatal hormones run amok. The way I saw it, it was *my* prerogative to stomp off.

Trouble was, I had nowhere to go and no way to get there.

"I make tea," Esperanza said somewhat desperately.

I stretched out on the sofa. "Is there any ice cream left?" I asked.

At six o'clock that night, I was ringing Danielle Bickerhelm's doorbell. I didn't have the latest Oprah pick. What I *did* have was an attitude, and my niece hovering at my elbow. Evidently, she and Sonterra had some kind of keep-an-eye-on-Clare pact going.

Danielle admitted us, coolly elegant in what looked like a

pair of Chinese pajamas. I introduced Emma. Danielle dismissed her after a once-over and "Glad to meet you, Emily."

"There are folding chairs in the dining room," our hostess called chattily, over one shoulder, long-legging it for what I presumed to be the kitchen. I was having trouble squaring this Danielle with the very bad girl boinking the mystery boyfriend in Micki's trailer.

The living room was small, and every chair was full. Chattering women everywhere, and the topic of conversation was Judy Holliday's grisly death. I gathered that there would be no funeral, just a memorial service in the high school gym on Friday night. A basketball game had been preempted for the occasion.

"We could leave now," Emma whispered. "Make a run for it."

"You're welcome to hit the road if you want to," I replied *sotto voce.* "I'm staying."

Emma sighed and turned toward the dining room, ostensibly to fetch a couple of folding chairs. Somehow, over all that womanly hubbub, I heard her gasp.

"Check this out," she said under her breath.

I followed her gaze and on the first pass, my brain didn't register what I was seeing. I did a double take. Sure enough, two skeletons sat at the antique table, one wearing a picture hat and pearls, the other, a bowler and an ascot. A china tea set sat between them, translucent in the lamplight. The pair was life-size and brown with age.

"Probably plastic," I murmured.

"Weird," Emma said. "It's not even Halloween."

No disputing either assessment. I took a step toward the tea drinkers. Stopped. Something about those two raised the hairs on the back of my neck.

"I wouldn't touch them if I were you," interjected a third voice, and I started. Turned to see a middle-aged woman in a green double-knit pantsuit. Madge Rathburn, the deputy's wife. I'd met her very briefly at the picnic after Sonterra's swearing-in.

Madge smiled warmly. "Danielle calls them Uncle Fred and

Aunt Doris," she imparted, as Emma made a belated show of claiming two folding chairs from the stack next to the china cabinet. "That's a small town for you. Full of eccentrics."

I dug up a smile, but it didn't feel stable enough to hold. The more I learned about Danielle Bickerhelm, the less I understood her. Which only made me more determined to find out what made her tick.

Madge nodded. She seemed friendly, but she was watchful, too. I figured she was as curious about me as I was about Danielle, and I also wondered if she'd expected her husband to be promoted to chief, instead of Sonterra, an outsider from the big city. "I see you didn't bring a book," she said.

It took me a moment to catch up. "A book?"

Madge smiled again. More gums than teeth, and they were that strange, purplish color. The gums, I mean. "This is a reading group," she said pleasantly, and held up an oversized paperback. "I wouldn't blame you if you opted for the Cliff Notes on this one. It's pretty dismal."

I nodded, and as Emma carried the two still-folded chairs past Madge, I followed. Not without a look back at those skeletons, though. Uncle Fred and Aunt Doris. I stifled a case of heebie-jeebies.

Emma found space in the living room and set up the chairs. Backs to the wall, clear view of the door. Was she afraid somebody would try to sneak up on us?

"The Hollidays were devastated, of course," a woman in a homemade dress was saying to the general assembly, as we sat down. "As soon as the coroner releases the body, they're having it flown back home for a proper Christian burial." The speaker had long, mousy brown hair, no makeup, and no jewelry, except for a plain gold wedding band sinking into the appropriate finger. I tried to place her, from the swearing-in or the picnic afterward, and couldn't. She might have been there, but she was the sort who fades into the landscape. Odds on, she belonged to one of those repressive churches and had an IN CASE OF RAPTURE, THIS CAR WILL BE EMPTY sticker somewhere on her car, the assumption being that

I, along with the rest of the unrighteous hordes, would still be around to get the message.

Danielle swirled in from the kitchen, by way of the dining room, carrying a big platter of cookies in both hands. "Has everyone met Clare and her niece, Emily?" she chimed. I recalled her strange fascination with the painting at her shop, and tried to square it with the skeletons in the dining room, not to mention the trailer-park rendezvous.

There is no figuring some people out. Not without a lot of snooping and a few trick questions, that is.

"Emma," my niece said.

My interest had snagged on the cookies. I scored a macaroon when Danielle set the platter on the coffee table. Good thing I was quick. The whole group dived, like sharks in frenzy, for the refreshments.

"Hello, Clare," everyone sang out at once, some with their mouths full. It sounded like the opening of an AA meeting. "Hi, Emily!"

"Emma," said Emily. "My name is *Emma.*"

Things went steadily downhill from there.

"Of course it is, Emily," Danielle said, taking the seat of honor with a flourish.

"Go," I told Emma, out of the corner of my mouth. "I know you and Sonterra synchronized your watches, but I'll be perfectly safe here."

She leaned in my direction. "Yes," she muttered back, "but will the macaroons?"

"I resent that remark," I said, helping myself to another cookie. If Emma was going to join Sonterra in the Fat Clare chorus, there would be trouble in paradise.

Emma favored me with an evil grin. "Well, I *do* have homework," she said.

"Don't let me keep you," I replied sweetly, as Danielle clapped her hands to call the book club meeting to order.

Emma got up, made her excuses, and hit the door.

"Good night, Emily!" I called after her.

Danielle leveled a look in my direction. She regretted inviting me, I could see that. I consoled myself with another macaroon.

"About *Threshings,*" she said pointedly, still glaring at me even as she picked up her own copy of the book from the end table beside her chair and waggled it for all to see. There were dozens of those little colored tabs attached to the pages, and lots of passages were probably highlighted, too. Maybe there were even little anal notes scrawled in the margins. "Who's read it?"

"I thought it was a load," Ms. Proper Christian Burial confided to those of us near enough to hear. Mentally, I ripped the rapture sticker off the back of her car.

As soon as Danielle's attention shifted, I scanned the room, looking for pictures of Bobby Ray Lombard in the flower of youth. Or even of a younger Danielle—I might be able to place her from a candid shot. I put checking the bookshelves and the china cabinet on my mental to-do list, along with getting married, avoiding a fiery vehicular demise, and searching the cemetery for the names "Fred" and "Doris." I wouldn't have been surprised if there were a couple of bodies missing. Not that I'd know, without digging up the graves.

Danielle's voice intruded on my dark ruminations. "What did *you* think, Clare?" she trilled. There's a reason that word rhymes with "drilled."

I blinked and reentered my body with a bone-jarring slam. "About what?"

"*Threshings,* of course." Her smile was thin, her gray eyes flat as dusty mirrors.

"Didn't read it," I confessed. I don't know what possessed me to say what I said next—it just popped right out of my mouth. "I've been a very bad girl."

Danielle's slate eyes flickered, and her cheeks seemed to recede a fraction of an inch behind a dusting of expensive blush. Clearly, the reference carried her back to last night's assignation in the bedroom of Micki's trailer. Then she must have decided there was no way I could know about her sexual adventures—God knows, ignorance would have been bliss in this case—because her makeup and her face reconnected. "Well, you *are* a new member, of course," she said generously. "You didn't really have time to give *Threshings* the attention it deserves. It's a literary masterpiece, you know."

She seemed to be implying that I moved my lips when I read, but that might have been my imagination, so I let it pass.

"Can we read a romance novel next time?" someone asked hopefully.

Danielle looked as though she'd like to leap to her feet, catch the offender by her hair, and fling her down the front steps.

Murmurs of agreement from the gathering only made matters worse, at least from Danielle's viewpoint. Her blush stood on its own again, and her mouth tightened.

"That would be fun," I said moderately, when some of the chatter died down. "We could meet at my house."

If the prospect of a juicy love story hadn't swayed everyone, the opportunity to poke a nose into our medicine cabinet and size up our furniture seemed to. A date was quickly set and a title agreed upon.

I smiled to myself as I took my Day-Timer out of my bag and recorded the pertinent details. I could feel Danielle's annoyance from across the room, and, all right, I enjoyed it.

The evening dragged on, the macaroons were wiped out, and I was the last to leave. I made several snoop-forays during the party, on the pretext of using the bathroom, and came up with next to nothing. There were no family pictures on the walls or any of the many surfaces, all of which were antique, but I did notice that the bookshelves were jammed with volumes on reincarnation, true crime, and a smattering of what appeared to be lesbian poetry.

Eclectic tastes, I thought. You can tell a lot about the inner workings of a person's psyche by what he or she reads. It's a virtual map of the unconscious, but decoding it can be a real bitch.

By the time I made the last run, the other guests were gone, and Danielle was waiting for me in the dining room, arms folded, skeletons partying ludicrously in the background. I'd never seen anyone seethe and smile at the same time, but Danielle managed it.

I thought she was onto me, so I was relieved when she didn't confront me right off. I've got no problems with confrontation, believe me, but it was too soon. I still had a lot of mental sorting and sifting to do before I got down to cases.

"I honestly can't imagine what you were thinking of, encouraging the group to spend a whole month of reading time on one of those silly little books," she said. "I'm disappointed in you, Clare. You're an educated woman, and I didn't expect this."

I smiled warmly, tarrying near the front door. My gaze went straight to the skeletons, and I had the fanciful thought that I might end up as the third member of the tea party if I didn't watch out.

I decided it wouldn't hurt to stir the waters a little and see what came up out of the silt.

"Have you heard from your brother lately?" I asked. Restraint is not one of my dominant qualities.

Danielle stiffened, watched me narrowly. "Bobby Ray had nothing to do with Dr. Holliday's tragic death, if that's what you're hinting at," she said.

"I'm not hinting at anything," I replied. It took more than an anorexic, skeleton-collecting book snob to scare me. Which did lend a certain credence to the idea that I might be a slow reader. "I joined the Pima County prosecutor's office today. The forensics reports on the crime scene ought to be in tomorrow, and if Bobby Ray left so much as a skin cell in Judy Holliday's house, I'll have him. You can bet your Victorian cradle on that."

For a moment, I thought she was going to lunge for my throat. Or throw her well-thumbed copy of *Threshings* at my head. "Micki's behind all of this," she said bitterly. "It's some elaborate, codependent scheme! I wouldn't be surprised if she'd killed Dr. Holliday herself, then gone underground, just so Bobby Ray would be blamed. She's that vindictive, the little slut!"

I refrained from rolling my eyes, but barely. "That's quite a stretch, Danielle," I replied. "No doubt Micki cleverly orchestrated her own battering, too. Goaded poor Bobby Ray into using his fists on her, so everybody would think he was a thug."

"Please get out of my house," Danielle whispered.

"Does this mean you won't be at the book club meeting?" I asked, reaching for the doorknob. I saw her knuckles whiten as her grip tightened on the thick spine of the tome.

She didn't answer. Probably a good thing.

"I'll let myself out," I said in parting.

I'd swear I heard *Threshings* strike the door as soon as I closed it behind me.

The other guests had long since left, but Madge Rathburn was waiting on the sidewalk. Her maroon Camry stood at the curb and, given Madge's air of urgency, subtle though it was, I was surprised the motor wasn't running. She looked like a woman who thought she might need to make a fast getaway.

"You really pissed her off," she said, in a pleased whisper, nodding in the direction of the house.

"All in a day's work," I answered, sounding more confident than I felt. I had a badge in my purse, but I was new in the investigation business. It would take some time to refine the process.

"I could give you a ride home if you want," Madge suggested.

I was only a few blocks from Cemetery Lane, and it was a nice night, warm and still and starry, suitable for walking off too many macaroons; but it was obvious Madge had more to say, and I wanted to hear it.

"Thanks," I said.

She nodded and went around to the driver's side, and I got in from the sidewalk. The ashtray was overflowing, and the smell of stale smoke felt solid in my nostrils.

"Tell me about the skeletons in Danielle's dining room," I said, as soon as we were rolling.

"Not much to tell," Madge replied. I knew she wanted a cigarette by the way her eyes kept straying to the pack on the dashboard, but she didn't indulge, and I appreciated the courtesy. "You mind riding around for a little while?" she asked. "I talk better when I'm driving."

Sonterra was working, and Emma, I hoped, was busy with her homework. "I'd like to see where those bodies were found, if the place isn't off-limits," I said. That was me. Respecter of law, order, and crime-scene tape.

Madge tossed me a curious glance. "Bodies?"

"The coyote victims." Jimmy Ruiz had been one of them, which made it a kind of personal pilgrimage, but I felt no need to confide that in Madge.

"Oh," she said somberly. "It's a ways out of town. Dave said it was the worst mess he's seen in all his years with the department."

Sonterra hadn't given me many details, other than that the bodies had been shot execution style, but my imagination filled in the gaps. It seemed, in that moment, as if Jimmy's soul passed through mine like a cold wind, and I shivered.

"Why would you want to see that place?" Madge asked. It was a reasonable question. Normal people aren't drawn to murder scenes.

But, then, I'm not normal.

I wasn't exactly sure how to put the need into words, without scaring her off, so I made something up. I decided to tell a partial truth. "Just to get a sense of what happened there, I guess."

"Those poor people," Madge murmured, with a shiver of her own. "It's a problem, all these illegal immigrants flooding into the country, but you can't help feeling sorry for them. Especially when something like that happens." She pulled onto Main Street and we whizzed through Dry Creek, heading northeast, into the desert. Madge clearly wasn't worried about getting a speeding ticket; like me, she had an in with the cops.

"How long have you known Danielle?" I asked, when a few moments had passed. I was back to wondering about the skeletons, but it was more idle curiosity than anything else.

"She moved to town five years ago," Madge answered, with another longing glance at the cigarettes. "Don't know where she came from, though. She and Oz were an item back in the day. That's Oz Gilbride, the former chief of police."

I nodded. Sonterra had said even less about Gilbride than the coyote victims, since we'd arrived in Dry Creek, a sure sign that the investigation was more sensitive than I'd guessed.

"They were an unlikely pair," Madge mused, and the cigarettes slid across the dash as she made a hard right onto a rutted track through the desert. "He didn't have anything but his pension, which I'm here to tell you wasn't much, knowing what Dave's going to get, and she was pretty high-toned, so we didn't know what to make of it. Danielle had the shop built, then Bobby Ray turned up one day."

"An even stranger pair, I imagine," I put in, as we bounced past a tall cactus with part of its skeleton showing. A lot of people think cacti are just pulp inside, but they have an intricate wooden structure.

"Dave ran a background check on him, on the q.t., of course. Found out he'd been in jail in Oklahoma—did three years for assaulting some old lady. It was odd, how Oz got so friendly with a yardbird like that."

"Did Bobby Ray work?" I asked, remembering Micki's assertion that he'd never made a payment on her trailer.

Madge made a harrumph sound. "He made some deliveries for Danielle once in a while. Packed stuff for shipment, things like that."

"Dry Creek's pretty small to support a store like hers," I observed.

"The locals don't buy much, that's for sure," Madge agreed, barreling through the darkness. Her headlights caught on various cacti as we jostled along; with their arms extended at all angles, it looked as if they were either trying to hitch a ride or wave us off. "We get our share of tourist traffic coming through this time of year, though. They spend plenty, on the way to and from Tucson."

I recalled how crowded Danielle's store had been when I drove into town for Sonterra's swearing-in, and she'd been selling things hand over fist when I'd stopped in.

"She does a big business on the Internet, too," Madge put in.

I made a mental note to go online when I got home.

Just then, a coyote—the four-legged variety—trotted into our path, and Madge laid on the brakes. The desert dog didn't break his stride.

"What was it you wanted to tell me, Madge?" I ventured, guessing that the moment was right. "You were obviously waiting for me to come out of Danielle's place."

She sighed, maneuvering between potholes. I wondered if she'd go home and tell Deputy Dave that the new chief's pesky girlfriend was a few cans short of a six-pack. "I just wanted to warn you about Danielle," she said quietly, almost reluctantly. "She's probably all right. But she's got influence in this town, and if she takes a dislike to you, she can make things mighty uncomfortable."

Too late, I thought.

We hit another pothole, and I braced myself against the dashboard with both hands. "Maybe we ought to turn back," I said. Now that I knew the approximate location, I could find the crime scene on my own, in the daylight.

"We're almost there," Madge said, and sped up. "Hold on. Here comes the gully." We were airborne for a second or two, and landed hard on the other side of a chasm, bouncing on the Camry's shock absorbers.

Once my heart slithered back down out of my throat, I asked, "Is Danielle involved with anybody now?"

"Those women at the meeting tonight? She's been to bed with half their husbands. Far as I know, there's nobody special."

I digested that. There weren't many secrets in towns like Dry Creek, at least not among longtime residents. Surely some of the members of the book club knew about Danielle's penchant for married men, and it seemed strange to me that they'd want to socialize with her. Human nature being what it was, they probably thought their own husbands were immune to her charms. That kind of thing always happens to somebody else.

Ask Loretta.

Suddenly, we were at the mouth of what appeared, in the headlights, to be a huge dry wash, and Madge brought us to a quivering standstill.

"Here it is," she said. She opened her door and reached for the cigarettes on the dash. Lit up as soon as she was clear of the car. "I don't like this place. I think it's haunted. Lots of caves and potholes out here, too. Every once in a while, some hiker gets swallowed up, and the search-and-rescue folks play hell finding the body."

I peered into the darkness. I saw tatters of yellow tape hanging limply in the glow of Madge's headlights, but not much else. The air seemed heavier, and colder, as I stepped closer, taking care to avoid rabbit holes and the sharp thistles that seem to jump off certain varieties of ground cacti, as if magnetized to human flesh. The bodies were long gone, of course, but the fear lingered, like some nebulous, ghostly force.

I couldn't help thinking of Jimmy, so young and so afraid. I blinked back tears and swallowed the lump of grief that constricted my throat.

Madge was right—the place *was* haunted. The silent cries of the victims still throbbed in the air.

"You be careful," Madge called after me, and hers might have been a disembodied voice, for all I could see of her. Just a vague shadow and the orange tip of a burning cigarette. "Dave would wring my neck if he knew I brought you out here."

Sonterra wouldn't be thrilled about the idea, either. Not that I intended to tell him, just yet, and it was safe to assume Madge wouldn't let the story slip to Deputy Dave, either.

I stood just inside the wash for several minutes. Although I had come to that awful place on purpose, it was an unwilling vigil. My feet had grown roots, it seemed, tangling around sharp plates of bedrock far beneath the dry, unyielding sand.

"We'd better get out of here," Madge said, uncertainly cheerful, her tone in direct contrast to her daredevil driving on the way out. "Dave'll be wondering where I got to. Tuesday nights, we usually catch up on our TiVo."

I nodded. I wanted to leave, too.

But I'd never forget that desolate place.

FOURTEEN

I was aware that I was dreaming. I knew I was lying in my own bed, safe beside Sonterra. I even knew that it was after midnight, though my eyelids were too heavy to lift.

I sat in the back pew of Father Morales's little church, surrounded by candlelight, flickering ineffectually against the shadows, by wafting incense and plaster saints. Francis of Assisi teetered on my right, cradling a blue bird with a chipped beak in the palm of one hand. The Virgin Mary, her delicate feet balanced upon a crescent moon, graced my left.

Up near the altar, a bride and groom stood with their backs to the odd congregation, the bride in full regalia, the groom standing straight in a rented tuxedo. Sonterra and me, I remember thinking, and nudged Mary to make sure she was paying attention.

"I now pronounce you man and wife," a male voice announced.

I felt a swell of anxious anticipation.

With a whoosh of flapping wings, St. Francis's blue bird took off, circled the sanctuary twice, then nose-dived into the middle of the wide aisle, shattering audibly into shards.

Meanwhile, organ music swelled to the rafters. I was sorry about the blue bird, but shit happens. My attention was riveted on the bride and groom, my breath raw in my throat.

I saw Sonterra's profile as he turned to face me—that *was* me up there, swathed in silk and lace, wasn't it? He was so handsome, so earnest, that I felt my heart quiver in my chest.

"You may kiss the bride," said the priest who wasn't there.

Sonterra tenderly lifted the veil, bent his head for the kiss, and recoiled. A skull grinned up at him from where my face should have been, brown like the ones in Danielle's dining room, with chunks of what looked like mummified flesh stuck to its cheekbone.

I screamed and shot bolt upright.

"Clare." Sonterra laid a hand on my arm. "Clare!"

I was still fighting my way out of the dream.

Sonterra switched on the bedside lamp, said my name again.

I blinked, and the bedroom came into dizzying focus. My whole body shook, slick with clammy sweat, and my breathing was so rapid and so shallow that I thought I was going to pass out from lack of oxygen.

"Easy," Sonterra said gently. "You were dreaming, Babe."

I was afraid to turn and look at him, in case he'd morphed into a skeleton, or I had.

He slipped an arm around me, pulled me against his warm, solid chest. "You're soaked," he said, brushing his lips against my temple.

I started to cry. I wanted to tell him about the nightmare, but I couldn't seem to assemble the words. I felt cold and, at the same time, feverish.

Sonterra used the edge of the top sheet to dry my cheeks. "Easy," he said again.

"I'm f-freezing," I managed.

He held me more tightly. "Want to tell me about it?"

"It was awful!"

"I gathered that much."

"Just hold me. I-I need a few minutes—"

He waited, and when I stopped shivering, he got up, fetched a hand towel from the bathroom across the hall. I was vaguely aware of Emma, standing in the doorway, and I heard

Sonterra tell her everything was all right, just a nightmare, go back to bed.

By then, my skin had dried to a goose-pimply chill, so the towel was unnecessary. I stayed on the bed while Sonterra helped me out of my nightshirt and into sweats. He even put socks on my feet.

"Better?" he asked.

"I love you," I said.

He grinned, standing over me, and leaned to kiss my fore-head. "I know," he answered. "You do your best to hide it, but word's leaked out. Want a glass of water or something?"

"How about a Blizzard?"

He chuckled. "No Blizzards," he said, lying down beside me. "Not at this hour."

I sniffled. "I dreamed I was sitting in the back pew at St. Swithin's. You and I were up in front of the altar, getting married. When it came time to kiss me, and you lifted my veil—" I stopped, and another shudder ran through me. *Get over it,* I thought, *it was a freaking dream.* But of course it wasn't that easy. "My head had turned into a skull."

Sonterra gave a low whistle, and I noticed he left the bedside light on. I was inordinately grateful for that.

I told him about St. Francis, and the Virgin Mary, and the kamikaze blue bird.

"Joseph Campbell would have had a field day with that one," Sonterra said. He was addicted to PBS. "Since he's not around, I'd have to say it means you're really scared to get married."

I looked at him, studied his face. His eyes were sad and watchful, and one corner of his highly kissable mouth curved in a forlorn attempt at a smile.

I shook my head. "That isn't it," I said, and I was fairly certain it was true.

"Okay, Sigmund," he agreed. "What's your take on it?"

"Danielle Bickerhelm has a pair of skeletons sitting at her dining room table. They're having a tea party, and she calls them Uncle Fred and Aunt Doris."

"Holy shit," Sonterra said. "What's with that?"

"Who knows? I ate a lot of macaroons, too."

Sonterra grinned. This time it was real, and there was nothing sad about it. "I'm not sure I follow your reasoning, Counselor." He rested his head in one hand, elbow pressing into the pillow. Something squeezed inside me.

"I think my subconscious mind took the skeletons and the sugar rush, poured on a few prenatal hormones, and made nightmare stew." I'd scanned Danielle's Web site and various online auction postings earlier, too, and even though nothing had really jumped out at me, it had left me with the niggling feeling that I was missing something important.

Sonterra reached out to turn off the light, pulled me back into his arms, and kissed the top of my head. "That's a recipe for crazy, all right," he agreed. His voice was low and sort of thick. "I'll be a good husband, Clare. I promise you that."

My eyes burned. "Yeah," I said. "But will I be a good wife?"

"It would be nice if you could cook," he teased sleepily.

I bit my lower lip. I felt safe, nestled in his arms, though ragged shreds of the dream were still with me. "I got Madge Rathburn to take me to the crime scene tonight, after we left Danielle's," I confessed, in a whispered rush. "The one in the desert, I mean."

End of cozy domestic moment. Sonterra sat up so fast he nearly sent me rolling off the other side of the bed, and snapped the lamp back on. "What?"

"Where the bodies were found."

"Christ," Sonterra rasped, and shoved a hand through his hair. "What possessed you to do that? What could you possibly have expected to find in the dark?"

"I don't know," I answered truthfully. "I just had to go there." I paused, trying to summon up my inner lawyer. All I got was the street kid from Tucson, and she wasn't up to her usual fancy verbal footwork. "No harm done, Sonterra. You and the feds have surely been over the place with a magnifying glass. Found all the evidence there is to find."

Sonterra's face softened, in the dim light of the quarter moon, but only slightly. "That's coyote country, Clare," he said. "Now that the heat's off, they might come back."

"That doesn't sound very likely," I reasoned. "They'd expect you—or the feds—to be watching the place."

"They know damn well we don't have the manpower," Sonterra said. There was something guarded about his tone, and I knew he wasn't telling me everything.

"Spill it, Sonterra. I'm not going to leave you alone until you do."

He must have believed me. "It's a dumping ground," he admitted. "The last batch of bodies was found there, too—about four years ago. Nice conversation to follow up a nightmare."

"Danielle's pretty pissed, too," I admitted, thinking I might as well get it over with. "I told her, in so many words, that I was going to book her baby brother a seat on Death Row. In my capacity as an investigator for the prosecutor's office, I mean. She told me to get out of her house."

"Did it ever occur to you, Sherlock, that if Bickerhelm *is* in contact with Lombard, she might be a lot more careful about dropping the ball, now that you've run off at the mouth?"

I was betting she'd panic and be *less* careful, but I knew Sonterra was persuaded otherwise, so I didn't try to convince him. "I have a legal right to investigate," I said. "Want to see my badge?"

Sonterra cranked off the light and slammed himself into the mattress. "Let me do my job, Clare." He didn't sound like he had a hope in hell that I would back off, and he was right about that. It was too late for Judy Holliday, but Micki and her daughter might still be alive. Sonterra was doing everything he could, but a fresh perspective—mine—couldn't hurt. "Lombard will blow it sooner or later. His kind always does. And once the cuffs are on, your new boss can prosecute him to hell and back for all I care."

"Go to sleep, Sonterra."

He threw back the covers, rolled out of bed, and did the lamp thing again. "Like I could," he said. He looked sexy as hell, standing there in his sweatpants and nothing else, with his hair all rumpled and his eyes shooting Latin fire.

I decided sex was probably out of the question.

"It's one-thirty in the morning," I pointed out. "What are you going to do at this hour?"

"I'll think of something," he told me, and stormed out of the room.

I wriggled over to his side of the bed and switched off the light. Maybe he didn't want to sleep, but I did. I plunked myself into the pillows and squeezed my eyes shut.

The skeleton bride came to mind.

I got up, grumbling, and went downstairs, tracking Sonterra to the small den at the front of the house, where he was logging on to the Web.

"This is ridiculous," I said.

He ignored me.

I went back to the kitchen, examined the contents of the freezer, and nobly decided against ice-cream therapy. I was sitting at the table, sipping herbal tea, when somebody pounded at the front door.

Sonterra was closer, and he got there before I did, but just barely.

A teenage boy stood on the porch, hyperventilating. I recognized him as the kid who, with his girlfriend's help, had pulled me out of the Escalade after the first vehicular attack.

I didn't recall his name and, between the hospital stay and everything else that had been going on since, I hadn't had a chance to thank him.

Sonterra pulled him into the house and sat him down in the living room. "What is it, Michael?" he demanded. Obviously, they'd had conversations in the meantime.

The kid's eyes were enormous, and he was trembling. "We shouldn't have been there—"

"Shouldn't have been *where?*" Sonterra pressed.

Michael swallowed hard. "The cemetery," he answered miserably. "We party there sometimes. Once, Lanna and I spent the night, on a dare—"

I sank onto the sofa. I knew there was a train coming, and it was too late to get off the tracks.

Sonterra crouched in front of the kid, looking up into his face. His voice was calm, even. "Okay, you were in the cemetery. *What happened,* Michael?"

Michael looked ready to faint, and I knew I ought to hurry back to the kitchen for a bottle of water, but I didn't want to miss a word.

"There's a naked woman, lying on top of one of the graves. I didn't want to touch her, but I think—I think she's dead."

Sonterra muttered an expletive and straightened. "Wait here," he said, and sprinted for the stairs.

Michael looked in my direction, but I don't think he was focusing. "She's all blue," he said. "And there's blood. Lots of blood."

My stomach rolled. I regretted the macaroons in a whole new way. "Did you recognize her?" I heard myself ask. I knew what he was going to say, but I was hoping I was wrong.

He nodded and dropped the bomb. Even though I was expecting it, the explosion practically tore me apart. "Micki Post," he said.

The cemetery was awash in the red-and-blue swirl of squad-car lights, and sure enough, my client and potential friend lay dead under a headstone that read BELOVED WIFE AND MOTHER. Both deputies were there, and the State Police were on the way.

I'd awakened Emma, told her to lock the door behind us, and jumped into the backseat of Sonterra's SUV just as he popped it into reverse. Michael sat in front, on the passenger side, his narrow, boy's shoulders moving with silent sobs.

Micki hadn't been posed. She was sprawled, arms and legs flung out, as if she'd been dropped from a great height. I wept silently, helplessly, and cursed Bobby Ray Lombard for the murdering vulture turd he was.

Michael, Lanna, and a few other kids stood at a distance, huddled with their parents. Like me, most of the adults were in bathrobes.

Where was Suzie? I wondered desperately. Where in God's name was the child?

Headlights appeared at the gates, and two unmarked cars pulled in, followed by a coroner's van. More townspeople began to materialize out of the surrounding darkness, moving woodenly to the perimeter of the scene, like the living dead roused from their graves. More squad cars pulled in, and I spotted Special Agent Timmons among the new arrivals.

"Everybody stay back!" Dave Rathburn shouted, while Sonterra crouched beside the body, talking with the crime-scene technicians and the new cop crop. Timmons showed his shield and muscled in, dropping to his haunches next to Sonterra. He wore a natty suit, in contrast to hastily donned uniforms and bathrobes, and I wondered if FBI agents slept fully clad, standing up to keep from wrinkling their clothes.

Then Emma appeared beside me, holding a blanket. She draped it gently over my shoulders.

I wanted to take the blanket off, use it to cover Micki, but I knew Sonterra and the others wouldn't let me get close enough. So I huddled inside the folds and waited, shivering hard. I'd thought the nightmare was bad, but this, of course, was infinitely worse.

Emma put an arm around my waist. "You shouldn't be here," she said.

I didn't state the obvious—that she shouldn't have been, either. She must have seen the flashing lights from her bedroom window, after we left, pulled on her clothes, and climbed over the fence between our back lawn and the graveyard.

"Come on, Clare," Emma urged, when I remained silent. "Let me take you home."

I shook my head. Micki had been my client. I'd filed for the restraining order that was supposed to keep Bobby Ray Lombard away. Fat lot of good that had done.

With my legal expertise and twenty-five cents, she could have made a phone call.

Sonterra stood and separated himself from the tight cluster

around Micki, like a cell dividing. He approached, his face grim in the nearly nonexistent moonlight and the eerie red-and-blue glare from the squad-car lights.

"Deputy Rathburn will take you home," he said tightly, looking straight at me and not bothering to comment on Emma's presence at all.

"Michael said there was a lot of blood," I responded, with no inflection in my voice. I didn't have the energy for anything but a monotone.

"Multiple stab wounds," Sonterra answered. I was surprised he gave up that much. "Go home, Clare. Please. There's nothing you can do here. Nothing anybody can do."

Rathburn loomed beside me. "Car's right over here," he said quietly.

I caved. Let Deputy Dave take my arm and lead me away. Emma stayed at my other side. Held my hand as we sat in the back of the deputy-mobile, staring at the metal grille designed to keep prisoners from assaulting the officers in front.

Next thing I knew, we were pulling into Sonterra's driveway.

Dave walked us to the front door, waited in silence while Emma produced a house key from the pocket of her jeans and did the honors.

"You'll be all right here," he said. "Be sure to lock up, just the same."

"Thanks," Emma told him, when I didn't speak, and pulled me inside. She locked up behind us, then walked me to the same chair where Michael had sat earlier, delivering the terrible news.

Waldo and Bernice hadn't barked when we arrived, and now, while Emma went to the kitchen for water, Waldo settled on my feet, and Bernice jumped into my lap. She pressed her paws into my chest and licked at the salty streaks on my face, and I didn't push her away.

Sometimes, you have to take your comfort where you can get it.

• • •

Loretta called at 7:00 A.M. sharp.

"Where have you been?" I demanded, testy from another trying night. "I've left half a dozen messages."

"With Kip," Loretta said quietly. "What's up?"

Kip. I'd seen an e-mail from him in my computer's in-box, but I hadn't taken the time to read it. I'd been completely absorbed in Danielle's Web presence the last time I'd gone online.

I took a slow, deep breath. "Your car is in the shop. Somebody bashed me from behind—in broad daylight, too."

Loretta gasped. "You know I don't give a damn about the car. Are you and the baby all right?"

Tears stung my eyes. "Yes," I said. "Sonterra says you're coming back for the wedding."

"Friday night is the ETA, but I'm looking for an earlier flight." A smile crept into her voice, albeit a weary and rather wartorn one. "Good news. Kip's credit cards still work. I bought you a surprise at Saks."

"Tell me!"

"Absolutely not. It wouldn't be a surprise then. Are Mrs. K and Shanda coming down for the ceremony?"

"Yes," I said, subdued by the reminder of the wedding. Come Saturday afternoon, I would no longer be a free agent. I recalled the skeleton dream and shivered. "Not to mention the whole Sonterra clan," I added.

"It's about time you bit the bullet, Clare," Loretta said. "Tony's a great catch. What do you say we learn to cook?"

Sometimes Loretta misses a segue and makes one of those conversational hairpin turns, and I have to lay some mental rubber to catch up. "Cook?" I echoed stupidly.

"You know—gather various raw food items and assemble them into something edible? Pots and pans are often involved, and a stove is usually helpful."

I laughed. "Is Kip rooming across from Martha Stewart or something? Since when do you have a domestic bone in your body?"

"Since I decided to simplify my life," Loretta said, and she sounded serious. "Kip is probably going to prison, Clare. Most likely, he'll serve five to eight months in one of those country club places. He has some offshore accounts, so I'll be all right for money. But I need something constructive to occupy myself in the meantime."

I took a few moments to absorb the idea of Kip Matthews cooling his swanky heels in a prison, fancy or not. " 'In the meantime'?" I queried. "You mean, you plan to stay with him?"

"Maybe, maybe not." There was a sort of shrug in Loretta's voice. "Time will tell. Right now, the plan is to simplify—sell everything but the ranch, pay off the creditors and as many of the investors as possible, and start over."

I didn't know whether to admire my friend or crawl through the phone wires and choke her. "Whatever you decide, I'll be with you," I said.

"I know, and I appreciate it, Clare." She paused. "This is the second time somebody's rammed your car. The question of the hour is, who's behind this, and what's their motive?"

Sonterra and I had been over and over the subject. He'd been scrounging for leads from the beginning, but they were few and far between, and the bottom line was, we still didn't have any idea what was going on.

I said as much to Loretta.

She was silent for a few moments after I'd finished, probably searching her own mind for a clue. "Any other developments I should know about?" she went on presently. "Besides the dents in the Lexus, I mean?"

I hesitated. "Some kids found a body in the cemetery last night. Naked, with a dozen or so stab wounds. Her name was Micki Post, and she was my client."

"Oh, God. This would be the battered wife you told me about over the phone? The one with the little girl?"

For a moment, I couldn't speak. "I should have protected her."

"How, Clare?" Loretta asked reasonably.

I bit my lower lip. I didn't have an answer, and Loretta probably didn't expect one. "Nobody knows where Suzie is. The daughter, I mean. God knows what Lombard has done to her—he might have killed her, too. I keep thinking another body will turn up—"

"You don't know that," Loretta broke in firmly. "Why go down that road before you have all the facts?"

I sighed. "I guess you're right." Up until then, I'd been curled up in a chair in the living room, like an invalid, with a blanket wrapped around me and the dogs curled up at my feet. Time to do something new. "You're really okay, Loretta?"

"Why wouldn't I be?"

"Well, you did say you wanted to learn to cook."

Loretta laughed. "I've been watching the Food Channel, between visits to Kip. We can *do* this, Clare."

"If you say so."

"I'll be at the Wagon Wheel late Friday night—unless I can get there sooner. Expect me on your doorstep Saturday morning at the latest."

I thought of the disabled Lexus. "Won't you need someone to pick you up at the airport?"

"I'm hiring a car. *Ciao*, Babe. Hang in there. Loretta is on the way."

I teared up again, tossed aside the blanket, and stood, wavering a little on my feet. "I can't wait to see you," I said.

"That sound you hear in the distance is a bugle. The cavalry is about to ride over the hill. In the meantime, try not to piss off any more crazed killers, will you?"

I promised, we said good-bye, and the line went dead.

I was still standing there, holding the receiver, when Esperanza came in with the fifth pot of herbal tea. She'd been a rock, arriving an hour early for work, getting Emma off to school, and screening phone calls, so I wouldn't have to come out of my cocoon before I was ready.

"You are feeling better?" she asked hopefully.

"Yes," I answered. Something about Loretta's call had shaken me out of my stupor. Maybe it was the threat of cooking. I felt recharged, and very restless.

I went straight to my computer, signed in, and opened the mailbox, calling Kip's e-mail up first.

Hello, Clare.

If you haven't deleted this by now, you're at least willing to listen, and that's all I can ask.

I know I screwed up, and since you're Loretta's best friend, you probably want to tell me off. I'm open to that. I deserve it. Mea culpa.

There's no excuse for what I did, let's get that out of the way first. I've made some bad mistakes, the worst of which was hurting Loretta. I got careless, I got busy, I got greedy. I forgot what really mattered—my wife.

You probably won't believe this, Clare, and under the circumstances, I can't blame you, but I DO love Loretta. I'm asking you to take care of her.

She's in a vulnerable place.

Keep her safe.

Kip

Tears stung my eyes as I hit the REPLY button and wrote a message of my own.

Nothing will happen to Loretta on my watch. Clare.

Ignoring the other e-mails, all of which had innocuous subject lines, I signed off.

A shower was the next thing on the agenda. Then I would sift through the messages Esperanza had taken down earlier, while I was incubating in the living room. That done, I planned to stroll down to the cop shop and hang around until I found out what was going on. If I had to, I'd flash my county credentials.

I felt like a new woman after the shower, even though I did have to pull on my fat jeans. I was standing in the kitchen, examining the messages—two from Eli Robeson, one from Mrs. K, three from Shanda, and one from a car dealership in Tucson.

I called Robeson first. We did a little verbal dance around the subject of Lombard—neither of us knew anything, and we commiserated. He promised to fax me the info on several cases he wanted me to check out.

Next, I gave Shanda a ring. She had news. My private client list had dwindled to squat, and she wanted to set up an eBay business to keep herself busy. She had a new boyfriend, one without a rap sheet for once, and her classes were going well. She and Mrs. K would be down Saturday morning for the wedding. Could she bring the beau?

I said yes, and moved on to Mrs. K. I got her voice mail.

That left the car dealership. Being in no mood for a sales pitch, I almost let that one slide. I'm not sure why I didn't, except that there was a slight tingle of curiosity in the pit of my stomach.

"This is Clare Westbrook," I said, when the switchboard operator picked up the call. "I'm returning a call from—" I squinted, trying to read Esperanza's Lilliputian handwriting.

"Jim Bonebale," the operator interrupted cheerfully. "Congratulations, Ms. Westbrook. This is some wedding present."

Before I could ask what she was talking about, Bonebale came on the line to introduce himself. "Your vehicle is ready for delivery," he said. "Will you be home this afternoon?"

"I didn't buy a car," I replied slowly.

"The order came from Mr. Anthony Sonterra."

I leaned against the counter for support. *This is some wedding present.* "Sonterra ordered a car?"

"Not a car, exactly," Mr. Bonebale said. "Our courtesy people are ready to bring it out to Dry Creek, if you'll be there to sign for it."

I was mystified. "Okaaaaay," I said.

Bonebale read off the Cemetery Lane address. "Is that correct?"

"Yes," I said, still at a loss.

"Good. Give us an hour. You're going to love this rig, Ms. Westbrook. Or is that Mrs. Sonterra?"

I felt as though I'd been punched. The curious thing was, it wasn't an unpleasant sensation. Who would I be after Saturday afternoon? Clare Sonterra?

Who the hell was Clare Sonterra?

"Still Ms. Westbrook," I said uncertainly.

The Hummer arrived one hour and seventeen minutes later. It was bright red and could have been used to invade Baghdad, lacking nothing but the antipersonnel swivel gun on the roof.

Bernice and Waldo barked hysterically, cavorting in the yard as the Red Marvel rolled up to the curb, followed by a van with the dealership logo painted on the side.

I'd been trying to get Sonterra on the horn ever since I'd learned about the delivery, but he didn't answer his cell phone—damn that caller ID—and when I called the cop shop, Deputy Jesse informed me that the chief was busy with "law enforcement duties."

A smiling young man with a shaved head and an earring climbed from behind the wheel of the Hummer. "Check out the license plate," he said. "Mr. Sonterra jumped through a lot of hoops to get it."

I walked around to the back. FNLY MNE.

I couldn't help grinning. *Finally Mine.*

"Take a look inside. Multiple CD-changer, global positioning device, the whole enchilada." The kid couldn't have been prouder if he'd built the Hummer in his dad's garage.

A clipboard was produced. I signed, and the young man handed me a set of keys, congratulated me, and got into the van on the passenger side. With a honk and a wave, the delivery team was gone.

I circled the Hummer, confounded and secretly jubilant. Sonterra had money, because of an inheritance wisely invested, but a ride like that had to have put a major nick in the funds.

Bernice and Waldo peered at me through the picket fence, tongues out.

"Let's take a spin," I told them. After dashing back inside for their leashes and my purse, I loaded the pair up, and Esperanza stood spellbound on the front porch, watching. I invited her along, but she shook her head and muttered something about cleaning the bathroom.

I climbed into the cab of the Hummer. It felt like a tank, after Loretta's Lexus. I fired it up, pushed it into gear, and off we rolled.

We hit Main Street doing at least thirty-five, and threw some gravel as we raced into the cop-shop parking lot. Sonterra's SUV was parked out front, along with a squad car and two state rigs.

I left the dogs in the car, with profound apologies and lots of air, and went inside.

Sonterra met me with a weary grin. He'd lost a lot of sleep since coming to Dry Creek, and I felt a pinch in my heart.

"How do you like your wedding present?" he asked.

If Deputy Dave and a couple of suits from the State Police hadn't been looking on, I might have flung myself at him and wrapped both legs around his waist.

"I can't believe you did that," I said.

"Believe it," he replied.

"I guess you couldn't get an armored car."

He laughed. "The ideal choice would have been a tank."

"It must have cost a fortune."

Sonterra shrugged. Some invisible cop signal must have passed between him and the others, because Dave and the staters disappeared into a back room.

I wrapped my arms around Sonterra's neck. "Thanks."

He spread his hand across my lower belly. "I want you safe until I nail these bastards," he said. "You and the baby."

"I didn't get you a wedding present," I told him. Suddenly, I was all choked up.

"You're all the present I need," he replied, and kissed the tip of my nose.

It was one of his days for saying the right thing. I wished he had more of those, but there you go.

"Then you won't mind showing whatever you've got on Bobby Ray Lombard," I said easily. The easy part was faked. When I thought of Lombard, I thought of Judy Holliday, swinging from a noose. I thought of Micki, sprawled naked and bloody on top of a grave. I thought of Suzie, who might be alive and might be dead.

Sonterra sighed. In small towns like that one, there are no jailhouse photo albums. Cops go online, to mugshots.com, or something like that, and call up the criminal in question.

Sonterra had the most recent image of Bobby Ray Lombard on the monitor and printing out in a few quick keystrokes. The rap sheet followed.

I studied the picture, scanned the sheet.

Lombard was the stereotypical criminal in appearance. Bad mullet, last washed during the Clinton administration. Acne scars. Mean little eyes that seemed to say, *Go ahead, get in my way, and I'll gut you like a fish.*

"Does he look familiar?" Sonterra asked.

I shook my head. I'd seen some version of Lombard a thousand times, in a thousand different arrest photos, but they'd all been variations on the same theme. Creeps Anonymous.

I lowered the printout to my side and held it tightly, just in case Sonterra thought I meant to give it back, which I didn't. Mentally, I'd already painted a target on that sheet of computer paper, and Lombard's ugly face was the bull's-eye.

"You need to get some sleep," I said uselessly. "Can't Deputy Dave hold down the fort for a while?" I lowered my voice. "And how come you haven't fired him? You were pretty pissed off when he left Judy Holliday's house unguarded."

The subject raised a charge in Sonterra, I could feel it, but I knew before he opened his mouth that he wasn't going to clear up the Deputy Dave mystery for me. "No way I'm leaving," he said. He gripped me by the shoulders and eased me into a chair. "Listen. Dan Post, Suzie's dad, got a call from her on his cell phone yesterday," he told me cautiously. "She said she was all right."

Relief can be as shattering as bad news. I went light-headed. "She's *alive*," I whispered. Then I snapped to attention. "Post waited until *today* to let you know this? Don't you think that's odd?"

"I called him on it first thing. He was feeling paranoid. Thought his phone might be tapped. People do crazy stuff when they're under this kind of stress, Clare."

"I take it you've already ruled Post out as a suspect? He wouldn't be the first divorced father to kidnap his own child, you know."

"Post is rock-solid. You're losing your edge, Counselor. I ran him through the computers as soon as the scene was secured at Dr. Holliday's."

"Suzie's alive," I repeated, just for the pleasure of saying it.

"*Maybe*," Sonterra clarified, fetching me a cup of water and holding it for me until I had a steady grip. "The ME puts Micki's death at roughly the same time, a little before the call, or a little after. Which means—"

"That Lombard could have killed Suzie, too. Especially if he caught her talking to her dad."

Sonterra nodded.

I swallowed a gulp of water. "Did Suzie actually say she was with Bobby Ray?"

"No," Sonterra answered. He squeezed the back of my neck lightly, then pulled up a chair of his own and sat facing me, taking both my hands in his. "According to Post, the kid was crying a lot. She told him she was scared and wanted to come home." He paused. "Post said he thought he heard a woman scream in the background, Clare. It could have been the TV, but—"

I closed my eyes. My stomach roiled with a sudden influx of acid. "Or it could have been Micki."

"We have to consider the possibility."

"I hate this," I whispered. I regarded him steadily. "How do you do it? How do you stand it, Sonterra? The bodies, the fear, the ugliness—"

"If I check out, the bad guys win. It's that simple."

I didn't point out that the "bad guys" win a lot anyway. After all, I loved the man, in my own semi-dysfunctional way, and he'd just given me a Hummer for a wedding present.

My cell phone sounded. I answered.

"Cl-Clare?"

A shard of emotion jabbed through me. I pushed the speaker button with my thumb so Sonterra could hear the conversation.

"Suzie?"

Sniffles. "Yes."

"Honey, where are you?"

"I don't know. It's dark. They killed my mama."

My stomach caught fire. "Who is 'they'?" I asked, as calmly as I could.

Sonterra was listening hard, but he didn't speak, and I was grateful. The balance was delicate; Suzie would hang up if she got scared.

"I'm not supposed to tell," she said in a small voice. "They said they'd kill me, too, if I do." Pause. "It's dark here."

Careful, I thought. "Whose phone are you using?"

"Dr. Judy's cell." Suzie began to cry harder. "It lights up. It had your number in it."

Sonterra scribbled something on a piece of paper and shoved it in my face. *Give me the number. I can put a trace on the call. And who the hell is "they"?*

I studied the caller ID panel, but it was blank. I was afraid to press any buttons, in case I broke the connection.

"They're coming back!" Suzie whispered, then she was gone.

Numbly, I handed the phone to Sonterra. He brought up the number and immediately got on a landline. I sank into a chair while he called Special Agent Timmons, updated him, and asked him to pinpoint the location of Judy Holliday's cell phone.

Just then, Deputy Dave came through the front door. I half expected Sonterra to tell him about Suzie's call, despite the palpable hostility arcing between the two men, but he didn't. I was an emotional Ping-Pong ball, bouncing between the good news

Suzie was still alive—and the bad news: She was being held cap-
tive in a dark place, by people who had already murdered her
mother and the doctor, possibly right in front of her eyes.

"That's some rig out there," Deputy Dave said, sounding a
touch too hale and hearty. He was clearly trying to get back into
Sonterra's good graces. "Does it have a GPD?"

"Yes," Sonterra said flatly. Definitely not playing ball.

My brain was shorting out. "A GP what?" My Escalade had
been a no-frills, closeout model. At the time I bought it, I'd been
poor too long to be all that comfortable with extras.

"Global positioning device," Sonterra said mildly.

Oh, great, I thought glumly, and with a twinge of resentment. *Now he'll probably be able to track me wherever I go.* I
gave him a look, but it didn't stick.

"You must be making a hell of a lot more money than I am,"
Dave offered, still pouring on the cheer.

Sonterra didn't answer.

"Dogs are raising hell," Dave went on, clearly determined to
strike up some kind of conversation. He probably wondered, as I
did, if Sonterra was already taking résumés.

I jumped to my feet at the reminder of the dogs. I'd forgotten all about Waldo and Bernice.

Sonterra pushed me gently back into the chair. "Sit there
until you catch your breath," he said. "I'll get them."

"Something going on?" Dave probed. His tone was good-
natured, but his eyes were watchful and slightly narrowed.

I looked to Sonterra.

"Not a thing," he said, and disappeared through the outer
doorway.

Dave looked baffled. "Everybody's on edge," he said with a
sigh. "Too damn many murders around here lately." He hung up
his hat, pushed back his desk chair, and sat. He'd been putting on
a façade while Sonterra was in the room. Now he let some of his
rancor slip out. "Just goes to show you, big-city cops don't necessarily have all the answers."

I bristled. "I wouldn't count on that," I said.

If the deputy picked up on my tone, he didn't let on. He began riffling through a stack of files. "Madge told me to ask you and the chief out to our place for supper tonight. Seven o'clock. She's making chicken spaghetti."

Sonterra returned, with Waldo and Bernice on their leashes, and caught the tail end of the invitation. "I can't make it tonight," he said. There was a slight edge to his voice. "How about a rain check?"

Dave smiled slightly to himself, sobered when he looked up and found me watching him. "Madge'll be disappointed. She's real proud of that recipe." He eyed the dogs, now sitting obediently at my feet, evidently waiting for their cue. "Maybe you could come, Ms. Westbrook. Bring your niece."

I was still jumpy over the call from Suzie. If I had to sit around the house all evening, waiting for the phone to ring again, I'd go crazy. Besides, if I was going to fulfill my duties as an investigator, I needed to know the townspeople as well as possible.

"Sure," I said.

Sonterra darted a glance in my direction, but he didn't comment.

"Good," Dave replied, and got up to fill his coffee mug. "Seven o'clock," he reiterated, as though I might have trouble following simple instructions.

I gathered up Bernice's leash, and Waldo's. "Can I bring something?"

"No need," Dave said. "We live over behind the high school. Green house with gnomes in the yard."

"See you then," I replied brightly, and made for the exit with the dogs.

Sonterra followed me outside.

"What was that about?" he asked.

"I might ask you the same question," I retorted. "You obviously don't like Dave Rathburn, but he's still got his badge."

"He's only a couple of years from retirement," Sonterra allowed. "He blew it the night of the Holliday murder, but I'm trying to give him the benefit of the doubt."

"And you don't trust him."

"He disobeyed an order, and the results were tragic. So, no, I *don't* trust him."

I studied him. "I think there's more."

"Think what you like. I need your cell phone, Clare. If Suzie calls again, I have to talk to her."

I was torn. Sonterra was the best of the best when it came to cool, calm, and collected, but if Suzie called, she'd be expecting to hear my voice, not his. She might panic and hang up.

I said as much.

"Timmons has the Bureau computers patched into Holliday's number by now." Sonterra held out his hand. "I can handle this, Clare."

"She must be so frightened," I whispered.

"Suzie knows me," Sonterra said, and I remembered how he'd introduced the child to Bernice and Waldo Friday afternoon, when we stopped by Judy Holliday's place, on our way out of town. They'd had a chance to chat while I was inside the house with Micki and the doctor.

I surrendered the phone, albeit reluctantly, and with a caveat. "If you hear from Suzie, I want to know about it. Right away."

"Cross my heart," Sonterra said.

My sarcasm detectors were up and scanning, but there were no blips on the radar. "I mean it, Sonterra," I warned, and put out *my* hand. "Swap."

He caught my meaning, and surrendered his phone as grudgingly as I had given up mine. Frankly, I'd expected an argument, or an outright refusal. After all, he took official calls on it. Too bad I didn't know the access code for his voice mail—I could have been up to speed on a lot of things in no time flat.

"I'll let you know if anything major happens," I told him.

Sonterra glared at me for a moment, then opened the back door of the Hummer and hoisted Waldo onto the seat. I set Bernice in front, on the passenger side, and climbed behind the wheel.

"What's your motive for going to supper at the Rathburns'?" Sonterra asked, with a distinct note of suspicion.

I smiled. "I like spaghetti," I replied.

I went home.

Esperanza was vacuuming the living room, so the dogs and I took refuge in the study, and I logged on to my computer to check my e-mail.

There were none from Shanda, and I was a little disappointed. My Phoenix practice had apparently sunk without a ripple. Pretty bad, when you can't even *give* legal advice away.

I was surfing, just to keep my busy mind occupied, when Emma came in from school. The dogs met her with their usual ecstatic greeting.

Esperanza had finished her work and gone home by then, so we had the house to ourselves.

"Whose Hummer?" Emma asked, looking thunderstruck.

I smiled and abandoned the Internet. "Mine," I answered. "Courtesy of Sonterra."

"Wow," Emma enthused. "Can I drive it?"

"Sure—when you get your license. We're invited to Dave and Madge Rathburn's place for supper. Seven o'clock."

"Geezers," Emma said, sounding both tolerant and dismissive. She was pale, and no wonder, after last night's gruesome scene in the cemetery. "I'd rather stay home, if it's all the same to you. I have homework, and I want to catch up on my e-mail."

I relented. Emma was tired, homework was important, and e-mail was her main means of keeping up with her friends back in Scottsdale. "Okay," I said. "I guess you could heat a can of soup for supper."

She smiled wanly. "Not a chance," she said. "Let's pile into the Hummer and hit the drive-through." She looked down at the dogs. "What do you say, guys? Cheeseburgers all around?"

Waldo woofed.

Bernice gave a happy yip.

I'd just been railroaded, but I didn't mind all that much.

We made the trip to B. Boop's, the only fast-food place in town, and I even forswore their version of a Blizzard, but I can't claim a lot of credit. My stomach had closed for business the instant I heard Suzie's frightened voice on my cell phone, back at the cop shop.

God knew how I was going to choke down a plateful of chicken spaghetti. I almost canceled, opting for a long bubble bath and a book instead, but I'd already agreed to make an appearance, and now Madge would be cooking for company.

While Emma plunked down at my computer to check in with the Scottsdale crowd, I chose an outfit—a blue floral sundress and sandals—and took a shower. I even put on makeup.

When I came downstairs, Emma and the dogs had migrated to the kitchen. Her books were open on the table, and her plain, precise handwriting filled half a page in her notebook.

"Are you really going to Deputy Dave's for supper?" she teased. "Or do you and Tony have a secret date?"

The idea of spending the evening with Sonterra, instead of the Rathburns, filled me with a sudden, fierce yearning. It was almost as if he'd been deployed on some secret and dangerous mission, of indeterminate length.

"I wish," I said, putting it mildly.

"You seem a little—I don't know—*nervous*," Emma reflected, serious again. "What's going on?"

I almost told her about Suzie's call, but I stopped myself. She was a teenager, not an adult, and, as much as I needed to talk the situation over with somebody, it wouldn't be right to worry her.

"Nothing," I said, and averted my eyes.

"Liar," she replied.

I glanced at the clock over the stove. Six-thirty. If I left then, I could swing by the supermarket and pick up a bouquet for Madge.

Fifteen minutes later, as I was dashing out of the store with twelve pink gerbera daisies in a plastic sleeve, Sonterra's cell phone rang.

I fished it out of the side pocket of my purse, fumbling a little. What if it was the FBI, or a snitch, or somebody calling to report another dead body? "Chief Sonterra's—office," I said.

Sonterra's chuckle vibrated in my inner ear. "Interesting

response," he observed dryly. "What am I supposed to say if *your* phone rings? Clare's Purse?"

I unlocked the Hummer, tossed the daisies across to the passenger seat, and climbed in. Not as easy in a sundress as it was in my fat jeans, earlier in the day. "Have you got a location for Suzie? Did she call again?"

When Sonterra answered, there was no trace of the chuckle he'd greeted me with. "One question at a time, Counselor. No and no. The satellite couldn't pick up the signal—either the battery's dead, or somebody destroyed the phone."

I rested my forehead against the steering wheel for a moment, almost convulsed with worry, dragging in breaths that seemed to go no deeper than my collarbone.

"Clare?"

"I'm okay," I said.

"Suzie's *alive,* Clare. Keep that in mind. We'll find her."

If I started crying, my mascara would run, and I'd look like a raccoon by the time I got to the Rathburns' house. It was touch-and-go, just the same. "She's so little—"

"We'll find her," Sonterra repeated.

"Where could she be?" I was thinking aloud. I knew Sonterra didn't have the answer—if he had, Suzie would be safe. Her dad would be on his way from Bisbee to claim her.

"Timmons figures she's within a twenty-five-mile radius of Dry Creek," Sonterra said. I could tell he didn't like parting with the information, but he knew I was frantic, and he was cutting me a break. Score one for SuperCop.

"How does he know that if there's no signal?"

"He checked with the provider, and they told him it was some kind of short-range, cheapo deal. You need a calling card to get long-distance minutes, and Doc Holliday didn't have any on the books."

I frowned as I hooked up my seat belt and got the Hummer fired up and rolling. "Does that seem strange to you? A doctor with a cut-rate cellular plan?"

Sonterra huffed out a sigh. Clearly, he was about to spill even more of the inside skinny, but he begrudged it. "The woman wasn't rich, Clare. She had student loans up to her earlobes, and she ran a charity practice. All her credit cards were maxed."

I remembered what a bare-essentials kind of place Judy Holliday's office had been. No receptionist. I hadn't even seen a phone, let alone the usual high-tech equipment common to any medical practice. Like her place of business, her house was also small and modest, and very sparsely furnished.

I recalled Esperanza remarking that Holliday had given her medication samples when her daughter, Maria, got sick. Obviously, she was an old-fashioned, caring kind of physician. Her loss was doubly tragic—the world needs more people like Judy, not fewer.

"You're still having dinner with the Rathburns, I suppose?" Sonterra asked.

"You suppose correctly."

"Have a good time," Sonterra said, sounding distracted. "I'll see you at home later."

I nodded. "Call me if anything happens."

He hung up, making no promises.

FIFTEEN

There were gnomes in the front yard of the Rathburns' rambling pink stucco house, just as Deputy Dave had said. Testy-looking little buggers, garishly painted and fashioned of resin or plaster, standing an average of three feet tall, they seemed to be plotting a home invasion. I imagined them kicking in the door, storming over the threshold, demanding to know Sleeping Beauty's exact whereabouts.

Madge greeted me through the screen, smiling and sporting a cotton apron over a clone of the double-knit pantsuit she'd worn to Danielle's book club meeting the night before. "Clare," she said, sounding pleased as she raised the little metal hook to let me in.

I handed over the gerberas. "I'm sorry Emma couldn't come along," I said. "She had homework."

"That's all right," Madge said. She didn't seem like the same woman who'd driven me out into the desert to a murder scene and stood chain-smoking beside her car while I walked around. "Dave's going to be late. He's on a call."

Madge had turned her back on me, heading toward the kitchen, so I took the opportunity to look around. Early American furniture, the kind that was in style in the fifties. A fireplace, the mantel lined with framed photos of children, boys and girls, several of them missing their front teeth. A TV in the corner, muted, with a newscaster mouthing all the latest local, national, and global atrocities. Hand-crocheted throws neatly draped over chair backs.

The scene was entirely normal, and yet it gave me an uneasy feeling. I could almost hear those gnomes murmuring in the front yard.

I followed Madge into the kitchen, which was cheery and filled with the savory aroma of supper bubbling in the oven.

"Have a seat," she said, indicating the old-fashioned chrome dining set in the breakfast nook. The walls were covered with copper gelatin molds, in the shape of various farm animals, and the linoleum floor gleamed with fresh wax.

I drew back a chair and sat down. Madge put the flowers into a vase and set them on the counter.

"It's a pity about poor Micki Post," she said, stepping lively to the stove and opening the oven door to peer in at a huge casserole dish. The luscious smell intensified for a moment, steamy and inviting. "But, then, she's always had a talent for picking bad men—except for the first one, that is, and of course that didn't last. Before Bobby Ray, she was writing to some yahoo in the penitentiary. Iced tea?"

I took a moment to negotiate the gap where the segue should have been. "Please," I said.

Madge took a pitcher from the fridge and poured tea into a tall glass with a cartoon character on the side. "There's sugar and packets of artificial sweetener on the lazy Susan, right there behind the napkin holder," she said, setting the drink down in front of me, along with a spoon, and bustling back to the counter, where a pile of salad makings waited on a chopping block.

"I'm sorry the chief couldn't join us," she told me chattily.

"He's kind of busy," I replied. There were no ashtrays in sight, and there was no tinge of cigarette smoke in the air. I figured Madge for a patio smoker.

"Don't I know it," Madge said, sundering a lettuce head with one swift blow of her knife.

I jumped slightly. "It was nice of you to invite us," I prattled.

Madge paused to smile at me, showing those purple gums again. "Nice of you to come," she replied, and started whacking away at a pile of green onions. "I like to get to know new folks. Make them feel welcome."

Except for the menacing band of elves in the yard, the place was homey. *Madge* was homey. "I saw a lot of photographs on your mantel," I said. "Your grandchildren?"

She nodded, without looking my way, and her neck pinkened faintly, probably with pride. "Six of them. We don't see them often, but the boys are good about sending pictures. Especially Dave, Jr., since he's a photographer."

"It must be hard, having them live so far away."

Madge looked at me in mild surprise. "Dave, Jr. lives in Nogales, on the Arizona side, and Mark's got himself a little air-conditioning repair business in Tucson."

Since she'd said she didn't see the grandkids on a regular basis, I'd assumed her family resided in distant states. Nogales, like Tucson, was within easy driving distance of Dry Creek.

Madge sighed, fumbled in her apron pocket and pulled out a pack of cigarettes and a lighter. "Let's step out onto the patio," she said, and headed for the back door.

I followed, iced tea in hand, sensing she was about to share a confidence, and, oddly, wishing I didn't have to hear it.

"Dave was too hard on those boys," Madge said, lighting up, inhaling, and puffing smoke out of her nostrils. There went the Happy Homemaker image. "Neither one of them will set foot in this house unless they know he's out of town."

How do you respond to something like that?

"I'm sorry," I said. It was a sincere statement, but lame.

"Me, too," Madge answered, and there was bitterness in her voice and in her manner. She dragged in another load of tar and nicotine.

"You're not saying Dave abused your sons, are you?" I ventured. Sometimes I know when to keep my mouth shut. Then there are the other twenty-three-and-a-half hours of the day.

"Took a belt to them on a regular basis, until I sicced Oz

Gilbride on him for it. Oz straightened him right out." She sighed out more smoke. "Just the same, once Dave, Jr. and Mark left here, they stayed scarce."

I'd been in a ton of foster homes in my life, and in a few of them, the volunteer parents had been more interested in the monthly check from the state than helping out a troubled kid. Still, in all that time, no one had ever laid an angry hand on me— not even my raving drunk of a mother.

My expression must have been bleak.

Madge summoned up an apologetic smile. "I don't know why I told you all that," she said with a shake of her head. "It's ancient history. Nothing to do with right now. And I wanted you to think well of me, too."

"Of course I think well of you," I protested. "It wasn't your fault—"

"It was," Madge insisted, grim again. I pictured her joining forces with the gnomes, trashing the house, and hitting the road. "I should have stopped him sooner. I should have left his sorry ass."

"Madge, did Dave—does he—?"

"Hit me?" Madge finished my sentence just as a car door slammed in front of the house. "That would make him look bad, wouldn't it?" She bent over a planter and snuffed out the cigarette hastily, not expecting an answer. "Best get supper on," she said, and headed back inside.

I hesitated, then went in behind her.

Dave stood in the doorway between the kitchen and the living room, still in his uniform. "I told the chief he ought to join us," he boomed jovially. "But he's locked away in the back office with that federal agent."

I was looking at the present-day Dave, but I saw his younger, angrier, belt-wielding self. Goose bumps spilled down my arms.

Madge, meanwhile, opened the fridge and brought out a can of cold beer. She didn't just hand it to her husband, she popped the top, got a chilled mug from the freezer, poured the suds, and carried it to him.

Dave took the beer without a thank-you, and his gaze never left my face. I'd have given a lot to know what he was thinking, and it's a safe bet that the reverse was true. There was a shrewdness in his eyes that I'd never noticed before.

"Supper's just about ready," Madge said.

"Why's that TV on in there?" Dave asked his wife, finally looking away. I felt like a captured butterfly with the pins just pulled from its wings. Inwardly, I flapped a little, ready to fly. "Nobody's even watching it."

"I was watching it," Madge told him evenly. "Then Mark called, so I turned down the sound."

Dave focused on me again, shaking his head. His hair was creased, sweaty and limp where his hat brim had rested. "The woman's never paid an electric bill in her life," he said, in a tone that made us buddies, even collaborators.

Inside, I was seething. Outside, I smiled.

Madge banged some plates onto the table, served up the food, and we all sat down. I still didn't have an appetite, but I was going to have to eat.

I started with salad, and Madge chattered on about Danielle's book club, and how relieved she was not to have to read another Oprah pick, since they never seemed to have a happy ending. Dave sat there like a lump, shoveling in food, and I watched him out of the corner of my eye.

At Sonterra's swearing-in, he'd seemed friendly enough.

He'd behaved in a downright gentlemanly manner, the night before, squiring Emma and me home from the cemetery in his squad car, after Micki's body was discovered, reminding us to lock the door as soon as we were inside.

Yes, he'd shown an antipathy for Sonterra, but I'd thought that was natural, and entirely human, given that he'd probably hoped to land the chief's job himself.

Obviously, there was another side to Deputy Dave.

My inclination was to tell him I thought he was three kinds of an SOB, but I was afraid he'd take it out on Madge after I left, so I kept my opinion to myself.

The spaghetti concoction was delicious, even if it did wad up in a ball in the pit of my stomach, like so much wood putty. Madge had made lemon chiffon pie for dessert, and I coveted it, but I knew it wouldn't go down. Remarking upon my modest appetite—I couldn't wait to share that one with Sonterra, along with my modified opinion of Deputy Dave—Madge cut three generous slices and popped them into a large plastic container.

"You can take these home with you," she said.

We cleared the table and loaded the dishwasher together, while Dave sat at the table, consuming a second piece of pie. I thanked them and made a graceful exit, and the minute I was outside, Sonterra's cell phone rang.

On the porch, I took the phone out and answered with a circumspect, "Yes?"

I didn't recognize the voice. "Is this Chief Sonterra's line?" a man asked.

"Yes," I repeated.

"Put him on," the caller snapped.

I started down the walk, casting one glance back over my shoulder to confirm an intuitive hit. Sure enough, Deputy Dave was watching me through the screen door, and he was scowling.

"Hello?" barked the grouch on the other end of the line.

"Who is this?" I whispered, hightailing it through the gnome horde for the Hummer. Somehow, purse, pie, and all, I got the door open and climbed inside.

I looked toward the house again, before starting the ignition. The squad car was parked in the driveway, and Dave was still watching me through the screen. By comparison, the gnomes looked friendlier.

"I beg your pardon? I called Sonterra's number, and I got you, whoever the hell you are. And *you're* asking *me* who *I* am?"

"There is no need to be rude," I said, cranking on the engine. "And I asked you first."

The caller swore and hung up with a crash that could be managed only on a landline. I certainly hoped he hadn't been calling to report a crime in progress.

Hell, if there was a crime, he was probably the perpetrator.

I keyed in my own cell number to relay word of a possible problem.

Sonterra answered in an urgent undertone.

I broke the bad news. "It's me," I said.

Sonterra swore.

"I love you, too," I told him peevishly. "And I only wanted to tell you that some misogynist just called, looking for you. He wouldn't give his name."

"Great," Sonterra said. "That's just great."

I frowned, maneuvering through the streets of Dry Creek, clipping the occasional curb. Those Hummers are big suckers, hard to drive with one hand. "Is there a problem?"

Sonterra was hardly more polite than Caller Number One. "Go home, Clare. If the guy calls again, give him this number."

I was in no mood to take orders, especially after a dose of Deputy Dave. "Whoever he is, his phone manners suck."

"So do yours. *Go home.*"

"Sonterra—"

He hung up. I stared at the phone, affronted, until I almost took out a fire hydrant, then tossed the cell onto the passenger seat.

I decided to cruise by the cop shop and give Sonterra back his stupid phone, along with a piece of my mind, but when I got there, the lot was empty, except for a single Crown Vic—Jesse's, no doubt.

Conclusion: Sonterra was in the field, which probably meant that one, they'd gotten a lead on Suzie, or two, there had been yet another crime committed in our sleepy little town.

The cell chirped. I retrieved it.

"Hello!" I yelled.

"Let's try this again," said the stranger.

SIXTEEN

I still wanted to grill the mystery caller, but I refrained. Sonterra hadn't actually *said* the guy was involved in the investigation of Suzie's disappearance, but I'd jumped on the clue train just as the last car passed. I rattled off my cell phone number and said he could reach the chief there.

"Thanks," was the terse response. The call disconnected just as I pulled into the driveway at home.

"You're so freaking welcome," I said into empty space.

Juggling the pie and my purse, I got out of the Hummer, locked it with the push button, and headed for the house.

When the dogs didn't rush to greet me the moment I opened the front door, I was instantly alarmed.

All the lights were on, and Sonterra's big-screen was tuned to MTV, but there was no sign of my niece.

My skin prickled. "Emma?"

I heard a faint but ominous woof in the distance, attributed it to Waldo, and tracked the sound to the kitchen, where Emma's homework lay forgotten on the table. The basement door stood ajar.

I called Emma's name again, louder this time.

"Come down here—please." Her voice echoed off the cinder-block walls of the basement, and there was an urgent note to it, but

I was so relieved to get a reply that I didn't immediately register her tone.

I set the plastic food container and my bag on the table and started down the basement steps. The dank, musty odor common to underground rooms, which are rare in Arizona, rose to meet me. Bernice came halfway up, yapping a belated welcome.

Because of the angle of the stairway, I couldn't see my niece until I was all the way down. She knelt on the concrete floor, peering into one of those odd little doors in the lower part of the wall, presumably opening onto a crawl space. A flashlight glowed, forgotten, in her right hand.

Looking at the elfin door, I thought of the Rathburns' ill-tempered gnomes. Anybody taller than they were would have had to crouch to get inside.

I started to ask Emma what was going on, but the question stuck in my throat when I registered the horrified expression on her face. She was pale, and even though the basement was cool, she was perspiring.

"Clare," she said hoarsely, with a nod toward the opening in the wall. "There are bones in here."

At first, I wasn't sure I had heard her correctly. *"Bones?"* I echoed stupidly. As many bodies as I've run across in my time, you'd think I'd be quicker on the uptake.

Emma nodded woodenly. Tried to speak, swallowed, and made a second attempt as I knelt to take the flashlight and peer into the black hole. Sure enough, the beam played over a human skull with its mouth wide-open, as if it had just uttered a primal scream, and the rest of the skeleton was there, too, but scattered, as though rats and other creatures had been at play.

"My God," I whispered. *"My God."*

"I c-came down here to wash my jeans, for school tomorrow—" Emma gripped my arm tightly, almost convulsively. "Waldo started scratching at the door and barking, so I opened it to show him there was nothing there—"

I put down the flashlight and wrapped both arms around my niece. "It's okay," I said, but my mind was racing, trying to make sense of the thing. I hoped my talent for finding dead bodies didn't run in the family. "It's okay."

She pulled back, shaking her head. It wasn't "okay," and we both knew it. "At first I thought it was just a Halloween decoration that somebody left behind when they moved—"

I got to my feet, pulling Emma with me. First order of business: call Sonterra. Second order of business: make a pit stop before I wet my pants.

"Who do you suppose it is?" Emma asked, with a shudder, as we started up the steps. Waldo and Bernice followed, and we were back in the kitchen before I realized Waldo had brought a pelvis bone along as a souvenir.

I took it from him and set it gingerly on the counter.

"I have no idea," I answered, a few beats after I should have, numb with shock. Once Emma was seated at the kitchen table, still shaking, I made my way to the phone and dialed Sonterra's number.

My purse rang.

I swore. He had my cell phone. I tried again.

"Sonterra," he said brusquely.

"You have to come home." It was all I could think of to say, at the moment. My gaze strayed to the pelvis bone on the counter, brown and nicked all over with the marks of rodent teeth. A chill gyrated through me, and I shivered in its wake.

I felt Sonterra shift from mild irritation—he was clearly in the middle of something—to red alert. "What is it?"

I couldn't answer.

"Clare."

"Bones," I said.

By then, Emma had recovered enough to cross the room and take the receiver out of my hands.

"Waldo found a skeleton in the cellar," she said matter-of-factly.

I groped my way along the edge of the counter, drawn to that fragment of a human being and, at the same time, repulsed.

"Okay," Emma responded, and hung up the phone. "Tony said not to touch the bones. He'll be here in fifteen minutes."

I nodded, still mesmerized. Had the victim been alive when he was placed in that dark cubbyhole with the rats? Dear God, I hoped not.

Emma and I were both sitting at the table, staring mutely at each other, when, some twenty minutes later, Sonterra unlocked the back door and burst in, closely followed by Special Agent Timmons and a couple of his cronies.

All of them homed right in on the pelvis.

"Waldo did it," I said.

Sonterra nodded, as though what I'd said made some sort of sense, and headed for the basement steps. Timmons caught my eye for a moment, then trooped after Sonterra. The other agents were right behind them.

I felt icy cold, as if an arctic wind had swpt through the room, wide as a river, but emanating directly from that grim little nook in the basement wall.

At least half an hour must have passed before Sonterra returned to the kitchen, accompanied by Special Agent Timmons, who was on his cell phone, calling for a crime-scene team.

Sonterra pulled back a chair and sat down between Emma and me.

"What's the story?" he asked quietly.

Emma bit her lip, then repeated what she'd told me earlier.

Sonterra listened, nodded when she was finished.

"Do you think it's Oz Gilbride?" I asked, referring of course to the remains. "After all, he disappeared, and this was his house—"

"We won't know for sure until we get results on the lab work," Sonterra replied, and something in his tone told me he was about to deliver breaking news. "If it is Chief Gilbride, he didn't rot alone. There are skeletons piled up in that hole like firewood."

I put a hand to my mouth. I had a thousand questions, and all of them scrambled into my throat at once, like mice fleeing a fire through a narrow pipe, and got stuck there.

Emma, steadier now, spoke up. "How come nobody figured out that there were bodies down there before this?" she asked.

"They must have stunk like crazy while they were decomposing." That's what happens when you have a fourteen-year-old who aspires to be a cop. They use words like "decomposing."

Sonterra gave a grim nod of agreement. He answered Emma, but he was watching me very closely the whole time, as if he expected me to suddenly come apart at the seams. "There's no possible way those people died here. I'd say they were killed else-where, then stashed after the flesh rotted away."

I grimaced reflexively as the obvious images cascaded into my brain.

Timmons, having completed his telephone call, leaned against the kitchen counter, inches from the rat-gnawed pelvis.

"They've been in there a while, though," he put in.

I shivered, remembering my skeleton dream, and wondering if I'd known all the time, subconsciously of course, that there were bones under the house.

Within an hour, our place swarmed with State Police, FBI agents, people from the Pima County ME's Office, and crime-scene techs. Emma, the dogs, and I waited in the living room, staying out of the way.

"This is way past creepy," Emma observed, her eyes wide. Now that the shock had subsided a little, she was intrigued. Although I didn't encourage it, I knew she read a lot of true crime and watched the same forensic science programs on Court TV that I did. "Don't you think it's weird that the graveyard is just over the back fence? It's like there was an underground earthquake or something, and a bunch of the bodies shifted into our basement."

I shuddered. "What a lovely thought," I said. "Unlikely that they'd all funnel into a crawl space, though."

Emma nodded in solemn agreement. "Do you think they're coyote victims?"

"Maybe," I said. I'd thought my despair couldn't run any deeper, but once the prospect was out in the open, I felt swamped by gloom. Sonterra had said there were a lot of skeletons down there, and I wondered, though he hadn't been specific, if some of them were women and children.

I heard Deputy Dave's voice in the kitchen. I didn't bother to play hostess. He'd find his own way to the cellar.

The news media arrived next, clogging the street out front with reporters, vans, and cameras. Timmons and his Bureau colleagues kept them at arm's length, but when the ME's crew began carrying the bones out in body bags, the yard lit up with eerie, flickering flashes. I could imagine what the pictures would be like.

Around midnight, Sonterra joined Emma and me in the living room, brushing cobwebs off his clothes.

"You might as well go to bed," he told me.

"Like I could sleep," I replied.

"Just think," Emma said. "We've been hitting the sheets every night, with no clue that there were a bunch of stiffs right under our feet."

"Emma." I sighed.

She pulled me up from my chair. "Tony's right," she said solicitously. "You need some rest."

Next thing I knew, Sonterra was undressing me and tucking me in. He kissed me on the forehead, took jeans and a T-shirt from his dresser drawers, and went across the hall. I heard the shower running, and took comfort in the normality of the sound.

I closed my eyes, listening.

When I opened them again, it was morning.

During those first few seconds of muddled, sleep-drugged thought, I believed I'd dreamed the whole thing. Reality was on me like a pit bull as soon as the fog cleared.

With a groan, I rolled out of bed—Sonterra's side hadn't been slept in—pulled on a robe, and crossed to the bathroom for a shower. When I was presentable, in navy sweats and sneakers, I went downstairs.

The kitchen brimmed with weary-looking FBI agents. Esperanza, shoulders stooped, stood at the stove, mass-producing omelets. Sonterra, still in last night's change of clothes, poured me a cup of coffee.

Timmons got up to give me his chair at the table, but I shook my head. Sipped the coffee. It seemed to have no taste at all, but it was hot.

"Now what?" I asked Sonterra.

He caressed my cheek, countered my question with one of his own. "You okay, Counselor?"

"Just great," I told him, looking around. No sign of Emma, or the dogs. "Where—?"

"Relax," Sonterra said, putting his hand to the small of my back and steering me out of the kitchen, through the dining room, and into the study, where we could talk privately.

"Tell me you didn't send Emma to school," I blurted. "The other kids will be all over her, not to mention the media."

"She's with Jesse's mother," Sonterra told me. "Bernice and Waldo, too."

"Who?" I asked, a split second before I remembered that— of course—Jesse was Sonterra's deputy. Significant, I thought, that he hadn't sent Emma and the dogs to Madge and Dave's place. "Are you sure they'll be all right?"

"Positive," Sonterra said, turning the chair in front of my computer around and pressing me into it.

"This is a nightmare," I murmured.

He huffed out a sigh. "No argument there, Counselor."

"Any IDs on the bodies yet?"

Sonterra shook his head. "Best guess, they're illegal immigrants."

I closed my eyes, rubbed my temples with the fingertips of both hands. The realization that I'd forgotten all about Suzie struck me then, with the force of a baseball bat. I gripped the arms of the chair, stricken that I could have let her slip my mind for even a moment. It was as though, by remembering, by keeping a conscious vigil, I could prevent her from dying.

"*Suzie,*" I whispered.

Sonterra gave my knees a squeeze. "Keep the faith," he said gruffly. "There are people combing the desert right now, looking for her."

"The desert?" I sat up a little straighter. "Did you get a lead? Is that where you were when I called you last night?"

He sighed. "No, I didn't get a lead. Yes, that's where I was. We were operating on Timmons's theory that the call came from within twenty-five miles of Dry Creek. The Bureau brought in a couple of scent dogs, and one of the TV stations in Tucson loaned us a helicopter and pilot to search from the air once the sun came up, but there are about 9 million caves out there."

I'd pulled him, and a flock of FBI agents, off the search because of a bunch of bones. Granted, the skeletons belonged to human beings, almost certainly murdered, but they'd probably been around for a long time. Their cause clearly wasn't as urgent as Suzie's.

Sonterra frowned, trying to read my expression. "What is it?" he asked.

"You might have found her by now, if I hadn't—"

"Stop," Sonterra interrupted firmly. "There must be a hundred volunteers out there. The situation is under control, and there's no point in beating yourself up."

A light rap sounded at the study door.

Sonterra closed his eyes for a second, then said, "In."

Timmons opened the door. "Sorry to bother you, Chief," he said, "but I just got a call from the field. They found something."

"*Something?*" Sonterra echoed tersely.

I couldn't speak.

Sonterra stood up.

"Not the kid," Timmons added quickly. "Evidently, one of the dogs picked up a scent and tracked it into a hole behind a pile of rocks. He came out with a sandal."

Sonterra was on the move so quickly that I had to hurry to keep up with him. I stayed on his heels all the way to his car and climbed into the back while Timmons took the front seat, reconnected with his field contact via the cell phone, in case there were updates. Either Sonterra was too distracted to insist that I stay behind, or he knew it would be a waste of breath.

Maybe he'd just resigned himself to my badge.

It was a bumpy ride, but we were on the scene within ten minutes.

By then, the searchers had found a cell phone, half-buried in the sand, and a few footprints. Two Bureau guys were already making plaster casts.

"Running shoes," one of them told Sonterra and Timmons, as we rushed over to investigate. Sonterra paused long enough to give me one of those stay-back looks, and I didn't press my luck. He could have me bodily removed from the scene if he wanted to, and worried about the consequences from Robeson's office later, and I knew he would if I got in the way.

The prints looked big, probably a size eleven or larger. There was a clear one, and three or four partials.

A tech came forward with a plastic bag, a tiny plastic sandal tucked inside.

My heart skittered, righted itself. Memory is a tricky thing. The unconscious picks up all kinds of details, catalogs them, and feeds them up later, when they become pertinent. Suzie had been wearing shoes exactly like that the one and only time I'd seen her—in front of Doc Holliday's house the previous Friday afternoon.

Sonterra's gaze sliced to my face, questioning.

I confirmed what the search dog had already figured out. "That's Suzie's," I said.

He gave a half nod and handed the bag back to the tech.

"Any tire tracks?" he asked one of the agents.

"Not so far," the man replied, after glancing at Timmons, silently seeking permission.

I became aware of the volunteer searchers, hovering in a little cluster under a lone, thirsty-looking mesquite tree. The dog handlers were already loading their canine cops into the back of a van, and the helicopter whirred in the distance, like a giant horsefly, headed toward Tucson. I had a crazy need to run after it, waving my arms, and shouting, "Come back! She's here some-where!"

By then, Sonterra was assessing the discarded cell phone, also bagged, having handed the sandal off to the tech. I felt a tear slip down my cheek and didn't bother to brush it away.

"Is everybody just going to give up?" I demanded in frustration.

Sonterra took so long to answer that I wasn't sure he'd heard me. Finally, though, he looked me in the eye. "Suzie's been moved to another location, Clare," he said patiently. "It's no use searching out here anymore."

I drew nearer, to examine the phone through the plastic. The battery had been removed. "Is that the one she used to call us?"

"Probably," Sonterra said bleakly. "We won't be able to tell for sure until it's operational again."

Just then, a squad car came bumping over the desert. Deputy Dave brought it to a rattling halt about fifty yards out, shoved open the door, and stormed across the distance in between.

"Maybe you forgot, *Chief,*" he ranted at Sonterra, "but I'm still a member of this police force, and I'd appreciate a call when something like this goes down!"

Sonterra didn't waver, nor did he raise his voice. "You put in a long night sorting bones," he said.

Rathburn looked apoplectic. "Yeah, and I wouldn't have known about *that,* either, if I hadn't had my scanner on. If you want me to turn in my badge, just say so, but don't leave me out of the loop again!"

I saw a tiny muscle bunch in Sonterra's cheek, but other than that, he was cool as a winter breeze. "When I want you," he told the other man evenly, "I'll call you. We'll discuss this privately— later."

The deputy blustered a little, but he finally caved. "Fine," he bit out. His gaze strayed to me, and I knew he wanted to ask what I was doing there, but he didn't quite dare.

Sonterra turned his back on Rathburn and started going over the surrounding area, following some mental grid. It didn't matter to him that the scene had already been searched—he had to see for himself.

Deputy Rathburn stood glaring after him for a few moments, sized Timmons up, then approached the milling volunteers with his questions.

Timmons crouched at the mouth of the hole where Suzie's sandal had been found, sweeping the interior with the beam of a flashlight.

He looked up at me. "You shouldn't be here, you know," he said mildly, and with a certain good-natured resignation.

I didn't bother to explain that, for all practical intents and purposes, I represented Pima County. The Bureau being what it was, he probably knew it anyway. "Has anybody been in there—besides the dog?"

"One of the techs got most of the way in," he said. "It's a tight space."

I measured the opening with my eyes and suppressed a shudder. It was the last place I wanted to go, but at the same time, I felt compelled to see for myself what might be in that hole. "I could make it."

Timmons straightened, shaking his head. "Why?"

"Because I'd like to see it for myself," I said.

He looked around for Sonterra, spotted him talking to one of the techs, then turned his gaze on me again.

"It's a crime scene," he reminded me.

Time to play the big card. "And I'm an investigator with the Pima County Prosecutor's Office. I can call for a warrant if you like."

He didn't smile—at least, not with his mouth. His eyes reflected a sorrowful kind of humor. "The chief won't like this even a little bit."

"Feel free to tattle," I replied. "As soon as I'm far enough in that he can't grab me by the ankles and pull me back."

Timmons tightened his grip on the flashlight and, an instant later, released it. I dropped to my knees and shimmied through the narrow mouth of the cave. It was deep, with only inches on either side. Suzie could have gotten in and out easily, but I wondered how her captor had managed it. Maybe he'd coaxed her somehow, but that didn't seem likely, either. She would have been terrified.

Sonterra was onto my game. His voice echoed through the passage. "Damn it, Clare!" he yelled. "Get out here!"

I ignored him and kept slithering, hoping I wouldn't meet a snake or a scorpion along the way. The air was close and dank, reminding me of the basement of the house on Cemetery Lane.

The space narrowed, and I fought a fit of claustrophobia. What if I got stuck? What if I died of suffocation, or just plain fright, before Sonterra and the others could get to me?

Assuming they'd even try, of course.

Just when I thought I couldn't stand it, a space about six feet wide and three feet high opened at the end of the flashlight beam. I paused, ran the light over the floor and walls. On the first pass, I saw nothing but root endings and a couple of sticks. I almost missed the crumpled scrap of paper—would have if it hadn't stuck to my shirt.

Heart pounding, I smoothed it and focused the flashlight beam.

It was ancient and yellowed, torn from one of those notepads they put in hotel rooms.

Palm Palace Hotel. Nogales, Arizona. There was a phone number, with an alphabetic prefix and no area code, but nothing else.

Frustration uncoiled in my throat.

What did it mean?

"Clare!" Sonterra called again, from above ground, where there was sunlight and fresh air.

Had Suzie been held at the Palm Palace Hotel? And how long had she been trapped in this hole? Had the mysterious "they" she'd mentioned on the cell phone bound her somehow, so she couldn't crawl out? Or had they covered the opening with something too heavy for a small child, hungry and thirsty and certainly in shock, to move? And how many people were we looking for? Two? Five? A dozen?

"Clare!" Sonterra again.

Clasping the bit of paper in one sweaty hand, I made a silent vow. *We'll find you, Suzie. No matter what we have to do, we'll find you.*

Sonterra was waiting when I squirmed out of the rabbit hole, like Alice on rewind. I didn't even bother to stand up—I just tossed aside the flashlight and handed him the only clue I'd found.

He scanned it, then pulled out his cell phone and keyed in the number.

We all waited—Timmons, Deputy Dave, and me—watching Sonterra's face as he listened to the rings.

Dave started to speak, and Sonterrra silenced him with an upraised hand.

Timmons gripped my elbow and helped me to my feet.

Sonterra said, "Hello? Who is this?" He listened, then switched to rapid-fire Spanish. I didn't get much of what he was saying, but I knew he'd asked a lot of questions, followed by a line of bullshit about a wedding. After a minute or so, he said *adios* and disconnected.

"What?" I prompted, none too patiently, when he just stood there for a long moment, assembling his thoughts.

"No luck," he said, too quickly.

I didn't believe it, and neither did Timmons, by the look on his face.

Sonterra turned to Dave, who obviously wasn't buying the dead-end story, either. "I need you to hold down the office for a while," he said, as though a harsh word had never passed between them. "You'd better get back to town right away."

"Jesse's already there," Dave protested.

"Jesse's barely more than a crossing guard," Sonterra answered.

Rathburn didn't budge right away, though it did seem that Sonterra's assessment of the younger deputy's abilities might have pleased him a little. "What are you going to do in the meantime?"

"Write you up if you don't follow orders," Sonterra said.

They glared at each other for a beat or two—it would have been a great place for the theme music from *The Good, the Bad, and the Ugly*—then Dave conceded the battle of the wills and stormed back to his squad car. He had the radio handset to his mouth as he sped by us, tires spitting hard sand.

"I don't think you fooled him," Timmons observed, eyeing

the paper as Sonterra slipped it into his shirt pocket. "Who the hell were you talking to just now?"

"The desk clerk of a rathole hotel in Nogales," Sonterra said. "On the Mexican side. I'm going down there."

"Wait a second," Timmons argued. "If you've got a lead, we can contact the *federales*—"

Sonterra was already on his way back to the SUV, and I tagged right along. Timmons double-timed furiously after us.

"Let me see that paper!"

Sonterra ignored him and kept going.

Timmons didn't give up easily, of course. "You don't have jurisdiction down there, Sonterra!"

"Neither do you," Sonterra threw back.

"Well, damn it, I'm going with you just the same!" Timmons growled.

"Not a good idea," Sonterra said, practically shoving me into the rig. "They're expecting a honeymoon couple. You tag along, *Special Agent* Timmons, and it'll seem odd, even in that part of town."

Timmons flushed with frustration. "I'll pull rank on you if I have to," he warned, as Sonterra got behind the wheel and cranked up the engine. "Don't think I can't have your ass stopped at the border!"

"Do that," Sonterra snapped, "and a little girl might die because of it!"

With that, we were rolling. I glanced into the rearview mirror and saw Timmons standing stiffly in the sand, scowling after us. I expected him to commandeer one of the other cars and follow, but he didn't.

"Good work, Counselor," Sonterra said.

I was still catching up. In fact, I'd barely had a chance to snap on my seat belt before we were off on our wild ride. "Do you have a good reason for cutting out the feds?" I asked when I caught my breath.

Sonterra looked even grimmer than before, and he was silent for a full minute or more. "Don't talk to me. I need to think."

"I wouldn't want you to hurt yourself," I said.

Sonterra didn't slow down at all as we hit the main road and screeched off toward Dry Creek. "The last thing I want is a bunch of suits and crew cuts closing in on the target and blowing the whole thing. The hotel *is* in Nogales, but it's on this side of the border."

"And the kidnappers might have taken Suzie back there?"

"Yes," Sonterra said.

"Tell me about the phone call you just made." I wasn't going to be put off as easily as Timmons had been.

Sonterra looked grim. "I greeted the guy in English, and he answered in Spanish. I guess he doesn't get a lot of calls in English, but he must have been expecting one, because at first he thought I was somebody else. Started spilling his guts right off the bat—said come quick, that the *chiquita* was *muy malo*. Then he must have realized his mistake, because he got testy. I played dumb and told him I wanted to rent a room for our wedding night."

I turned in the seat to look back. We had the road to ourselves, except for a tractor traveling about three miles an hour. "I'm not sure you made the right decision back there. Now you've pissed Timmons off, and the feds might actually have been useful, for once."

"Right," Sonterra said. "Nobody would suspect a thing if thirty guys in brown shoes suddenly appeared in the lobby."

"Timmons is probably on the horn having a roadblock set up even as we speak. We'll be lucky to get through Dry Creek." I paused for a breath, pushed back my hair, which was peppered with dirt. "Deputy Dave would love that—you on the wrong side of the cell door and him holding the keys."

"If Timmons is on the phone, he's calling the border patrol," Sonterra replied. We took a country road I'd forgotten was there, skirting the town entirely.

My high school Spanish began to kick in. "*Muy malo.* That means 'very bad.' You *could* call the Nogales police, you know. If Suzie's in this hotel, and she's sick, they should take her to the hospital!"

"I can't take the risk, Clare. The hotels in that neighborhood are all dives. These are the kind of people who crawl under rocks when they smell a cop. A word from them, and the perps will grab Suzie and disappear again, maybe kill her in the process. God knows how long she was in that hole in the ground, and if they gave her food or water, there was no sign of it. There's no telling how much more she can stand."

I settled back in the seat, trying to relax, or at least *seem* relaxed. "What are we going to do when we get there?"

"I don't know yet," Sonterra admitted.

"They couldn't have known she had that phone."

I imagined Suzie huddled in that gravelike space, with no light except for a tiny panel on a cell phone.

"I think she expected somebody to find that cave," I said.

"Or we just got lucky," Sonterra countered. He paused, and I studied his profile. He looked haunted. "We got the dogs out there as soon as we knew what a limited range the doc's cell phone had, but we're still talking about a lot of desert."

"Don't beat yourself up, Sonterra," I counseled, though I probably would have done exactly the same thing in his place. And I had my share of regrets—if I'd personally seen that Micki and Suzie took refuge in a shelter before I left Dry Creek for Scottsdale, instead of leaving them at Judy Holliday's place, knowing Bobby Ray had been released on bail, they might both be safe, and Judy wouldn't have been such an obvious target.

Hindsight.

Like they say, it's always twenty-twenty.

SEVENTEEN

Nogales is a small, dusty town, straddling the border between Arizona and Mexico. Sonterra seemed to know it well—he'd had a misspent youth of his own, as it turned out, and Nogales had been his Dry Creek—and he wasted no time getting there. Normally, the trip would have taken a little over an hour, but he brought the SUV to a stop on a shabby side street in forty-seven minutes flat, by the clock on the dashboard.

"Where's the hotel?" I asked, looking around. All I saw were littered sidewalks, bums, and boarded-up shops, marred with graffiti.

"Three blocks east, if it's the one I think it is," Sonterra answered, leaping out of the car and pulling his service revolver and shoulder holster from under the driver's seat. He pulled up his T-shirt and strapped it on while I stood there wishing I'd brought a gun, too. "If we show up at this dive in a late-model rig, they're going to guess there might be a problem. Give me back my cell phone."

I handed it over. The thing had been giving intermittent beeps all the way from Dry Creek.

Sonterra pushed the speaker button and tapped into the messages, then set it on the hood to make sure his revolver was loaded. Out of the corner of my eye, I saw the bums make him for a cop and pull a collective vanishing act.

Message one: "Sonterra? This is Timmons. You owe me big for this one. Really big."

Message two: "Hi, it's Loretta. I caught that early flight I was looking for, and Clare's not answering her phone. Where the hell IS everybody?"

Message three: "Chief Sonterra? You probably don't remember meeting me at the picnic, but my name is Becky Peakes, and I'm calling to report a missing person. I work for Danielle Bickerhelm, and she didn't come into the shop this morning. I went to her house, but nobody answered the door. So I let myself in—I have a key, you know, in case she needs me to fetch something—and she wasn't there, either. But the place had been ransacked—" A beep sounded, then another message began. The voice was still timid, but even more nervous than before. "Sorry about that. It's Becky again. I tried your office, but there was no answer. Will you call me when you get this message? Please?" She left a number, and hung up.

"Shit," Sonterra said, shutting off the phone and shoving it into his hip pocket. "Dave and Jesse should *both* be in the office. They're probably at the Doozy Diner, pigging out on doughnuts and grousing about about how the department's gone downhill since I took over."

"Aren't you concerned about Danielle?"

Sonterra looked down at his T-shirt, which bulged under his left armpit. "Right now, I'm concentrating on finding Suzie. Here's the way I want this to go down, Clare. We walk into the hotel, playing lovey-dovey newlyweds. Then I say I'm going out for the luggage, and you sit in the lobby for five minutes, like you're waiting for me. Got that? *Five minutes*. Then, no matter what, you come back here, get into the rig, and lock the doors." He tossed me the car keys. "Got it?"

"I want to help you find Suzie."

"I don't give a crap what you want right now. Just once, do as I tell you. If you mess this up, Suzie might be the one to pay the price."

I sighed. He was right. I hate it when he's right.

The Palm Palace Hotel turned out to be anything but a palace. Made of old brick, the whole depressing structure seemed to lean slightly to the right, and the windows were painted black. It was the classic flophouse, the kind of joint junkies and hookers frequent.

Later, when the pressure was off, I intended to ask Sonterra why he knew where it was.

Who was going to believe that Sonterra and I actually wanted to check into that place?

I looked down at my sweats, filthy from my trip down the rabbit hole out there in the desert. Noted my reflection in the grimy glass door leading into the lobby.

Just about anybody would believe it.

"Drunk," Sonterra cued me, draping an arm around my shoulders and slapping on a goofy smile.

We went in.

There were a registration desk, a few dusty potted palms, and a ratty couch that reeked of urine. A general miasma of mildew, vomit, and b.o. completed the olfactory onslaught.

A small, rodentlike man of Spanish extraction stood behind the desk, sizing us up.

Sonterra addressed him in slurred Spanish, giving me the occasional rummy glance as he spoke. As far as I could tell, he was asking if they rented by the hour.

The clerk, wearing an outfit that resembled a vintage band uniform, replied in the universal language of greed, thrusting his palm toward us.

Sonterra made a show of fishing out his wallet, all the while holding me close against his left side. I finally realized that my main function was to cover up the service revolver under his T-shirt, which was bruising me. I smiled dreamily up at him, trying to look like I was on something illegal.

Fumbling, the way drunks do, Sonterra finally extracted two twenty-dollar bills and laid them in the desk clerk's hand.

More Spanish was exchanged. I thought the desk clerk looked suspicious, but then, working in a dive like that, he probably had plenty of reasons for taking a dim view of humanity in general.

He gave Sonterra a key, and the game was under way.

According to plan, SuperCop steered me toward the urine-soaked sofa. I wanted to retch, but I refrained, and actually sat down amid the stains and burn holes from dropped cigarettes. I comforted myself with the fact that I could always dip myself in bleach when we got back to civilization.

Sonterra weaved his way out the front door, pausing on the other side of the dingy glass to ripple his fingers at me and grin like an idiot.

I waved back, incorporating the middle digit.

Five minutes can be a very long time when you're sitting in a place like that, watching crack addicts and diseased hookers come and go. At four minutes, thirty-five seconds, gauged by surreptitious glances at my watch, I looked back at the desk clerk. He'd been observing me the whole time; I could feel his gaze prickling the back of my neck.

I thought about asking where the bathrooms were, to make conversation, but when he told me, I'd have to go in there if I didn't want to arouse his suspicion. No way I'd set foot in the facilities in an armpit like the Palm Palace, let alone use them.

"I wonder what's keeping my husband," I mused aloud, realizing a moment after the fact that I'd sounded too sober. Discretion being the better part of valor, I made a beeline for the front door.

Sonterra had told me to go straight back to the car, and wait there for him, but of course I didn't. I slipped around the back of the hotel, found a rickety fire escape on the alley, and slouched my way up the stairs.

On the first landing, I had to step over a junkie of indeterminate gender, curled up in a fetal position. If he—or she—hadn't blinked, I would have been forced to check for a pulse. Believe me, this was not someone I wanted to touch, but I felt a twist of pity, just the same. This shaggy, grime-caked specimen was somebody's child. "Is there anyone I can call?" I asked.

The creature shook its head and closed its eyes.

Silently, I offered what could pass for a prayer, and tried the first-floor fire exit.

Security just isn't what it used to be. The door opened with a little shoulder action on my part, and I stepped into a dark corridor.

I'd thought nothing could smell worse than the lobby. Here, people had relieved themselves against the walls. I almost tripped over a rat carcass and another zoned-out user, before I started turning knobs, and what I wouldn't have given for a pair of Esperanza's cleaning gloves. Like the fire exit, the doors were unlocked, and occasionally, the rooms were occupied. I waited, on each threshold, for my eyes to adjust.

More junkies.

More hookers.

Just the sort of place a bride dreams of spending her wedding night.

The last door on the right was locked. The floor creaked overhead, and I figured Sonterra was doing the same number up there.

I felt a little thrill of dread and anticipation and knocked lightly.

"Suzie?" I called, keeping my voice low and pressing an ear to the panel.

I thought I heard something inside.

"Suzie?" I repeated. "Are you in there? Make a noise if you are."

Seconds passed, taking their sweet time. Then something crashed to the floor.

My heart seized, and sweat broke out on my upper lip. The Palm Palace was a roach trap, but the doors were the old-fashioned kind, solid wood. I wasn't going to break this one down without a bulldozer.

Fortunately, I knew just where to find one.

I located the inside stairwell and beat feet up a flight, bursting into the corridor. There was Sonterra, with his revolver out, and he had it aimed and ready to fire before he realized I wasn't some low-life resident about to jump him.

Even in the gloom, I saw the color drain from his face. He swore under his breath as he lowered the gun to his side.

"Quick!" I blurted. "I think I found her!" I retraced my steps to the door on the floor below, and Sonterra followed, elbowed me aside when we got there, and tried it.

Still locked.

"You're sure?" he asked.

I nodded. "Hurry!"

He stepped back and kicked hard with his right foot.

"Hey!" somebody yelled from a nearby room. "Wha—?"

The lock gave way, but the security chain held.

Sonterra used his shoulder the second time, and we tumbled in. I slammed hard into his back.

Suzie lay on the floor next to a bed an animal wouldn't sleep in, amid the shards of a shattered lamp base, her hands and feet bound with duct tape. Apparently, she'd hurled herself off the mattress in the process of knocking over the lamp to let me know she was there. And she'd used the last of her strength to do it.

She looked up at Sonterra and me with the terrified eyes of a trapped animal bound for some diabolical testing laboratory.

Sonterra laid the revolver within easy reach, crouched beside her, and cut away the tape with his pocketknife. "It's okay, Suzie," he said. "It's me, Chief Sonterra. And here's Clare. You called her on the cell phone, remember?"

She nodded mutely, but she looked feverish, and I wasn't sure she was tracking.

He scooped her up in his arms, held her for a moment. "Don't be scared. We're going to get you out of here," he told her. Then he handed her to me and reclaimed the revolver. "I'll go first," he said. "If it goes bad, hold on to Suzie and run like hell."

We'd barely crossed the threshold when the desk clerk appeared at the top of the stairs, a wiry little shadow in the gloom. Opened his mouth to protest, or maybe to yell for help.

"Don't make a sound," Sonterra warned him, and cocked the revolver.

He looked at the gun and nodded.

We hurried for the fire exit.

"Watch out for the junkie on the landing," I said.

The desk clerk, still inside, let out a loud yell. Now that Sonterra wasn't aiming firepower at him, he'd sounded the alarm.

"Hit the ground running," Sonterra told me, stepping aside so I could go out first.

I heard several new voices shouting behind us as we rounded a rear corner of the hotel and sprinted down the alley. Footsteps pounding down the fire stairs.

How many people were after us? I didn't take the time to look. I clutched Suzie with all my strength and fled.

Shots pinged against the walls of the other ancient buildings lining the alley. I'd thought I was traveling full out, but now I was jet-propelled. Suzie made a pitiful, nonsensical sound and burrowed into my chest, as if trying to melt into my body.

"Sonterra!" I called, without looking back, my heart thumping in my throat.

"Run!" he shouted in reply, and a bullet struck the side of a Dumpster as I shot past it.

I kept picking them up and putting them down, breaking my own speed record. I had no choice, with Suzie depending on me to get her out of there, not to mention the little passenger in my uterus. Still, a part of my mind stayed back, with Sonterra.

Had he been hit?

Tears burned in my eyes and throat like battery acid. Sonterra wasn't invincible, after all; nobody knew that better than I did.

Sirens whined in the distance. Too far away, too far away.

I ran harder, stumbled as I erupted onto a sidewalk. Nearly knocked an old lady and her pushcart flat in the process.

Suzie began to wail, a strangled sound that hurt my soul.

"Jesus," I cried, under my breath. "Jesus, Jesus, Jesus—"

I think I was praying. I'm not sure.

Finally, I rounded a corner, and there was Sonterra's SUV. Juggling Suzie's now-inert frame, I pried the keys out of the pocket of my sweatpants and managed to open the door.

The thought of leaving Sonterra behind, maybe wounded, maybe outgunned, maybe even dead, weakened my knees. But I knew what I had to do.

I laid Suzie on the backseat—she was unconscious by then—and jumped behind the wheel. Where was the nearest hospital?

I watched anxiously for Sonterra.

I was trying to figure how long I dared wait, given the condition Suzie was in, when he suddenly bounded out of the alleyway, half a block ahead. I threw the SUV into drive, and the automatic lock engaged. I gave the engine a shot of gas, flipped the button that would open the locks, and screeched to a brief stop so Sonterra could jump in on the passenger side.

"Go!" he yelled.

I floored it.

We streaked out of that neighborhood in the proverbial hail of bullets.

Thank God, the bad guys were lousy shots.

EIGHTEEN

Several desperate minutes after our hasty departure from the Palm Palace, I pulled over to the side of the road, laid my head on the steering wheel, and drew deep, slow breaths, trying not to dissolve into hysterics.

Sonterra caressed my nape. "Take it easy, Babe," he said. "The worst part's over."

I wasn't sure that was true. Suzie was obviously in very bad shape.

Now that nobody was shooting at us, I whirled in the seat to look back at the child. She was still, and her eyes, though partially open, had rolled back in her head.

"I don't know where the hospital is," I wailed.

Sonterra pulled me close and kissed my forehead. "Shhh," he said. "Get in the backseat with Suzie, and I'll drive."

My knees were weak, but I jumped out of the SUV, jerked open the back door, and wriggled inside, pulling Suzie gently onto my lap. Meanwhile, Sonterra rounded the car and took the wheel.

I held Suzie against my chest, felt her breath, faint as the beat of a moth's wing, on the underside of my chin.

"She's alive," I said, and began to rock her in my arms. Maybe I was rocking my own baby, too, and myself.

I don't know how much time passed before Sonterra whipped

into the emergency entrance of a hospital. He shoved open the driver's door, waggled his badge, and shouted, "Police! We need help!"

Suzie was wrenched from my arms, whisked away on a gurney.

Sonterra opened my door, already on his cell phone.

"Mr. Post?" I heard him say. "We found your daughter—"

I stopped listening.

The emergency room doctors took charge and did what they could to stabilize Suzie, but it was a small hospital, and they weren't equipped to provide the kind of specialized care she needed. Almost immediately, they dispatched her to Tucson by ambulance, and Sonterra and I followed in his car, having updated Dan Post by cell phone so he could meet us there.

When we arrived, a few minutes behind the ambulance, Sonterra sat me down in the lobby waiting room.

I stared into space, pulling myself together.

"She's pregnant," I heard Sonterra say to someone in blue scrubs. To this day, I couldn't tell you whether it was a man or a woman. Their response sounded like the teacher in the *Peanuts* comic strip. *Blah-blah-blah-blah-blah.* I remember hearing Sonterra say, "About seventeen weeks."

I was given the requisite disposable garb, whisked to an examining room, checked over, and soon proclaimed to be disgustingly healthy, if a little the worse for wear. When the medicos were through with me, I stretched out on a couch in the lobby and went to sleep. A delayed reaction to stress, I guess.

When I opened my eyes again, Sonterra was leaning over me, sprouting a seriously attractive five o'clock shadow, and grinning. "You know," he said, "you'd make one hell of a cop."

"Is Suzie all right?"

The grin faded. "She's alive, Clare. That's what matters."

I sat up and clutched at his arm, probably left a few scratches in his flesh. "Tell me the part you're holding back!"

"She's catatonic."

I closed my eyes. "Dear God."

"Suzie is *safe*—that's the important thing. She's being treated, and her dad and stepmother are with her."

I tightened my grasp on Sonterra's arm as another thought rose out of the fog in my brain to slam me. "Bobby Ray—or whoever took her—might think she can talk, give him away—we could have been followed—"

Sonterra smoothed my hair back, helped me stand. "Easy," he said. "There's a guard outside Suzie's door. Nobody's going to get to her. I promise you, Clare. *Nobody is going to hurt her.*"

I bit my lower lip, wanting desperately to believe him.

"Meanwhile, the State Police are all over the Palm Palace, looking for any trace of the desk clerk, the perps, or the shooters. If they find anything, they'll let us know."

"I want to go home," I said.

"Me, too," Sonterra agreed. The grin was back. "Just out of curiosity, what part of 'stay in the car' did you not understand?"

I sighed, aggrieved. "Are you going to start ragging on me about that—now, after all that's happened?"

"No," he answered, his arm still around me as we crossed the lobby and stepped out into the cool twilight, "but it's on the calendar."

"It's a good thing I didn't do what you told me," I argued, ever the lawyer. Sonterra's car was still in the ambulance bay. "At the rate you were going, you'd never have found Suzie. And didn't you just say I'd make a good cop?"

Sonterra unlocked the SUV and helped me into the passenger seat. "I got carried away."

I waited until he came around and got behind the wheel. "I'm glad you weren't shot," I told him.

He grinned wearily. "Well, thanks for that, anyway. I'm glad I wasn't shot, too, and even gladder that *you* weren't."

We headed for our place in Dry Creek, land of the free, home of the bones. Both emotionally exhausted, we didn't talk much on the way.

Special Agent Timmons, Loretta, and Emma were all seated around the kitchen table, when we came through the back door, finally home. Timmons looked like the head of a war council.

Emma and Loretta took one look at me and simultaneously leaped to their feet.

"What happened?" Loretta demanded, rushing to take my arm. She looked well, for someone who had been visiting her cheating husband in a federal holding cell.

"I see you got an earlier flight," I said.

Loretta sighed. "What *happened?*" she asked again.

"It's a long story," I answered. I met Special Agent Timmons's inscrutable gaze. "We found Suzie, though."

"You're wearing hospital clothes," Emma said worriedly.

I looked down at my scrubs, stuck for an answer.

"Look at you," Loretta said, steering me toward the back stairway. "You're on the ragged edge. You need to lie down for a little while and recharge your batteries."

The miasma of the Palm Palace was still with me. "I want a shower first."

"Stay with her," Sonterra told Loretta.

She did. That's the mark of a true friend. Somebody who will hose you down, put you in your pajamas, and tuck you into bed like a baby. Even more important, someone who knows you'll rally, and believes in your strength, not your weakness.

I slept like a dead woman.

NINETEEN

"I'm supposed to get married tomorrow," I told Loretta the next morning, in the sunny kitchen on Cemetery Lane. Emma was at school, Sonterra was working, and I'd given poor Esperanza the day off with pay. Wednesday night's archeological discovery in the basement had nearly done her in, and little wonder. I was still pretty shaken by it myself.

"If you don't manage to get yourself killed in the meantime," Loretta said. She'd arrived twenty minutes before, hiking over from the Wagon Wheel B&B, carrying a large shopping bag from Saks. Switching on the TV, she got Esperanza's Spanish soap opera and, thumbing the remote, scanned until she located the Food Channel.

I was about to snoop in the bag when the phone rang, and I leaped on it, expecting an update from Sonterra on the newest mess: Danielle Bickerhelm's disappearance. I was more concerned about Suzie, and I'd been calling the hospital at one-hour intervals since I woke up.

The answer was always the same. Condition critical, and unchanged.

"Hello?"

"Clare?" Big, booming voice. Eli Robeson.

I perked up. "Speaking."

"I hear you and Chief Sonterra found the little Post girl alive and got her out of a nasty situation. Good work."

I let out a sigh, staring out the window in the back door at the graveyard behind our house, remembering what it was like to see Micki's body lying there, naked and blue and bloody. "Thanks," I said. "But Suzie's not out of danger yet."

"I know," Robeson said kindly, "but she'd probably be gone by now if it weren't for the two of you."

Suzie was suffering from the effects of shock, severe dehydration, and exposure. I couldn't bear to imagine her dead, but maybe it wasn't such a bad thing that she was still unconscious. She'd have a lot to deal with when she woke up—her mother and Doc Holliday murdered, her own ordeal at the hands of her captors.

"I don't know how she's going to come back from this," I murmured, and caught Loretta watching me with concern. Behind her, a woman was chatting cheerfully on the TV screen and wrestling a lobster toward a pot of boiling water.

"Kids are resilient, Clare," Robeson said quietly.

I realized that my free hand was resting on my abdomen, shielding my unborn baby from a world where little girls were bound with duct tape and hidden in holes in the ground, and in seedy hotels, surrounded by the dregs of humanity. Where lobsters were tossed, flailing, into a simmering kettle.

"I'm afraid I haven't followed up on those case files you faxed over," I said.

"You've been a little busy," Robeson replied. "When Bobby Ray Lombard is apprehended—and he will be—I expect you to have a rock-solid case ready."

"I will," I told him.

Mercifully, Loretta turned to the Travel Channel, and I didn't have to watch the lobster die.

"Good," Eli said. "I'd like you to come in on Monday morning for the staff meeting. Nine sharp. Can you be here?" He paused. "If you're not going to be away on a honeymoon, that is."

"No honeymoon," I said. "Not right away, at least."

"We can expect you at the meeting then?"

"Yes."

"Good," Robeson answered. "Oh—before I hang up—I sent along a little wedding present. My wife specifically asked me to tell you that she had nothing to do with it." He chuckled.

I blinked, confused. I'd never met Mrs. Robeson. What kind of wedding gift would cause her to issue a disclaimer to a complete stranger? "Okay," I said warily.

"In the meantime, take care of yourself."

"I will," I promised, and we hung up. "What's in the bag?" I asked Loretta.

She smiled, evidently reassured by the return of my acquisitive side. "Open it and see," she said, setting aside the remote.

I plowed through the tissue paper and found a wedding veil inside, a gossamer creation spilling from a wreath of pink-and-white silk roses.

Loretta beamed. "I got you a dress, too," she said. "I left it at the B&B. Too bulky to carry over here on foot."

"You bought me a wedding gown?"

"I was afraid you'd show up for the ceremony in sweats and sneakers if I didn't," she joked. At least, I *thought* she was joking. "We'll have lunch at the Wagon Wheel, and then you can try it on."

I stared at her mutely.

Loretta's delight wavered visibly. "It's okay, isn't it? I mean, I know women usually pick out their own—"

I crossed the room and threw my arms around her. "Thank you," I blubbered.

Tentatively, Loretta hugged me. "Oh, Clare, you poor thing," she said. "You're positively on your last nerve."

I pulled back, sniffling inelegantly. "I'll be fine," I replied.

"Right," she said, looking unconvinced. "Go change. I won't be seen in public with a woman wearing her boyfriend's clothes."

I glanced down at Sonterra's boxers and muscle shirt, and laughed. God, it felt good to laugh, even a little bit.

I went upstairs, showered, and put on a pair of fat jeans and a loose blouse, pausing briefly to wonder if Loretta had had the foresight to buy a wedding dress with an elastic waistband. I wasn't huge, but I was expanding pretty rapidly. If she'd grabbed my usual size eight off the rack, we were in trouble.

We took the Hummer. Loretta's Lexus was ready to be sprung from the body shop in Tucson, but no one had had time to retrieve it. She'd used a car service to get from the airport to Dry Creek.

As we passed Danielle's house, I slowed. No police tape.

Loretta had never met Ms. Bickerhelm, so I filled her in, finishing with, "I know her from somewhere. I can't remember, and when I have time to think about it, it drives me crazy."

"High school?"

I shook my head.

"Maybe you were in the same foster home," Loretta speculated.

Something clicked, deep down. I'd been in at least a dozen of those, and the names and faces ran together, but I knew I'd never encountered anyone called Danielle while I was in the system, and said so.

"She could have changed her name, Clare," Loretta pointed out.

Duh. I hadn't even thought of that.

I went out of my way to drive past the antique shop. Open for business and packed, as usual.

All through the soup-and-salad special at the Wagon Wheel, I riffled through mental files, searching for anyone who even vaguely resembled Danielle.

Zip.

Loretta picked up the lunch check—I wasn't supposed to notice, but I think she held her breath until her credit card went through—and we headed for her casita, and the waiting wedding gown.

"I got it for half price," Loretta said proudly, pulling a cloud of ivory taffeta from the huge dress box waiting on the bed. A faint, nervous blush suffused her perfect complexion. "It's a twelve, but I thought we could baste it."

I let her off the hook, but knew she'd deliberately chosen a larger size. She was trying to be diplomatic, and I couldn't fault her for that. "It's beautiful," I said, and I meant it. "Do we have time for the alterations? The wedding is tomorrow."

"Of course we do. I used to sew, before I got rich. Try it on."

I did.

Thank God it needed to be taken in.

When we got home, there was a package waiting on the front porch, propped against the screen door. I was wary of explosive devices until I remembered that Eli Robeson had mentioned a wedding gift. Sure enough, the name and return address in the upper-left-hand corner were his.

Inside the house, Loretta and I greeted the dogs, and I opened Robeson's package. It was elegantly wrapped, the card signed with warm regards.

I tore open the box, raised the lid, and laughed out loud.

"What is it?" Loretta asked. She'd been occupied with the wedding dress, shaking it out and hanging it in the coat closet next to the front door.

I held up a Kevlar vest.

The expression on Loretta's face told me she didn't get it.

"Bulletproof," I explained.

Life has a funny way of hinting at future events.

One of these days, I'm going to start paying attention.

Loretta and I were trying to cook when Emma came in from school that afternoon. With the lobster's cruel demise a thing of the past, we'd tuned in to the Food Channel again, and we were whipping up something called Easy Beef Surprise.

It was going to be a surprise, all right, and Sonterra was the most likely victim.

Emma took one look at us and burst out laughing. "Whatever that stuff is, I'm not having any," she announced, craning her neck to peer into our mixing bowls from a safe distance. "It looks radioactive."

"A little moral support, please," Loretta said with a twinkle. "I'm poor now, and I have to learn to cook."

My niece set aside her schoolbooks and turned a wry gaze on me. "What's *your* excuse?" she asked.

"Prewedding jitters," I answered, and I was only half-kidding.

Emma opened the refrigerator and peered in. The pickings had been better since Esperanza had signed on, and she copped some rice pudding and a few slices of American cheese. "I figured you'd use the bones in the basement as an excuse to postpone the ceremony," she said mildly. Eli's Kevlar vest was still on the table, in its fancy gift box, and my niece paused to admire it. "Sweet," she said, in a tone some teenagers would reserve for cashmere. "Can I try it on?"

"Be my guest," I said. The woman on the Food Channel had gone on without us, and now Loretta and I were in culinary no-woman's-land.

"We could log on to the Web site," Loretta suggested. "Print out the recipe and fill in the gap."

"Just add sawdust," Emma put in.

Resigned, and a little relieved, I set my bowl down on the floor for Waldo and Bernice. Waldo took a sniff and backed off like a bomb-dog scenting nitroglycerin. Bernice took his word for it and wouldn't go near the stuff, either.

Observing, Emma laughed again and unwrapped a piece of cheese for each of them. "You'd think they'd been trained at CDC headquarters," she said. "Biohazard division."

"Very funny," I replied, but I couldn't help grinning a little.

Loretta looked disappointed. I think she seriously thought she would starve to death if she didn't learn to whip up an Easy Beef Surprise.

I patted her back. "Don't sweat it," I said. "I'll go online and get the recipe for you right now."

My friend sighed again and shook her head. "It's probably

not edible," she said. "I don't think we were supposed to put in a whole box of baking soda. That was for soaking the pan afterward."

Emma snickered into her pudding cup.

"Just for that," I told my niece, putting a consoling arm around Loretta's slightly slumped shoulders, "we're tuning in to the next episode."

"Oh, great," Emma said. "Is there any ipecac?"

Loretta giggled, then refocused on the TV, squinting. "That looks like some kind of chicken dish. Do we have chicken?"

Sonterra dragged in just about suppertime and eyed the supermarket pizza boxes waiting on the table with good-natured disdain.

Loretta and I played cards, working around the delivery cartons, while Emma stood at the counter, chopping vegetables for a salad. I knew she'd caught the expression on Sonterra's face when she said, "Look on the bright side. The Chicken De-light didn't turn out any better than the Easy Beef Surprise."

Sonterra looked momentarily mystified and crossed the room to lean down and kiss the top of my head. "Don't play the jack," he said.

I threw in my cards and gave him a look of mock-exasperation.

"What's the deal with Danielle Bickerhelm's disappearance?" I asked when he went to the fridge and helped himself to a beer—like Emma's after-school snack, the six-pack was there by the grace of Esperanza.

"We're looking into alien abduction," he answered, and tipped the beer can.

Danielle and I wouldn't be turning out an Easy Beef Surprise together anytime soon, but I *was* concerned that she was missing.

"You could show a little more concern," I pointed out.

Sonterra sighed. "I stopped by the hospital to visit Suzie this afternoon," he said. "She's coming around, but she hasn't said a word. When I asked her if Lombard was the one who kidnapped her, she turned her face into the pillow."

"Sounds like a yes to me," Emma said, scraping a colorful pile of veggies off the cutting board and into the salad bowl.

"Has it occurred to you that Lombard might have snatched Danielle?" I asked Sonterra.

He widened his eyes at me. "Gosh, *no,*" he said, plucking a piece of green pepper from the salad bowl and munching. That was when he spotted the vest. "Whose Kevlar?"

"Mine," I answered. "Eli Robeson sent it as a wedding present."

Loretta brightened, abandoned the game of solitaire she'd begun after I folded, and rushed out of the room. It must have been the word "wedding."

"What's up with her?" Sonterra asked.

"She's poor now," Emma said. "And desperate enough to cook."

"God help us," Sonterra remarked, still admiring the vest.

Loretta burst in with the wedding dress. "It's a size twelve," she announced, "but we're going to take it in."

Sonterra's mouth twitched upward at one corner. "Tomorrow's the day," he said, watching me. "Did I tell you Eddie's coming? He won't look all that great in the pictures, but he's up for best-man duty. Riding down with *mi familia.*"

Okay, so I was a little slack on the logistics. I'd been busy.

I jumped to my feet in a fit of panic. Shanda and Mrs. K were planning to attend as well. "Where are we going to put all these people?"

"Relax," Loretta said. "They can stay at the ranch."

I sagged into the chair again.

"Darn," Sonterra teased, his eyes laughing. "Now we can't postpone."

The phone rang. Sonterra sighed again and grabbed the receiver since he was the closest.

"Sonterra," he said.

So predictable.

He frowned as he listened. "Sure," he told the caller. "No, no—it's no problem. I'll be there in a few minutes."

"Who was that?" I asked. So *predictable,* taunted the voice in my head.

"Father Morales," Sonterra answered, still frowning.

"Is something wrong?"

"I don't know," Sonterra said, heading for the door again. "He said he wants to talk. Probably something to do with the wedding."

"Then maybe I should go, too."

"Or not," Sonterra answered, and went out.

TWENTY

About an hour later, when Sonterra got back from St. Swithin's, I was standing on the coffee table with my arms outstretched like a scarecrow, while Loretta pinned and stitched the hem of old size 12. To look at her, you'd have thought she knew what she was doing, but I had tiny holes in my sides to prove she'd been exaggerating her sewing skills.

"It's bad luck for you to see the bride in her dress before the ceremony," Loretta put in, only to be ignored.

"So did Father Morales talk you out of getting married?" I asked Sonterra.

He looked thoughtful. "No," he said, giving me a puzzled once-over, like he'd never run across a woman perched on a coffee table in an inside-out wedding dress before.

"Well, what did he want, then?"

"Could you please stop being a lawyer for five minutes?"

"Sure," I answered. "If you'll stop being a cop."

Loretta looked up at me, rolled her eyes, and stabbed me in the ankle. I'm not sure, but I think she did it on purpose.

Sonterra took in the dress again, in a long, rueful sweep, and shook his head. "Did you leave enough room for the Kevlar?" he asked Loretta.

I put my hands on my hips. "Sonterra."

He sighed once more, ran a hand through his hair. "It was weird. He seemed so anxious on the phone, but when I got there, he was all smiles and took me on a tour of the place. Showed me the back room, where they used to hold bingo games before the American Legion got blackout and ruined their action."

"Maybe he's trying to get you to join the Knights of Columbus or something," Loretta offered. "Launch a campaign to take back bingo. Do the Knights of Columbus do that sort of thing?"

Sonterra looked at her as if she'd just volunteered to throw together a batch of Chicken De-light and serve it to people on liquid diets.

"Just trying to help," she said lightly, and stabbed me again.

I flinched. "That *is* weird," I agreed, albeit belatedly.

Sonterra was still staring at Loretta. "If you can't afford your medication," he said, "I'll be glad to float you a loan."

"*Sonterra,*" I repeated.

"Stand still," Loretta said, unperturbed.

Sonterra scanned the room. "Where's Emma?"

"Upstairs, doing her homework," I answered, watching him the way he'd watched Loretta a few moments before. "Sonterra, what's the matter with you?"

"I don't know," he said. "The whole thing with Father Morales—"

I was concerned, and not just about Father Morales. Sonterra had been up to his armpits in dead bodies ever since we arrived in Dry Creek, and he'd stayed relatively cool. Now he was oddly jumpy.

"Are you finished, Loretta?" I asked.

"I can take a hint," she said.

"I'll drive you back to the Wagon Wheel," Sonterra told her.

I put a hand on Loretta's shoulder for support and stepped down off the coffee table. "I'll do it," I said.

For a moment, it seemed that Sonterra would put up an argument, but in the end, he didn't. "Is there any of that pizza left?" he asked.

"I hope that isn't a reference to the size of my wedding dress," I responded.

Sonterra crossed himself, à la Esperanza, and ducked into the kitchen.

"You don't have to leave," I told Loretta. "You can sleep on the couch."

"Whoop-de-do," Loretta said.

I went upstairs, exchanged my wedding gown for fresh sweats, came back down again, with the dress over my arm, and drove my best friend to the Wagon Wheel.

"Thanks, Loretta," I told her, pulling up in front of her casita. It looked lonely and very small, huddled there in the dark.

She gathered the gown from the backseat, game for a long night of stitching. "For what?"

"For buying the dress. For trying to cook. For not hitting Sonterra over the head with the nearest blunt object when he made the crack about medication."

She grinned. "See you in the morning," she said, and climbed out of the Hummer. "You're going to make a wonderful bride, Clare."

I teared up again. Maybe it was the pregnancy. Maybe it was the stress of my daily life. Maybe it was the narrow escape from Easy Beef Surprise.

I waited until Loretta was safely inside the casita, then zoomed back to the house on Cemetery Lane.

I should have marked that day on the calendar.

Nobody called to report a body.

Nobody shot at me or tried to run me off the road.

Nobody uncovered a cache of skeletons anywhere on the property.

Red-letter, for sure.

Sonterra was in bed when I got upstairs, reading a battered Dean Koontz paperback. He gave me a tilted grin.

"You'd look better without those sweats," he said.

I pushed the door shut, kicked off my sneakers, and stripped.

All Sonterra did was look at me, but by the time I dived into bed with him, I was hot as a flea-market pistol.

Sonterra rolled on top of me, resting on his forearms. Nibbled at my lower lip. "Last night for illicit sex," he drawled. "This time tomorrow, we'll be an old married couple."

"This time tomorrow," I said, punctuating the sentence with a little whimper when he slid a hand between my legs, "we'll be doing exactly what we're doing right now."

Sonterra slid down far enough to tongue my right nipple to rigid attention. "We might be doing this—" He kissed his way along my sternum, to my belly. "Or this—" He parted my thighs and slipped under the covers. "Or this."

I bit back a yelp of passion and gripped the headboard with both hands.

Sonterra teased. He tasted. And when I lost control, he reached up and covered my mouth with one palm while I bucked against his mouth.

I'd no sooner recovered from that orgasm when he was inside me, and driving me steadily toward another one. And another.

Like I said. Red-letter day.

The next day would be redder, for a whole different reason.

Loretta hoofed it over from the B&B around 9:00 A.M., bringing the dress. There were a few last-minute alterations, involving pins and the inevitable puncture wounds. Then Mrs. K arrived, with Shanda and a shy, good-looking young man named Lamont. Alex Sonterra, his wife, Alberta, and Eddie got there soon after that; Sonterra's brother, sisters, and aunts were still en route.

Eddie was still bruised, but mobile. Sonterra was in his element, with his former partner *and* his dad and stepmother seated around the kitchen table, drinking coffee and catching up.

"Lamont's majoring in systems analysis," Shanda confided to Loretta and me, in the living room, where I was enduring the final fitting. By then, her boyfriend had joined the other group. "I like him a lot."

Mrs. K seemed to look through us all, rather than at us, but she was in a good mood. "Ghosts everywhere," she commented cheerfully. "I've never seen so many in one place."

"They probably belong to the bones," Emma commented as she came down the front stairway. Her faithful canine companions, fresh from the backyard, ran to meet her. Judging by my niece's tone and manner, one would have thought the conversation was entirely normal.

Ever the trouper, Mrs. K shook off the semitrance. "I could use a drink," she announced. "Anything alcoholic."

Shanda gave a shudder, and I knew it had nothing to do with Mrs. K's request for booze at that hour of the morning. "Skeletons in the basement," she marveled, hugging herself and making her eyes big. "That is such a *Clare* thing to happen."

"So how's the online auction business going?" Emma asked. "And how's the boyfriend?"

Shanda smiled at her, then glanced at me. "I'm not spending a lot of time on the eBay thing," she said. "I always get my work for you done first."

"I know you do," I told her, grinning. "Tell us more about Lamont."

"Some people," Loretta put in, "would be more concerned about the ghosts."

Shanda was still on the Lamont link. She wet her thumb, struck the air with a long stroke, and made an eloquent hissing sound.

"Hot," she said.

"Awesome," Emma said.

"Dozens of them," Mrs. K remarked lightly. "They're everywhere. How am I supposed to get a bead on the wedding with all these spirits blocking my view?"

I patted her shoulder. "I'll get you that drink," I said. All I had to offer was some of Sonterra's beer. "It'll steady your nerves."

When the day was over, we'd all want to swill the stuff.

TWENTY-ONE

St. Swithin's was jammed with Sonterra's relatives, my brave little band of friends, and a number of curiosity-seekers bold enough to crash the party. Loretta and Emma were bridesmaids—Loretta in a smart blue suit, Emma in a red sundress. There were flowers, thanks to Father Morales's secretary, but alas, no wedding cake and no photographer.

I simply hadn't thought that far ahead.

Sonterra's stepmother, Alberta, made an impromptu dash from the church to the nearest convenience store for a bag full of throwaway cameras, and Shanda called the supermarket on her cell phone to order up a couple of sheet cakes, promising to collect them after the ceremony. I heard her say she'd take anything they had sitting around.

I stood just inside the main entrance, next to Alex Sonterra, who was giving me away, perspiring in my altered size 12, my gaze fixed straight ahead. Father Morales was sweating, too.

Organ music swelled, seeming to push at the very walls.

Emma started up the aisle at a nudge from Loretta, who followed a few moments later. Sonterra looked more than handsome, standing up there in his wedding getup, with Eddie flanking him as co–best man, along with his older brother, Mike.

At a nod from Father Morales, Alex and I started up the aisle.

I flashed on my scary wedding dream, imagined myself standing up there at the altar, Sonterra lifting the veil, my head replaced by a bare skull.

I shivered, and Alex patted my hand.

I locked eyeballs with Sonterra, and felt a slight tugging sensation deep inside, as though an invisible string stretched between us, and he was pulling on the other end.

I kept going, but the floor felt strangely soft beneath my feet, and my head was spinning.

We made it to the front, and I let out the breath I hadn't realized I was holding.

"Who giveth this woman to be married?" Father Morales asked.

Alex replied, "I do," and stepped back to join his wife and Sonterra's beaming sisters and elderly aunts in the front pew.

The priest, his face glistening, his dark gaze darting periodically around the sanctuary, opened his book, and the ceremony began.

I spoke, as prompted, though Emma had to elbow me a couple of times. The whole thing was going off without a hitch, so I shouldn't have been nervous.

"I now pronounce you man and wife," Father Morales said, at long last, and smiled nervously. "You may kiss the bride."

Sonterra turned to face me, lifted the veil, and winked down at me before planting a smacker on my mouth.

Cheers erupted. The organ piped up again, and flashbulbs went off all over the place. Father Morales stepped between us, smiling for the throwaway cameras Alberta Sonterra had supplied, and that was when it happened.

I heard a sharp *pop,* and Father Morales dropped, folding slowly to his knees, then pitching forward down the altar steps.

"Everybody down!" Sonterra yelled, tackling me and managing to take Emma to the floor in the same move.

Screams of panic echoed off the walls. Out of the corner of my eye, I saw blood spreading around Morales's head.

"Stay here!" Sonterra rasped, and rolled off me to run down

the aisle, with Eddie right behind him. Special Agent Timmons walked the full length of a pew, jumped into the aisle, and dashed after them.

Still prone, I groped for Emma's hand, then Loretta's.

Outside, tires squealed on dry asphalt.

"Are you both all right?" I asked.

My bewildered bridesmaids murmured insensibly, clearly stunned, but unharmed as far as I could tell.

Alex low-crawled to Father Morales, turned him over. The bullet had struck him in the forehead, and his eyes were open wide, staring toward heaven.

More squealing of tires. Sonterra, Eddie, and Special Agent Timmons, chasing the shooter, no doubt.

I'm not Catholic, but I crossed myself as I sat up. The skirt of my wedding dress was blood-spattered; I felt the sticky wetness against my legs, and it was all I could do not to rip the thing off in revulsion, then and there.

Sonterra's brother was on a cell phone, calling for an ambulance.

Deputy Dave lumbered up the aisle, crouched beside Father Morales, opposite Alex. I wondered distractedly where he'd been sitting; I hadn't noticed him when I swept the assembly, coming up the aisle. "Police," Dave explained glumly, at Alex's questioning glance. "Looks like the padre is a goner."

My father-in-law's jaw tightened, and I was struck, once again, by the family resemblance. In twenty years, Sonterra would look just like dear old dad. I decided I could live with that.

"You could put it that way, yes," he said.

I got to my feet, but the floor had gone spongy again, and Emma took a quick, firm grip on my arm. Held me up until she was sure I could stand on my own.

I looked out over the crowd, most of them just rising from beneath and behind the heavy wooden pews. Somebody snapped another picture, and I blanked, as dazed as if the flash had gone off an inch from my nose.

"Is anyone hurt?" I asked when I'd recovered.

"If it hadn't been for those damn ghosts clogging up the channels," Mrs. K complained, rising from the floor and dusting herself off, "I would have foreseen this and warned you."

I stepped closer, put an arm around her. "It's all right," I said.

She looked down at Father Morales. Shook her head sadly.

Deputy Dave finally went into cop-mode. "Did anybody see the gunman?" he thundered, surveying the gathering.

Everyone looked blank, which was answer enough.

Shanda, breaking out of Lamont's protective embrace, hurried up to me. "We've got to get you out of here, Clare," she said. "Whoever fired that shot might have been after you, and there's no telling if they'll try again."

I didn't think there was any real danger of that. The shooter would be too busy trying to elude Sonterra and his sidekicks to do anything as fancy as doubling back.

Alex remained by Father Morales's side, and Alberta came to join him, but she was watching me. Sonterra's siblings attended to the aunts, who were understandably shaken. "Clare, your friend is right," the elder Mrs. Sonterra said. "You might not be safe here."

I looked down at poor Father Morales.

No safe places, I thought.

"I want to stay until they take him away," I said. "It wouldn't be right to leave him—"

Alex raised his gaze to my face. "Go," he said. "You must think of the child now, Clare. I will wait with Father."

And so it was that I left the church as a married woman, with my gown soaked with blood and my groom off chasing an armed killer.

Loretta had driven Emma, Shanda, Mrs. K, and me to the church in the Hummer, before the ceremony, while Sonterra, Eddie, and Lamont brought the SUV, and the Sonterra clan traveled in their own vehicles. My all-female entourage and I piled into my rig, though this time, Shanda drove.

Lamont had decided to stay behind with Alex and some of the other men.

The house filled up fast with murmuring wedding guests. We hadn't planned a formal reception, but people tend to go into huddles after an experience like the one we'd just shared.

Shanda followed me upstairs and helped me out of the ruined wedding gown. I showered and put on a nubby bathrobe with a zipper up the front. I couldn't seem to get warm.

Loretta was serving coffee as fast as the pot would brew it, and somebody had made a run to the supermarket to fetch the cakes Shanda ordered earlier. One of them had "Happy Birthday, Hernando" written across the top in hot pink icing.

"Maybe we should cook something," Loretta whispered.

"These people have been through enough trauma for one day," Emma put in, studying the hodgepodge of cakes. "Who's Hernando?"

"I don't know," Loretta said. "But they must have canceled his birthday."

I thought sadly of Father Morales. His next birthday had been canceled, too, along with any others he might have had coming to him.

The all-too-familiar wail of sirens sounded in the distance. The State Police, I presumed, along with paramedics and a contingent from Tucson PD.

Dry Creek was getting to be a regular hotbed of crime.

Despite the piles of presents on the dining room table, the gathering felt more like a wake than an impromptu wedding reception. Guests, many of them townspeople we were just getting to know, sought me out, offering hugs and condolences, and I wandered aimlessly from one part of the house to another, unable to stand still.

I was back in the crowded kitchen when Sonterra appeared, with Eddie and Timmons. I knew by their faces that they'd lost the shooter. Dry Creek is a small town, but there are a lot of places to hide.

Sonterra weaved his way between guests to reach me. Drew me close. "I'm sorry, Babe," he whispered, close to my ear. "This is some wedding day."

I nodded against his shoulder, letting myself cling a little. Then I drew back far enough to look up into his eyes. "Did you get a look at the gunman?"

Sonterra shook his head. "He was driving an old GMC pickup, though. Red. Lots of rust. He was just rounding the corner by the time we got the SUV rolling. No sign of him anywhere, which means he's probably holed up in a garage somewhere. I radioed the State Police to put up roadblocks on both ends of town, and I'd like to think we've got him sewed up, but he could have ditched the truck and headed for the desert on foot."

It took me a couple of beats to catch up. "Do you think it could be the same guy who ran me off the road that night?"

Sonterra nodded. "It's possible. I stopped by the station for a look at the paint-chip reports. They jibe with the truck we saw."

"What are you going to do now?"

"Work," he said. He kissed the tip of my nose. "You'll be okay?"

I swallowed, nodded. I wasn't scared for myself, but I didn't like the idea of Sonterra out there doing a door-to-door search, and maybe coming face-to-face with a firearm.

"I'll make this up to you somehow," he said, and tried to smile. Then he gave me a chaste kiss and went upstairs to change out of his suit. When he left the house, Eddie and Special Agent Timmons went with him.

Presently, Alex and the rest of the family arrived on the scene. Alex looked strained, and there were blood spatters on his pant legs. Someone brought his suitcase in from the car and, after a shower, he came downstairs in jeans and a white cotton shirt, open at the throat.

"My son is out chasing a madman on his wedding day," he lamented, when we got a chance to talk. "He should be here, with his wife."

"It's his job," I said gently.

"He needs a different job," Alex maintained. "Tonio could have worked with Mike and me, in the landscaping business. It's a good life. But oh, no. *He* has to be a cop."

"He'll be all right," I insisted.

"Will he?" Alex asked.

"We have to believe he will." ·

Alex kissed my forehead. "I'm very sorry that your wedding day turned out like this, Clare Sonterra."

Clare Sonterra.

I liked the sound of that, though it would take some getting used to. "At least your son finally made an honest woman out of me."

Alex smiled. "You were *always* an honest woman," he said. Then we both began to circulate again. I felt like a fish swimming against the current.

After another hour or so of excruciating small talk and the expected isn't-it-awfuls, the crowd began to dwindle, and I was grateful for that. In the end, it all came down to Shanda and Lamont, Mrs. K, Emma, Loretta, and me. Even Alex and the rest of the Sonterra bunch made their excuses and headed home to Phoenix. There's nothing like a murder to spoil a celebration.

The rest of us gathered around the kitchen table, and what was left of Hernando's birthday cake, and Mrs. K brought out her well-worn tarot deck, always somewhere on her person, and began to shuffle.

It was disconcerting, somehow, even though I'd seen her do it any number of times before.

Nobody batted an eye when she threw the Death card.

Then she tossed the Three of Pentacles after it. I blinked. The card showed two people in medieval dress, faces upturned to a third person, standing on a platform or bench. An ornate cathedral window showed clearly in the background.

"The gunman was *inside* the church," Mrs. K said flatly, after studying the card for a while. "And he had two accomplices."

"He must have stepped through the door, fired, and run out again," Loretta concluded. "I remember hearing his tires screech."

Mrs. K shook her head very slowly, and her gaze moved from one face to the next until it locked onto mine. "That was a distraction. He—or she—was *already inside*. Another person was driving the truck."

"But someone would have seen him!" I protested. What had happened to Father Morales was terrible. The idea that the killer might have been sitting among the guests through the whole ceremony, just waiting for his chance, only made it worse. Who was he, and who were his partners in crime?

"There's the choir room, and that hallway leading to the restrooms," Loretta recalled. "The shooter could have been lurking there and blended in when everybody dived for the floor. There was a lot of confusion." She paused. "Anyway, once they figure out the trajectory, they'll know where he was standing when he pulled the trigger."

I flashed on Deputy Dave, back at the church. It had seemed then that he'd appeared out of nowhere. He'd abused his children, and almost certainly his wife, and there was no love lost between him and Sonterra, but now that I'd gone over the incident a hundred times in my mind, I knew neither Sonterra nor I had been the target. The hit was too precise for that.

Father Morales had been the intended victim all along. But why?

What possible reason could Dave Rathburn have had for killing him?

He'd been a very kind man, beloved in the community. What possible reason could *anyone* have had for ending his life that way?

Mrs. K's hands shook a little as she put her cards away. "I'm not feeling well," she said, without looking at anyone in particular. "I need to go home."

"I thought you were going to spend tonight at the ranch," Loretta said.

"I need to go home," Mrs. K repeated. "Right now."

Shanda and Lamont exchanged glances.

"I'll drive," Lamont said.

I scraped back my chair, worried about Mrs. K. I'd never seen her quite so upset before. Now that I really looked at her, I realized that she'd aged ten years since morning, and there was a frightening, bluish tinge to her lips.

I took her arm and led her into the dining room. "Are you all right, Mrs. K?" I asked, clasping both her hands.

She looked at me, blinked. "Have you seen her?" she asked, in a strange tone, with no inflection at all.

"Seen who?"

"The apparition. The second Clare."

"No," I said. "Not since that night at Loretta's."

"You didn't see yourself wearing a wedding dress? You're absolutely sure?"

"No," I repeated, even more worried than before.

"This is a warning," Mrs. K whispered, staring at me as though I were opaque, reflecting her own image back to her. "She must have been trying to prepare you for the incident on the road, when you saw her before." She considered that, then shook her head, but in the next instant, she seemed herself again. She was focused, and in deadly earnest. "Clare, listen to me, for your baby's sake and for your own. Something terrible is going to happen if you stay in this town. It's an evil place—"

I cupped her papery cheeks in my hands. Her skin felt hot against my palms. "I promise I will be careful," I said slowly, and as gently as I could. "That has to be good enough, Mrs. K. I can't run away. I *won't* run away."

Tears shimmered in her eyes. "I know," she said with resignation and real despair. "There are times when I wish you were a coward, and this is one of them."

I kissed her forehead. Mrs. K was like a mother to me, and I loved her dearly. "Trouble has a way of sticking to my heels until I face it head-on. There's really no other option."

She nodded sorrowfully, pulled a hankie out of her skirt pocket, and dabbed at her eyes. I hugged her.

I felt a deep sadness when she left with Shanda and Lamont.

"That woman needs psychiatric treatment," Loretta said when they were gone. "Ghosts. Death cards. Killers hiding in churches—"

Emma opened the freezer door, took out three TV dinners, and glanced at the instructions. "Mrs. K is stone sane," she remarked, almost idly. "If she says the killer was in the church all along, then he was."

Loretta shuddered. "If I hadn't sworn off liquor," she said, "I'd ask for a martini right about now."

I patted her shoulder. "I'll make tea."

My best friend stared at me. "How can you be so calm? This is your *wedding day*. The priest gets blown away, right in front of you—"

Emma put down the TV dinners, crossed to Loretta, laid hands on her shoulders, and pressed her into a chair at the table. "Chill," she said. "You're going off the deep end."

Loretta buried her face in her hands.

I filled the teakettle, plugged it in, and got out cups and tea bags. The truth was, I was as shaken as Loretta, but I figured I could hold off the creepy-crawlies if I kept myself occupied.

"How can you sleep in this place?" Loretta asked.

I assumed she was referring to Mrs. K's ghosts. "They were here first," I said reasonably. "Anyway, they'll probably move on, now that the bones are on the winding forensic route to eternal peace."

"Maybe we should hide out at the ranch," Loretta said, looking at me oddly. I think she was wondering if I'd finally gone around the metaphysical bend.

I shook my head firmly. "I'll tell you what I told Mrs. K. Nobody—and I mean nobody—is going to scare me off."

"You're too brave for your own good," Loretta argued.

"Maybe," I agreed. "But I'm not going anywhere."

Emma took one of the TV dinners out of its carton, popped it into the microwave, and dropped a bomb. "I think Father Morales knew something was going to happen."

Loretta looked confused. "What?"

Emma glanced at me, then turned to set the timer on the microwave and push the START button. "He was sweating like a pig," she reflected. "Am I the only one who noticed that?"

"No," I admitted, leaning back against the counter and folding my arms while I waited for the kettle to boil. "I saw it, too." My mind went into rewind, past the wedding, past last night's hot sex with Sonterra, to the point where he came home from St. Swithin's. He'd gone there at Father Morales's request, I remembered, and been puzzled when he got to the church because the priest gave him a tour and made small talk.

It was weird, he'd said.

I saw that Loretta had caught on, too. Her eyes went wide, and her mouth dropped open. *"Last night,"* she said. "When I was altering your wedding dress, and Tony was in such an odd mood."

"Maybe Father Morales wanted to tell Tony something important, or ask for help," Emma pondered, after we brought her up to speed, still hovering next to the microwave. "Then—who knows why—he lost his nerve."

"You know what else I just realized?" I asked, pushing away from the counter. "Esperanza wasn't at the wedding. She was looking forward to it. Why didn't she show up?"

"Maybe we should ask her," Emma suggested. The microwave dinged, and she removed the tray. "Who wants lasagna? The other two are meat loaf and"—she examined the third carton—"Swiss steak."

Loretta opted for the lasagna, and Emma brought it to her, along with silverware and a paper napkin.

"*We* aren't going to ask Esperanza anything," I decided, looking around for the keys to the Hummer. "She'll be scared to death if we all show up on her doorstep at this hour."

"You're not going alone," Loretta said.

"Freakin' A," Emma agreed. "Swiss steak or meat loaf? And don't say you're not hungry. You haven't eaten anything since breakfast."

"Meat loaf," I said, resigned.

After we'd eaten, Loretta, Emma, and I fired up the Hummer and headed for the Hidy Tidy. Esperanza's place was dark.

"She might be pretending she's not home," I speculated, and

got out of the rig. There was a slight nip in the air, and I wished I'd worn a coat.

Loretta and Emma hurried after me.

"Tony would be pissed if he knew we were here," Emma said.

"He's resilient," I answered, and mounted the porch steps to knock on the door. "Besides, he *doesn't* know."

I knocked a second time.

Nothing.

"Esperanza," I called. "I know you're in there."

The curtain covering the little window in the door fluttered.

"I'm not leaving until you talk to me," I added.

The latch snapped, and the door opened. Esperanza peered around the edge. "I have to quit, Mrs. Clare," she said in an agitated whisper.

"You know something about what happened to Father Morales," I said. It was no great deductive leap: There was only one Catholic church in town, and Morales had been Esperanza's priest and confidant. She'd mentioned speaking to him when she went to St. Swithin's to light candles and pray for Micki and Suzie, after Judy Holliday was murdered. "I need you to tell me what it is."

Esperanza glanced behind her, then faced me again, shaking her head. "I don't know anything," she insisted. "My sister, she is sick. In Mexico. I go back."

"Esperanza, Father Morales is *dead. Somebody murdered him.*" Morales could have known a little too much about the coyote operation. I was sure he wouldn't have gotten involved for the money, but he might have provided sanctuary for a few of the illegals, helped them get papers, jobs, places to stay.

Esperanza unhooked the chain and skulked out onto the porch, then stood there shivering. "This very dangerous, Mrs. Clare," she said, and there was a plea in her voice. "Please—you will leave it alone. We will *all* leave it alone."

I leaned in. "Read my lips, Esperanza," I said. "I'm not going anywhere until you give me the straight story."

Esperanza paled, and made the sign of the cross. "These are very bad people! They kill Father Morales, they kill me. Or my Maria. Or *you*. They don't care. Get in the way, they *kill*."

"*Who*, Esperanza? That's all I want to know. Give me names, and I'll go."

There was a long pause, and I thought I'd gotten through to her. But she turned, quick as a desert mouse bolting for its hole, and slipped inside the trailer. I grabbed for the door latch, but I was too slow. The lock engaged with a hard click.

"Great work, Clare," Emma said. "If you were going to do bad cop, you could at least have given me a chance to jump in with good cop."

"You're not *any* kind of cop, either of you," Loretta pointed out. "You're civilians, damn it!"

"I'm calling Sonterra," I said, ignoring Loretta, jamming a hand into my jacket pocket and raising my voice. "Do you hear me, Esperanza? I'm calling Chief Sonterra!"

It would have been a terrific plan if I hadn't left my cell phone at home.

"Maybe she really doesn't know anything," Loretta argued. "Let's get out of here." She looked across at Micki Post's trailer, and I followed her gaze. Crime-scene tape rippled forlornly in the chilly breeze. "This place gives me the willies."

"Give me your cell phone," I said.

"I don't have one anymore," Loretta replied, starting down the porch steps. "I'm cutting back on expenses."

"*Damn* it," I muttered.

"Tony's probably at St. Swithin's," Emma said, following Loretta. "Let's go find him."

It made more sense than standing there on Esperanza's porch, trying to wait her out. But Sonterra *wasn't* at St. Swithin's, unlike every other cop in Pima County.

We tried the station.

Deputy Dave sat behind Sonterra's desk, playing solitaire with a ragged deck. No sign of anybody else, and he didn't bother to get up when we came in.

"Do you know where the chief is?" I asked, putting a slight emphasis on the word "chief." Occupying Sonterra's space, in his absence, was a petty rebellion, the kind of passive-aggressive behavior people engage in when they don't have the guts to be direct.

I watched him narrowly, trying to decide if he could really have been the one to shoot Father Morales. Even with his nasty temper, it seemed hard to believe. He *was* a cop, after all, and as intense as my suspicions were, I had nothing substantial to go on.

"Out making the world safe for democracy, I guess," Dave said.

My dislike for him intensified. "I missed Madge at the wedding today," I told him, though in truth I hadn't realized she'd been absent until that moment. From my tone, you would have thought it had been an *ordinary* wedding, not a murder scene. I'd already thrown out the bloody dress, and it would be a long time before I opened any of the presents.

"She's sick," he said, without particular concern, frowning down at his cards in concentration.

"Maybe I'd better look in on her," I replied. "Make sure she's all right."

That got his attention. He lifted his head and gave me a narrow stare, and I saw that he knew what Madge had told me when I visited their house for supper the other night. And a chill ran down my spine, because he wasn't above taking it out on her. "Like I said, she's sick. It wouldn't do to disturb her."

I hated myself for the rigid smile I summoned up then. I was more inclined to spit in Deputy Dave's face, but if he went home and bounced Madge off the walls for spilling the family secrets, the responsibility would be partly mine.

"Okay," I said brightly. "Just give her my regards, then."

He mulled that over for a few moments, and I couldn't tell if I'd convinced him with my backpedaling or not. He slapped a queen of clubs down under a king of hearts.

"Will do," he said, without a hint of sincerity.

Loretta, Emma, and I trooped outside and piled into the Hummer.

"What now?" Loretta asked. I could tell she wanted me to say we'd call it a night. It was equally clear that she wasn't holding out any real hope that I would.

"Sonterra must be in the field somewhere," I said, backing out of our parking spot. "Which means we swing by the Rathburn place to give our best to Madge, then we park in front of Esperanza's trailer and wait."

"Cool," Emma enthused. "Surveillance!"

"Cool," Loretta echoed—without the enthusiasm.

Madge didn't answer the door, but I could see light between the drawn drapes, and her Camry was in the carport. She knew I was there, all right, and I had a pretty good idea what she was doing.

"Wait here," I told my fellow crime stoppers, and started down the steps, glancing back over one shoulder to make sure they stayed put.

"If Deputy Dave pulls in," I said, "get into the Hummer and lock the doors."

Emma tried to follow when I walked away, but Loretta caught her by the sleeve and held on.

"Be careful," my best friend called after me.

I went around the side of the house, and sure enough, Madge was hiding out on the patio, puffing away on a cigarette. In the light spilling from the kitchen, I saw that both her eyes were blackened.

She started when I appeared, and then let out a sigh, her shoulders slumping a little. I bit my lower lip to stem the torrent of sympathetic words pounding at the back of my throat and wedged my hands into the pockets of my windbreaker.

Madge blew out a long stream of smoke. "You shouldn't be here," she said calmly. A tiny smile crooked one corner of her mouth. "As you can see, it's a dangerous place."

"Dave did this to you?" It wasn't really a question.

She drew on her cigarette again, and in the red glow, I saw that her lip was split. "He didn't want me to go to the wedding," she said softly, and with a wistful note. "Was it nice?"

Was it nice?

"You haven't heard what happened?"

"I was—indisposed," Madge answered with another infinitesimal and slightly spooky smile.

"Father Morales was shot to death."

Madge's cigarette dropped to the patio stones, forgotten. *"What?"*

I took a step toward her. Put out a tentative hand, the way one might approach a wounded deer, taken by surprise on a twisty path through the deep woods. "You need to see a doctor, Madge. You may be badly hurt."

"I'll be all right."

"I don't think so," I argued gently. "Come with me. Please. Let's get you some help."

She shook her head. "There's no help," she replied. "No escape."

"That's what Micki said," I reasoned. "She could have gone to a shelter, but she wouldn't. And now she's dead."

"I envy her," Madge said.

I took her arm. "Don't say that."

"She's free."

The words were so hopeless, so full of resignation. Tiny, invisible ice cubes spilled down my spine. "We'll get you to a hospital," I said. "Then I'll call your sons to let them know where you are. Everything will be all right, Madge—I promise you that."

"Do you?"

"Clare?" It was Loretta. She stepped out of the darkness, stopped cold when she got a look at Madge's battered face. "Dear God," she breathed. "What happened?"

"Deputy Dave happened," I answered tersely. I tugged at Madge's arm. "Come on. We're out of here."

Loretta took Madge's other arm, and we hustled her around the house, through the gnome mob, and into the Hummer. Emma was already there, with the engine running.

"He'll stop us," Madge said, but she let Loretta and me hoist her into the backseat. "He knows everything that happens in this town."

Loretta climbed in next to Madge, buckled them both up, and put a protective arm around the older woman's shoulders. "Let him try getting in our way," she said.

Emma scrambled over the console to batten down on the passenger side, and I took the wheel. "I'm calling Tony," my niece said, studying the GPD buttons on the dashboard. One of them functioned as a phone, and I had no clue how to operate the system, but Emma would probably figure it out.

"Go ahead," I answered, and pointed the Hummer toward Tucson. "Tell him to bust Dave Rathburn on assault charges—and have his hands checked for powder residue."

Madge leaned forward, clasped my shoulder hard enough to leave marks. "Don't mess with him, Clare," she pleaded. "You have no idea—"

"I think I do," I said.

Emma sifted through the manuals in the glove compartment, came up with one for the communications device, and pushed the appropriate button on the dashboard, spouting Sonterra's cell number and giving the "dial" command.

His voice mail picked up.

"Crap," Emma said, in disgust, waiting for the beep. "Tony? This is Emma. We're in the Hummer, Clare and me and Loretta—and Mrs. Rathburn. She's hurt, so we're taking her to a hospital. Call us." She looked at me. "What's the number for this thing?"

"No idea," I said.

"You're a cop," Emma told Sonterra's voice mail. "Find it." With another push of the button, she ended the call.

A squad car whipped in behind us, lights whirling, just as we passed the Dry Creek city limits. I glanced anxiously into the rearview mirror and kept going.

Madge made a strange, low sound in her throat.

"Maybe it's Tony," Emma said.

I shook my head. "He'd call." The town had been sealed off

after Father Morales's shooting. Where the hell were the road-blocks? Where were the staters and the Bureau types?

I floored it.

Deputy Dave switched on the siren.

"We won't get away," Madge said. "Nobody gets away—"

Nobody gets away. I filed that thought for later review. Provided there *was* a later.

"The hell we won't," Loretta replied. "Duck down, Emma, in case he starts shooting."

Emma didn't duck.

The siren intensified to a shriek, and the squad car eased up on the left, almost even with the rear bumper. I wrenched the Hummer in that direction, straddling the white line. Deputy Dave swerved, fell back a car length or two, and revved his engine. The siren screamed, numbing my eardrums.

"For God's sake!" Madge screamed. "Stop!"

I ignored her. Dave was trying to come alongside again, this time on the right, and I knew he'd run us off the road if he succeeded.

"Emma!" I yelled, fighting the steering wheel as the Hummer zigzagged this way, and then that. *"Get down!"*

She crouched on the floor, and a ringing sound came from the dashboard.

It had to be Sonterra.

It was. And he didn't bother to say hello. "What the hell is going on?" he demanded.

"Tony!" Emma cried in anxious relief. I had to concentrate on my driving, so I didn't say anything, but it was better than good to know we had Sonterra on the line. "We need help! That crazy deputy—"

"Tell me where you are," he said.

Emma pinpointed the location as best she could, with some help from Loretta.

"Keep going," Sonterra instructed. "I'm on my way. Emma, hit the emergency button on the dashboard—it's the one with the red cross. Tell the operator what's happening. I'll contact the

State Police, but the GPD will give them your exact location. Got that?"

"Got it," Emma said, her voice shaking a little.

Sonterra disconnected.

Emma jabbed the emergency button.

Deputy Dave rammed the rear bumper hard enough to rattle the fillings in my teeth.

Déjà vu all over again.

Madge began to wail in panic, a raw, wounded sound that trembled in my bone marrow and competed with the siren.

"Good evening, Mrs. Sonterra," chimed the operator. "How may I help you?"

"You can send a whole shitload of cops!" Emma cried. *"Now!"*

"What is your emergency?"

Loretta leaned forward, shouting to be heard above Madge's continued lament. "A maniac is trying to run us off the road, and that sound you hear in the background is somebody screaming in terror, you idiot!"

The operator responded with unruffled competence, as though such calls were commonplace, shrieks, insults, and all. "We're contacting the police," she said. "Would you like me to stay on the line until they get there?"

Deputy Dave crashed into the bumper again. I wondered, from that odd, detached place in a back corner of my mind, how he planned to explain the damage to the Crown Vic, which was, after all, municipal property.

He didn't seem overly worried.

"Brand-new," I muttered. "This car is *brand-new.*"

"The Arizona Highway Patrol is en route to your location," the operator announced. "Is there anything else I can help you with, Mrs. Sonterra?"

"Maybe dinner reservations," Emma quipped, and grinned up at me from the floor. Then she added, "Thanks for everything," and pushed the button.

The GPD phone rang again.

"I'm with you," Sonterra said, his voice coming from every speaker in the car. "Special Agent Timmons and I are closing in fast, and the staters are up ahead. When you see them, pull off the road and don't make any sudden moves. They'll be nervous."

"Check," I replied, glancing in the rearview mirror. Sure enough, I saw what must have been Sonterra's lights in the distance, and so, apparently, did Deputy Dave. With a squeal of tires and a lot of smoking rubber, he swung off the road and bumped to a stop in the desert. The red-and-blue lights continued to spin dizzyingly, and the siren stayed on the banshee setting.

"Dave just ditched," I told Sonterra.

"I can see that," Sonterra replied. "Keep moving."

"Be careful!" I warned. Dave was probably on foot by then— it was too dark to see—but he might be planning to dig in for a showdown, too. Had I been alone, and not pregnant, I probably would have spun a brody in the middle of the road and gone back.

But I didn't have that option.

I slacked off on the speed, and when I saw four squad cars approaching from the other direction, I followed Sonterra's instructions, pulled off the road, and laid my head on the steering wheel, woozy with the release of tension.

State Patrolmen surrounded the Hummer.

Madge's cries trailed off to little whimpers.

"Open the door and step out of the vehicle with your hands up," one of the cops yelled.

"They don't look happy," Loretta observed.

"It's routine," I said, lifting my head and pushing open the door. I left the engine running, in case Sonterra tried to get through on the GPD phone. "Right now, they can't be sure which side we're on." I unfastened my seat belt, stepped down to the pavement, and raised both hands, heeding Sonterra's warning. In situations like that one, emotions run high. Guns are drawn. Best to play it very cool.

Loretta, Emma, and Madge took the same tack.

Flashlights played over us, blindingly bright.

One of the staters called, "Mrs. Sonterra?"

I wanted to laugh, all of a sudden. Hysterically. *Mrs. Sonterra.* I could get used to that.

"That's me," I said.

He scanned the four of us. Loretta and Emma were holding Madge upright between them. "Anyone else in the vehicle?"

I shook my head. My vision narrowed, then widened again, all in a few seconds.

Gunfire sounded in the distance. A distinctive *pop,* a pause, and then two more shots, in rapid succession.

Sonterra.

Madge gave one last bloodcurdling scream and started to run back down the highway toward the colorful sweep of lights. Toward Dave. Remarkably, after everything he'd done to her, and to her children, she was afraid for him.

One of the patrolmen sprinted after her, caught her easily, brought her back. "It's all right, ma'am," I heard him say. "It's all right." Then, to one of his companions, "Where's that ambulance?"

I tugged at the sleeve of the nearest officer. "Help him," I said. "Chief Sonterra—he's back there—"

The radio on his service belt crackled, Special Agent Timmons's voice, disembodied.

"Officer down," he said with no inflection at all. "We need assistance."

This time it wasn't Madge who broke into a run, it was me.

TWENTY-TWO

I was younger and faster than Madge, but I couldn't outrun the long arm of the law. Within a dozen strides, I was caught and restrained, though I fought like a scalded cat. Two of the four State Patrol cars shot past, headed for the tangle of lights a quarter mile back along the highway.

Even from a distance, I heard the dashboard phone in the Hummer go off.

Emma did, too, and she dived for the button as I ran toward her. "Hello?"

"Is my wife there?" Sonterra asked.

I gave a strangled shout of relief, elbowing Emma aside. "Are you hurt?" I choked out.

"No," Sonterra answered. "Are you?"

I shook my head.

"Clare?" Sonterra prompted.

"She's okay," Emma said, standing almost at my elbow. "We're all okay."

An ambulance roared into view and arrowed right past us. Madge was sitting in the backseat of a squad car, her head in her hands.

"What happened?" I asked, though I knew the answer.

"Dave's dead," Sonterra answered quietly. "He fired on us, and Timmons took him out."

Madge was too far away to have heard what Sonterra said, but she lifted her head just the same. I thought I saw her eyes glitter, in the darkness, like those of a wild creature, catching the briefest flash of light.

Sonterra said he'd catch up with me as soon as he could, and rang off.

In the meantime, a second ambulance arrived, pulling in behind the car Madge was sitting in. Two attendants got out, unloaded a collapsible gurney, and snapped the legs into position underneath it.

I wandered toward Madge.

"You're safe now," I told her.

"He killed Oz," she murmured. "He killed Father Morales. He didn't want anything to stop the money coming in—"

Her eyes rolled back in her head, and she convulsed.

The EMTs loaded Madge onto the stretcher, treating her on the move. I tried to squeeze her hand, but she was out of reach.

I watched as Madge was loaded into the back of the ambulance, numbly processing the last words she'd said to me. *He killed Oz. He killed Father Morales . . .*

Loretta approached. "Maybe one of the EMTs should check you out, Clare," she said, taking hold of my arm. "Just in case."

I shook my head. "I'm all right. I want to follow the ambulance to the hospital, though. Make sure Madge is okay, and look in on Suzie if I can." Sonterra would be occupied for a while, of course, and I was feeling a lot stronger, now that the crisis was over and the shock was wearing off.

Loretta nodded and got into the Hummer on the driver's side. I rode in the backseat, while Emma took the shotgun position, calling Sonterra to give him an update on our whereabouts.

"Anybody ever tell you you're hell on cars?" my best friend asked, pulling out and gunning it to keep pace with the first ambulance. The second one was already headed farther along the highway, toward the scene of the shoot-out with Deputy Dave.

"Wait till I tell you about my wedding day," I replied. "Oh, *that's* right. You were there."

Emma's face appeared between the front seats, so pale that her freckles stood out even in the dark. "You're not bleeding or anything, are you?" she asked.

I took a mental inventory. "No," I said.

"Do you hurt anywhere?"

"No," I repeated firmly.

"You might want to consider incorporating the Kevlar into your everyday wardrobe," my niece suggested. "Do they make a maternity line?"

"Very funny," I said, then I laughed, but it came out sounding a little raw.

"Keep talking to her," Loretta told Emma. "I think she's in shock."

The Hummer picked up momentum.

I remembered my promise to Madge, that I'd let her sons know what had happened. "Fire up the dashboard phone again," I said.

"Why?" Emma asked.

"I've got to call Madge's son. His name is Dave, Jr., and he lives in Tucson."

I listened while my niece got the number from information and made the connection. Leaning between the seats, I calmly related the facts, at least concerning their mother. I would leave it to Sonterra, or the FBI, to break the news about their father.

When we reached the hospital, I tried to see Suzie, but there was still a guard posted at her door, and I couldn't go in.

Half a dozen of Timmons's men showed up soon after we arrived—I recognized them from the bologna-sandwich assembly line that day in our kitchen—probably waiting for a chance to question Madge about Dave's involvement with the coyotes.

We exchanged polite nods.

Loretta and Emma sat with me awhile, then went off to the cafeteria for coffee and sandwiches.

I didn't have an appetite, so I settled in the main waiting room, on the first floor, to read outdated magazines. Loretta and Emma came back, and, when two hours had passed and Sonterra still hadn't shown up, we piled into the Hummer and went back to Dry Creek.

It was after one when I heard Sonterra come in. I sat up in bed and switched on the lamp.

"Are you okay?" I asked anxiously, the instant he stepped through the bedroom doorway, while his words ran over mine. Same question.

Sonterra gave a raw chuckle and kissed my forehead. "Yes," he said.

I slipped my arms around his neck, remembering Timmons's ominous words crackling over the police radio earlier that night. *Officer down.* "I'm so glad you're home," I whispered, clinging a little.

"Me, too," Sonterra said. He held me for a while, then pulled back to get out of his clothes. He pulled on a pair of boxers and crossed the hall to brush his teeth.

"Exactly what happened out there?" I asked a few minutes later, as he slipped into bed beside me. "In the desert, I mean."

"I thought you'd never ask," Sonterra said, turning off the lamp.

I cuddled close. "Spill it," I said.

"Dave took a potshot at us from behind the passenger door of his Crown Vic. Timmons popped him. End of story."

"It wasn't about Madge," I said.

"What wasn't about Madge?"

"The car chase. Rathburn killed Oz Gilbride, and he shot Father Morales, too. Madge told me. He must have realized he'd pushed her too far after that last beating."

Sonterra listened pensively.

"Well?" I prompted when he didn't jump in with a reply.

"Plausible," he said, yawning. "Even probable. I'll have a warrant by tomorrow morning. We can search the Rathburn house then, and if there's any evidence, we'll know for sure."

"I don't suppose that 'we' includes me?"

"I was referring to myself, Timmons, and his crew."

"Did anybody question Madge?"

"Couldn't. She's in surgery."

I sat up, leaned across Sonterra, and turned the lamp back on. "Surgery? Nobody said anything about surgery when I was there—"

Sonterra pulled me down beside him again. "Internal injuries. Rathburn broke one of her ribs, and it punctured a lung."

"My God," I whispered. Madge had been on her feet when I found her on the patio. She'd tried to run back to her husband when we heard the gunshots, out there on the highway. Either she was the toughest woman on earth, or she'd been beaten so many times that she'd built up a tolerance to pain. Her body must have finally cried "uncle" when she had the convulsion alongside the road.

"Will she be all right?"

"I don't know, Babe," Sonterra said, and I knew by the way he hesitated that there was more bad news coming.

"What?" I pleaded.

He kissed my temple. "Suzie," he said gruffly. "She's taken a turn for the worse. She's on life support."

"No."

"Dan Post and his wife are with her. There's always a chance—"

"But not a good one."

"No," Sonterra admitted. "Not a good one."

I squeezed my eyes shut, trying to make the world go away. "I hate this planet," I said. "It's a crazy, rotten place!"

Sonterra held me very tightly. "Babe," he said.

I clung to him. He doused the light again. "Why do we try?" I whispered. "Why do any of us even *try* to go on?"

Sonterra shifted onto his side, facing me, and laid a hand on my belly. "Because we might be able to make it better," he said.

I broke down and cried then—for Suzie, barely holding on, for her mother, and for Judy Holliday. For Madge and Father Morales. Somebody else would have to cry for Dave Rathburn.

"It all sucks," I said when I'd exhausted myself.

Sonterra kissed away my tears. "*Some* of it sucks," he answered. "But then there's the baby, and Emma, and Loretta." He paused. "There's Mrs. K and Waldo and Bernice—"

"Keep talking," I sniffled.

"There's you and me." He lowered his voice to a breath, close to my ear, and a sweet shiver went through me. "There's hot, slick, wet sex. There's fresh coffee, and sunrises, and Christmas trees with those little bubbly lights in the branches. There's baseball, and old movies, and watermelon on the Fourth of July—"

"I love you, Sonterra."

He nuzzled my temple, and tightened his embrace. "There's that, too."

"More," I said.

"Waking up in the middle of the night and realizing you don't have to get out of bed for hours. Rain on the roof. Choices. Four years between presidential elections. Dr. Seuss. Jay Leno's monologues."

"I prefer Letterman."

"You would."

I nudged him.

"Chocolate. Train whistles. Making love by firelight, with an Anita Baker CD smoking on the stereo—"

I closed my eyes and gave in to sleep, like a child listening to a lullaby.

To my surprise, Esperanza showed up for work Monday morning, acting as if nothing had happened. Of course, word had gotten around about Dave Rathburn, and her presence confirmed my belief that she knew something. With Rathburn dead, the heat was off.

Sonterra popped in at home around ten o'clock, after I'd dropped a protesting Emma off at school. Loretta was probably still recovering over at the B&B, and Esperanza was dusting the living room. "I just left the Rathburns'," SuperCop informed me, pouring himself a cup of coffee. "We found a Glock, with one bullet out of the clip. The ballistics test isn't back yet, but the consensus is, it's definitely the same gun used to kill Father Morales."

I wasn't really surprised, but I was briefly speechless, partly by the confirmation and partly by the fact that Sonterra was sharing that kind of information with me.

"Nothing on Bobby Ray or Danielle, I suppose?"

Sonterra sighed. "Zip," he said.

For the merest fraction of a heartbeat, I was under the bed again, in Micki Post's trailer, while Danielle Bickerhelm banged the mystery man. Then I heard Madge's voice, in the car, after the book club gathering.

Those women at the meeting tonight? She's been to bed with half their husbands.

"Damn," I said. "It was *him*."

"Who was him?" Sonterra demanded, frowning.

"Never mind," I said. Danielle and Deputy Dave? It was only a hunch, and Sonterra would shoot it down if I told him before I had any evidence.

"Clare." He scowled. Clearly, he wasn't going to let it go.

Nobody ever died, I decided, from having holes punched in a hunch. "I was just thinking Dave Rathburn might have been the man Danielle boinked that night in Micki's trailer."

"Why?"

I sighed. "There's where you've got me. I don't exactly *know* why. It's just a theory. The night of the book club meeting, Madge told me Danielle had slept with half the members' husbands."

Sonterra checked the clock, poured out his coffee, and sighed. "You're right," he said. "It's just a theory. Let me know if you get anything solid." A brief pause. "Esperanza's here, right?"

Ah. The real reason he'd stopped by in the middle of a workday.

"Yes," I answered, just as she came through the dining room doorway.

She stopped when she saw Sonterra, visibly steeling herself.

"I have some questions I want to ask you," Sonterra said.

Esperanza swallowed, glanced at me, then nodded.

"Sit down," Sonterra told her. He tried to sound cordial, but it was an order just the same.

Esperanza drew back a chair at the kitchen table and sank into it. I took one, too, just in case Sonterra thought he was going to elbow me out.

Sonterra stood behind a third chair, bracing his hands on the back and leaning in a little. Esperanza's gaze slipped to the basement doorway, then dodged back to Sonterra's face. She looked small, forlorn, and determined, sitting there, and I reached out to squeeze her hand.

"Clare told me she visited your trailer last night," Sonterra began. His tone was no-nonsense, but he was making an obvious effort not to intimidate Esperanza. "What do you know about the coyote operation?"

Esperanza lowered her eyes to her hands, now clasped on the tabletop, and raised them again. "Father Morales," she began. "He was not coyote."

Sonterra waited.

I held my breath.

The housekeeper glanced at the cellar door again. "When we come here," she said tremulously, "my family and me, I am meaning, was two years ago. They hide us down there. Locked door from this side." She trembled. "My Maria, she get fever, while we are waiting for the false papers they promised. No one come, so I break out window, downstairs, climb out with her. I go to church, wanting help. Father Morales, he get Dr. Holliday. He ask who bring us here, to United States, who hide us. I was afraid to tell." She fell silent, obviously flustered.

I watched Sonterra's face while we waited out the silence. I should have had an award for self-restraint.

Tears welled in Esperanza's eyes. "It was Oz Gilbride," she said. "He pick us up in desert, bring here."

Sonterra nodded slowly. "Who else was involved?"

Esperanza bit her lower lip. "I don't know. But I think Rathburn, because it go on after Mr. Gilbride disappear, and I hear things. From other Mexican people. Father Morales, he thought so, too. He wanted proof first." She blinked several times, rapidly, but the tears fell anyway. "He must have found something. He die." She crossed herself.

Sonterra spoke carefully. "What did you do after you went to Father Morales, that first time? When Maria was sick?"

I'd been wondering the same thing. Oz or one of his henchmen would surely have noticed the broken window and counted noses. Finding two "clients" missing, they would have started a search, fearing word would get out that the chief of police was harboring illegal immigrants in his home.

Esperanza sniffled, and Sonterra brought her a paper towel to wipe her eyes. "Father Morales, he keep us until the bad men stop looking." She paused and smiled shakily. "We all alike to them."

A chill went down my spine. "The others, in the basement with you and Maria—what happened to them?"

She covered her face with the paper towel for a long moment, and her shoulders trembled. Eventually, she looked up again, fixing her gaze on Sonterra. "I not see any of them again. I think they go to other towns, or back home, but maybe—"

"Do you remember exactly how many people were with you and Maria, when you were here?" Sonterra asked very quietly. I knew he was thinking about the skeletons in the crawl space, as I was, and wondering if Esperanza and her little girl had narrowly escaped joining them.

She shook her head. "I never count. It very crowded. We get water from laundry sink and use buckets for—" She stopped, closed her eyes again. "It was summer. Very hot. No air. Maria so sick."

"You didn't report what was going on because you didn't know whom to trust," Sonterra concluded. "And because you were afraid of being sent back to Mexico."

Esperanza nodded, groped for her purse before she realized it was still on the kitchen counter, next to the door, where she'd left it when she came in that morning. She looked at it with longing, but made no move to rise out of her chair. "I have card now.

Father Morales help me get card. Maria do so good in school, and I get job—" She turned pleading eyes to me.

"You still have a job, Esperanza," I assured her.

Sonterra rounded the table and laid a hand on her shoulder. "Nobody's going to send you back," he told her. "But if you know anything else, it's really important that you tell us."

She shook her head. "I do not know more," she said earnestly. "When Father Morales shot, I am so scared. I panic. I think, maybe coyotes find out somehow. Remember us, Maria and me."

I got up, filled the teakettle, and plugged it in to boil. Esperanza definitely needed a little TLC. I thought back, as I worked, to the way she'd crossed herself repeatedly the day I hired her and often since. It must have been almost more than she could do just to enter that house again after the experience she'd had.

Sonterra broke the bad news. "You might have to testify in court," he told Esperanza. "Do you understand what that means?"

She nodded. Smiled. "I watch Court TV sometimes, at neighbor's place," she said.

Sonterra and I both laughed, and, after a moment of hesitation, Esperanza joined in.

"I really think you deserve a day off with pay," Sonterra told her, a few minutes later, as she sipped her tea. I agreed, and on his way back to work, he dropped Esperanza off at the Hidy Tidy.

I was relieved when Loretta finally turned up at the front door half an hour later, because my mind was going about ninety miles an hour, and I needed a distraction, but my delight faded a little when I got a good look at her face.

"What?" I asked anxiously.

Loretta swallowed visibly and leaned to give each of the dogs a halfhearted pat on the head. "Kip pleaded guilty this morning, to avoid a trial. He's on his way to a minimum-security place in Connecticut. Twelve months."

I steered her into the living room, sat her down, and perched on one arm of the sofa. "Oh, Loretta," I said. "I'm sorry."

"It happens."

"It shouldn't have. Not to you."

"I'll deal with it, Clare."

"How?"

She blinked back tears and tried hard to smile. "I guess I'll get by with a little help from my friends," she said.

"Count on it," I told her.

I missed the Monday morning staff meeting entirely. Dave Rathburn's funeral was held a few days later, in the high school auditorium in Dry Creek. Madge didn't attend, since she was still in the hospital, nor did her sons, but the FBI was well represented, and just about everyone else in the community showed up, too, including a large contingent of Latinos. I figured a lot of them just wanted to make sure old Deputy Dave was in the box.

I know that was my motive.

"They're still out there," I said afterward, thinking of Suzie, when we were alone in Sonterra's SUV. "The people who hurt her are still out there."

"I'll get them, Clare," Sonterra promised. "If it's the last goddamned thing I do, I will get them."

"Danielle may already be dead, like Micki and Dr. Holliday," I mused on, not really expecting any immediate input from Sonterra. "But where the hell is Bobby Ray Lombard?"

The ballistics report on Dave Rathburn's gun had come back from the FBI lab early that morning, and so had the ID on Oz Gilbride. His had definitely been one of the skeletons secreted in our basement. And either Deputy Dave had been loaning out his Glock, or he'd executed Jimmy and the four other coyote victims in the desert, too. The striation marks on the slugs recovered from the bodies were exact duplicates.

"Madge hasn't issued a statement?" I ventured, watching Sonterra out of the corner of one eye. I'd tried to visit her once or twice, but the nurses wouldn't let me in. Suzie was still unconscious, and holding on by a thread.

Sonterra's jaw worked. "Let it go, Clare. For five minutes, just let it go."

"I can't." Furious sorrow rose in my throat, sticking there like a clump of cactus spears. "Suzie could die, and even if she survives, she's going to be traumatized, maybe for life. *Somebody* is responsible for that, and I want to know who it was. I want Robeson to prosecute them from here to the Needle Room."

"And you think I don't want the same thing?"

I sighed, rubbed my right temple with my fingertips.

"Clare?"

I gave in. "I know you do. It's just hard to be patient, that's all."

"Tell me about it."

I drew in a deep, restorative breath, and released it slowly. "What now?"

"I'm taking you home."

My body was willing, but my mind wanted to push. "Have you and Timmons even looked for Danielle and Lombard?"

"We've been a little busy," Sonterra pointed out.

I had to concede that one. "It bugs the hell out of me. I'm positive I know her, but I still can't figure out where from. Loretta suggested that Danielle and I might have been in the same foster home."

"Try the Internet," Sonterra said. "With your connection to Robeson's office, you ought to be able to get into county files."

I nodded. The stuff my boss had given me to do so far was pretty easy. With Lombard still at large, I was at loose ends. Loretta had flown back East the day before to visit her husband at Camp Cush, and I missed her with a vengeance. Esperanza wasn't a lot of company, and Emma was in school all day. I was going to be alone a lot, for the time being at least, and all of a sudden, I hated the idea.

As soon as we got home, Sonterra changed out of his suit and into a uniform, and left me to my own devices. I swapped my black dress for sweats and sneakers, let the dogs have a supervised run in the backyard, and slapped together a quick lunch for all three of us. They had kibbles, I had a peanut butter and banana sandwich.

With a cup of herbal tea close at hand, I settled into my chair in the study and logged on to the computer. Thanks to the inveterately sentimental, there are thousands of remember-when sites, clogged with goofy school pictures.

I started with first grade.

No sign of Danielle, but there I was, small and unsmiling in one of my sister's hand-me-down dresses, eyes already shadowed with defiance.

I felt a twinge of grief.

Around sixth grade, I got bored with my own image and tapped into Child Protective Services. After wandering through a cyber maze—I didn't need my county credentials, since a former client, David Valardi, had shown me how to hack with relative impunity—I opened my records, hoping to find a list of the foster homes I'd passed through on the rocky road to Gram's double-wide.

I found them, but I found something else, too.

Something that made my tailbone tingle. My birth certificate.

It took me a second or two to realize that it wasn't the same one I had tucked away in the file cabinet.

I stared at the cyber version of the document, confused and very uneasy. I guess my subconscious mind had already picked up on the discovery I was about to make.

The information was typewritten.

Name, date and time of birth, weight and length. The usual. But in the slot for comments, someone had scrawled, in tiny letters I had to squint to see, *Surviving twin.*

I sat back in the chair with all the force of someone who's just been slapped across the face.

"'Surviving twin'?"

Waldo, lying at my feet, looked up at me in one-eyed wonder.

I was a *twin?*

Mom had never mentioned that, nor had Tracy or Gram, though *they* might not have known. I wanted to call someone, demand an answer, but there was no one to call. Emma and I were the last of our noble line.

I leaned forward again, my nose a few inches from the monitor screen, found the attending physician's name, and scribbled it on a notepad.

John C. McVere.

What were the chances he was still in practice, after more than thirty years? He could easily be dead.

I reached for the phone, called information in Tucson.

"John C. McVere," the operator repeated thoughtfully.

"M.D.," I specified.

"I'm sorry. There's no listing under that name."

"Any other McVeres?"

"Cynthia P.," came the reply, reverberating with good-natured patience. "Would you like that number?"

"Please," I said, trying not to be terse. The woman was only doing her job—it wasn't *her* fault that I'd just found out I was living in a bad soap opera.

"I could connect you. Of course there would be an additional charge."

"Do it." So much for not being terse.

One ring. Two. Half a dozen. Then, just as I was about to hang up, an elderly woman answered with a teetery, "Hello?"

"Mrs. McVere?"

"Miss McVere." A prim emphasis on the "Miss."

"You wouldn't by chance be related to a Dr. John C. McVere?"

Definite chill. "Who's calling, please?"

I summoned up a telephone smile and a lawyer's line. "I'm sorry. My name is Clare Westbrook. I'm doing some research, and Dr. McVere is listed on my birth certificate as the attending physician. I'd like to ask him some questions."

"I'm afraid that won't be possible, Mrs. Westbrook," Miss McVere told me. "My father died eight years ago."

"I don't suppose you still have his records?"

"Heavens, no," she replied. "He was in practice for half a century. His files would fill the house."

"I see," I said. "Thank you, Miss McVere. Sorry to bother you—"

"Of course there is the microfilm," she said.

My voice came out as a croak. "The microfilm?"

"Papa was ahead of his time. He always planned to write a memoir someday. God bless him, he never got around to it. But I know he had some of his charts put on film. My brother Charles was in charge of the family archives." She gave a slight sniff. "He's dead, too," she went on, without the regret she'd shown for her father's demise, "but his widow, Helga, might have the films. She holds on to everything, just in case there might be a nickel in it somewhere. I don't have her number, but it's probably listed. Let's see—Harry came after my dear brother, and then Ross—"

I waited, literally on the edge of my chair.

"Jasper. That's it. Clyde Jasper. He owns a wrecking yard in Gila Bend. I wouldn't have thought he'd be her type, but then, he *is* a junkman." She gave a bitter, crackly little chuckle.

I smiled, scribbling. "Thanks, Miss McVere. Thank you very much."

She hung up in my ear.

I immediately called information again. There was no private listing, just one for Jasper Scrap Iron and Car Parts. Gila Bend isn't exactly a metropolis, so I felt that small, quivery thrill in the pit of my stomach that usually means one of two things—I'm on the verge of an important discovery, or someone is about to go for my jugular. On occasion, it's both.

Mr. Jasper, the proprietor himself, answered on the third ring, barking out the name of his business. Either it was a bad day in the Bend, or he was inherently cranky.

"Mr. Jasper, my name is Clare Westbrook, and I'm actually looking for your wife—er—Helga?"

"I know my wife's name," he snarled. "And I'm trying to do taxes, here. Damn government. Take, take, take, that's all they do. A man works hard and what does he get for it? Penalties. Surcharges. They're all the same—Republicans, Democrats. Bunch of moneygrubbing bastards—"

"Is Helga around? I checked with information, but they didn't have a home number."

"That's because we don't have a phone over to the house. Helga runs up the bill, calling those foreigner relatives of hers. My guess is, she's down at the casino right now, poking the grocery money into the slot machines. Likes the Double Diamonds."

I smiled to myself. Poor Helga. If she'd married Clyde Jasper for his money, as her former sister-in-law seemed to believe, she'd made a bad bargain. "I see," I said warmly. "Does Helga carry a cell phone, by any chance?"

"Like I'd let her have one in a million years. Them things can run ten dollars a minute and up when you're calling overseas." He paused, and I could almost hear the gears shifting in his head. Now that Clyde had poured out his disenchantment with the government, foreign relatives, phone bills, and slot machines, he wasn't going to be so forthcoming. "What do you want to talk to her about, anyways? I don't even know who you are."

I repeated my name and explained carefully, without too much detail, that I'd heard Helga might have Dr. McVere's medical records, and I was hoping mine, or my mother's, might be among them.

"She's got all kinds of stuff stashed in a storage unit outside of town," Clyde allowed. "Do you know what those places charge? Highway robbery."

"They are expensive," I agreed mildly. "I wonder if you would ask Helga to call me? Collect, of course."

More suspicion. The avaricious kind. "You writing a book or something?"

"No," I answered.

"Because if you are, Helga's got a right to some of the money. That doctor should have left her fixed, but she didn't get much."

"I'm *not* writing a book," I said quietly. "But if the records I want are there, I would be happy to pay for them."

"How much?"

I picked a figure out of thin air and hoped it would fly. "Five hundred dollars," I said. Money wasn't an issue with me, but that didn't mean I wanted to be fleeced.

"She'll call you," Clyde said with certainty. "Whose file are you looking for again?"

"Anybody named Westbrook. Specifically, Vanessa or Clare."

"How do you spell that?"

I spelled, and gave Clyde both my cell and landline numbers.

After I disconnected, I sat still, stunned by the twists life can take. Then the reality of Suzie's situation caught up with me again, and I reached for the phone, to keep it at bay for another few minutes.

"Hello?" Mrs. K answered, sounding worried. "Clare, is this you? Are you in trouble?"

"I'm not in trouble," I said quickly. Of course, that had a way of changing from moment to moment, but it just so happened that nobody was holding a gun to my head, so I considered it a truthful answer. "But I just learned that I might have been a twin. Am I crazy, or could that have something to do with—well—seeing myself?"

Mrs. K drew in a sharp breath. "Has it happened again?"

"No," I hastened to say. "I guess I'm just grasping at straws, here. Trying to find an explanation for something that can't be explained—"

My friend was quiet for a long time. "I hear little Suzie Post isn't doing very well," she said. "I'm sorry, Clare."

"Does that mean you think she'll—that she won't make it?"

"I don't know," Mrs. K said sadly. "I can't always see clearly."

The muscles in my nape knotted, and I rubbed my temple again, trying to keep it together. "What if she dies?"

"No one really dies, Clare," Mrs. K said gently.

Tears sprang to my eyes. "It sure as hell looks that way from here," I said.

"I know. But your little friend might not *choose* to stay, and you should be prepared for that. She may decide to go on, and be with her mother."

Sometimes, kindness breaks down my defenses. "That would be terrible."

"For you, and for the others she would leave behind, yes. But not for her. Don't hold on to her, Clare."

I wiped away my tears with the back of one hand. It was a weak moment. Report me to the spine police. "Why is there so much tragedy? Why is the world such a brutal place?"

I'm not psychic, but I could tell that Mrs. K was choosing her words. "Perhaps because you see it that way," she said softly and at considerable length. "We attract what's inside us, dear."

I didn't speak. I wasn't exactly offended, but I wasn't inspired, either. And I certainly wasn't comforted. But it *was* true that I'd been in street-fight mode ever since I could remember.

"I know, I know," Mrs. K said with a sigh, as if I'd spoken aloud. "I've told you over and over again that you're in danger. What I *should* have said was, 'look into your heart.' Look, Clare, as deeply as you can. Somewhere in yourself, you've taken the offensive. Perhaps the universe is merely giving you what you've come to expect."

I bit my lip. My instinctive response was, *I didn't call for a bunch of New Age mumbo jumbo.* But I *had* called to ask if I was being haunted by my unborn twin.

"You're angry," Mrs. K prodded quietly.

"Confused," I countered.

"Think about it," my friend said. "I'll get back to you on the twin question. I need to meditate and do some—" She paused, chuckled, *"New Age mumbo jumbo."*

I'd had a number of similar experiences with Mrs. K, but she could still catch me off guard. I gasped.

"How do you do that? Read people's minds, I mean?"

She laughed, a little ruefully, I thought. "I wish I knew," she said. "Then maybe I could turn it off and live like a normal woman."

"How does a 'normal woman' live?"

"I don't know," Mrs. K replied succinctly. "I've never met one."

My mind shifted back to Danielle Bickerhelm, and our connection, whatever it was. I decided to run it by my personal Swami and gave her a brief recap.

"Foster home," Mrs. K said, barely missing a beat. "Green house, white shutters. Black spaniel. She went by another name then and had a fixation about reincarnation. You'll have to take it from there. I'm due at WalMart."

I blinked, flipping through the mental files. Before I went to live with Gram, I'd lived in a lot of places, with a blur of people.

Green house.

Black spaniel.

Another name.

I mumbled my thanks and a good-bye and hung up. There was too much to think about, including the fact that I'd have to tell Sonterra about seeing myself one of these days. I'd use the twin news as a segue.

"I need a nap," I told Waldo and Bernice.

Both of them yawned in agreement.

We all trooped into the living room, and I collapsed onto the couch, the cordless phone within easy reach on the coffee table. I dreamed I was tied to a stake, in a Venetian piazza, with dried sticks piled around my feet. Danielle—but that *wasn't* her name, and she was wearing the wrong face—carried a torch, and laid it delicately, almost gracefully to the wood . . .

I woke in breathless panic, groping for the jangling phone.

"S-Sonterra residence," I choked out.

"I'm trying to reach someone named Clare Westbrook," a woman's voice said with a tinge of disappointment.

"Speaking," I replied, still muddled. The dogs, lying nearby, looked up at me pityingly.

"This is Helga Jasper. My husband said you would be willing to pay five hundred dollars for some of Dr. McVere's records?"

I sat up, pushed back my rumpled, sweat-dampened hair. I could almost feel the nightmare flames licking at my lower legs. "Yes," I said. "Anyone named Westbrook—specifically, Clare or Vanessa."

"Yes," she said. "Clyde gave me that information. I'll take a look and get back to you."

My heart began to pound. "When?"

"As soon as I can, Ms. Westbrook," Helga answered. "I need that five hundred dollars. I'll have to go through the boxes, but I think the films are labeled alphabetically. I can look at it at the library, print copies, and fax the information to you. After you pay me, of course."

"I'll give you a hundred-dollar deposit," I said firmly. "As soon as you send me a page or two, so I know they're really my records."

Helga hesitated. I waited her out.

"Okay," she said, at some length. "Two pages. Then I want my money."

"Of course," I said, letting out a breath. We exchanged e-mail addresses, and I gave her the fax number. She promised to let me know if and when she found the files, and send them as soon as my down payment turned up in her PayPal account.

When Emma came home from school, two hours later, I was hunched over the computer in the office, waiting for an e-mail confirmation from Helga Jasper. I accessed my PayPal account during the lull, sent in the hundred dollars, and racked my brain, trying to remember the foster home Mrs. K had seen in her psychic flash, but no luck.

Emma laid a hand on my shoulder. "I hear you went to Deputy Dave's funeral."

I nodded. Since a lump had formed in my throat, this time of rage, I couldn't answer. It seemed to me that he'd gotten off easy, the bastard, even if he *was* dead.

"Maybe it's over," she said philosophically. "Everybody at school thinks Deputy Dave was behind Father Morales's murder, and the coyote killings, too." She stopped and took a bite of her grilled cheese sandwich. "Busy guy."

"That still leaves the skeletons in the basement," I reasoned, after swallowing hard. The FBI was taking their time, IDing the remainder of them. "Oz Gilbride was a victim for sure. Danielle is still missing. And then there's Doc Holliday, Micki, and— Suzie."

We attract what's inside us, dear, I heard Mrs. K say.

The computer did a musical riff, and I turned back to the monitor. Helga's e-mail address popped onto the message screen, with "I Found It!" in the subject line.

I opened the e-mail and devoured it. *I didn't find your name, but I did come across a Vanessa Westbrook after some searching. She was cross-referenced with a Vanessa Gennaio. It was a thick file, so I need $23.50 for the extra copies. I'll send the two pages, and as soon as I get notice from PayPal that your deposit arrived, I'll fax the rest. Better put lots of paper in the machine.*

Right on cue, the fax kicked in.

Three pages ground their way out, including a cover sheet from one of those public mailbox places. I scanned the other two pieces of paper. They looked like the real deal, and my stomach did a flip.

I went back to the computer, clicked to PayPal, lowered one of my bank accounts by another $423.50, logged off, and scanned the pages I had while I waited.

"What's going on?" Emma finally asked.

"Long story," I answered.

"Aren't they all?"

"Research," I said. "For a case."

"You're lying," Emma accused, splitting the remainder of her sandwich into two pieces and giving one to each of the dogs.

"Okay," I admitted without looking at her. The paper tray in the fax machine was a little low, so I opened a new ream and added to the supply. "I'm lying. I might be a twin. A slot-machine-playing junkyard owner's wife is about to fax me your grand-mother's medical records."

Emma sighed. "That's just crazy enough to be true," she said.

The fax machine started up again, sucking up a piece of paper for the cover sheet. I held my breath.

"Have you heard from Loretta today?"

"No," I said, scanning the cover sheet and tossing it. "Why?"

"Just wondering when she'll be back."

I glanced at my niece. "Why?" I asked again. We all loved Loretta, but she'd traveled a lot ever since she met Kip, and we were all used to her periodic absences.

"I have to go to school all day, and Tony has a job. Esperanza always looks like she's going to jump out of her skin, and she's only here part of the time. We need somebody to keep an eye on you."

I snatched page one of my mother's medical chart from the fax machine and felt a peculiar, pitching sensation in the pit of my stomach as I scanned it. Name, address, height, weight—nothing I'd really wondered about. So why was my heart shinnying up my windpipe?

"I'm perfectly capable of taking care of myself," I said.

"Oh, right," Emma scoffed. "You ought to be in protective custody."

"If that's what I have to look forward to when you finally become a cop," I said, "you should go into cosmetology instead."

"Very funny," Emma retorted, but she was standing at my shoulder, peering at the second page of the file. I read the diagnosis notes.

Stomach flu. Prescribed bed rest.

"Stomach flu," I muttered. "Try alcoholism, and she got plenty of bed action, if not much rest."

"Clare?" Emma asked, looking at me as though I might have a fish bone caught in my throat.

I blushed. I'd been pretty honest with Emma about her mother's childhood, and mine, but I wished I'd had a better grandmother to report on.

The information I was looking for came pages later—*Pregnancy. High risk, considering acute alcoholism. Danger of fetal alcohol syndrome.* So, Dr. McVere had finally caught on. *Suspect twins.*

"You *were* a twin!" Emma marveled. She was a born speed reader, and not a bad snoop, either. She'd make a good cop, whether I liked the idea or not. "Holy *Days of Our Lives*!"

The last page came through, with a little, grinding sputter.

My birth date seemed to stand out from the scribbles and type-written information.

Twins delivered at 6:30 and 6:37 a.m., today. Both female. One live birth, one stillborn. Mother doing as well as can be expected, given the alcoholism. I suggested contacting Social Services, but the patient refused.

I sank into the desk chair, weak-kneed. And furious.

"Why didn't she tell me?"

I already knew the answer, of course. Mom wasn't into heartfelt exchanges—unless they were with drunken bikers she'd known for at least five minutes. She probably hadn't told Gram or Tracy, either.

"What difference would it have made, Clare?"

I hadn't told Emma, Sonterra, or Loretta about the other Clare. Only Mrs. K knew, and it was probably crazy to associate the hallucination with my stillborn twin, anyway.

"None, I guess," I answered after a long time.

When Sonterra turned up, an hour later, I was in the kitchen, trying to make dinner from a recipe I found on the back of a soup can.

"Don't worry," Emma said glibly from her place at the table, where she was doing homework. "It isn't Easy Beef Surprise."

Sonterra looked relieved. He took off his gun belt, put it in the usual place on a high shelf in the pantry, and crossed to the counter to kiss the side of my neck.

"What is that?" he asked, daring to glance into the mixing bowl.

"Some kind of meatballs," I answered glumly.

"Let's go out to dinner," he said with a little grin.

Such a diplomat. Trouble is, I saw him wince before he suggested the restaurant.

"Great idea!" Emma cried, and the way she leaped to her feet reminded me of a sailor jumping up and down on the deck of a sinking boat, trying to attract the Coast Guard's attention. "I've been wanting to try the Doozy Diner."

"I was thinking of Tucson," Sonterra said. "Do us good to get out of Dry Creek for a little while."

I perked right up. "I'll change."

"Me, too," Sonterra replied, indicating his uniform.

We shared the shower, after making sure Emma was still downstairs.

Sonterra leaned me against the wall, kissed me crazy, and proceeded to enjoy my breasts at his leisure. After that, he knelt and parted me, letting the shower spray tease the nub of swollen flesh he'd revealed.

I was already groaning by the time he took me into his mouth. I got the full treatment, and by the time he lowered me to straddle his thighs, there behind the shower curtain, I was in a delicious daze.

He shocked me out of the afterglow with one smooth, deep thrust, and within seconds, I was going off again, bucking on his lap, stifling my cries of release in the curve of his neck. He finally stiffened, with a groan, and I ground my hips to make it as intense for both of us as I could.

It took a while to recover, and then we soaped each other, and rinsed, and Sonterra used his fingers to make me come again, just to ensure a mellow mood for the rest of the evening.

Bastard.

"I found out something interesting today," I confided to Sonterra, later that night, at the brightly lit restaurant on the outskirts of Tucson. Emma was whiling away the food wait by playing a video game in the entryway.

"What?" Sonterra asked with a sort of wary innocence.

"That I was a twin."

He leaned forward, took my left hand, turned my plain gold wedding band with the pad of his thumb. "Wow," he said, and I could tell he was trying to read me so he could react appropriately.

If I'd told Sonterra that aliens had landed in the front yard, set up camp, and made s'mores, or that I'd witnessed a case of spontaneous combustion at the supermarket, he'd probably have said, "Wow."

"It makes me feel like a stranger to myself," I said.

He moved to the chair beside mine. "Yeah," he said. "I suppose it would."

Emma glanced in our direction, looking worried.

"Something else happened, too," I added, on a roll.

Sonterra slipped an arm around me, and my heart pinched. "Like what?"

"Mrs. K told me that I'm attracting all these dead bodies."

"Mrs. K," he said calmly, "is a crazy old bat."

"It doesn't happen to other people."

"You're not 'other people.' You're Clare."

"I'd just like to be ordinary."

He grinned. "And your second choice would be—?"

The waitress appeared with our dinners. They looked a lot better than my aborted meatballs. Emma homed in from the video arcade.

We lapsed into what was, for us, regular dinner conversation.

"Forensics analyzed more of the bones Waldo hauled up from the basement," Sonterra announced, buttering a dinner roll. "No specific IDs. Safe guess that they're Mexican immigrants, given what Esperanza told us."

I'd been about to attack my chicken-fried steak, but my fork slipped out of my hand and clattered to the floor.

The waitress, an observant soul, brought another fork. I waited until she was gone before I spoke again.

"So how come you're spilling your guts all of a sudden, Sonterra? Usually, I can't get a word out of you."

"You told me about your twin. I figured it was only fair to cut loose with a secret of my own."

"Some secret," Emma observed wryly. "It's probably going to be in the newspapers tomorrow morning."

"Probably," Sonterra agreed.

"You've got more than that," I said suspiciously. He'd tossed me a crumb, but he was still holding out on me.

Sonterra wriggled his brows.

I considered stabbing him with the fork.

"Cut me some slack, Clare. You're a lawyer. If I tell you what we have, the case could be compromised and the feds would hang me by my"—he glanced at Emma—"thumbs," he finished.

"Just tell me if there's any connection between the whole coyote mess and what happened to Doc Holliday and Micki." I couldn't bring myself to add Suzie's name to the victim list, but I knew she was within an inch of being there.

"Nothing we can find," Sonterra said.

"Somebody say something cheerful," Emma put in.

"Okay," Sonterra replied. "I hired Eddie Columbia today. He's taking over Dave Rathburn's job."

I was happy for Eddie, but I had other concerns. "This is beginning to sound more and more permanent," I said carefully. "I thought we were only staying in Dry Creek for six months."

"I *like* Dry Creek," Emma said.

"So do I," Sonterra agreed.

"Do I get a vote?" I asked.

"Yes," Sonterra said, as he and Emma exchanged glances, "but I think you're outnumbered."

"It's not a bad town," Emma reasoned, "and I love the house."

"If you don't mind bodies dropping on the other side of the back fence," I said, "and bones moldering in the basement, it's just wonderful."

"Isolated incidents," Sonterra said. He took my fork, cut off a piece of chicken-fried steak, swabbed it through the gravy, and held it to my mouth. "Things will settle down a little now."

I took the steak, chewed, and swallowed. "Oh, really? What makes you think that?"

"I'm not at liberty to say."

"I hate it when you get like this."

"Yeah, I know." He grinned, though there were shadows of sadness lingering in his dark eyes—sadness over Suzie's condition, I knew, and Jimmy Ruiz. And all the nameless, faceless ones who had taken a chance on a better life and ended up lying facedown in the desert with bullets in their skulls.

I relented, remembering the fun we'd had in the shower, and touched his cheek. Sonterra brightened. "So," he said. "Would it be okay if Eddie bunked on the couch for a while?"

TWENTY-THREE

I met Loretta in baggage claim, at Tucson International Airport, around 10:30 A.M. the next day. She looked, as Gram used to say, like somebody who'd been dragged backwards through a knothole.

Seeing me standing there, in expando pants and one of Sonterra's sweatshirts, she smiled wearily. We'd spoken only once while she'd been gone, when she'd called to let me know when her flight would get in.

"How've you been?" she asked, while we stood waiting for her Louis Vuitton to dump out on the luggage carousel.

I was still raw, mostly because Suzie wasn't any better, but things had settled down to a dull roar. No new murders. No bones, discovered in inappropriate places. No attempts on my life. "Sonterra hired Eddie Columbia to replace Deputy Dave," I reported, "and he's sleeping on the couch."

Loretta arched an eyebrow. "Is that good or bad?"

"Somewhere in between," I answered. "It's nice to have him around, and a change of scene will help him. How's by you?"

Suitcase #1 swung by, and neither of us reached for it. "Kip asked for a divorce," Loretta said. The blue of her eyes seemed to deepen, to the color of bruises. She bit her lower lip. Shook her head at my unasked question. "It isn't what you think," she added quietly.

"And what *do* I think?" I inquired gently, as another bag went by. "If you don't mind my asking."

"Probably that it's because of her. The other woman—she-who-must-not-be-named."

A third Vuitton passed, followed by a fourth and final one. Loretta must have been traveling light—she owned a twelve-piece set. "Don't tell me he's decided to do the honorable thing," I ventured. I wondered if he'd been bullshitting me, when he sent that heartfelt e-mail asking me to take care of Loretta.

"Okay," Loretta replied, snagging a weekender off the carousel and setting it at her expensively booted feet. "I won't tell you."

I grabbed a second bag. "Like I'd let you get away with that."

She sighed, and her shoulders slumped. Tentatively, I put an arm around her, squeezed.

"I must be the mother of all codependents," she told me sadly. "I still love him."

"Maybe you're just a grown-up," I said.

She blinked. Whatever she'd expected me to say, it wasn't that.

"You ladies need some help with those bags?" a porter asked, pushing in close with a large, flat cart.

"Yes," I told him, and pointed out the remaining two, which were still making the rounds.

"Where's the lecture on pride and independence?" Loretta pressed, studying my face.

"You expected a lecture?" I countered, a little affronted.

"Of course I did," my friend said.

Inwardly, I sighed. "No lectures forthcoming," I promised. "Whatever you decide to do, fight for your marriage, or let it go, I'll be rooting for you."

"Thanks."

"This all of it?" the porter interrupted.

Loretta did a glance count and nodded.

Fifteen minutes later, we were in the Hummer, with the bags loaded, ready to roll out of airport parking. I paid the lot attendant and merged with the traffic.

"Everything Kip and I owned is up on the block," Loretta confided, putting on her Versace shades. "Except for the ranch house and about five acres surrounding it. His lawyers are handling all the arrangements."

"Ouch," I said. "Naturally, you've got a lawyer of your own."

She grinned ruefully. "Yeah. You."

I nodded. I'd review the papers, when the time came, and make recommendations. If she needed a barracuda, I'd see that she got one.

"In a strange sort of way," my friend went on, "it feels good to be letting go of all that *stuff*. I called Rosa and offered her a job at the ranch, but she says she's ready to retire and spend more time with her grandchildren. Thank God her pension fund wasn't touched."

I felt a little nick of sorrow at Rosa's departure, sharp as a razor jab. She'd been a mainstay at Loretta and Kip's place in Scottsdale for a long time—a good housekeeper and, by extension, a good friend to Emma and me.

"Now what?" I asked, after giving things a few moments to settle.

"Well, I'm not going to sit on my ass and wait for Kip to get out of jail, that's for sure," Loretta said. The spirit in her voice cheered me up considerably. "I think I'll get a real estate license, to start. Maybe I'll skip sales and go straight to brokering. Or I could turn the ranch into some kind of resort."

"What about the divorce?"

"I told him I'd fight it. I want to see who we are, Kip and I, without all those stocks and bonds and fancy houses." She turned slightly in my direction. "You think I should cut my losses and run, don't you?"

I thought for a few moments. Shook my head. "Not necessarily," I said.

Loretta drew a deep breath and let it out slowly. "I'm not

sure of many things," she told me. "But I know I still love Kip. The real Kip—the man I married."

"Then you ought to give him a second chance."

A tear slid from under her Versaces, and she didn't bother to wipe it away. "I always thought I'd kick him to the curb if he ever cheated on me," she reflected. "I wonder what Dr. Phil would say about all this."

I laughed, though I had to blink back a few tears of my own. Loretta was hurting, so I was, too. "Guess you'll have to work this one through without him," I said. "You're not a stupid woman, Loretta. You have choices, and, last I heard, access to a Swiss bank account, which puts you way ahead of most people. If you want to give the marriage another try, do it. If it's a bust, you'll know you did your best."

We were quiet for a while.

"Catch me up on all the latest at Dry Creek," Loretta said, after she'd repaired her eye makeup.

I gave her the condensed version.

Loretta listened thoughtfully. "What else?" she asked, when I was finished.

"What do you mean, 'what else'?"

"I know there's more. I can tell when you're holding back and, besides, this is too easy. Your life is a freak circus, Clare."

"*Thanks.*"

"Don't try to deny it."

I smiled. "Actually, it's more like a soap opera these days."

"Tell," Loretta ordered.

"I'm a twin."

Loretta was suitably impressed. "You mean, you have a long-lost sister roaming around out there someplace?"

I thought of the times I'd glimpsed the other Clare, and felt sad again. I'd had a while to think about the phenomenon—it was far-fetched enough, seeing myself as a separate person, without concluding that I'd been visited by my dead twin's ghost, as if she'd grown up in some parallel universe and found some way to bleed through into my dimension in a crisis.

"No," I said firmly, addressing my own newly discovered fanciful side, as much as Loretta. "She was stillborn."

"Oh." Loretta reached across the console to pat my arm. "Nobody ever mentioned her to you?"

"Mom certainly didn't. I don't think Tracy or Gram had any idea that she ever existed, either—but I'll never know for sure."

"How does that make you feel?"

"Talk about Dr. Phil," I countered.

"It's a fair question. I've read about these things. Sometimes, when one twin dies, the other feels a void, a kind of loneliness they can't explain. As if a part of them is missing."

I *had* had that feeling many times in my life, but I'd always connected it to my mother's chronic neglect and repeated experiences with the child welfare system. "Sonterra thinks I ought to have counseling," I said with a dash of resentment. I'd told him about the twin discovery, and I'd planned to come clean about the hallucinations, too—until he mentioned a shrink. After that, I'd dug in my heels, and Mrs. K hadn't gotten back to me with the results of her psychic scan, if she'd done one.

"And you took that as an insult."

"I'm already seeing an obstetrician," I pointed out. In fact, I was scheduled for a sonogram in Scottsdale on Friday. Sonterra and I were still debating whether we wanted to know the baby's sex, or wait for the unveiling in June.

"It isn't the same thing," Loretta argued, "and you know it."

"I'm not crazy."

"You've had therapy sessions before. Time for an update. A professional could help you make sense of things."

"Like what?"

"Like why a great guy like Tony Sonterra practically had to drag you down the aisle, for a start."

"Look what happened when I got to the altar," I said, as the vision of Father Morales taking a bullet unfolded in my head. We'd talked away the distance between Tucson and Dry Creek, and now we were on the outskirts of town. "Where to?" I asked. "Our place, or the B&B?"

"Actually," Loretta said, after another deep breath, and an exhalation that made her shoulders slope, "I thought I might bite the bullet and go back to the ranch."

We'd passed *el rancho* twenty miles back, but I saw no need to state the obvious. "You're sure you're ready for that?"

"I'm sure it won't get any easier if I wait," she answered. "But don't turn around yet. I want to say hello to Emma and Tony." She grinned, and I glimpsed the old Loretta. "Maybe we could tune in to the Food Channel and whip up something interesting for lunch."

"And commit another culinary atrocity? No way."

I stopped at the supermarket, and we bought fried chicken and potato salad at the deli. Good thing I picked up extra, because when we got back to the house, Sonterra was there, along with Eddie and Special Agent Timmons. They were having some kind of confab at the kitchen table, over coffee and a box of doughnuts.

Like any good cop's wife, I refrained from commenting on the doughnuts.

Sonterra rose from his chair, politely waited until both dogs had been greeted, then kissed me lightly on the mouth.

"Hey, Loretta," he said, gruffly kind. "Welcome back."

She nodded, and didn't take her sunglasses off right away.

"Kip okay?"

Loretta nodded again.

Sonterra introduced her to Timmons—she'd met Eddie before, of course—and both men stood, after some chair scraping.

"Guess I'd better get back to work," Eddie said. He looked gaunt in his new uniform, but purposeful. His bruises were fading, too. I wondered if he missed plain clothes—Sonterra did, though evidently not enough to turn in his badge and return to homicide duty with Scottsdale PD. "I've got a place of my own now, Clare," Sonterra's former partner added hastily. "I'm renting a trailer at the Hidy Tidy. I can move in anytime."

"No hurry," I said.

Eddie grinned. I saw a mischievous light in his eyes and rejoiced, because I knew he was coming back from whatever dark place he'd been caught in since his marriage started to fall apart. It might be a long, slow trip, but he was headed in the right direction. "Much as I love sleeping on that couch," he joked, "I wouldn't mind a real bed."

I nodded, and the men went outside to confer briefly on the back porch, out of Loretta's and my hearing. Then Sonterra came back into the kitchen, and Eddie and the fed left in separate cars.

"Where's Esperanza?" I asked, looking around.

"The school called and said her daughter was sick," Sonterra answered. "Eddie took her to pick up Maria in the squad car, then drove them both home."

"Is it serious?"

"I don't think so," Sonterra answered.

I was unpacking the food, filling plates for Loretta and me. "Want something to eat?" I asked Sonterra.

He shook his head. "Too many doughnuts," he said. "Anyway, I'm due back at the station."

"Any trace of Danielle Bickerhelm?" I asked, as casually as I could.

Sonterra didn't buy casual. Maybe because I'd been nagging him for answers for days. "No," he said with exaggerated patience. He stepped into the pantry and came out buckling on his gun belt. "But I'll be sure and keep you in the loop."

He crossed the room, kissed me again.

"You are so full of it," I said with affection.

"I love you, too, Mrs. Sonterra," he answered.

When he was gone, Loretta picked through the chicken carton for another wing. "Let's do something we shouldn't," she said.

"I'm game," I replied. "Any suggestions?"

"We could go over to Danielle's house and poke around a little. Look for clues."

"Great idea. Except for the distinct possibility that we'll be charged with breaking and entering—a definite embarrassment to SuperCop—I can't see a problem with that."

"Like that stopped you when you checked out Micki Post's trailer."

I helped myself to a drumstick and inspected it closely before taking a nibble. "It was dark."

"We could go to her shop, then. I noticed that it was open for business when we came through town."

I thought about the painting of the young Venetian contessa and her lovely, doomed children, and a shudder ran down my spine. All of a sudden, that seemed even creepier than the skeletons in her dining room. "Why would we want to do that?"

Loretta shrugged. "We can grill the clerk. Might find out something the cops missed."

"What brought this on?"

"I guess I'm in a Nancy Drew kind of mood," Loretta said. "Besides, if I sit still too long, I start thinking about Kip. How he's on one side of the country, behind bars, and I'm on the other. How we probably have a snowball's chance in hell of making this marriage work. How I want a baby."

I was too stunned by the baby comment to address it. "You could always rent an apartment near the prison and ride out his sentence," I suggested lightly. "Watch the Food Channel between visits and bake him little surprises."

"That *would* be codependent," Loretta replied.

"It would also be assault," I said.

Loretta made a gee-that's-SO-not-funny kind of face.

I finished off the drumstick, washed my hands, and reached for the Hummer keys. "So," I began casually, "were these visits you made to Kip conjugal?"

She grinned mysteriously. "Maybe. You might say he's doing hard time."

"Droll," I said. "He made love to you, then asked for a divorce?"

"No," Loretta replied. "He asked for a divorce, then I seduced him."

It seemed like a good time to change the subject. And, like Loretta, I was in a Nancy Drew kind of mood.

"Let's do some sleuthing," I said.

Two minutes later, we were on the move.

As we pulled up in front of the antique store, a young woman crouched in the display window setting tiny pieces of furniture in the rooms of a massive wooden dollhouse. I vaguely remembered her from my visit, when she'd been ringing up sales in the back of the store.

She was thin, dressed in old clothes, and her brown hair had that little-Dutch-girl-just-awakened look that *will* go out of fashion if there's a God in heaven, along with those baggy cutoff jeans teenage boys love to wear.

She looked us over warily as we crossed the sidewalk, and worked up a smile. Evidently, business was slow that day. There was nobody else in the shop.

"What happened to the cradle?" I asked, surveying the contents of the window as the clerk stepped down to the floor.

"I sold it over the Internet," the woman said, studying us curiously. "Some collector." Had she made us for nonshoppers? I could see where she'd rule me out as a potential customer, but my sidekick had "platinum Amex card" written all over her.

Loretta approached the beautiful but creepy painting. "An amazing piece," she said thoughtfully. "How much?"

"It's worth in excess of fifty thousand dollars," the little Dutch girl informed us, running her palms down her thighs. "I've told Danielle she ought to sell it, but she—wouldn't." A pause, a blush. "She's missing, you know."

I nodded, watching her. "I'm Clare Westbrook—"

Loretta shot me a look.

"Sonterra," I finished.

"Chief Sonterra's wife?"

"The same," I answered.

Dutch Girl put out her hand. "Becky Peakes," she said. "I'm assistant manager. Not that there's been anybody to assist."

We shook, and Becky's palm felt moist against mine. I remembered hearing her message on Sonterra's cell phone, while we were in Nogales, rescuing Suzie from Hotel Hell. She'd reported Danielle's disappearance, and she'd sounded agitated.

"The police have probably asked you a lot of questions,"

Loretta observed, still pretending a keen interest in the painting. At one time, she could have afforded it, but it would never have worked at the ranch, even at the height of her spending power. The décor there was distinctly Southwestern.

"You can't even imagine how many," Becky replied.

"I think I can," I said.

Becky did the thigh-wiping thing again. "Nobody seems to want to find Danielle. I know she's difficult, but—"

I considered patting her shoulder and decided against it. Loretta was doing enough overacting for both of us. "How long have you known Danielle?" I asked.

"Forever," Becky said. "We were in the same foster home together."

Bingo.

I squinted at Becky and did a reverse-aging sequence in my brain, but I couldn't place her. I pegged her age at around twenty-five or so, but she might have been younger—or older. "Really?" I asked, careful not to seem too interested. "We have something in common, then. Foster homes, I mean."

She looked distinctly uncomfortable, and I wondered if Danielle had instructed her not to talk about the wonder years. "It was a long time ago," she said.

"I had an alcoholic mother," I said lightly. "What's your story?"

"My folks died in a motorcycle crash, when I was five," Becky answered, and for a fraction of a second, I glimpsed the bewildered child she'd once been. "I didn't have anybody else, so I became a ward of the state. I was so scared and confused. If it hadn't been for Wanda—"

Wanda.

In that instant, my recalcitrant memory finally kicked in. Of course—that was Danielle's real name. I was ten when I knew her, and she was probably thirteen or fourteen. We—the other foster kids and I—had dubbed her Wanda the Witch, because she wore black lipstick when the state-sponsored roboparents weren't around, and once chalked a pentacle on their laundry room floor.

Since the Fredricksons belonged to a strict church, Wanda/Danielle disappeared back into the system as soon as the last load of towels went into the washer.

"What was Wanda's last name?" I asked.

Becky blushed. "I didn't mean to say Wanda. I don't know what I was thinking. I've been so upset—"

"Cut the crap," said Loretta, really getting into the spirit of detective work now, "and answer the question."

I took her aside. "Cool it, Sherlock," I whispered.

Loretta looked offended, but she cooled it.

"Wanda Heighton," I said, as the rest of the memory train rolled into the station, long overdue.

Becky put a hand over her mouth, and her eyes widened.

"Are you afraid of Wanda?" I asked.

She shook her head, but the expression on her face told a different story. "Of course not. We were—*are*—friends. She wanted to make a new start, that's all. Put the past behind her. So she changed her name and asked me not to tell anybody."

I didn't move. The situation was fragile, and I thought Becky would run like a startled rabbit if I spooked her. "So you didn't give this information to the police?"

"No," Becky admitted weakly. Then, quickly, "It wouldn't matter—it really wouldn't. She's the *victim* here, not the criminal!"

"Becky, do you want Danielle to be found?"

"Yes!"

"Then you need to tell the police everything you know." I reached into my bag, pulled out my cell phone. "My husband will talk to you—"

"No!" Becky cried. "Stop! I can't trust the police—look what Deputy Rathburn did to Oz and Father Morales—"

I dropped the phone back into my purse. "Rathburn was a rogue," I said quietly. "Chief Sonterra is a good cop. The real thing. He can help you."

"*Please*," Becky pleaded. "I *promised* Danielle—"

"If she's still alive," I said evenly, "she's in trouble. Don't you want to bring her home?"

"She *is* alive, and she's not in trouble!"

I waited a beat. "How do you know that?"

Nothing from the Dutch Girl.

"Because you've either seen or talked to her since you reported her disappearance, that's how," I guessed aloud. Out of the corner of my eye, I saw Loretta open her mouth, and I held out one hand in a bid for silence. "If you *have* been in touch with Danielle," I went on, "the police will be able to trace her through your phone records. So you might as well tell the truth."

"Maybe I talked to her once," Becky said miserably.

"Where is she?"

"I don't know—I swear I don't!"

I got the cell phone out again.

"Don't," Becky pleaded. "Oh, God, she's going to kill me—but *please* don't involve the police."

I didn't really have a choice, since I was married to one of them, but I decided to play along and see what came of it. I lowered the cell phone to my side.

"Danielle called a few days after she disappeared. I asked where she was, and she said she had to hide out for a while. She told me to keep the store going and tell the police, when they came around, that I hadn't heard from her." Becky paused, her eyes enormous, luminous with pleas. "It wasn't because she did anything wrong. She was afraid of Deputy Rathburn, and he knew everything that went on at the station, so I didn't dare go to Chief Sonterra."

"She was having an affair with Rathburn," I mused.

"It wasn't like that," Becky protested. "She loves—"

Loretta and I waited. Becky's eyes darted from one of us to the other.

"Me," she finished. Then her eyes flashed with defiance, and her cheeks seemed to burn like hot plates.

"She keeps you a secret," Loretta guessed, and I gave her points for having a killer instinct. "Like there's something wrong with the two of you falling in love."

That time, I didn't signal her to shut up. She was getting the hang of the good-cop, bad-cop routine, so I let her have her head.

"It's only temporary," Becky said, with less spirit than before. "Wanda loves me."

"That's what they all say," Loretta replied.

Now that I knew who was supposed to be the good cop, and, by process of elimination, the bad one, I jumped in again. "Give her a break, Loretta," I said. "She's in love. She wants to help Danielle, keep her safe." I met the scorned lover's gaze. "Don't you, Becky? You don't want anybody to hurt Danielle."

Becky swallowed.

Loretta kept her mouth shut. Sure as shit, she'd been watching reruns of my perennial favorite, *Law & Order*. In Loretta's case, this was certainly preferable to the Food Channel.

"She didn't want to be with Dave Rathburn," Becky said. "She said he was disgusting. She was trying to keep Bobby Ray out of jail, that was all. Now that Rathburn is dead, she'll come back." A lift of the chin. "To me."

"If she can," I said gently, and waited, while the words sank in.

Becky went pale. "What do you mean, 'if she can'?"

"If she's with Lombard, she's got one of two problems. He's the primary suspect in two murders—Judy Holliday's and Micki Post's, and"—I paused—"he was probably responsible for what happened to Suzie, too. She's six years old, Becky. There's a possibility she's suffered a psychotic break, and she's barely alive. Either Danielle's in very grave danger, or she's going to be implicated."

"Call her," Loretta urged, watching Becky. "You know the number."

"I *don't*," Becky insisted.

"Okay," I said.

Loretta stared at me. "*'Okay'?*"

I shifted, so that I was standing almost shoulder to shoulder with Becky. Her and me against an uncaring world. "She's told us what she knows," I said. "I believe her."

Loretta opened her mouth, closed it again.

"Look at the time," I said, then remembered to check my

watch. "Emma will be home from school soon. Since the bone incident, she doesn't like to be in the house alone, so we'd better boogie."

Loretta consulted her own watch. "But it's only—"

"They're getting out early," I interrupted. "Teachers' conference." I turned to Becky, handed her one of my old cards from Phoenix, with the new information scribbled in. "If you hear from Danielle again, call me. Her life might depend on it."

Becky hesitated, nodded glumly, and pocketed the card without looking at it.

"What just happened in there?" Loretta asked when we were back in the Hummer. "She was on the verge of telling us everything."

"She's panicking," I said calmly. "Which means, if we watch her, there's a good chance she'll lead us to Danielle."

"Wait a second," Loretta said. "*We* can't follow her. It might be dangerous. Tony's the cop—let him do the following."

"Oh, yeah. Maybe he could take one of the squad cars, and flash the bubble light for drama. She'd never suspect a thing."

"Clare Westbrook Sonterra, we are *not* going to take the law into our own hands!"

"Of course we're not," I said. "We'll find out where Danielle is, then we'll tell Sonterra and stand back admiringly while he does the rest."

"I think even Becky might notice a red Hummer on her tail," Loretta countered. "This is a *bad* idea, Clare. If Danielle *is* with Lombard—"

"We can use your Lexus," I said. "Are you in or out?"

"I could tell Tony what you're up to. That would be the end of this whole stupid plan!"

"You wouldn't, though. Don't take up poker anytime soon, Loretta. You can't bluff for shit."

Loretta sighed. "*Damn* it."

"Let's go out to the ranch and pick up your Lexus."

"What about Emma?"

"Emma?"

"Yes, *Emma*. Your niece. The one who's getting out of school early and afraid to be home alone?"

"Oh, *that* Emma. She's doing some research for a paper in the school library after her last class, and by the time she gets home, Eddie and Sonterra will be there, too. Even if they weren't, she wouldn't be scared. The kid wants an overnighter in the Lizzie Borden house for her fifteenth birthday."

"You were lying the whole time. About everything!"

"Go figure, Loretta. If you don't want to go with me, we can just swap cars."

"Of course I'm going with you," Loretta huffed. "Obviously, I don't dare let you out of my sight for more than five minutes."

TWENTY-FOUR

At dusk, we parked the Lexus in front of the Doozy Diner, just up the street from Danielle's shop.

"So this is what a stakeout is like," Loretta said.

I sighed. If Sonterra caught us, there would be hell to pay, but he was busy back at the house, going over the coyote case with Special Agent Timmons. They may have pinned Oz Gilbride and Deputy Dave down as the ringleaders, but there were still a lot of desert dogs out there, doing the legwork. Loretta and I had left the Hummer at the ranch, when we swapped it out for the Lexus, and Sonterra believed we were shopping in Tucson. I hadn't exactly lied to him when I called—I just told him I needed maternity jeans, which was true, and let him draw his own conclusions.

At seven o'clock sharp, Becky Peakes closed the shop, shutting off the lights and locking the door. We watched as she walked, slump-shouldered, hands wedged into the pockets of her denim jacket, down the sidewalk in the general direction of Danielle's house. She'd probably been living there all along, sharing her boss's bed whenever there was a vacancy. I wondered where she'd been during the book club meeting.

Loretta moved to start the Lexus.

"Don't," I said.

"I thought we were going to tail her."

My friend's cop lingo made me smile. "Before we can do that, she'll have to go someplace," I said. "Give the girl time to get home, feed the goldfish, and put in a call to Danielle."

"Good Lord," Loretta lamented, anxious to begin her career as a crime buster. "That could take hours."

"That's the nature of a stakeout," I replied. We'd buzzed through the drive-in for burgers and fries, and I munched on the last of my dinner. "Becky might not turn a wheel tonight. For all we know, she doesn't even own a car."

"Then why are we sitting here?"

"Because I could be wrong."

"I didn't ever think I'd hear you say those words."

"Wonders never cease."

I let half an hour go by, during which we debated the pros and cons of Loretta's plan to get a real estate license versus turning the ranch into a business, then gave her the nod. At my suggestion, we parked at the top of the alley behind Danielle's house and doused the lights.

Another forty-five minutes passed, then our patience, as they say, was rewarded. Becky came out of the house, approached the door of the ramshackle garage, and fiddled with the padlock. Next thing we knew, she was backing a battered blue sedan into the alley.

I flashed back to the day I'd gone to Tucson for the job interview with Eli Robeson, driving Loretta's Lexus. I couldn't be sure, but I had a strong hunch that this was the same car that had bashed into me from behind and sent me spinning into that busy intersection.

"Holy shit, Batman," I muttered.

Loretta speared me with a look. "What?"

"I think that's the same car that smashed into the back of your car in Tucson. Back up and head for the main road. She's going to notice if we bump down the alley behind her. Better yet, let me drive."

"Not a chance," Loretta said, throwing the car into reverse. "I've never done this before. I want the experience."

"For what? Your memoirs?"

"It's part of the new, proactive me."

"Great," I said, but I didn't argue.

We headed for Main Street and, sure enough, Becky's taillights appeared up ahead. She was moving toward Tucson and not paying much attention to the speed limit.

"Go slowly," I warned Loretta, who was clearly in a pedal-to-the-metal state of mind. "If Deputy Jesse happens to be on patrol, we might get pulled over."

We stayed about ten car lengths behind, and when a farmer driving an old cattle truck got between us and the quarry, I told Loretta not to pass.

"Poop," she said. "I was up for a high-speed chase."

"Get over it, Clint Eastwood," I answered, keeping an eye on Becky's back bumper. Had she been the one to ram me in Tucson and, if so, why? I'd never met the woman before today. What could I have done to piss her off that much?

"It must have been Danielle," I decided aloud.

"What?" Loretta asked reasonably.

"She must have been the one driving, that day after I left Robeson's office."

"How can you possibly know that?"

"I don't," I said. "I'm speculating. Brainstorming. Running things up the flagpole to see if anybody salutes."

Becky took a side road, about ten miles out of town. I made Loretta cruise on by, then double back once the blue sedan disappeared around a bend, into a cluster of cottonwood trees.

"Where do you think she's going?" Loretta asked.

"To Danielle, I hope." I glanced at my watch and squirmed. Like Loretta, I wanted to step on the gas.

"She's going to get away," my friend fussed.

"Not unless she's planning on some off-road driving," I replied. "There's nothing back there but an old chicken ranch."

"Again—how do you know that?"

"I called the Psychic Network."

"Bitch," Loretta said with a sort of grudging fondness.

I relented. I could see Becky's taillights, far ahead, blinking red between the trees. "During my misguided youth, a group of us used to come to Dry Creek to party. This was one of our favorite haunts."

I tried to remember the layout of the property. There was a barn, dwarfing the house and leaning distinctly to one side. There was a spring-fed pond, too slimy to swim in.

And there were trees.

I thought back to the town picnic, the day Sonterra was sworn in as chief of police. Danielle had wanted to buy the house on Cemetery Lane, because of the cottonwoods. *The city council refused to sell,* I recalled her saying. *It's the only house in town with trees in the yard.*

"Not the *only* place, Danielle," I muttered. "But, then, you knew that, didn't you?" I could have kicked myself for not thinking of the chicken ranch, with its cottonwood guardians. They were no secret, after all. I'd driven past them a dozen times, on my way to and from Tucson, and never really noticed.

"If you're going to 'brainstorm,'" Loretta said, "would you mind including me?"

I leaned forward to peer through the windshield at the sky. The moon was in its last quarter. "Shut off the lights," I said, "and drive slowly."

Loretta did as I asked, but I noticed a definite reduction in enthusiasm. "I think we should call Tony," she said. *"Right now."*

"Not yet," I answered. "Suppose Danielle's not here? Becky could be up to something else entirely. Sonterra will want an explanation if we drag him out here, and it turns out we're wrong. What are we going to tell him then?"

"He'll want an explanation anyway, when he finds out about this," Loretta reasoned, leaning forward and squinting at the dirt road ahead as we jostled along. "Fortunately, that's *your* problem. I intend to take the Fifth."

An explanation and a pound of flesh, I thought dismally.

"Keep going," I said, scanning the trees ahead. No lights, no nothing. "Stop just this side of that boulder, where the road bends. We can walk the rest of the way."

"Are you kidding? I'm wearing four-inch heels."

"An oversight on your part," I said. "Feel free to wait in the car if you'd rather."

"And let you bumble into yet another *situation,* all alone? Not an option."

"This isn't going to be a 'situation,'" I replied. "We're not going to confront anybody. We'll just take a look around, then come back to the Lexus. If Danielle is here, we'll call in the law."

"What if she's *not* here?"

"Then we'd better come up with a couple of pairs of preggo jeans," I answered. "Sonterra will expect evidence of shopping."

"*Or* you could just tell him the truth," Loretta suggested.

"What a concept," I said, opening my door, getting out, and closing it quietly behind me. I left my purse behind, but I had my cell phone. I also had the presence of mind, remembering the near miss at Micki's trailer, to switch it to vibrate. The last thing we needed was a Johnny Cash concert while we were trying to sneak up on the chicken ranch.

Loretta locked her own purse in the trunk of the Lexus, then removed one of her Manolos, looked sadly at the towering Lucite heel, and broke it off on the boulder. The other soon met the same fate, but at least she wasn't teetering as we sneaked through the trees toward the hideout.

"This is so crazy," she whispered.

"You were the one who suggested we get wild," I whispered back. "And be *quiet*. If you so much as glimpse either Danielle or Lombard, turn around and run like hell for the car."

She nodded, and we went on.

The chicken ranch had been spooky back when I was a kid. Now, having had roughly twenty years to disintegrate further, it looked like something out of a horror movie.

Becky's car was parked in front of the barn, which, by some miracle of architecture, was still standing; but there were no other vehicles in sight and no people. The house had fallen in, and the thin moonlight played over an old wringer washer, rising like a rusted phoenix from the ruins.

A shudder inched down my spine.

"Let's get out of here," Loretta mouthed.

I shook my head.

Voices played on the chilly night air, but I couldn't make out the words or identify the speakers, though obviously Becky had to be one of them. The general tone was angry. Recriminations were flying.

I stepped out of the trees.

Loretta grabbed for me, then let out a strangled scream.

I whirled to see what was wrong and came face-to-face with a living mug shot.

I'd seen Bobby Ray Lombard on the Internet, and here he was, in person. He had Loretta in a chokehold, the filthy plaid sleeve of his ragged shirt cutting off her wind. Her eyes were huge with fear.

"Let her go," I said.

Lombard gestured with his free hand, and I saw the nine-millimeter semiautomatic. "Hello, Mrs. Sonterra." He grinned, revealing both bad intentions and a whole lifetime of dental neglect. "Who's your friend?" He jerked his arm hard, and Loretta's eyes rolled back in her head. She slumped, and he let her fall.

I hoped to God she was faking. When I moved to find out, Lombard slammed the butt of the gun into my head.

When I came to, I was inside the barn, duct-taped to one of the support beams, Joan of Arc style. There was no sign of Loretta, but then, I had blood in my eyes, so she might have been there somewhere.

Danielle/Wanda stood facing me with a plastic fire-lighter in one hand.

"Hello, Clare," she said sweetly.

My head throbbed, and she kept going in and out of focus. I couldn't decide between throwing up and wetting my pants. "Hello, Wanda," I said. "Where is Loretta?"

She didn't even react to my use of her real first name. "The blond chick? Bobby Ray's taking care of her. She's probably dead by now."

"You'd better pray she isn't," I answered. I might have been jelly on the inside, but my survival instincts had kicked in the moment I regained consciousness, and I had one objective—to keep my baby alive. And of course that meant I had to survive, too. If anything had happened to Loretta—

But I couldn't afford to follow that thought too far down the primrose path.

"You killed my children," Danielle said. "You escaped retribution back then, but you won't get away this time."

A whimper sounded, somewhere off to my left, and I saw Becky sprawled facedown on the floor of the barn, bleeding from the head. Sick fear roiled through me. *What had they done to Loretta?*

"What the hell are you talking about?" I retorted, still playing the only hand I had—a bluff. The painting of the Venetian woman and her children loomed in my mind, vivid in every detail, along with their tragic story.

"Don't you remember? You murdered them. Your name was Elisabeta then."

I swallowed a throat full of bile. "You don't seriously believe that."

"I *know* it," Danielle said. Her eyes glinted.

"Wanda, don't!" Becky called. "Please—don't do this—"

Lombard entered through the barn door, but Loretta wasn't with him.

"Bobby Ray," Becky begged, trying to get up. "Do something."

He did something, all right. He walked over to Becky, drew back one foot, and kicked her hard in the side. The thud made my gorge rise again, and I squeezed my eyes shut for a moment.

Then he approached me. Ran the knuckles of his right hand along the length of my face and neck in a way that made me shudder with revulsion. Tension coiled inside me, like the spring in an old-fashioned watch, wound too tightly.

"Where's the other one?" Danielle asked, batting his hand away from my cheek. "You dealt with her, right?"

"She's gone for good," he answered, still staring at me. "Gave her a little baptism in the pond."

I spat in his face. The spittle glistened on his cheek.

He slapped me so hard my ears rang. If I hadn't been taped to that pole, my knees would have buckled, and I would have crumpled to the floor. "Wanda, here," Lombard leered, slowly wiping his face, "she's got what she figures is a decent reason to kill somebody. Me, I just like to watch people die."

"You killed Micki, and Judy Holliday."

The grin didn't falter, and it was worse than the gleam in Danielle's flat gray eyes. "Damn right I did."

I waited out a visceral urge to claw off his face. "You as good as killed Suzie, too," I breathed, "you bastard."

"Wanda here, she's got a thing for kids. We kept the brat alive, but I always figured it was a temporary thing. After all, she was a witness."

I wanted to spit again, but I knew he'd hit me harder the second time, and I needed to stay conscious. "Why? Why did you do it?"

"Because that bitch Micki filed charges against me. And that lesbo doctor probably figured on sleeping with her—if they weren't doing it already."

I glanced in Becky's direction. She lay very still, maybe unconscious, maybe dead. I wet my lips as I met Lombard's gaze again, tasted blood.

Danielle's face hardened, and she glared at me in warning.

"What's the matter, Wanda? Haven't you told Brother Bobby the truth?"

She flicked the Bic, used one foot to scrape dry straw up around my feet. I caught sight of the red pickup then, the one that had been used to ram me in the Escalade that night on my way to Loretta's. The one that had screeched away from the front of St. Swithin's after dropping Rathburn off, so he could shoot Father Morales.

"You were in on the coyote thing, with Rathburn and your old lover, Oz," I accused, watching her.

"Shut up," she snapped, and leaned down to set fire to the straw.

Up until that moment, I guess I was in denial. Or maybe it all just seemed too incredible to be true. This woman actually believed I was a reincarnation of the governess who'd drowned those children and escaped punishment. How do you reason with somebody that crazy?

Wanda Heighton, aka Danielle Bickerhelm, actually intended to burn me at the stake.

"You and Becky—"

"Don't say it," she warned.

"What do I have to lose?" I countered.

At that moment, Becky lifted her head and cried, "Wanda loves me!"

Bobby Ray, who had been growing more and more agitated all the while, developed a tic under his right eye. "What the hell is she talking about?"

Danielle bent again, but this time, she touched the lighter to the straw. Flames licked at my pant leg. "Nothing," she said, rising.

Somehow, I stayed calm. "What about the skeletons in your dining room, Danielle? Are they real?"

It was Bobby Ray who answered, placing the splayed fingers of one hand on his chest. "Dear old Daddy and Mama," he said. He glanced down at the flames, amused. "Like I said, I like watching folks die. It was especially good with them. Daddy was a mean drunk, and Wanda's mama turned both of us over to the child welfare folks so she could crawl into the bottle with him. Theirs was a marriage made in hell, I can tell you right now. It was a special pleasure, for sure, killing those two—wasn't it, Wanda? But you might be even more fun, Mrs. Sonterra."

"Danielle, tell him about us!" Becky pleaded.

I tried to kick some of the smoldering straw away, but my ankles were taped, and I couldn't move, except to writhe. I felt my forehead and the skin between my breasts slicken with sweat.

My baby, I thought, in desperation.

The straw consumed itself, and though my pant legs smoked, they didn't catch fire.

Determinedly, Danielle looked around for something flammable. Not a difficult search, in an abandoned barn.

Meanwhile, Lombard stomped over to Becky, grabbed her by the hair, and wrenched her head back so he could look into her earnest, terrified face. "Talk," he said.

"Don't do it, Becky," I heard myself say.

Danielle seemed to have disassociated from the whole nasty business by then. She broke an old fruit crate into pieces and piled them around the base of the stake. Moving mechanically, single-mindedly, she proceeded to gather other things—ancient scraps of newspaper, old pieces of rope. All of them went onto my funeral pyre.

"I'm going to kill you anyway," Lombard told Becky, fingers entwined in her hair in a brutal grip. "So you might as well die with a clear conscience." What had Micki and Judy Holliday suffered at those hands of his? I stopped short of imagining what he might have done to Suzie. Bottom line, I couldn't bear to know.

"Danielle won't let you kill me!" Becky proclaimed. "She loves me! We were going to take Suzie somewhere safe, where nobody knew us, and raise her as our own—"

Lombard slammed Becky's face into the dirt and rotten straw covering the barn floor. She went limp.

"Wanda!" he roared, storming over to her, turning her by the shoulders from the old sawhorse she'd been trying to demolish with bare, frantic hands. "You'd better tell me that bitch was lying! Bad enough you slept with half the men in Pima County—but I draw the goddamned *line* at doing it with women!"

She stared up at him, blinked. He might have been a troublesome stranger, asking directions in a parking lot, instead of a semi-incestuous lover, half-wild with jealousy.

"Help me get the fire started," she said, almost plaintively. "She drowned my babies. I figured it out last year, when I saw her picture in the paper—"

Lombard stood with his profile to me, and his right temple

leaped with the promise of a rupture. "Tell me you weren't *sleeping with no freakin' woman!*" he bellowed, and shook her so hard that I thought her neck would snap.

A flicker in the doorway distracted me from the drama, as well as my own impending barbecue. Sweet Jesus, it was Loretta, eyes blazing with determination and abject terror, her clothes wet through and clinging to her body. She had a cell phone pressed to one ear.

I prayed Lombard wouldn't notice her, tried to will her away, out of sight. I knew she'd called Sonterra. I also knew he couldn't possibly get to the chicken ranch before I went up like a dead tree in a forest fire.

I kept my gaze fixed on the scene unfolding between Lombard and Danielle.

"*Tell me!*" he bellowed, and backhanded her so hard she stumbled backwards, only to be grabbed by the front of her blouse and dragged back.

"It didn't mean anything, Bobby Ray," she said, smiling oddly. "You know it's only been you, ever since your daddy married my mama."

He put his hands to her throat, started to strangle her. "You bitch!" he bellowed.

She gazed up at him in adoring bewilderment.

Far, far in the distance, I heard sirens.

Unfortunately, Lombard heard them, too. He let go of Danielle and spun toward the door, spotted Loretta. She'd dropped the cell phone in favor of a pitchfork, but I wouldn't have given two cents for her chances. Lombard rushed her with a nerve-freezing roar of rage.

The sirens drew nearer, but they weren't close enough.

Loretta hesitated for a fraction of a second, then thrust the tines of the pitchfork into Lombard's midsection, putting all her strength behind it. He screamed in pain and furious surprise, and fell forward, driving the metal rods in so hard and so deep that they came through the back of his shirt.

Danielle shrieked, scrambled for the lighter she had dropped in the fracas with her stepbrother, and crawled, sobbing, to put it to the newspaper at my feet. This time, the flames wouldn't fizzle out. I heard them crackling, looked down to see them traveling in little orange lines from stick to stick.

I'm sorry, Baby, I thought, *I'm so sorry.*

Loretta, forgetting Lombard, rushed toward me.

Danielle met her in the middle of the barn floor, and they fell, rolled, kicking and flailing and screeching.

I felt the heat, and my pants began to smolder again. I struggled, but the tape only tightened.

Danielle got Loretta by the hair and slammed her head down hard. Loretta shrieked and threw a wild punch, connecting with Danielle's jaw.

Becky stirred, tried to get up, fell again. I saw her gaze dart, with horror, from Lombard's skewered body, spouting blood, to me. Then, dazed, she took in the catfight between Loretta and Danielle.

Her eyes widened. She grabbed for something—a rusty horseshoe, it turned out—and headed for the fray.

My ankles began to blister. "Loretta!" I screamed. "Look out!"

But it wasn't Loretta Becky was after. She raised her hand, high over her head, and brought the horseshoe down between Danielle's shoulder blades with the force of a sledgehammer. *"You said we didn't mean anything!"* Becky screamed. *"You said it's always been just you and him!"*

Danielle stiffened and fell facedown in the moldy straw. Becky hit her again, and a third time.

Loretta rushed to me, kicked away the burning paper and wood, and tore at the duct tape with both hands. Over her shoulder, I saw Becky kneeling over Danielle, calmer now that she'd spent her fury, resting her forehead on the very places where she'd struck her with the horseshoe.

The duct tape began to give way, but it was a slow process, and the flames Loretta had scattered began to catch here and there, cheerfully greedy. I watched in partial stupor as they licked

at the other support beams, found their way to Bobby Ray
Lombard's bloody shirtsleeves, nibbled at his pant legs, explored
the soles of his boots.

And the sirens reached a deafening pitch.

Loretta's hands were bleeding where she'd tried to free me.
Thwarted, she looked around frantically, found Danielle's lighter,
and used it to burn through the webbed tape. It was quality
stuff—flame-resistant.

Smoke rolled up from the floor, and the fire raced toward
flash point, dancing in a merry circle around Danielle and Becky.
Becky noticed the flames, at last, though she seemed oblivious to
the sirens, and began to beat at the flames with her bare hands.

Loretta and I both started to cough, and my eyes burned as
if they were already ablaze.

Sonterra burst through the barn doorway, closely followed
by Special Agent Timmons and Eddie.

The fire started up the tinder-dry walls, sneaked under the
red pickup, searching with supple red fingers for the gas tank.

It all seemed surreal by that point, an incident in a dream.

Sonterra tossed Loretta to Eddie, who rushed her toward the
exit. Timmons looked down at Lombard, shook his head, and ran
for Becky, grabbing her around the waist and dragging her, kicking and struggling, to safety.

I was finally free, but my legs were bloodless. I folded, and
Sonterra caught me on the way down, lifted me in both arms.

"Get the hell out!" he roared at Eddie, who had come back
for Danielle.

Eddie sidestepped him and barreled past, and the whole
place went up with a whoosh.

I screamed.

Outside, Sonterra hurled me bodily into Special Agent
Timmons's arms, turned on his heel, and dashed back into the fire
for his friend.

The roof caught.

There were more sirens, but I barely registered them over my
own raw-throated cries. I fought Timmons with all my strength,

but he held me against his chest, as stiff and unyielding as a bronze statue.

"Sonterra!" I shrieked.

The barn roof collapsed, sending up a spire of sparks.

At the same moment, Sonterra and Eddie catapulted from the inferno, dragging Danielle's motionless body between them. Their clothes were on fire, and both of them dropped and rolled.

Timmons finally let me go. I ran, stumbling, toward Sonterra.

He was lying facedown in the grass, his jacket scorched and melted.

I knelt, wrestled him over onto his back, sobbing his name.

He opened his eyes and grinned. "Are you ever in a shitload of trouble," he said.

I fell to him, kissing his face, his hair, his chest.

He caught my cheeks in his hands, held me just far enough away to sit up. Then he dragged me close and held me.

Eddie, too, was okay, if a little singed around the edges. He sat up, shook himself, and put his fingers to the pulse at the base of Danielle's throat. I knew even before he looked at us that she was dead.

Two fire trucks careened into the yard and spilled volunteers. There were no hydrants on the chicken ranch, so it was hand-to-hand combat. The paramedics showed up next, tending to each of us in turn.

Loretta's hands were bandaged.

I was treated for minor burns to my lower legs, but I didn't feel the pain. That would come later, along with a few scars to remember the occasion by. As if I could ever forget it.

The EMTs hustled Becky into an ambulance, and we learned later that night that she'd died on the way to the hospital. The diagnosis was a ruptured spleen, courtesy of Lombard's steel-toed boot, but I'd put my money on a broken heart.

They were all dead—Lombard, Danielle, and now Becky.

"Thank you," I told Loretta, as Sonterra rubbed burn cream on my shins and calves, later that night, in the master bedroom of our house on Cemetery Lane. Emma huddled in the doorway, pale with residual fear. Bernice and Waldo tried to lick my wounds, and Sonterra elbowed them gently aside.

"It was nothing any superhero wouldn't do," Loretta said, and grinned wanly. She looked a mess, but she was beautiful to me.

I choked on a sob. "I thought he'd killed you—Lombard, I mean—"

She watched as Sonterra continued to doctor me. "He tried to drown me in the pond," she said. "I played dead, and he bought it. I found your cell phone on the ground and called for help." She paused, shuddered. "I might take a while to get over the pitchfork thing," she confessed.

"I'm sorry," I said. "If it wasn't for me—"

Sonterra caught my eye. For a long moment, we just stared at each other.

Here it comes, I thought. I was going to catch hell, and I deserved it. Sure, we'd gotten the bad guys, but it could have turned out so differently.

He grinned. "God," he said, "I hope our kid has more sense than you do."

My smoke-reddened eyes burned with tears. "Me, too," I replied.

Sonterra leaned in to kiss my forehead. "Do me a favor and rest for a while, okay?"

I nodded.

He kissed me again. Switched the bedside lamp to dim.

Emma backed out the doorway, and Loretta and Sonterra left the room. The door clicked shut behind them.

I lay there, blinking away tears. My head was caked with dry blood, and the blow from the butt of Lombard's pistol pulsed, but it wasn't a serious wound. I needed a shampoo, but not stitches.

I sighed, settled back into the pillows fluffed behind my back, and closed my burning eyes.

When I opened them, she was standing at the foot of my bed.

The other Clare.

I sat up, stiff with surprise.

There wasn't a mark on her. She smiled.

I knew she'd vanish if I closed my eyes. "Are you—?"

My voice dried up, like the moisture on my eyeballs.

She was as solid as the walls of that room. She wore jeans and a white blouse and a tweed blazer. Studying her, my heart pounding, I noticed that her hair was a lighter shade of brown than mine, her nose slightly tipped at the end, where mine was straight. She was an inch or two taller than I was, and at least ten pounds lighter.

"Don't go," I said, and started to move, intending to touch her. If I touched her, she'd be real.

The pain in my legs stopped me.

She smiled again, waggled her fingers in farewell.

I stared, a thousand questions battering at the back of my throat. I couldn't utter a one.

Eventually, I had to blink.

When I looked again, she was gone, and I knew it was for good.

Who was she? Maybe she was a hallucination. Maybe she really *was* the ghost of my dead twin.

I'll never know for sure.

And maybe I don't need to know.

EPILOGUE

Tucson General Hospital

Sonterra and I stared in wonder at the two tiny forms on the screen of the sonogram machine. Our babies. Our boys.

"Will you look at that?" Sonterra marveled, clutching my hand. "Twins."

I merely nodded, too stricken to speak.

"They look and sound healthy," observed the doctor with a relieved smile. "Any names in mind?"

I chose the first one, for two of my favorite men. "Anthony Alejandro."

Sonterra nodded in rapt agreement, reached out to trace the small forms with the tips of his fingers. "And Edward James."

Edward for his former partner and now deputy, of course. And James for Jimmy Ruiz. My throat tightened with emotion.

"It's a good world," I said, when I could speak.

The doctor nodded, waited a few more moments, then lifted the handheld scanner off my belly, switched off the machine, and left the room.

Sonterra patted my stomach. "It gets better," he said.

I searched his face. "Tell me."

"While you were getting set up for this, I looked in on Suzie. She's not talking yet, but she's conscious. It'll be a long road back." He paused, swallowed, blinked away the moisture in his eyes. "Her dad and stepmother are determined to get her all the help she needs, and they obviously love her very much. She's going to be okay, Clare."

I put a hand over my mouth, and my vision blurred.

Sonterra kissed my belly button and covered me up with the sides of my paper hospital gown. "Maybe this isn't a good time to talk about this," he said gruffly, "but the city council offered me a permanent job. They'll sell us the house if we decide to stay."

"If *we* decide to stay?" I took his hand, and our fingers interlocked.

"It's as much your decision as mine," Sonterra said. "If you want to go back to Scottsdale, we will. No questions asked."

I raised his hand to my mouth, brushed my lips along the ridges of his knuckles.

"I think we ought to give Dry Creek a chance," I said.

His eyes lit up, and a smile quirked at the corner of his mouth.

"Anyway, I wasn't about to give up my job with the prosecutor's office," I added.

Sonterra laughed. "I love you, Counselor," he said.

I kissed him. "It's a damn good thing. Think I'll make it as a cop's wife?"

He caressed my stomach. "So far, so good."

Since we were having a heart-to-heart, I decided to tell him about the other Clare. He helped me into my clothes as he listened, and I waited anxiously for his response when I finished.

"Weird," he said.

"That's all you've got to say?"

"Well, I do wish you'd told me sooner. Why didn't you?"

"Because I didn't want you to think I was crazy."

He grinned. "I've known that all along," he said.

I reached for my purse, and we ducked out of the sonogram room.

"Any more secrets?" he asked, as we approached the elevator.

"Not a one," I told him. "How about you?"

"Hell," he said. "My life is dull compared to yours." The elevator doors whooshed open. Sonterra pulled me inside and kissed me deeply when we were alone.

"In a strange sort of way," I said, when the kiss was over, and I'd caught my breath, "seeing myself that last time seems like a turning point. Like the end of an era. Maybe I'm not going to trip over dead bodies anymore. Maybe nobody's going to try to kill me."

Sonterra curled a finger under my chin. "We can only hope, Counselor," he said. "We can only hope."